D0445059

ALPHA AND OMEGA

BARNES & NOBLE REDISCOVERS

ALPHA AND OMEGA

Stories by
ISAAC ROSENFELD

Foreword by Saul Bellow

BARNES & NOBLE

NEW YORK

To

Eleni and George

This 2009 edition published by Barnes & Noble, Inc.,
by arrangement with Viking, a member of Penguin Group (USA) Inc.

The stories, with one exception, first appeared in
*Epoch, Furioso, Harper's Magazine, The Kenyon Review,
Modern Writing #1, New Directions 10, The New Republic,
Nugget,* and *Partisan Review.*

Barnes & Noble, Inc.
122 Fifth Avenue
New York, NY 10011

ISBN: 978-1-4351-1024-3

Printed and bound in the United States of America

10 9 8 7 6 5 4 3 2 1

PUBLISHERS' NOTE

Not long before his death in 1956, Isaac Rosenfeld had prepared a collection of thirteen of his stories that had appeared in magazines over the preceding fifteen years. The volume was never published. *Alpha and Omega* reproduces the contents of that original collection—as well as its dedication, to the author's children—but also includes four other stories: "Joe the Janitor," "The New Egypt," "The Misfortunes of the Flapjacks," and "Wolfie," the first of these unpublished, and the last published posthumously. The arrangement of the stories is chronological, with one exception; the date at the end of each story is that of its original publication or, in two cases, the year of its writing.

CONTENTS

Foreword

⌒

ISAAC HAD A ROUND FACE AND YELLOWISH-BROWN HAIR
which he combed straight back. He was nearsighted, his eyes
pale blue, and he wore round glasses. The space between his
large teeth gave his smile an ingenuous charm. He had a belly
laugh. It came on him abruptly and often doubled him up. His
smiles, however, kindled slowly. He liked to look with avuncular
owlishness over the tops of his specs. His wisecracks were often
preceded by the pale blue glance. He began, he paused, a sort of
mild slyness formed about his lips, and then he said something
devastating. More seriously, developing an argument, he gestured
like a Russian-Jewish intellectual, a cigarette between two fingers. When he was in real earnest, he put aside these mannerisms,
too. A look of strength, sometimes of angry strength, came into
his eyes.

He had a short broad figure. His chest was large. But he was
round rather than burly, and he could move gracefully. His lazy
lounging manner was deceptive. He was quick with his hands and
played the flute well, and the recorder superbly. He was haunted,
however, by an obscure sense of physical difficulty or deficiency,
a biological torment, a disagreement with his own flesh. He seldom enjoyed good health. His color was generally poor, yellowish. At the University of Chicago during the thirties, this was the
preferred intellectual complexion. In the winter Isaac was often
down with the flu or with attacks of pleurisy. He was told that his

skin couldn't bear much exposure to the sun. But during the war when he was Captain Isaac, the entire crew of a barge in the New York harbor, he had good color. He read Shakespeare and Kierkegaard on the water and found it agreed with him to be in the open air. He had friends on the waterfront. In such circumstances Isaac would never be the visiting intellectual. He never went slumming. It was impossible not to be attracted by the good nature of his face, and I assume his ineptitude with ropes touched the hearts of the deckhands on the tugboats.

I am among his friends perhaps not the best qualified to speak of him. I loved him, but we were rivals, and I was peculiarly touchy, vulnerable, hard to deal with—at times, as I can see now, insufferable, and not always a constant friend. As for him, his power to attract people might have made more difference to him than it did. He wanted their affection, he wanted also to return it...but then these matters we have learned to speak of so simply have not thereby become simpler.

He had one of those ready, lively, clear minds that see the relevant thing immediately. In logic and metaphysics he was a natural. He had a bent for theology, too, which he did everything possible to discourage. His talent for abstraction displeased him; he was afraid it indicated a poverty of his feelings, an emotional sterility. To the overcoming of this supposed sterility, a fault fed by his talents themselves, exaggerated by them, he devoted his best efforts, his strength. He didn't like to be praised for achievements he regarded as largely mental. Heartless abstraction filled him with dread. Originally his purpose in coming to New York was to study philosophy. During one of his bouts of pleurisy, he went through Melville and he wrote me that after reading *Moby Dick* he could no longer be a logical positivist.

There followed a period of exaggerated "feelings." But whether he gave himself over to the Theory of Signs or exclaimed sentimentally over the poor sprouting onions in an impoverished grocery, Isaac never went very long without laughing.

He was a playful man. He loved hoaxes, mimicry, parody, and surrealist poems. He was a marvelous clown. He imitated steam irons, clocks, airplanes, tugboats, big-game hunters, Russian commissars, Village poets and their girl friends. He tried on the faces of people in restaurants. He was great as Harry Baur in *Crime et Châtiment*, the inspector Porfiry Petrovitch, smoking cigarettes with an underhand Russian grip. He invented Yiddish proletarian poems; he did a translation of Eliot's "Prufrock," a startling X-ray of those hallowed bones which brings Anglo-Saxons and Jews together in a surrealistic Yiddish unity, a masterpiece of irreverence. With Isaac, the gravest, the most characteristic, the most perfect strokes took a comic slant. In his story "King Solomon," the magnificence of Jerusalem mingles raggedly with the dinginess of the Lower East Side. The great king, also mortal and slovenly, sits in his undershirt. He fondles children in the park. They sit on his knees and smudge his glasses with their thumbprints.

He preferred to have things about him in a mess. I have an idea that he found good middle-class order devitalizing—a sign of meanness, stinginess, malice, and anality. The sight of one of his rooms with Isaac hard at work, smoking, capably and firmly writing on his yellow second-sheets, would have made Hogarth happy. On 76th Street there sometimes were cockroaches springing from the toaster with the slices of bread. Smoky, the rakish little short-legged brown dog, was only partly housebroken and chewed books; the shades were always drawn (harmful sunlight!), the ashtrays spilled over. There was no sweeping, dusting, mopping, or laundering. The dirt here was liberating, exciting. Later, downtown, it was a little less gay. In the intricate warren of rooms called the Casbah and on Hudson Street it was simply grim. Toward the end of his life, on Woodlawn Avenue in Chicago, he settled in a hideous cellar room at Petofsky's where he had lived as a student. The sympathetic glamour of the thirties was entirely gone; there was only a squalid stink of toilets and coal bins here. Isaac felt that this was the way he must live. The disorder had ended by becoming a discipline. It had acquired an ascetic significance for him which, at least to me, he never explained.

By now he had given up the Reichianism which for a time had absorbed us both. He no longer questioned people impulsively about their sexual habits or estimated the amount of character armor they wore. His homemade orgone box did not follow him in his later travels. He had at one time (in St. Albans) experimented with tomato seeds kept in the orgone accumulator; they produced better fruit, he claimed, than seeds which had not been exposed. Friends with headaches were urged to put on the tin crown or "shooter." He treated the neighbors' sick pets in his box. But during the last years of his life all his quaintness—incomparably charming and accompanied by brilliantly persuasive lectures and arguments—was laid aside. His wit was clearer and sharper, purged of crankiness. There had been a quality in him in earlier days, described by one of his friends as "hard-headed *Gemütlichkeit*." For eight or ten years his mood was anything but *gemütlich*. He judged people harshly, he was not less harsh with himself.

I am convinced that in his view the struggle for survival, in the absence of certain qualities of life, was not worth making. Without heart and without truth there was only a dull dogged shuffle about things and amusements and successes. Singlemindedly, Isaac was out for the essential qualities. He believed that heart and truth were to be had. He tried to fix them within himself. He seemed occasionally to be trying to achieve by will, by fiat, the openness of heart and devotion to truth without which a human existence must be utterly senseless.

He was perfectly aware that in this America of ours he appeared to be doing something very odd. To appear odd did not bother him at all. Nor did he ever pursue eccentricity for its own sake, for its color. He followed an inner necessity which led him into difficulty and solitude. During the last years of his life he was solitary, and on Walton Place in one of his furnished rooms, he died alone.

—SAUL BELLOW
1962

PART I

The Hand That Fed Me

My Landlady

Joe the Janitor

The Colony

The New Egypt

The Misfortunes of the Flapjacks

THE HAND THAT FED ME

Dear Ellen,

It was very sweet of you to send me a Christmas card. It was really a wonderful gesture, and so simple! When you prepared your Christmas list you included me—and that's all there was to it.

You know, in that one day of ours I never did manage to find out who your friends were (not that I wasn't eager to!). But I imagine your list went something like this: aunts, uncles, cousins; girl friends; boy friends. It amuses me to think that I must have been included in the latter group, in the company, let us say, of John, Bob, Steve, Chick, etc. I am quite willing to share the honor with them, even though the names of my colleagues must be entirely imaginary and even though you probably put my own name last on the list. But perhaps you had me in mind all along, knowing what a gesture that would be! Naturally, you must have assumed I'm not in the army. I'm not quarreling with you, but there's something a little glib in that assumption. Why, so far as you are concerned, should I *not* be in the army? Is it simply a habit of thinking so that whenever—rarely!—you do come to me, you immediately say, "Joe? Oh, he's still around." I can see no other way, unless, God save my mind, you've taken to obtaining information from my friends, whom you have sworn to secrecy. But how should you know who my friends are, since I never found out yours?

Of course, I may have mentioned Otto to you—he was very much on my mind that day. Would you believe it, while we were walking down Hoyne Avenue and I was, permit me, impressing you with all I had, I kept wondering what Otto would do in similar circumstances, and I was gloating, sure that he would never have been able to give such a fine account of himself! Furthermore, I still gloat over it although—for all the fine impression I made— you never answered my letters and even once, when I called on you (for perhaps the tenth time), you actually hid from me. I know all about it. Your brother came to the door and he seemed to have half a mind to admit me; but behind him I could hear a commotion of shushing and whispering, and I'm sure it was you, ducking into the pantry and telling them to say you were out and on no account to let me in.

Of course, what makes all this slightly ridiculous is the fact that it happened three years ago. But why did you wait three years before sending me a card? What was wrong with the Christmas of the very same year, or the one of the year following? Ah, I know how your mind works. On Christmas, 1939, you *suppressed* all thought of me. In 1940 you allowed yourself to think, but only to the following extent: "If I send him a Christmas card now, he'll think I've been unable to forget him. So we'll wait another year or two. By that time it'll be quite clear, when he gets my card, not that I've been *unable* to forget him, but that I have so good a memory that I can even recall the name and address of a man whom I saw only once, three years ago." Am I right?

But it's a trivial thing and why attach so much importance to it? I suppose you would have me believe that. You would have me believe that your card was only a way of acknowledging a pleasant day that you had hitherto failed to acknowledge. Something brought it to your mind—say, an onion you had eaten recently. And so the card, yes?

Not on your life, Ellen, not for one moment will I believe it. For if it were only a trivial matter, would you have waited three years? You would have sent me a card at once, or even phoned me on the following day, as you'd promised. Trivialities are the things women rush into, feeling they're important. The important things, however, are what they mull over, plot, deliberate, all to no end. It took you three years, Ellen, to convince yourself that a single afternoon you had spent with me was trivial!

So there you are.

But one more thing. On your card you have written, "From Ellen. Do you remember me?" A pretty little disingenuous note! I assure you, your card was sent in the deepest conviction that I had not once ceased to think of you. I'm sure of it. If you thought I'd forgotten you, you wouldn't have dared send a card. What, a man should receive a card from a certain Ellen and wonder who she is? Any time you'd leave yourself open! Or, on the other hand, was it a rather coy way of insinuating that you'd all but forgotten me? You see, if you are willing to admit that I may have forgotten you, isn't that another way of suggesting that you barely, barely manage to remember me?

Nonsense! I know perfectly well that you've never forgotten me.—But who are you, Shakespeare, that the smallest scrap of your writing should be covered with commentaries? Enough of that.

> Do you remember me?
> Indeed!
> Joseph Feigenbaum

Dear Ellen,

It just occurred to me that while I wrote to you at some length, yesterday, I forgot the obvious subject of our correspondence— Xmas. So I'm writing you again to wish you a merry Xmas.

> Yours,
> J. F.

P.S. Of course, I could just as well send a Xmas card.

Dear Ellen,

Since I wrote to you twice, I might just as well have said something worth saying. After all, even if we have "forgotten" each other, we still have our three years to look back on—years, may I add, all the more interesting because we did not, in any way, spend them together.

Please understand my motive. If it seems sentimental to you, then you're a fool, and I've no fear of offending you when I say so. And besides what can you do about it? Can you threaten to break off our friendship? Can you threaten to stop writing? You see, Ellen, by avoiding me you've put yourself completely in my power. But that's hardly worth pointing out.

Our whole meeting comes back to me. I remember that summer, no work, no friends, no conversation, the realization I was meant for WPA. What a wonderful summer of self-discovery! Believe me, chaos is the mother of knowledge. It's a distinguished family: indolence, poverty, frustration, *seediness*—these are the blood relations of that little monster, Mr. Knowthyself. I shall never again be afraid of turning myself inside out, like an empty pocket—what treasures of lint and fuzz! Do you follow me, Ellen? I mean to say, it is sometimes a good thing to shake yourself out, and go around unhappy—you lose most of your delusions. A happy man takes a great risk—of believing that he is what he seems to be.

Well, I was forced to go on WPA; forced outwardly, that is, for inwardly I went as a free man, as to my true station in life. A career. My friends ("my generation" as it became fashionable to call them) were all on one cultural project or another. I would go on the Writers' Project and fill out a time sheet with the best of them. WPA was a great social invention, the State altered its course on our account. For the first time in history, writers had official existence. Do you appreciate what it means for a writer to exist officially? Not merely in the circle of his unpublished friends who take in one another's work with a barely muffled groan, but *officially*—on file! But what's all this? I merely wanted to say a few things it was impossible to say when we walked out of the relief station together, and I find I am overdramatizing myself.

I hadn't thought there would be such a long line at the CRA office, so many old men. Not a single applicant for the Writers' Project among them. It is so much better to be an unemployed writer than an unemployed anything-else that I felt especially sorry for them. An unemployed plumber, for example—a man who is starving because there are no toilet bowls for him to fix. There is something so pathetic in that! A writer, at least, is always writing. Whatever happens, he records it. It begins to rain—he says to himself, it is raining. He walks down the stairs—he says to himself, I am walking down the stairs. He is always writing in his head, and it does him good. But what good does it do a man to go around fixing toilet bowls in his head? Pig misery! So there I was, looking at the men around me and recording them, putting down their coughs, their leanness, the dirt, the stubble on their faces, and meanwhile thinking: here am I, a writer, this is me, etc., etc.

Ellen, you look at yourself only in mirrors. Relying on a piece of glass the way you do, you probably have little notion of the actual figure you cut. That day, when you were not smearing on lipstick while looking into a compact-mirror, you were sucking the point of a pencil, and rolling it between your lips. That you, who refuse to write to me, should have come into my life at the point of a pencil!

Now I might almost begin to flatter you—to dwell on the image of a girl, a little above average in height, more than ordinary in appearance, a girl, though I suspect the word, quite beautiful, standing there in the basement among all the coughing old men, surrounded by steam pipes, benches, notices plastered on the wooden walls: *Bekanntmachung, Aviso.* And all the while this girl rolls the point of a pencil in her mouth. Do you know, after you had caught my eye, you stuck your tongue out at me. First the pencil, and then the tongue. Ellen, Ellen!

It would have meant very little. It would only have been a study in violent contrast, squalor and flirtation, sex and the relief office—and, as a matter of fact, I was not sure at the beginning that it meant anything more. But immediately the element of personal worth entered. Almost at once I talked to you, you will recall, as though you were more than a pretty girl with a pencil stuck in your mouth. It was you who did the flirting, made the advances. Do I wear make-up? Do I carry a purse full of compacts, powder boxes, lipsticks? Understand, I accuse you of nothing. I am glad you behaved as you did. Perhaps because I am not thin and old and coughing, you saw to it that I should notice you. But it was I who saw to all the rest.

I want you to observe that you were ahead of me in the line. When your preliminary interview was over and your preliminary papers were filled out, you could have gone home. I expected you, at any moment, while you were idling around the basement, I expected you to break away, perhaps with a slight nod in my direction, and go home. But I knew you would not. I said nothing, you will remember, I even pretended not to notice you. But how carefully I watched you, and how pleased I was! There you were, waiting for me, and it was all voluntary on your part, and even somewhat embarrassing. The pretexts you invented! First you sat down on one of the benches and stretched and yawned as though you were tired. Then you removed your shoes and rubbed your feet—such pretty feet, if I may say, and just barely dirty! By that time I thought I might dare acknowledge that I knew you were waiting for me. I smiled. I motioned to you. But you would not admit it. You wouldn't look at me. You curled up on the bench where you sat and pretended to go to sleep—a wonder no one saw you and put you out. I knew you were waiting for me, that you had already acknowledged me even more deeply than I had acknowledged you—since at the outset I was only responding to a flirtation, but what were you responding to? I don't flirt. You were therefore responding to me! It made me so happy, somewhat dizzy, it was even slightly alarming. I sang a song, I joked with the man who stood ahead of me in line, a short and chubby fellow whom I liked immensely. I offered him cigarettes. When he took only one, I forced more on him; he was now my friend. Having become your friend, I was everybody's friend. I even smiled at the relief worker who interviewed me, a bitter hag who resented my happiness and detained me with unnecessary questions, as though to extract my secret. And when I was through with her and came out, startled to find you absent from the bench, only to see you standing at the door, so clearly, so obviously waiting!

That whole afternoon, Ellen, the walk to your house, your friendliness, your kindness in asking me up and inviting me to have lunch with you! Even now I can hardly believe that I should ever have received such gifts of kindness. Such absolute friendship, comradeship, trust, good will, and with it all the constant promise of intimacy: one moment you are at my shoulder, the next, you take my arm, or my hand, or you pretend a mosquito has landed and you slap my cheek. And what a lunch! Rye bread and borscht, served by your father, and with such good nature, even after he had learned my name and drawn certain unavoidable inferences. Borscht, furthermore, with bits of green onion floating in it. I was so happy to learn you were Russian! I consider myself a Russian, you understand. As a Jew, I am also a German, an Italian, a Frenchman, a Pole, I am all Europe—but a Russian, foremost.

I am sure that all this did not come to naught because I am a Jew. To begin with, you are the kind of gentile who knows how to say "goy"—a word I distinctly heard you use. There is only one nation on the earth—the nation of those who call the rest of the world "goyim." We Jews use it in contempt, because of our fears, but it is capable of elevation into a word of pride and brotherhood. No, that is not the reason why we "broke up." There are only two possibilities, one very flattering to me, the other, degrading.

To take the base one first, I observed, when I entered your house and when I was eating lunch, that you avoided all reference to WPA. You presented me to your father, and later to your brother, as an old friend from school whom you bumped into downtown while looking for a job. You would not admit that you had applied for WPA, and you would not have them know that I, too, had done so. What a false and wicked pride, and—since you evidently know something about such matters—what utter disloyalty to your class! Your father, a carpenter as I recall, was obviously unemployed. He had that look about him. And your brother, who was building a model airplane in the middle of the day, evidently had nothing better to do. So what was there to be ashamed of? And what if your mother, as I gather from her absence, was the only one working in the family? What of it? Must you be ashamed? But perhaps you were even more ashamed of me than of yourself. Perhaps the very fact that you met me in a relief station was enough to queer me. Then why flirt with me and bring me to your home?

But apart from all that, what a fool you were not to go through with your WPA application. I scoured all the rolls, inquired at all the projects where you might conceivably have been taken on, but no one had heard of you. Ah, what you missed! Myself, I went on to the Writers' Project and compiled a hundred-thousand-word report on pigeon racing in Chicago, including a life-size biography of Josiah Breen, the pigeon fancier. And what did you do? Pickle works, belt-buckle factory, typist, stenographer, secretary? You are a traitor to your class, Ellen, to your better instincts and your better capacities, and you allowed what we call "the most crucial experience of our generation" to slip by you. But this is a digression.

As I say, you may have been ashamed to know me, or to continue seeing me because I was going on WPA. Or perhaps, even because I had caught you in the act, applying for the national dispensation. This, of course, is only a possibility; and I may be wrong. Assuming that I am, and that you had your own and better reasons, there remains another possibility, which I am very eager to entertain. It does me good.

This is mystery. It involves a whole world, of which you are the hub. At the center, beside you, let me place a young man, of respectable, and somewhat better family than your own, a man whom we shall call Willard. Am I warm? When we met, you had already known Willard for a period of two years. He, a serious fellow, perhaps a student of law, or already a lawyer, could not help but have serious intentions. He doesn't laugh very often, your Willard; and when you do, opening your mouth wide, it disconcerts him. Furthermore, when you suck pencils in his presence, or show him your tongue, he is more than a little embarrassed. But what can you do about it? You were to marry him. You were then, I should judge, twenty-four, the age when one begins observing a woman is not growing any younger. Besides, you are *used* to him, miserable habit. He is good to you, he's solid, he looks down on WPA, he smokes cigars. What then? How else are you to act when this wistful, melancholy, timid, cynical, and so appealing young writer comes along and speaks to you as a man has never spoken before, and dwells on you, and intimates, and sighs, and stares? It is, after all, shocking to discover that one's fiancé is not the ultimate man on earth, and that another, a man you met in a basement, who has never kissed you or walked you through the park, is capable of pre-empting the emotions you have already consigned and wrapped and, furthermore, of providing you with new ones. *Nyet, krasavitsa moya?*

Ellen, if this be true, then your reticence is a tribute! Thank you for ignoring me, thank you for your silence. For it means you realized, in those few hours, that going with me would make irrecoverable your whole past life and its commitments. After all, women have been known to keep several men on a string. Thank you for not binding me. For it means you feared the string, and where it might lead you. And what if the string should break? The fear that a string might break is the fear of love!

But look at all these pages I have written, and where will I find an envelope large enough? Ellen, unintentionally, I have invoked more of the past than I had intended. It has brought me back to that helpless, pitiful state of mind—I despise it—where a man lives on promises. I have drugged myself into believing what I believed three years ago—your promise to call me, to write to me, to see me again. Now I know you will write, if only a few words, and I know you will answer me at once.

Always yours,
Joe

DECEMBER 29

Dear Ellen,

Christmas passed, and nearly six days have gone by. I tell myself that you have been very busy over the holidays, that you haven't found time to write. But I know full well that if you were going to write, you would already have done so. Why do you deny me this? Is it your pride or my presumption? Have I touched too sensitive, too deep a point? Or could it be that I have merely bored you?

I tell myself I have bored her. But how can that be when I still believe in the love she seemed to have offered me? Is it possible? If the world were made up of such haphazard, ill-fitting emotions, no pattern at all would exist—it just wouldn't hang together.

Excuse me if I have used the word love in vain. But the more I have thought of you, the more I have grown to believe that I have a right to use it. It is almost as though I have written these letters to make myself believe that you love me. God knows what I have written! God knows why I go on!

I suppose every man sometimes has the urge to pour himself out, release all the stops and let go. My sense of caution should tell me that few men have the right to confess; only murderers and hardened criminals, never men who are merely unhappy. Those who have really committed crimes, those who have an actual guilt lying over them—they have something to say. But the rest of us—perhaps we become liars when we open our mouths, liars or pathetic wishers, and half of what we say may be false, and the other half merely the result of a ridiculous striving for a sense of personal history.

Then why do I go on? Why do I persist in writing to you in the face of what must surely amount to a personal humiliation? I'll tell you why—and may the telling damn you! A man feels humiliated only when he is cast down from one position to a lower one. Some men never learn their lesson. No sooner humili ated, they attempt to injure someone else in return. These are the unpleasant characters, the personalities charged with an explosive that any touch may set off. Your Willard may be of such a type—not because he is mean; he may even be sweet in his own way—but only insofar as he lacks subtlety. But our other type of man is a different sort entirely. When he is humiliated he does not bound back with a rage that destroys his perception. Instead, he learns. He sees most clearly what concerns him most closely; and he accepts it and makes it a part of himself. When he has been utterly humiliated, he observes that he has touched bottom; having reached bottom, he knows there's no lower he can fall. There's a comfort, a perpetual cushion in certain kinds of misery—you rest on it, just as a contented man rests at the top of his career. Top or bottom, either way—but no struggling in the middle!

Does this succeed in explaining myself to you? Most likely not. I feel you must learn something about the way in which I live, in order to understand why, after three years have passed, I shower you with letters, to which I expect no answer.

I live in what I consider to be a state of exile. Among the friends I have at present is a certain Zampechini, an Italian refugee, and a certain Lutzek, a German refugee. I have told them, "Boys, we are in exile together. Not from our separate countries—but from history." But why proceed in this fashion, at this level, away over your head? It is enough to state briefly the following conditions:

1. I am alone.
2. There is a war on and I am out of it on all fronts; neither losing nor profiting by it, and not even employed.
3. I live in a rooming house, on the allowance my father very grudgingly gives me.
4. The last six women I approached unconditionally turned me down.
5. Ever since WPA folded up,

but never mind the rest.

I was going to tell you more. I wanted, first, to tell you everything; then, a little; now, nothing. Ah, what's the difference? I cannot bear to tell you what I have suffered, because I am proud of it, and it would only bore you. Enough. Let this be a last effort at explanation in a letter full of abortive efforts. As a man who, quite confidently, has touched bottom, both in what he has suffered and in personal esteem, I feel nothing I do can injure me. Your rebuffs are *not, definitely not* a further humiliation. I understand myself too well. I am of the brotherhood of paupers who endure everything at their own expense. And so, if I go out of my way and out of my time to reach after a promised happiness of three years back, this, too, a deliberate delusion, is also at my own expense. And perhaps even the greatest irony is my knowing that while you refuse to answer my letters, you also fail to understand them.

But, no fear, I shall plague you no longer.

Feigenbaum

Dear Ellen,

Contrary to the word I had given, I called on you yesterday. I am writing today to identify myself, to make it perfectly clear that it was I, and no one else, who called.

He said you were out. Who, I do not know. Perhaps it was "your Willard." I believed him, made no further inquiries. I left no message and no name. In a fit of humiliation I withheld my name. I am writing today to repudiate that humiliation. It was not of the bottom variety; it was of the rising sort that struggles midway between its origins and its hopes. It was not true to nature. My humiliation admits no hopes.

Now that there can be no doubt in your mind as to the identity of your caller, I may go on to the next point. By calling on you I satisfied a partial longing. Naturally, complete satisfaction would have come only with my seeing you. But as it is I saw your house, the door which opened, the stairs that led up, the door that closed in my face. Willard does not count. I am indifferent to him. My point is that with yesterday's closing of the door I accepted as closed our whole relationship. I shall no longer plague you with letters, no longer make any attempt to see you. And this is the truth. You may rely on it, not because I have promised you—my promises are evidently as little to be trusted as yours. But it is so because I have at last accepted it, and have willed it to be so. I find that this decision, against which I have been fighting ever since your Xmas card came, has, surprisingly, liberated me.

For what I have to say actually has nothing to do with humiliation. Very simply, Ellen, I love you. It is so easy to say, and one can say it as well as another. Why did I have to torture myself?

I love you. And why do I love you? Because you came to me. Because, in the basement of the relief station you noticed me before I noticed you, and because your flirting was not in response to an act of mine, but an overture, an opening entirely of your own. For this, all my gratitude. Because, at a moment when you did not yet exist for me, I already existed for you. Isn't this reason enough?

No, it needs further explaining. I feel that the more I love you, the less you understand me. You must know that a man like myself, so deeply displeased, dissatisfied with himself as I am, can only be saved by an act of graciousness. A blessing, external and gratuitous, must come to him. For he will destroy whatever is internal, whatever comes out of himself. The lower he falls, the more he will demand and the louder he will clamor for salvation. An absolute beggar demands the entire world.

This is why I love you. But if I love you because you flirted with me, I am, at the same time, inclined to disapprove your flirtatiousness. I could understand flirtatiousness in a nun. But in a woman like yourself, Ellen! A nun, let us assume, is repressed. But you! Not repression but *bonheur,* bliss at every pore. Now that I no longer need withhold anything, now that I am free, I may tell you what I felt when I first saw you. Believe me, and here enters another irony, my first sight of you was intuitive proof that I would have you! That is what is called spontaneous love. Love pre-exists in the heart, and when it finds its object it leaps out and enters it and does its business, establishing a conviction, while the timid soul still tells itself it has no more than an "interest." But I do not delude myself. I saw and at once believed, and I knew what I saw and what I believed, and so strong was my conviction that even the three years that passed and the frustrations of the last week have not deprived me of it. Yes, I was sure. Furthermore, I still am. For it will not go away. I still see you as I saw you then, excited, plump, in a tight black dress, your arms bare, your hair loose, your feet in sandal-shoes. I have torn that dress from you a thousand times, but I have done it reverently, in my mind observing that same delicacy, that attention to detail I would observe in fact. Thus I have seen you naked, and I do not revile myself with the thought that what is only imaginary for me must be actual for one or many a man. It is my own possession. The nakedness with which I have endowed you is solid and unique, both in the actuality it has for me, and in its expression, which is entirely its own and not compounded of other women. Nor is the look of the body a wish fulfillment, for I do not assemble you out of separate female perfections—that art of day dreaming! No, for your breasts, as I imagine them, are even too large for my preference and your thighs could do with a little less hair. I have, furthermore, distilled a set of odors to go with your hair and your armpits, and these, again, are distinctive; and I have supplied your skin with textures, and have given you appropriate sounds—laughter for love play, a sharp intaking of the breath for passion, and a wildness of hissing and moaning devoid of all language. This is that solemn nakedness to which we bring not only our passion, but our capacity for a sensual revenge. But it is not brutal; it is tender. And above all it is persistent in the face of a thousand complications I can never make out.

And then the pencil in your mouth, the tongue stuck out at me, and the conversation and your waiting for me and the walk and the invitation to your house, the lunch, and your promise and the happiness almost, almost reached, and the conviction established beyond overthrowing! Was it from this that I was to expect denial?

We lean toward the imperfect—it was too good to be true. But this is no explanation. It will satisfy only a shallow, a skeptical intelligence. The perfect must be true! What else is perfection, and why do we demand it? But however I explain it, I still do not understand. I refuse to believe my own reasons.

What then? I love you enough to think evil of you. I am angry enough to know that what I saw and believed, you, too, saw—but did not believe. You acknowledged a conviction without sharing it. And nothing human can be colder!

Look how similarities endanger us. You, with the pencil in your mouth, knew me well enough, from your own traits, to destroy me. I am of the same erotic type as you, I, too, must be fed. My whole life can be explained by hunger. You knew you would have to offer, give, yield. If only you had not known! If only your perception had been clouded with that animal stupidity for which we are, occasionally, so grateful in women! Or, if only I had known better! I should have known that a woman will make a concession on one point only when she has prepared some reservation on another. As it was, you managed to concede everything, yet withheld everything. The evil in your flirtatiousness was that it went beyond flirtation; it offered love, real love, in order to snatch it away. It was the old game played to its fullest, criminal in its intelligence, the *absolute* cheat.

Well, it's over and done with. Of course, in outdoing me you also had to deny yourself. But a woman will count her self-denial at a small cost when the game is so large and she masters it. But it's over, it's over. Yet it persists. Certain patterns are dangerous. We form them once and follow them always. And if a man will attach, as I have done, a whole morality to a single incident, he will always be at the mercy of "incidents." The insight he will gain will give him no peace. He will be forced to employ it everywhere, with all the subtle damage it can do him. And at a time like the present when there is no place for unhappy men, no understanding they can count on, no mood they can share, what good will their insight do them?

But, Ellen, I release you. I go back to my own cares, reluctantly, I admit, but with a certain confidence. My place in the world—see how quickly one can spring from his place in bed to his place in the world! Can a woman do as much?—my place in the world is assured, no matter how difficult it be, for I am my own assurance. I am that man—and there are many like me—whose place is entirely contained in his own being. So long as I exist, that is my place; my function. I do not justify myself. I merely point this out: I have so little, so little pride, so little belief, so little outward appetite, I am so pared down to my own core, that I cannot help believing I am an essential man. And besides, WPA will come back, have no fear. Do you think I wrote my report on pigeon racing for nothing? It stands there in the files, waiting, ready to be taken up again. Some day, when the war is over, and the machines have been removed from the old buildings, after the dust has settled and the activity has died down, the steel vaults will be unlocked and the steel files will be brought out, and the pigeons will flutter again. Once again the world will take account of us—we bare, pared, essential men. The earth will once again acknowledge loneliness, as real as her own mountains. What else can be done? We may be a generation—we may, as well, be an eternity. But perhaps a new wrinkle in disasters? Perhaps the night and the wolves and the waves we howled about back in the thirties—when there was still a little twilight—will really come down to blot out, swallow, and wash us away? What will be will be.

One looks only to his own accountable and natural future. But here, I shan't write much longer. The New Year is coming. Ellen, Ellen, at last I am free. One moment you were my great bitterness, and now I am in the clear, rid of you. My life will find another bitterness, perhaps a higher, fresher quality, perhaps even a bitterness in some successful thing. What does it matter? I am cushioned at the bottom and only look forward to what I may expect. For after all, what is humiliation? It does not endure forever. And when it has led us underground to our last comfort, look, it has served its purpose and is gone. Who knows when new heights may not appear? A man has only so much in common with his experience. The rest he derives from God knows where.

I believe some men are capable of rising out of their own lives. They stand on the same ground as their brothers, but they are, somehow, transcendental, while their brothers are underground. Their only secret is a tremendous willingness—they do not struggle with themselves!

Ellen, all I mean to say is this: I still believe in human happiness, and in my own to boot. If I cannot make my claim on you, I will make it on life, demand that existence satisfy the longings it arouses. It must, it must! For that is happiness: the conviction that something is necessary.

But how dare I speak of happiness? After all, I was once convinced that you were necessary. And what is necessity without fulfillment? Is it possible? I shall say it is. Be gentle to the unfulfilled, be good to it. We are accustomed to sing the joys of the happy, the fulfilled men. Let us also sing the joys of the desolate, the empty men. Theirs is the necessity without fulfillment, but it is possible that even to them—who knows—some joy may come.

I forgive you and release you, Ellen. You are beautiful—go. But God, if you only knew, if you only knew how willing I am—always—to take the risk of my happiness!

Happy New Year!

> Love,
> Joseph

[1944]

My Landlady

LISTEN TO ME WHEN THEY TELL YOU THERE IS NO HOPE FOR mankind. I say that the simplest person may have a virtue of the soul great enough to redeem all the evildoers who are quick with life and some of the sour dead who still linger within recall. In fact, all I need to send my heart thumping with hope for the world is just one good solitary example—and that will keep me going for six months, at least. My present luminary is my landlady, and there is a source of light for you! Surely there is hope while she yet lives. In consequence of which I cannot pass her in the hall without a wave of love instantly rushing over me. Why, it is an indecency to pay her rent. And yet her good husband may sleep in peace, for nothing shall come of it. Nothing more than the following, that is, for there already exists an imperishable intimacy between us. At night, sometimes, I steal out into the spring air in the yard, and there, resting under a tree, I watch my landlady through her window while she moves about her kitchen busied with her dishes, pots, and pans—and it seems to me that everything she touches glows responsively.

This is how it happened. One wintry Saturday of the holiday season I came home late from my work in the hospital. I was tired as usual, but this time I did not throw myself onto the bed to spend the first few moments recuperating in oblivion. Instead, I sat down in the chair at the window, and not troubling even to turn on the light or to remove my hat and coat, I leaned on the window sill and stared out into the snow-covered yard. My window was open, and the cold wind blew in on me, but with a feeling of sadness and disgust I shrugged my shoulders as if to say, "Let it blow—who cares?" I had been working that day as usual, mopping floors, but in the afternoon, shortly before quitting time, when I was already emptying the bucket of dirty water, a small woman clutching a shopping bag came running distractedly down the hall, crying "Oh, oh, oh!" and nearly losing her footing on the wet floor. "Mister! Mister!" she cried, seeing me. "Where is the children's hospital? I've lost my way—oh, what am I going to do?" "Careful, there, or you'll fall. What's the matter with you?" "My purse!" she cried, tears running down her face, "I lost my purse. Where is the children's hospital?" "Around the corner to your left to the end of the hall, then down the stairs to the basement, where you take the passageway." "Come with me, please! Quick, come with me!" and she began running in the direction I had given her. I dropped my mop and ran after her, fearing she was crazy. Catching up with her, and holding her by the arm, I ran at her side, trying to silence the commotion she was making. "Quiet please, collect yourself, this is a hospital." But she broke away from me and ran on ahead calling out, "My purse, my purse, oh my little girl!" We raced through the passageway in the basement, then up the stairs to the children's hospital, the woman laboring for breath. The nurse in attendance on the second floor took her in hand and made her control herself. "Where did you lose your purse?" "I don't know!" exclaimed the woman. "I was with my little girl, and I laid it on a bed. Do you think I could have left it there? Oh, let me go look!" "Visiting hours are over now. I'll have the girl on the floor look. What ward is she in, please?" "Two D. I'm sure I left it there. I remember now, I laid it on a bed next to my little girl's, it was an empty bed. Oh, I should control myself, but I had all my money in it." "There is no purse in Two D," said the floor nurse coming up to the desk where we stood. "Let me look!" cried the woman, "I am sure I laid it on the bed." "You heard the nurse say it wasn't there," said the nurse in attendance. "You must have picked it up when you went out. Where else did you go?" "I went to the washroom. Yes, I remember," said the woman, looking ashamed. "I had it with me because I laid it on the washstand with my shopping bag, and then I didn't miss it until I went down to the cashier to make a payment for my little girl. I got so frightened I ran in the wrong direction. Oh, I was so nervous." "Have you looked in the washroom?" asked the nurse. "Thank you, thank you," said the woman, walking to the washroom. She came running out. "No, it isn't there!" "You will have to be quiet," said the nurse. "You are in a hospital. Have you looked in your shopping bag?"

"Yes, I've looked," said the woman, frantically emptying it again. "It was stolen!" she cried. "My husband's pay check for the week was in it. I have to pay for my little girl. What am I going to do?" "You had better go down to the desk and make a report," said the nurse. I walked back to the desk with her. "It was stolen," said the woman. "Can you imagine, who would do a thing like that? In a hospital, too. You'd think they'd know a person in a hospital needs their money." "Was there anyone in the washroom with you?" I asked. "There were some other women there. One of them must have taken it. And right under my own eyes in the hospital. Who would do a thing like that?" "This woman had her purse stolen," I said to the clerk at the desk in the lobby, going through the details for him. "Maybe one of the janitors picked it up, in which case it will be turned in," said the clerk, looking at me a little peevishly for standing in the lobby in my dirty work-clothes. "No," I replied, "this only happened about fifteen minutes ago. The janitors go through early on Saturday." "In any case," said the clerk, loftily to the woman, "we will take your name and address. It may be handed in." "My name is Mrs. Anderson," said the woman, quietly now, but without hope. "I know it was stolen and

I won't ever see it again." "Wait here a minute," I said to her, "I'll be right back."

I ran to empty my bucket, and hurriedly dressed in the locker room, punched the time-clock and came back to the lobby. "We have given Mrs. Anderson carfare," said the clerk. "Perhaps the purse will be recovered." "I have an extra dollar," I said to her, "which I would be glad to let you have." "No, I couldn't take it," she said in a low voice, quickly looking about her, and turning to go out of the hospital. Outdoors I urged her again and she finally accepted it with great embarrassment. "Will you do me another favor?" she asked. "Will you go with me as far as the street car?" The lights from the Christmas tree in front of the hospital entrance colored her face with an incongruously happy red and orange flush. "No Christian person would do a thing like that," she said while we walked to the street car. "They must have a pretty black heart. My poor little girl just had her appendix out. I don't know what we are going to do." "I live your way," I said to her. "If you don't mind, I will ride with you." The street car was crowded and we had to sit on opposite sides. On the way to her home she called out "Thank you" several times across the aisle.

Mrs. Anderson lived in the poor district near the stockyards. "You've been so nice to me," she said, "I would ask you up, but I left the house in a terrible mess. And it's so late now I think my husband is home." Still she did not say good-by to me but remained hesitating at my side. "Perhaps I should come up anyway," I suggested, "it might be easier if I were along." "If you wouldn't mind," she said eagerly. She led me through a passageway and up the rear stairs. She climbed ahead of me, and on the way up turned once and smiled down at me with a sudden youthful smile. She pressed my hand before ringing the bell and said, "Well, here goes."

Her husband opened the door and we stepped into the kitchen. Around the stove in the center of the room sat three little children. Mrs. Anderson rushed at them as she entered, crying, "I've told you a hundred times not to play on the floor," and without stopping to remove her hat and coat shooed the children into the bathroom. Her husband looked at me mistrustfully. "My name is Joe," I said. "Joe Feigenbaum." He looked at me with suspicion for a few moments and then hurriedly offered me his hand as if to destroy the impression that he had forgotten to do so at the proper time. He had been drinking coffee and he now returned to the table and invited me to sit down. "No thank you," I said, "I shall be leaving in a moment." I remained standing. I felt it would be better if I told him before his wife came back into the room, but I was uncertain how to begin. He was a lean, sharp-featured man with hazy eyes and, I feared, a temper. I was worried about the outcome, but I remained standing uneasily under his scrutiny and looked about the kitchen. A pile of unwashed dishes lay in the sink, and leaning in a corner stood a thin, ragged Christmas tree, unmounted. Mrs. Anderson re-entered the room. She had changed her dress for a clean apron and was smoothing her hair and putting in the last few pins as she entered. "How is Jennie?" asked her husband. "Jennie is doing fine," said Mrs. Anderson, speaking with a hairpin in her mouth. "Did you pay the hospital bill?" She cast a quick look at me before answering him. "You lost the money!" he cried, springing up from the table. "The purse was stolen from me, George." She was attempting to speak calmly. George made a quick gesture with his arm as if to strike her. "Oh, please, George!" she cried, catching his arm. "This man was with me, he works in the hospital. He was so nice, George, he let us have a dollar." "A dollar!" cried George. "What are we going to live on for the rest of the week? How are we going to pay that bill?"

"I am getting paid on Monday," I said, stepping forward. "I will be very glad to help you." "That's so nice of you," he said, "and I suppose you'll pay the *whole* bill too? Oh, that woman— she can't hold on to money to save her life. Now how are we going to pay the bill? How are we going to live this week? Answer me that!" He moved forward, threatening her. She looked at me pleadingly, motioning to the door. The powder she had applied before re-entering the room showed white on her face. "Go on, get out of here!" cried her husband at me. "Don't stand there lying to me that it was stolen. Get out!" Mrs. Anderson nodded her head insistently at me. "I hope everything will be all right," I said. "I will be glad to help you." I went out, closing the door cautiously. I had gone down a few steps when I heard the sound of a blow coming from the kitchen followed by a woman's scream. I heard another blow and another, louder, scream. Rushing back up the stairs, I heard a sound of falling dishes followed by a slamming door, and then a quiet sobbing.

I sat now at the window letting the cold wind blow in on me and hearing in my mind the woman's screams and her long-drawn-out, peaceful sobbing. I felt a tenderness for her distracted fear, for the innocence with which she had reacted to evil, and for the sudden flirtatious warmth she had shown me when I accompanied her into her home. Nevertheless, I knew I could not reach her in her suffering. And sitting in my dark room I felt removed from the world, and with a sudden philosophical emotion I saw all humanity before me suffering from evil, while I alone looked on and could see the cause. Why, since it was the holiday season, should not purses be filled instead of stolen? Why shouldn't somebody have slipped some money into the purse as it lay on the washstand, even a penny? I saw the result of this act, Mrs. Anderson helplessly caught up and frantic, and I saw the necessity which led to her husband's blows, he, too, helpless. I wanted to call out against this necessity, to cry, "Stop! You do not understand!" But it was merely given to me to be a witness, to look on and be alone in my understanding, and this only increased my loneliness.

But as I sat at the window I heard faint music floating in toward me, and I recognized a Russian song sung by a chorus and accompanied by an accordion. I listened to the sweet, sinuous melody, and all of a sudden I saw a summery plain on the out-skirts of a village, and there, in peasant costumes, a group of young boys and girls were dancing in the sun, dipping and wind-ing, snapping their fingers, gesturing with their arms, and calling out in lusty voices.

I rose from the window and, throwing off my hat and coat, ran out into the hall. The sounds were proceeding from the floor below me and, following the music, I came to my landlady's door and stood for a moment listening. Without knocking, I entered, motioning to her to remain seated. She was sitting in the corner by her Victrola, her hands folded in her lap, smiling faintly and nodding her head in time with the music. I threw myself into a chair and listened, following the young dancers over the plain.

The record came to an end, and my landlady, smiling with embarrassment, said, "I am all alone in the house on a Saturday night, so I was playing a record. My boy went out and my hus-band hasn't come back yet. Sometimes when I'm alone I like to play a folksong. Is there anything you want, Mr. Feigenbaum?"

"No, no!" I said. "I want to hear it. Play it again!"

She released the catch and set the needle to the record. There came the rollicking introduction of the accordion, and then the chorus, softly at first, and then swelling out, the music increas-ing in tempo. My heart melting, I sat up in the chair, waving my arms and softly snapping my fingers. My head was thrown to one side and I smiled, feeling an ecstasy rising within me. I could see my landlady watching me with a kind bewilderment, and then smiling back at me, she began waving her arms, and throwing her head back in answer. Suddenly she bent down in her chair, removed her shoes and stepped out on the floor holding her arms spread above her. Delicately kicking to either side with her stock-ing feet, she went into the dance. She spun around the room, waving her hands at her wrist, her feet making a soft thud on the rug. "Oh you are good!" I cried out and I could see in this stocky middle-aged woman the soul of the dancers on the plain. Her body whirled around, heavy, unused to the dance, but for me it had grace; her large, round bosom was thrust forward, but in it I could see the heart twinkling; her arms were moving through the air but I could see in them that same embracing softness, and they were acting out the human goodness of the dancers of the plain.

The music was still playing, but suddenly my landlady stopped in her dance and her hands remained elevated at her sides. I looked to the door and there stood her husband, swaying unconsciously and clumsily to the music, and a look of astonishment on his face. The record ended; the needle whirred and scratched. My landlady walked over to the Victrola in her stocking feet, stopping the record, and it came to a halt with a slow, shrieking skid. Then she bent down and began putting on her shoes. I looked into her husband's face, in which a silly, glass-eyed, and still widening astonishment remained, and I looked at his thin, spent figure; then I looked at my landlady, her dark face flushed and her eyes flashing, and at the breath coming heavy in her now vigorous body. I sensed the embarrassment between them, but I was ready to leap for joy for the vision of goodness I had had. I alone could have explained to them what this awkward scene really meant, but instead I asked her, "What is the name of that piece?"

" 'Dyerevna.' By the Village."

"It is very nice," I said. "And thank you for dancing it for me. You danced it very well." Oh, but the words I could have spoken then!

Turning I went out of the room, and as I passed her husband I realized what a profound and sympathetic attachment had grown up between my landlady and me.

Oh landlord, I could pull you up by the ears, kiss you on the head, tweak your nose, tickle your ribs—what a wife you have!

[1941]

JOE THE JANITOR

MANY PEOPLE THINK THAT I AM MAD. NOW, SEE HOW EASY it is to say "many people." Actually, I know only a few. But allow me. If I had a woman I know what she would think. Suppose we had finished our supper, and outside there were a magnificent sunset and I, after looking at it, turned to her and said, "Ninotchka, it is beautiful, it is a work of God!" "Yes, it's very pretty," she would say. "But why do you always have to drag in God?" Find me a woman who wouldn't say that. But then, can you blame them? There is an intensity in my nature which always seeks the highest expression. Where others find peace in sleep, I find it in exaltation, in vivid internal excitement. Ah, then I feel good! Energy surges in me, the spirit rages, I am alive! Naturally, this is something the world does not understand. And yet I am no demon. I am a mild-looking young man, a little below average height, with watery eyes and an ear for music, and all in all a pleasant individual. So why, really, should the world think ill of me?

The reason is clear. People look at me and say, "He is always alone, he is a janitor in a hospital (and such an educated young man—imagine, a janitor!), and he talks to himself." But no harm is done in talking to myself. I have observed it and it is always to the point. And what if I am a janitor? It is good work, I swindle no one, and I love to mop floors—the rhythm of it soothes me. And as for my being alone, I am really not so isolated. I am surrounded by the world. Everything that lives presses in on me.

I think everything has a soul. Take my mop that I use at work. What a busy little woman it is! Gray little housewife, tangled, juicy, pussycat. Of course, it has a low-grade soul, one of the lowest of the low. All it knows is water. But other objects that your well-dressed family man will pass so blindly, they are full of soul. Take dogs. Dogs are so mute, so pining; in them a soul is imprisoned. Dogs are always sad, they have a burden. But it's no great matter, it is even disappointing when you see what they want. They want to be like their masters, own cars and open up a business. They have the soul of a well-dressed man. Whenever I see a dog struggling with his identity, wagging his tail, rolling on his back, imploring with his tongue, I cannot help but smile. For if you gave him his liberty and opened the gates of his heart, what do you think he would do? He would tell you what's proper. Lover of dogs that I am, that is why I do not have a dog. I prefer other people's dogs. I am too sensitive.

One of my favorite occupations is to walk in the park. It is here that I meet my dogs. Here is one, a tawny shepherd with a lank smiling jaw, full of teeth. He has great strength. With him is his master, a mean man. I look at the two of them as they are standing on a little hill and I realize that I could express myself to the dog more easily than to the master under any circumstances. What a man he is! While he and the dog are playing, it is he who growls, he who bares his teeth, utters sharp cries, strikes out with his arms and fists. In his face is all the hatred, all the cruelty in the world. He takes a little stick, throws it down the hill and calls to his dog, "Get him, Pal, sic 'im, tear 'im apart, that a boy, kill 'im, kill 'im!" The dog catches the stick in his mouth and trots back with it to his master. That is what hurts. Could it be that the dog is fallen too? Could the master, seeing me pass and taking on a sudden hatred, call his dog on me? Would his lank jaws clutch me at the shin bone, crush and penetrate with hatred, snapping my leg in two? No. I know it cannot be done. For as I go by, the dog recognizes me, and I see him grow tense and whimper. He runs up to me and wags his tail. His eyes look into mine and he says, "I love you, comrade, you have a pure heart. Have no fear, I would never bite your shins." But then he sniffs at me and I know he is making a mental reservation. "My master is better dressed than you," he is thinking. "C'm here, Pal!" cries his master in a jealous voice, enraged. The dog trots off, looking back at me over his shoulder and saying, "Well, comrade, farewell. I must go to him. After all, I am only a dog."

Now you think that's not very profound of me. Anyone can tell you that dogs have a soul. Very well, take something else. Take a grocery store. There is a small grocery store near my house. Sometimes it catches me as I go by, and I stand and stare in the window. I see a few loaves of bread, their brown crusts cracked and shiny, a few sweet rolls, a box of cheese, a pyramid of halvah. Ah, how sad I feel when I look into that window! In it is all the sadness in the world. I remember how I once entered that store. I came up to the counter feeling sad and sorry for the small store, for the sweet rolls, the tub of herring, for the gray-haired lady behind the counter. "What do you want?" she asked me in a surly voice. She didn't like the way I was staring and abstractedly nodding my head. "What do I want." Ah, what sadness! On the floor was a box of onions. I picked up an onion and laid it on the counter. It was wrinkled, old and dry, and it had begun to sprout. "What do you want?" she repeated. "What do I want." I saw a package of marshmallows on the counter and I pointed and said, "Give me this." She gave me the marshmallows with an injured look. What do I want with marshmallows, and especially these that are cracked and dry?

Or with a Teddy bear that I see in the window of a toy-shop? I look at it and suddenly I feel that life is precious, ah, so precious. I smile at myself for staring at a silly toy, but at the same time I feel a burden, and I cannot throw off my burden. I would smile at myself, but as I stand before the dusty fly-specked window it is like staring deep, deep into the heart of things.

Then how can you say I am alone when I go around like this day after day? I am cheerful and my heart is light, but also sad, filled with a sad, wistful cheerfulness. In me are gathered all human desire and all human frustration. Everything that lives presses in on me. How precious life is! I think of Teddy bears, dogs, surly women, dry marshmallows. I think of myself, of everything, the dust in the street, and I realize that the world is eternal and that everything has a soul. I struggle to give voice to this, I try to find words. How tight my heart feels, how pressed! I want to sing and cry.

The boys at work have given me a character. I am their pet, their "professor," and although they respect me, their "queer guy." I am a little to blame for this—you see, I am vain. I could well have been just one of them, merely Joe who eats sandwiches and drinks coffee out of the Thermos bottle. Or at least I could have been the silent type in their eyes: a young man, none too strong and none too bright despite his education, who never says a word, but is still a dependable worker. But no, I had to have my ego-pleasure. I would occasionally come early to work bringing a book with me and sit and read in our locker room until the rest of them arrived. Sometimes I would even write a few observations—nothing dramatic or sustained, for I do not fancy myself a writer. Well, this is all right, it is casual. A man is lonely, so he reads in a room where there are old clothes and shoes, brushes, towels, dust mops, a room where other people will soon arrive. Or, his room is cold, so he writes a word or two in a place where his fingers are not cramped. There is nothing self-conscious about this, and if he really wants to pass unnoticed then he can put aside his occupation in time before the boys come in. Ah, but you are dealing with me! I would always feel the impulse to continue until the other janitors showed up. I would even go out of my way and read a book that bored me, write when I had nothing to write. Naturally, they caught me at it. "What are you doing, Joe? What are you writing? Are you a writer? Let's see what you've got!" They snatched the paper from my hands and read aloud some of the lines I had written. "Hey, boys, Joe, here, is a writer! Write about us, Joe. Write about the mop." Well, I made my point, so let them kid me a little. I don't mind. In fact, I am secretly pleased, and I now wait for them to allude to it. Kid me all you want, boys. There is no harm in your voices. It is milk and honey, you are angels, all of you.

Then there was the time when I made myself out as a bit queer. It was when I had first begun to work and I was not yet used to the labor. Perhaps the exertion of swinging a mop made me a little faint and light-headed. There I was standing on the wet floor, my arms aching, my hands blistered, and sweat pouring from me. Click-clack, slip-slop, went my mop. I no longer felt the exertion. I felt only a tenseness at my heart, a tightness, a sadness without weight and yet the most unbearable of burdens. Soon, soon it would burst on me. Soon I would spread, flow in all directions. And suddenly it came on. I was flooded with cheerfulness. There was cheer in my eyes, in my ears, at my heart, and still the sadness remained, mingling with it. I heard a voice saying, "This is you, Joe, you swinging the mop." I felt my whole personality welling within me, I tasted it with my entire being. "Swing the mop, little brother, swing!" it cried. It was time to quit. The boys were beginning to put away their tools. But I ran back dipping my mop into the bucket and crying, "Once more, once more, I love it!" And back on the floor I ran, swinging my mop, pushing it into all corners in a fever, sweat pouring from my face, and within me the voice, the dear clear voice whispering, "This is you, Joe." "He is nuts," I heard the boys laugh. It pleased me to hear them say this. I could have embraced them all.

This feeling of self, it is so precious, so good to have. It is as precious as life itself. Without it I don't know where I should be.

It has saved me many times from boredom, from hating myself or my work, from feeling like a failure, even from fearing death. How lonely I should otherwise be! Thank God for it, thank God that sometimes holding my mop or walking in the park I meet myself face to face.

Not long ago I came near a breakdown. I was bored with my work and I hated my mop. It became for me a lewd spinster, a symbol of my drudgery. I picked my calluses from my hands, I washed incessantly, I was obsessed with the desire to be clean. "You are a man with an education," I told myself. "A boy with a B.A. and several credits toward a master's on the very campus where you are now mopping the floor. You've missed the bus, dropped your cue, let the silver cord slip from your fingers. You are lost, Joe. Go look in the dustbin. Has anyone seen Joe? You are lost, Joe, lost." I lay awake at night feeling sorry for myself. But gradually my self-pity changed to fear and I lay awake thinking that I must die, and fearing death. In despair I called up to my mind the image of a young girl, naked, clean, brimming with life. I clasped her to me, trying to enter into the stream of her life and share her undying beauty, but she kept slipping away from me and I was left to die alone, unredeemed and filthy. I broke out into a sweat and I sat up on the edge of my bed and turned on the light. I looked at the clock which pointed so desolately, so eternally to seven minutes after three, the loneliest hour in the world. "What will become of you?" I began to cry. I sobbed, snickered, urged myself to cry. I clenched my fist and struck myself on the head. I unclenched my fist and picked my calluses, mourned for each particle of dead skin, a flake of the dead me. "You are rotting on your bones, go clean yourself!" I ran to the bathroom and stripped and washed, going over my entire body with a washrag for the third time that night. I changed pajamas, I lay back in bed with my head where my feet had been, I piled on extra covers, but still I shivered with the sickening fear of death. I longed to be clean, fresh, vivid. I longed for life and for vivid, exalted peace, and for the voice which would come and whisper to me. Instead I heard only a nursery rhyme which went round and round, jangling incessantly in my mind:

> *Water, water we must drink*
> *To keep our bodies fresh and pink.*

For several days I went around like this. Then one night coming home from work and walking through the campus I heard music. There was a concert in the court. I was very tired, feverishly exhausted from work, from lack of sleep. I sank down on the edge of the crowd, shut my eyes and rested. They were playing Tchaikovsky, the *Romeo and Juliet* overture. "Tchaikovsky!" I said aloud, and suddenly Tchaikovsky was part of me and part of my odor of sweat and I could feel Tchaikovsky in my nostrils. I opened my eyes and looked about me.

What is this? Hundreds of people packed the court sitting on chairs and benches, lying on the grass, on newspapers, on blankets, crouched in doorways, leaning out of windows, side by side, twos, threes, fours, touching. And over them all the music. And more people arriving, coming from all corners, silently walking forward, drawn together to the edge of the crowd. I sat alone, but I could feel excitement and exaltation rising in me. I looked at the hundreds of people, each one separate, each a center of feeling and consciousness, and I felt them all merging and joining together in me. And as I sat there hearing the music and seeing the people arriving, arriving, still driven on, light from the orchestra reflected in their eyes as they moved forward, it seemed to me that these were their souls walking, not they. This was Judgment Day, and the souls were arriving, kneeling on the grass, lying on their backs and in each other's arms. And those who were still coming were coming to stay and not to leave, until all who were waiting would hear the final trumpet bringing them deliverance in shattering, vivid peace. By my side were a young boy and a young girl so near to me I could have touched them, kissed them both. Before me sat a bald man so near I could have kissed his gleaming head. Together we were, all our souls, and I was no longer alone. I was lying in the girl's arms, I was resting on the bald man's lap. We were all one substance, one stuff, one soul, and judgment was pouring forth on us.

And then tears rose in my eyes while I heard the voice whisper, "You, Joe, this is you." And I joined it crying, "Life is precious, let me hold to it, oh let me live forever, yes forever, dear sweet life. Let me always feel myself, know that I am I to the ultimate change in nature, past death, past grass, past stone." "Have no fear, but only praise and yearning," answered the voice. "This is you, Joe." And desire for immortality, the greatest joy, the greatest yearning rose in me and welled out with my tears.

It was over. There was applause from unclasped hands, shattering the air. The bald man, rising, stepped on my foot. No matter, bald one, I have lain in your lap. No matter, girl, do not smooth your dress about you. I have lain in your arms. No matter, people, breaking apart, falling off, going. We will live, we are one. You will carry me home with you.

I, too, rose and went home. I climbed the stairs, washed, went to bed. I felt the cool sheet about me urging me to sleep, and I yielded, and it was good to yield to the pillow and the sheet. Good to yield although I was alone at night, good to submit unafraid, though alone, though clinging only to myself. It was good to give myself back to life, to precious, delicate life, knowing I might always give myself, without fear, and with belief in my yearning.

[WRITTEN 1941; UNPUBLISHED]

The Colony

⌒

1. Satya and the Indefatigables

Satya knew that his arrest was imminent.

For several months he had been living in a village on the outskirts of Allaban, the capital of the Central Province. Having adopted the way of life of the lowest peasants, he had established himself in a mud-hole. His hut had walls, ceiling, and floor, but it deserved no better name than the one in the native language meaning mud hole or hole-in-the-ground by which dwellings of this type were known. During the rainy season it was all but unbearably damp, in the dry season the heat grew intense and the walls chipped and needed constant patching with mud. A few slits served him for light and ventilation. A cotton rug lay on the floor, where Satya worked and slept. A stove and a row of cooking utensils occupied one wall; against another leaned a low couch on which he received visitors.

Three Indefatigables now guarded his door. They relieved one another at eight-hour intervals and contrived, somehow, to meet three times during the day—at sunrise, noon, and sundown—when they would stand together uniformly tall and white, wearing the new furry headgear, their buckles gleaming. When all three stood together they completely hid the house behind them.

No general orders for the arrest of party leaders had as yet been issued. The authorities were allowing the fifth-year general party meeting to be held in the Central Province, in the hope that a violent session, a public incident, or even a strongly-worded resolution would provide grounds for beginning the oppression. But, as everyone knew, and as the higher, and therefore more cynical, officials admitted, they were desperate and might begin without pretext, if finding one demanded too long a wait.

During the week preceding the opening session, Satya busied himself with the preparation of his presidential address. He was of poor memory for all but his own words; while he could have reproduced nearly intact any speech he had ever delivered, he was always unable to prepare a fresh one without the use of a library. And since he lived simply—in "ostentatious poverty" as he called it—and therefore kept neither reference works nor bound newspapers, he had found it necessary to apply to the district commander for permission to visit the library of Allaban.

The interview was humiliating. First, Satya was kept waiting in the antechamber while others—whites—who had arrived after him were admitted to an audience with the commander. Then a secretary came out and informed him that, by a new ruling, natives were required to wait in the reserved antechamber. Satya was led behind a screen into a small, square, unventilated, and unlighted room, where there were neither benches nor chairs. He was determined to stand, to bear indignity with dignity; but, his legs tiring, he squatted in a corner, and finally sat on the floor. As soon as his eyes had become accustomed to the darkness he discovered a row of mops and brooms hanging from the ceiling. The room, however, was not a porter's closet, but had rather been decorated to resemble one. This he ascertained by examining the mops and brooms and a stack of pails that he found in one corner; all were new and unused. There were also a pair of sandals and a glove, such as a porter might wear.

An hour passed before he was admitted into the official chambers. The commander, receiving him, declared, "Satya, old boy!"

attaining, thereby, a perfectly ambiguous insult. To call a native "boy" was to follow custom, while to speak his name, adding the adjective, "old," was to indulge in a play at equality. Officials adopted either form of address, but only the highest used both; for while all whites were practiced in arrogance, only the elite had mastered ambiguity.

The commander did not let him begin. He insisted on showing Satya about his office, which was furnished as deliberately as the porter's closet. The commander dragged down an elephant's tusk that had been hollowed out and filled with gold, and urged Satya to "get the heft of it." It was hefty and, as far as Satya was concerned, thoroughly disgusting; he was, if anything, even further humiliated. "Just throw it anywhere," said the commander. "Here, I'm sure you'd like to see these gems.—Oh, I say, would you mind putting it back where it was? You can use that chair." The commander, who was taller than Satya, had risen on his toes to reach the top of the bookcase. Satya did not remove his sandals before stepping onto the satin covered chair; but he felt the petulance of his gesture, and he feared it had cost him dignity. The gems he was invited to see had been set in a hand mirror to form the coat-of-arms of the mother country. This, too, had been done with deliberate vulgarity. The commander shrugged his shoulders, as if to say, "We wouldn't normally go in for that sort of thing, but you people rather expect it of us." Observing Satya's displeasure, he remarked, "Perhaps a little inappropriate. You know, they come from one of your temples. Forget which. Either in Bagputana or Charnadras. One that goes like this . . . Middle period." He drew the outline of a temple in the air.

"I came," began Satya, "to . . ."

"Oh, do sit down, at once. Don't stand on ceremony." The commander offered him a cigar (Satya did not smoke); a drink (Satya did not drink). "Well, you know, it's been such a long time. You boys used to be much more communicative." He said this with an ambiguous wink, which may also have been the tic of a burdened administrator; the tone of his voice, however, was unmistakable. It was as if he had said, "Politics is politics, let's not delude ourselves. Instead of playing your silly old game, you could be holding down a good spot as a magistrate."

Satya, in an unfriendly, severe, and formal tone, finally made his request. The commander, enjoying a paradox, replied that in an efficient society, where government fulfills its proper functions, even those elements who seek to destroy it must depend on it for support. "You want us to put our properties at your disposal," he continued, in weary and ironic condescension, "so you may write a speech that would send everything crashing down."

Satya remarked that the library at Allaban was hardly a government property, since all its books were in the native language, as the commander could ascertain by a visit; and that a speech intended primarily for the overthrowing of the government did not require research. One had only to say the obvious, with no more than natural emotion, to arouse, if one wanted, the most violent reaction. Satya, however, had to do some research, for his speech—and here, with his most insolent courtesy, he pretended to take the commander into his confidence, which was as insulting to the official as the latter's courtesy had been to the native—his speech was to survey the last five years, and he would find it very embarrassing if the party's younger intellectuals caught him in error while he reported events in which he himself had been prominent.

The commander smiled delicately as if to show that he, too, was acquainted with the ways of intellectuals. And, to demonstrate his superior irony he replied, repeating himself, "It's quite well that you come to us. By inviting government to participate in its own destruction, you learn to depend on it. And so you strengthen us. You are unable to take a step without us."

He therefore thought it would be unsporting to grant Satya's request. "Your tactics are wrong. I cannot—as one commander to another—" and here he raised his lip again, spreading the bristles of his moustache—"allow you to pursue such poor tactics. My good man, I must refuse!"

Satya therefore announced that he would proceed without permission. The years of self-discipline and control were in vain. He felt himself grow angry and he knew that he was on the verge of haranguing the commander with a review of the party's history and of recalling, to his complacently short memory, the number of times that the party had shaken the government by its disobedience movement and brought it to the verge of falling.

Party members had long since refused to bow themselves out of an official's presence. Satya stiffly walked away. "One moment!" the commander called after him. "Hey, boy! Not that door— out the other way!" Satya, disobeying, did not turn back.

In the courtyard he recognized two of his guards, who had evidently followed him to the city. Thereafter, one of the three Indefatigables was detained at the mud-hole, while the other two, in furry headgear, accompanied him to the library, to the stacks, and about the city in the blazing sun. As he sat and worked, one guard stood on his left, the other on his right. When he walked in the street one preceded him and the other followed. The Indefatigable at the head of the procession, never knowing which way Satya would turn, was constantly wandering off in the wrong direction or being left at street corners and always had to be recalled.

Ever since the death, some three years earlier, of Bapu, who had led the resistance party for nearly half a century, Satya had been the head of the movement. His official title was party president, which, in itself, meant little, for he had held the same office for ten years, while Bapu had still been alive. The old man had preferred to serve without office and had withstood all urging with his well-known stubbornness, replying, when pressed, that he was obviously unfit for politics. "There is only one office for which my poverty qualifies me—treasurer," he had said on one semipublic occasion, at a conference of district leaders. Later, in private, Satya had reprimanded him. "Bapu, allow me to say, you take too much pride in your humility. You make it conspicuous."

"Dear boy," Bapu had replied, which was all he had to say, for his moral command over his followers was such that anyone who accused him of pride thereby stood accused of greater pride. The old man had never failed to illustrate his beliefs through his own character. He had shown the extraordinary force that resides in gentleness, the obduracy of the sweet and self-effacing smile, the tyranny of sacrifice. While he had inspired the greatest love and reverence even in nonreligious men, while simple souls had proclaimed him a saint, and the complex, and more modern, had secretly agreed, he had, nevertheless, by a universal but timid acknowledgment, also been considered something of a crank. Thousands had willingly died for him, but never, thought Satya, without a trace, a spoor, a particle of resentment.

But Satya did not question his indebtedness to Bapu. He had accepted the doctrines laid down by the old man and defended them in the party. There was, in fact, very little criticism of Bapu's work. A few extremists, who had always dissented, argued that the growth of government oppression confirmed their views. But the majority of the party held that the old man's policy had been sound, and that no one could have foreseen, he least of all, the drastic changes in the country's administration that had been introduced after his death. The strategy Bapu had followed— refusing to call it a strategy, he had sought only moral justification for it—was correct not only morally, thought Satya, but politically. It was, he admitted, a curious political counsel that turned to a study of Scripture rather than economics; and yet, saintliness had succeeded where mere political shrewdness would have failed. No other doctrine would have gained such a large following among the superstitious and illiterate masses. Even the lowest peasants in the remotest corners of the country, men so degraded and stupefied by oppression that the most elementary significance of political struggle remained inaccessible to them, nevertheless venerated Bapu's name and, regarding him as a God, improvised, through the devotions of a cult, some of the very measures he would have had them adopt by reason alone.

Bapu had feared in his youth that the country was not ready for liberation. Several times he had called off the resistance movement, doubting that his followers were prepared for the struggle. In his later years the old man had seen that freedom would not be achieved in his lifetime. It had, perhaps, been a kind of vanity that had led him, toward the end of his life, to intensify the struggle. Some believed that he had died a disappointed, an outraged man. But, apparently, he had not expected to attain his goal. He knew he would die in the desert, a Moses; during the last period he had taken to calling Satya "Aaron."

But if the country was not ready for freedom now, it never would be. It is possible, thought Satya, that a nation's deepest need cannot be considered a responsibility. Freedom is more than a responsibility to men; it is a higher obligation, and while they may not be prepared to receive it, they must, they absolutely must, live only to obtain it. The old man's teachings had therefore been wrong in assuming that there was ever a moment when men's readiness for freedom could be determined. But he had at least recognized that the need was always present; if he had preferred to wait, out of prudence, or out of a desire for moral perfection, he had nevertheless been wise enough to impose his restrictions at a time when prudence and perfection were still practical. But virtue had never been so impractical as it was now.

The new government—or the new administration—for the country had always been administered rather than governed— which took office during the crisis brought on by Bapu's death, soon proved itself to be no mere colonial bureaucracy. Where previous regimes had been cruel and corrupt, the present administration was only cruel. And if bureaucracies by nature are corrupt, they are known to be so only when approached with bribes. The bureaucracy that now held office made itself unapproachable, and therefore outwardly honest. But it was skilled in arithmetic, even if it refused to employ its talents in counting up bribes, and it followed the same thumb-to-tongue rule of carefully fingering the issues of state that its predecessors had observed in the traffic of banknotes.

Against the present, as against previous regimes, the party was carrying forth the nonviolent struggle in which Bapu had instructed it. Essentially religious, an elaboration of the ancient faith, nonviolence had, under the old man's guidance, made its way into politics. It was the only means, so the party intellectuals had reasoned, whereby, after the failure of all the violent struggles that had arisen in Europe and in parts of the East after the war, men might still attempt to attain a measure of decency, that is, moral success, as well as political success in the effort to free themselves.

Perhaps one needed religious capacity really to take nonviolence to heart. But Satya was not a religious man. He had once in his youth endeavored to learn Scripture and to follow the old religion in all its precepts. But he had begun too late, for the literature of the West was known to him (he had been educated abroad) and he was still struggling with the first chapter of the Text, when he had already read the works of European socialists. He understood the destiny and the suffering of his country far better by looking to a socialist future than by considering the religious past. As for acquiring merit, he realized he would never learn the full list of sacred vegetables, or receive more than sentimental satisfaction from prayer. Even during the early period of his association with Bapu, which had been marked by incessant controversy, he had felt no need—a self-confidence rare among the old man's

followers—to apologize for his Western instincts. He accepted
science; he believed himself a materialist, and he hoped that some
day the country would be fully industrialized. And yet politics is
politics, practical truth lacks symmetry and even the most consistent revolutionary is, at heart, a foe of progress. If, as he was convinced, a violent struggle was not feasible, if an unarmed country
could never oust an armed oppressor by bloodshed, then one
should be thankful for backwardness insofar as it is the condition
of that country's liberation. For nonviolence could draw on endless resources: poverty, misery, disease, humiliation, even ignorance and superstition. But what little supply of arms a violent
revolution could amass would soon be exhausted and violence
would be reduced to a useless expenditure of lives.

And then, was there any assurance, even if the country
were armed, that violence would prove a success? War after war
had been fought, revolution after revolution—why, some revolu-
tions had even been "successful"—but all they had ever accomplished might as well never have been attained, for a single war
had wiped out every trace of enlightenment and left a ravaged and
exhausted world, its strength squandered, its culture degraded,
its men turned into beasts, whose only instinct now was to prepare for further violence. The West had died. All that had survived was what it had set out to destroy. The achievement of
liberation and the establishment of a socialist society required a
more reliable means than violence. And the only alternative to
violence was nonviolence.

There was also to be considered the desire for power, characteristic of all ruling groups. Satya had warned the people against
the expropriation of power by their own party leaders in an anonymous article he had written, attacking himself. The authorship
of the article was soon discovered and the word spread, but it had
carried its point remarkably well; he had won greater confidence
among the masses, to whom it appeared that a leader so well

guarded against himself would never become a tyrant. But it took more than such devices to curb the appetite. To tell the truth, he did not absolutely trust himself. "Perhaps," he had wondered, "I stooped to trickery. Hadn't I known that the article would soon be traced to me?" Without the deepest, almost religious belief in the ends to which nonviolence was dedicated, without the constant attempt to overcome the vanity and the greed, the desire for power, and the other corrupting impulses to which the political leader was subject, he might, even if he achieved his ends, easily transgress against them, and pervert the general gain into a private or a bureaucratic exploitation.

But was nonviolence still possible? The present administration, while it had not yet fully shown what it was capable of, had already indicated that it was better prepared than its predecessors to protect the aims of government—to maintain the rule and not to yield. It had the advantage of freedom from public opinion in the mother country. There the oppression had already been established. On the pretext of rebuilding the national economy the whole country had been subjected to military discipline—or rather, the war in which it had been engaged for seven years had never been declared at an end. The army and the navy were maintained at full fighting strength. Trade unions were regulated and long hours were still exacted from factory workers, with strikes forbidden. All expression of protest was gradually curbed, and finally stifled. Parliament had not convened in three years and no election had been held in more than a decade. Political parties had been realigned for the duration of the "national emergency"— which meant that they had all been placed under the control of the political council, so that, while they differed in name, they now had the same leadership. Moreover, "experimental prisons" had been introduced and were rapidly overflowing with subjects for experiment. For the first time in history, a colony found itself not much worse off than the mother country.

The administration had good reason to fear its own ambitions. The colony was so vast that, at least until recently, there had not been enough arms at the government's disposal to coerce even an unarmed population. Millions of rounds of ammunition (their calculations must have amazed the government statisticians) would be needed to enforce the same discipline upon the colony that the mother country already enjoyed. Nor were there enough sites available for experimental prisons, which required large tracts of land in the less populous regions of the country, suitably drained and reclaimed. The administration had therefore embarked upon an intensive land development project in the northern provinces, improving for slavery the earth that it had considered good enough for freedom. And such enterprises were unprofitable. Altogether, it was a tremendous task, requiring careful and extensive preparation. It was understandable that the administration should show some reluctance to proceed with the oppression.

The district leaders, meeting in Allaban in pre-convention conference, were in very low spirits. Abvan Singh, Dr. Ramdas Sodha, and Givot Pandalamchari, who had journeyed (third class) from the Northern Province, were especially pessimistic as they gave their reports of the preliminary steps the administration was taking to incite the Resistance Party to violence. Several provocations had occurred in the North, the most serious being a charge of rape brought, curiously enough, against a white surveyor by a group of farmers and a white tax collector. The surveyor, who had recently arrived in the district and had not yet made any enemies, was accused of criminally assaulting a native woman, the wife of a tenant farmer. Her body had been found mutilated and several days dead in an irrigation ditch. The surveyor had concluded his work and was about to return to the Central Province when he was arrested and held in a local jail, some forty miles from the nearest court where criminal trials were usually staged.

The jail was in Lokhamadra, a city of fair size, known for its jute industries. The body of the woman was also taken to Lokhamadra, some twenty-five miles away from her own village, on the outskirts of which the alleged crime had occurred. This was an irregular procedure, since the local police in the town of Bhingat, only three miles away, was of adequate size to conduct a preliminary investigation and the facilities of a morgue and coroner were available there. The dead body had been placed in an open car, exposed to the view of the natives, and had slowly been driven through the streets of Bhingat and of the other towns on the way to Lokhamadra. The news had meanwhile been broadcast and as the body approached Lokhamadra, an angry crowd began to gather. By the time the dead woman reached Lokhamadra, the whole city was aroused; demonstrations were held in the bazaar and in the public squares. The body, scantily guarded, was left in the open for several hours. The delegates from the North considered it remarkable that no violent incident occurred.

The surveyor meanwhile had been placed, not in the large jail outside the city, but in a small police station in the bazaar where the natives soon discovered him. It was apparent that no precautions had been taken against a public uprising. Some believed that the station's normal complement of police had been dismissed; others, that they had fled. Whatever the case, the jail had been unguarded. The accused, who was in an outside cell, could easily have been reached from the street. But here, too, the people had restrained themselves and there was no violence, although several natives, who were later shown to be provocateurs, had tried to incite the crowd.

No storm had broken, for which the party was thankful; but the resentment had not been dissipated. A strange mood had come over the people. They were completely unconcerned in the trial (the murdered woman's funeral had been sparsely attended); and yet they showed an unprecedented bitterness. They knew even

before the party had been able to point it out to them, and
even before the trial had established it beyond doubt, that the
government had arranged the entire incident as a deliberate provocation. And while they had maintained perfect calm after the
initial demonstrations, it was a calm—so bitter was it—that could
exist only in the absence of a means of reprisal. Which had given
to the party leaders an indication of the danger now present in the
mood of the people, and to the administration whatever success it
had achieved in the affair. The trial itself had been dismissed when
the authorities saw that they had overplayed their hand and had
nothing more to gain. The surveyor had disappeared, returning, so
it was believed, to the mother country where he received a promo
tion in the civil service.

The delegates were now debating whether to bring the incident
before the party. The news had not, of course, reached the other
provinces, and had in fact not been known outside the densely
populated Northern Province. Satya advised the delegates to place
the affair on public record, to warn the people that they would
soon be exposed to similar provocations and incitements to riot.
It would also show how strong and efficient the censorship had
become, when it could arbitrarily restrict information to a single
region, and yet use every means of public dissemination radio,
newspaper, and rumor—to spread that information throughout
the area.

All had incidents to report; and all having traveled third
class, they had been subjected to the usual humiliations with a
few new annoyances, such as having to fill out in triplicate the
lengthy travel applications at each government inspection station
they had passed. (Some had encountered as many as twenty stations on the way, had missed their trains and been held over for
days without accommodations. The papers had previously been
carried by the traveler from origin to destination. The new ruling,
which had never been published, and which, the delegates were

certain, had been applied only against them, required that a complete set be made out at the beginning and surrendered at the end of each stage of the trip.)

The delegates spoke freely of their fears, confessing to Satya that, in Bapu's time, they had never known such pessimism. He felt no jealousy, no resentment. He himself shared in the general depression, the grief over losing a leader whom, he freely admitted, he himself could never replace. Nor did he remind them, in self-defense, that the administration had changed since Bapu's time. What colored man did not know this?

A few of the delegates had been placed, with Satya, under preliminary, or ambulatory, arrest and could go nowhere without the company of Indefatigables. Satya's own guard had been reduced by the removal of one of the soldiers—the one who had gone in advance of the procession and had never known which way to turn. The remaining Indefatigable now walked at Satya's side, the better to be seen. He had acquired the white man's usual arrogance. In private he called Satya "boy." But in public, whenever they passed a group of white officers in the street, he would address Satya by name while the officers were still within earshot, lest anyone fail to recognize his charge. Once, while they were abroad on a hot afternoon, he removed his headgear, wiped his forehead, and forgot himself to the extent of uttering a word of criticism of the administration that made him wear fur in summer. Satya also forgot himself and remarked, in all friendliness, and with an unforgivable assumption of equality—if not of actual superiority—that the soldier could consider himself fortunate that he was not stationed in the mother country, where his duties would have been more severe and degrading, since he should have had to oppress his own people. The soldier replaced his headgear, lengthened his stride and, prodding Satya along with his stick, reminded him that familiarity with the armed forces was not permitted to natives.

He was a fair young man of the blond type that turns red and irascible in the tropics; the sort of man who disintegrates as a person and is held together only by the external restraint of his uniform, without which he would go mad. The sweat that poured down his forehead had caused sores to break out among the sparse, fine, colorless hairs of his eyebrows; sticking flies troubled him. The skin under his headband was raw, and a vein beat in his throat. The Indefatigable grew more and more arrogant, showing his authority on the least provocation. He required Satya to open doors for him and to stand in the blazing street while he rested in the shade; envying the freedom of Satya's loose clothes, the full, unbinding trousers and the thin homespun jacket, he tried to impose military posture upon him, prodding his shoulders with his stick whenever Satya slouched, and ordering him to keep in step. The soldier wore boots; Satya wore sandals and his feet were soon blistered.

Public comfort stations were unavailable to colored men, who had to use segregated and foul latrines (All natives carried "toilet-cards," long strips of cardboard, ruled off in squares, which they had to insert in stamping machines that stood at the entrance.) The soldier, on the same day that he had forgotten himself and criticized the administration in Satya's presence, accompanied him to the latrine—a measure of the reinforced discipline he should now have to suffer. Satya, knowing he had never entered a native latrine, warned him of the unpleasantness. But men who had recently come from the mother country showed a curious avidity for pain. The Indefatigable went in and stood guard over him. Later, feeling the need to relieve himself, he made Satya come with him into a comfort station—tiled and white, equipped with washstands and electric dryers. Before entering one of the spacious stalls, he made Satya lock himself into the adjoining one, ordered him not to use it, to remain standing, and under no circumstances to step out until given permission to do so.

2. The Last Free Men

The meeting began shortly after sunrise, with a mass prayer during which the delegates knelt, facing the sun. The people were assembled in a large field, a natural theater shaped like a saucer with a broken rim, which was closed on three sides by a rise of ground and shallow at the farther end where the platform had been raised. Over the shallow the sun rose, and as those who knelt faced the sun, they seemed also to be praying to the leaders on the platform, the party's banner, and the cloth streamers, covered with slogans in all the native dialects, that were strung along the trees. This put a taint of idolatry on the prayer, confusing religion with politics in a manner which Satya, who sat on a dais and therefore seemed to be the object of worship, found extremely distasteful. But it could not be helped; there was a similar confusion in the country itself, an intermingling of tradition, chance, and necessity, which made irony inevitable and contradiction the rule of life.

Satya sat with his legs folded under him, his thighs forming a deep bay—the traditional human lap of generation and reception, which even the earliest gods had learned to imitate. So, level with the earth, they had poured forth their seed into furrows and valleys and, in return, received human offering, having discovered that this was the best position for the intercourse they held with men. The language in which the hymns were sung had once been a human language, but, now forgotten, it had become divine. So, too, the spreading of genital laps in the sign of nature pointed to a discontinued intercourse; and the gods, who were all split beings, owing half their existence to nature and half to man, had become one, as the original soil and the mark of human handiwork had merged. They had entered reality, acquiring their own natures, because, and this was all Satya would grant to the sacred metaphysic, it is what we put away from us that becomes real, not what we handle and use. That which dies acquires its own life.

Children were singing the hymns. They were ranged around
the platform many rows deep, their heads bowed, their hands
clasped at their breasts, their white gowns and bare feet, with
dully shining nails, making a natural uniform. The blue-black
straight glossy hair of the girls, parted in the middle, was bisected
by rows of white scalp and tightly drawn back in braids, forming
a pattern as of loaves or folded wings. They sang the sacred words,
not understanding them. Overhead fluttered the banners and the
political slogans—land, bread, freedom, self-rule—these, too,
words of a litany.

Satya neither prayed nor sang. His dry lips moved from time
to time, without forming syllables. His expression as usual was
melancholy, his large eyes, staring, the lines around his mouth
drawn into their habitual cast of pity or pain. He was now com
pletely gray and his complexion had an ashy undertone, combin-
ing the pale olive of nature with the infirmity of jails. He was at
once impatient and in repose, absorbed in himself yet conscious
of the crowd, withholding from prayer in the expression of his
individual conscience and yet, thereby, contributing to his public
image. It was the division of the inner and outer man, inseparable
from political life, both a conflict and a poise, neither wholly private nor wholly public, for neither in itself was whole. Thus, he
could look at the scene about him, enjoy its color, enjoy the spread
of caps and turbans, the crossed legs and arms, the deep almost
coal-black of the southern people, the lighter skins and finer features of the men from the North—all this he could enjoy, and also
the profusion of banners and flags, the costumes of the various
castes, the physical conformation of the tradesmen and artisans,
the stunted, homogenous bodies of the peasants—he could feel
himself part of this crowd and participate in its being, where he
should merely have been a spectator. Yet, knowing their misery,
their humiliation, recognizing signs of disease, malnourishment,
and deformity, knowing also the ignorance of the people, he felt

himself withdrawn, observing where he should have been moved to participation through sympathy. Bapu had never suffered the complexities of a divided nature. His faith had been whole, proceeding without deviation from the heart; his life and his work were identical. He had not known what it meant either to love the crowd or to stand off from them. Bapu had sat before them, his legs turned under, his lap spread out, and the dirt of the soil and the mark of handiwork—both visible—were one.

And yet Satya could feel a simple, positive joy, not to be subtilized, when he rose on the platform at the conclusion of the singing and received the ovation of the delegates. It was the joy of being with his people and of discovering again, in the moment of pride, who he was and what he was, when the inner life, expanding, merged with the outer and proved itself equally great. Then all humiliation was forgotten, all doubt and all fear. The warmth of the moment superseded consciousness and in an instant the public devotion, overleaping politics, met its reward out of time. The country was a nation, free, its ends accomplished.

It was only a metaphorical joy. A cordon of police had been drawn around the crowd. In the distance, coming down the slope of the outer range of hills, could be seen another troop of provincial police, and several magistrates, riding on elephants.

"Comrades," he began, "I am aware that your prayers were offered lovingly for one who was with us five years ago, at our last general session, and today is no more." His voice was loud and high; it reached clearly to the edge of the crowd. "I join you in that prayer. No one has known better than I how great a loss was the death of Bapu." He knew that his mind would take up its accustomed critical position, a little to the left of him—he felt it actually in terms of space—and run a commentary on his words. Already he was aware of duplicity—he had spoken of "joining in prayer" when, as everyone knew, he never prayed, and in his very first reference to Bapu he had inserted the words "at our last general session," as if he were careful to grant Bapu no more than his due and to restrict the attention to the present and therefore to himself by withholding complete reverence.

"It is now my painful duty to correct a misconception. Some have paraphrased the speech I delivered at Bapu's funeral as a sigh of relief, as though to say, 'Now watch our speed!' Nothing is further from the truth. You will recall that I said: 'Though this loss is inevitable, it is one from which we may never recover. It may also be inevitable that we fail.' " (He was aware of the pride he was taking in his memory.) "I should repeat those words today. I cannot recall a general party session which met under more unfavorable, more threatening circumstances." He described a wide arc with his arm to accompany these words; his hand swept over the line of soldiers and police ringing the crowd. The magistrates had dismounted from their elephants and had been brought, in golden sedans, carried by natives, to points of vantage on the surrounding hills. The administrators—governors, commanders, and bureaucrats—sat in a small grandstand at the side of the field shaded by large squares of bamboo, which, when worked with ropes, could serve also as fans.

"But it is true that I should like to hurry you, our time is running short. I do not want our steps to be ill-chosen; they must be firm and wise. I do not recommend recklessness in the name of action; we must now more than ever consider the wisdom of our policy, question it, improve it, enlarge it. But we must act and we must act quickly. We will soon have to face the greatest crisis in our struggle for liberation. The oppressor stands ready to strike his blow, and ours, too, must be prepared!"

Satya took the applause of the crowd with his accustomed sternness, standing erect and unyielding, as if to show that he could outface all emotion; he was the mover who would not in turn be moved. His glance passed beyond the people and rested on the cordon of police and soldiers, which had been reinforced and drawn up several rows deep along the edge of the meeting. He could make out the native interpreters busily translating his speech to members of the administration. Some of the administrators were deaf, and their interpreters kept bending down to relay the translation directly into their ears. At the edge of the platform he recognized his Indefatigable, who was boasting to a group of his fellows, stamping his heels, tossing his furry headgear, and pointing at Satya. Today the Indefatigables were all armed with carbines.

As the applause was dying out, one of the natives near the platform noticed the troops that had been stationed at the edge of the crowd. He called out, "Long live Satya!" and pointed to the police. The crowd at the shallow end of the field, their attention drawn to the surrounding troops, redoubled their applause and also raised the shout, "Long live Satya!" They rose to their feet and surged forward, applauding in the native manner with their arms extended over their heads and their palms meeting stiffly. They were awkward at applause; it was only at political meetings that they found occasion for it. But they were in the habit of expecting miracles, and their eyes, as they looked up to Satya, were full of a wild and unreasonable hope which—arousing both his pride and his displeasure—declared him their savior. He raised his hand for silence.

The next part of his speech drew no applause, but called out murmurs, sighs, expressions of pity and sympathy, and cries of outrage. He reviewed briefly the events of the preceding five years, the gains the party had made and the activities in which it had engaged. It was this part of his speech that he had carefully prepared, and he put on a pair of spectacles while he read it. His voice was pitched lower than before, modulated to avoid dullness, more closely resembling his natural tone and lacking the inflections of the agitator. Then he turned to describing the growth of government oppression. He removed his spectacles, put aside his notes and raised his voice again. It rang out to the edge of the field as he spoke of the insults and humiliations that the colored people had suffered; he spoke of the provocations in the North, telling in some detail of the false case the government had built against one of its own underlings, and his voice was full of indignation; he described the efficient working of the censorship and warned against future provocations, and his voice dropped and took on the well-practiced and sustained sinister tone, the slow and crafty and evil intonation, sibilant and harsh, that mimicked the oppressor's evil. The crowd responded as a body, expressing its anger, murmuring or crying out its protest. The little girls who had sung the hymns now wailed in distress, and Satya paused at appropriate moments to let them mingle their young voices with the grief of their elders. The sun rose and the morning heat grew. Satya sweated, and the crowd sweated with him. The natives were now pulling on the sheets of bamboo that hung over the grandstand.

"And what have they?" he cried out, his voice once more hard and clear in its anger, "what have they in their own country?" He wheeled sideways, and stood with his left shoulder and arm raised, his right arm drawn back—the pose of a javelin thrower about to let hurl at the crowd. "What of their boast that they have abolished poverty and disease and unemployment? What of the promises they hold out to us? I have thanked them for their good intentions—I have expressed the people's gratitude to them. We say: No, thank you! Far happier is our own wretched peasant with his acre of unproductive ground and his blistered hands, with his broken back and cut and bleeding feet—far happier is he, so long as he resists their rule, than anyone of their own well-fed and athletic race who submits to it! We say: No! Little do they realize that the crust of freedom which we treasure with our sacred hunger is better than the bread that they must eat. What are their goods to us?—the corruption of riches, the greed that fastens on the land, the lust and the luxury in which the few wallow and in the envy of which the many are ground to death. We know what their goods are, and we are not lured by them. We say: No! We say: your poverty persists in spite of all your efforts to abolish it, and it always will persist. It persists in your movie houses, where, not the bright screen, but the darkness of the theater truly mirrors the life you lead. It persists in your levers and cranes, your contrivances and inventions, to all of which we must say: No! Your poverty persists in the poisonous fruits of your industries, your instruments of destruction, your bombs and your guns, your rockets and flame-throwers, your ships that prowl under the ocean and your trains that fly through the air. And what is the standard of living of which you boast, the material wealth that you accumulate? To us, they are the instruments of death, even as the bombers bring death. To our clearer eyes, your civilization is dying and the agony you now suffer, the discipline and the dictatorship, the cruelty of your prisons, the brutality of your cities, the vast cemeteries into which you have converted all that was fertile in your life, all that was humane in culture and productive in industry—all this prolonged dying is but the final torment of the initial disease: the degradation of man. We say: No! Even as slaves, we have more freedom than our masters. Even if we knew that this was to be the last day, the last hour, of our present misery, we would still prefer it to your way—we would rather have our misery than be damned by your blessing! We have chosen between your life and ours, and our answer is: No! We say: No!"

"No!" cried the crowd.

"No!" cried Satya. "No! No! No!"

And the crowd answered him: "No! No! No!"

He paused during the outcry, and seeing how he had aroused the people, he let down his arms, and stood empty-handed, the javelin discarded. He wiped the sweat from his face, adjusted his cap, which had nearly slipped from his head, and waited for the demonstration to subside. When he began speaking again, his voice was lower and calmer, as if he regretted having played on the people's emotions and felt he had done them an injury.

"We must observe what the real issues of politics are. They have to do not only with obtaining freedom, but with discovering freedom—with discovering what are the bases, in spiritual independence, of the freedom we would build on earth. Our whole life, had we time enough, would be a constant choosing and rejecting among truths and falsehoods. But we must make practical choices, and even the ideal ends that we set for ourselves must have practical justification. Thus, we must again consider whether nonviolence, to which we are pledged, is practical. Moreover, a dying world looks to us for a way out of the undying horrors to which its perpetual injustice has doomed it. We must be sure that nonviolence, our weapon, will not fail us, and will not fail the earth's oppressed millions who look to us for help."

He missed the tension of the crowd, and while he had resolved not to let himself be carried away by fervor—which was no more than the desire to hear his name shouted—he looked once more at the ranks of soldiers on the field, the administrators in the shaded grandstand, the magistrates on the hills, and Satya scowled at the visible oppressor, as if to recharge his energy for another leap at the crowd.

"The world looks to us for a way out. What shall we do? Shall we take up arms? Forget for a moment that we are pledged to peace, that all our aspirations and the very history of our movement forbid it. Consider—where would we get arms? We have no industry. And if we nevertheless acquired arms, what would we do? Our numbers are large—but there stands an army, already assembled and trained to kill. It is an army equipped in force. It is ruthless, it recognizes no check of conscience or public opinion against its fury. Had we resorted to arms and violence in the past, when the oppressor was relatively weak—that is, when he had a conscience—we should now, perhaps, be prepared to venture the struggle. But it is too late. Our decision has been made—and, I say, wisely! We have only the naked force of our faith, our persuasion, with which to defend ourselves. We are equipped to resist evil only with the knowledge of what evil is, and we must conquer violence even as we abhor it!

"But will they not ride over us and trample us down? Will they not drop bombs and containers of gas, strafe us from the air, crush us on the unprotected ground? What defense is there against death, carefully, scientifically prepared? There is no defense— but one—willingness to die!" He was again raising the javelin. "Consider our thousands of martyrs who faced machine-gun fire, who marched, singing their defiance and chanting their prayers, holding the holy images aloft, directly into the path of rifle and cannon! Consider the thousands who were massacred and beaten and burned—the centuries of violence we have already withstood, without fear, without losing courage, and without once failing, in the end, to wrest the instrument of death from the hands of the oppressing soldier and send it dashing to the ground.

"Consider the sacrifices of the great Bapu"—a shout rose at the mention of his name—"the saint who lived among us, how his frail body endured torment after torment, languished in prison, lay starving and tortured, and how, always defiantly, he sprang again to the head of our ranks, to reaffirm our faith and to lead our struggles. Consider these things, and then ask yourselves: are you willing?"

"Willing!" roared the crowd.

"Then this is what you must do!" cried Satya, without waiting for the shout to die down. "This is what you must do!" He threw his voice over the roar of the crowd. "Disobey! Adhere to our disobedience program, extend it. Extend it into every corner of your lives. Do not recognize their language. When they issue a command in their own tongue—when one says, 'Open the

door,' or, 'Get off the street,' do not understand, do not obey.
When the signs say 'whites only' in the comfort station, in the
theater, in the park, do not read, do not understand, do not obey.
Also when the sign says 'natives only.' We all wear clothes of our
own manufacture, refusing to touch what their hands have spun.
So, also, must we avoid them. Not only must you disobey overt
commands, you must avoid even opportunities for unconscious
obedience and cooperation. Just as the touch of Midas turned all
things into gold, so must your touch make all things anarchic.
Disobedience is our gold. Disobey! Refuse to return or recognize
the nod of condescension in the street, the luxury of friendly
greeting with which the administrator pampers you. Do not hold
out your hand to the fallen, raise your cap to the lofty, bow to the
powerful. Despise and disobey!"

"Despise and disobey!" cried the crowd, recognizing a new
slogan.

The troops had begun to move. Several squads had marched,
rifles slung, onto the hills and taken up commanding positions.
The administrators in the stands had dismissed the translators
and had gathered together, conferring among themselves. Native
runners, naked except for loin cloths and turbans to which their
badges were pinned, could be seen leaving the field, bearing messages in official envelopes. The native pullers had been disaffected
by Satya's speech; they now refused to operate the ropes, which
they had left swinging idly over the stands. A few of the bamboo
squares stood upright overhead, balancing in the still wind, and
casting no shade.

"You have learned disobedience of the major laws—gov-
erning taxes and rent, and property rights," Satya went on, his
voice high and piercing and beginning to crack. "Now you must
learn and put into effect disobedience toward the entire social
structure. Disobedience of the minor laws and of the unwritten
laws; disobedience of the assumptions of society. They have a

community among us, and we must destroy their community by withholding recognition, by withholding consent, by withholding respect even for the most elementary pledges that they put upon us. Do not recognize their forms of life! Do not acknowledge the common air and the sun they share with us! Uproot them thoroughly from your consciousness, from your fear, your concern. Deprive them of being, of the human support that even the most degraded heart requires. They will be unable to go on living in a country where they no longer exist!"

"That was a good line," he thought—and then was appalled. Even at this moment he was ruled by vanity.

"Do all this without hatred," continued Satya, feeling he owed the injunction to his inner self. "Hatred is a form of cooperation, a form of recognition, the opposite of love, but just as binding. Do not hate. Steel yourselves! Be cold. Again, not the coldness of fraudulence or of suppressed heat that burns within. Be cold as their prisons are where the sun never falls. Be cold as the cell is when the light is shut off. Emit no light!

"And so will you defeat them. An army conquers only another army that cooperates with it in murderous enterprise. But a disaffected people, above all a people who are not afraid to die, and who stand only to fall, is a greater army and it employs a weapon that none can withstand. We have an abhorrence of killing and of blood—but not of our own blood. If it must be shed, it must be, as it has been shed before. I demand this of you. I will be harsher with you than Bapu was, and drive you to that extreme before which he always hesitated. The time is short and the time demands it. We will attain the extreme of nonviolence, where it transcends all violence and overcomes all force, becoming itself the greatest force!"

At the mention of Bapu's name, the crowd rose to its feet and took up the cry, "Bapu, Bapu, Bapu!"

"Despise and disobey!" cried Satya, again raising his voice above the crowd and redirecting their attention to himself.

"Despise and disobey!" chanted the crowd, crying out their new slogan.

To despise, he thought, checking himself as he was leading the delegates in the chanting of the slogan, to despise is also to hate. It was impossible to speak clearly.

"Now this is the duty that I charge you with," he cried, making a final attempt at self-justification through rhetoric. "Be brave! Remember your responsibility not only toward your country but toward the world! The world looks upon you as its only hope! You, the enslaved, are the last of the free men, and knowing this, you shall not fail in your effort to create the new society!"

It was the demonstration of the crowd rather than his own effort that reassured him and put him at peace. He stood on the platform, stern as before, but smiling inwardly. "It was a good speech," he thought, and yet he did not think this, for to think would have been to re-create the division in himself between inner and outer man. The applause of the delegates, the singing of the girls, the high adoration, and the hope as they all looked up to him, told him that he was one—at one with his own words and at one with the duty to which he had called his countrymen.

But even as the demonstration was going on, amid the applause and the singing and shouting, the surging forward in joy, shots were fired which at first were lost in the noise of the crowd. Then men began to fall and the shouts turned to screams. Panic broke out as the riflemen on the hill fired down their volleys and as the cordon of police began drawing in on all sides, also firing on the crowd. Simultaneously a troop of Indefatigables, carbines leveled, rushed onto the platform, surrounded the party leaders and handcuffed them, each selecting a man to himself. Satya's own Indefatigable closed the bracelet on his wrist. The leaders were all dragged to a van that had been drawn up behind the platform, locked in, and driven away.

The oppression had begun.

3. The Third Alternative

Satya found himself in jail. But precisely where he was, he could not be sure, for the entire journey, which had lasted nearly a week, had been made in the closed van. The party leaders, shackled to one another, had been let out of the van and allowed to stretch their legs and relieve themselves only at night, when it was impossible to tell what part of the country they were in. For all but the last day of the trip, they had been chained together wrist to wrist; the chains had not been unfastened even when they were let out to relieve themselves. It proved embarrassing; though all had been transported to prison before, they had never been subjected to such indignity. Chained in this manner, they had been unable to tend to their needs at the same time, and some had had to stand and wait, hiding their disgust, while the rest squatted or turned aside to avoid wetting or defiling one another. The administration had determined that terror was best approached through humiliation, and humiliation, through the violation of cleanliness. On the last day the van made many stops, and only then were the chains struck as the party leaders were removed, one by one, each apparently to a separate jail. The original group of some forty men had been reduced until Satya was alone, borne to his own destination. His wrist was still manacled; but as there was no one to whom he could be shackled, the free end of the long, empty chain had been fastened to a hook in the wall of the van.

It was obviously prison country; and this, one might as well suppose, was an experimental prison. From the length of the journey and from what he had tasted of the air, feeling it growing rarer and colder on the way, he gathered that they had penetrated to the Northern Foothills. But he was not satisfied merely to know in what province or section he found himself. As he had been cut off completely from contact with the world, he felt it might lessen his isolation to know exactly where he was, for then he would still be defining his life with reference to his country and his people. Therefore, he set about imagining a landscape suitable to experimental prisons; and bearing in mind that they were far North, and yet not actually in mountain country, and that furthermore, the administration would prefer to keep him in a sparsely populated region, he concluded that the jail was situated somewhere in the forest of Kananda. At once he remembered the river that bordered the forest on the south and that ran through the mountain town of Achalabad, which lay, he judged, some thirty miles to the east. It was from this town that he had set out, several times in his youth, to climb the northern ranges.

Because Satya was a political man, he had become incomplete in himself, and now found it necessary to believe in the reality beyond his present experience; by imagining the landscape, the river, the town, and the people in it, he was keeping alive the image of himself that existed out there, and without belief in which he, locked in prison, would lose identity. He settled back into his obscurity, accustomed to prison life but encountering, as he had each time in the past, a new desolation and a fresh anxiety that he would not be able to sustain himself.

Quite apart from its indignity, it had been a heartbreaking trip. The party leaders for the first few hours were militant and resolute. They had been arrested and dragged off the platform so quickly that they were spared the sight of the massacre, and while they had heard the first shots and seen the first of their followers fall, they were removed before the assault had reached its full proportions. Therefore, they were unbroken in spirit, and their admiration of Satya—to whom, on this occasion, some of the worship reserved for Bapu had fallen—reached a degree remarkable even in a party inclined to charismatic excess. At one point their ecstasy had been such that though they were all bouncing about, chained and bound in the dark and crowded van, they insisted on embracing him, and they fell over one another in the effort to throw their arms, and their chains, around his neck. His speech, they declared, exceeded even Bapu's speeches in fire and eloquence. Now they could understand why Bapu, no matter how passionately he spoke, had always failed to satisfy them. Now that one thought of it he was inclined to ramble and repeat himself, especially in the later years. Satya need have no fear, they assured him; he had raised the people to greatness, and they would not fail. Even in the precious moment of agony, which they had been allowed to share with their comrades, one had seen how they had risen fearlessly and overwhelmed the soldiers with their faith. They would carry on the struggle, even as he had directed them; the very attack to which the administration had resorted was proof of its weakness, and the people, whom no power on earth could stop, would see that it fell, completely crushed, never to rise again. "Long live Satya!" they had cried over his protests.

Thus they fell to singing hymns and their voices, bearing the divine and forgotten words, blended with the purr of the motor.

But the hymns ended and the darkness persisted. It grew close and hot and finally one of the prisoners fainted. The driver refused to stop and the military guard did not allow them to have water until it was time for their meal, at sundown. They had great difficulty reviving the invalid. Then, after they persuaded him to sit near the door, where it was cooler, the whole company circled about inside the van to bring him to the door and a number were injured, knocking their heads against the walls.

This had broken the silence. Thereafter complaints of suffering were heard—physical, mental, and finally political. It had not been such a good speech, after all. Satya had neglected the special problems of the castes. The speech had served only to provoke the authorities, who—as everyone knew—had been reluctant to act. No, argued one of the moderates, more than the speech was at fault. Satya was wrong to have convened the general party meeting in a time of crisis. Bapu would have acted differently, argued another. He would have done thus and such. Or else, so and so. They spoke openly now of the collapse of the resistance movement and held Satya responsible for the misfortune. But by now they were weak with hunger, having refused, on religious grounds, to eat the rotten fish which the guards threw to them at nightfall.

Of one thing Satya was sure, as he sat cross-legged on the floor of his cell—the charges his comrades had made against him, were, in the sense that only politics allows, strictly true. History is everything, and there are no causes. He had devoted his life to the movement, striving to contribute his will to the general effort, in the hope that out of the common will might emerge a force which could act as a cause. But he had been only an agent, a means, and never a cause, and through his agency had passed events that he had never intended and in which he could never recognize him self. And thus it was true to say that while he had never done any thing for which he need feel shame or regret—it was true to say that he was the cause of the defeat of the movement. Insofar as any man could be a cause, he was also the cause of this.

And yet he knew that there were many throughout the country who still revered his name, who thought him a martyr and a hero and prayed for him and suffered with him. For them he still existed as a man, and they would not let history dissolve him. But what had become of them—those who wished him well, and who, undoubtedly, were in the majority? Satya knew that whatever he should have to endure in prison, he would suffer most from isolation. . . .

Weeks ran by. The prison routine was as he had always known it, and there was no evidence of experimentation. He was in sol itary confinement, and solitary confinement was the same as it had always been. With, however, the following exceptions: his cell was not part of a block, but stood alone, a small stone hut isolated from all others. It was surrounded by a twenty-foot wall built at a distance of five feet from the hut. He was let out once a day and allowed to walk in the passage between his cell and the prison wall. For all he knew, he was the only prisoner. He could not look over the wall; nor did he hear sounds of life. When he asked for books they were given to him—one was long in coming and when it arrived, he found a note pinned to the cover, apologizing for the delay and explaining that it had been necessary to send to the library at Allaban, no other copy being available. When he asked for writing materials, these, too, were given to him. Only when he asked for news did the prison authorities deny him. He kept himself alive in the hope, not so much of his release, which he was willing to admit he might never obtain, but of learning, someday, what had become of the resistance movement, and of again establishing contact with it.

After several months had passed, he began to keep a diary. His entries were undated (he had lost all track of time), and, at first, sporadic.

> At a time like this, a diary! Not enough, the whole world has its eyes on me—I, too, have to steal a glance.
> I assume it is true that the world has its eyes on me. And how I hope it is true! With all my heart. I am not ashamed to confess it.

> I have led two lives—in jail and out. The two are unrelated to each other. No single life can be both free and bound, and that is why each prisoner—and especially a political prisoner—is in reality two persons. Or three, or five, or any number, so long as it is not one. Freedom is now a memory, and at times even a meaningless one. It amazes me that I should ever in the past have had command of it. This, this stone world is now real, the chamber pot, the five-minute walk in the yard in the morning. The dish of food shoved in through the door and removed half an hour later.

Jail at A—, jail at B—, jail at C—, jail at D—. I have lost count. I have been through an entire alphabet of jails. One-third of life is normally lost in sleep. And one-half of the remainder in jail. Leaving one-third of life free, which I persist in regarding as the real life. But on that count I have lived only about eighteen years.

But I must be forgetting my true history, which is that of imprisonment. For with two-thirds of life wasted, I should never have been able to become the Satya who lives on out there. This prison, although the same in all other respects, differs from its predecessors in that I really am cut off; is this the element of experimentation? At other jails I kept in touch with the movement, issued directives, wrote long letters on policy, received visitors, did some of my best work. There is now at least one consolation: that I cannot look out. How many nights have I spent in jail looking out at the moon and the stars! I know what terrible things the stars are. If I had a window to sit at, and spent my nights looking at the sky, I am sure I would go mad.

At last, evidence of experiment. This morning, stubbed my toe on one of the paving blocks in the courtyard, and was surprised to see that I had knocked it out of place. I bent down to replace the block and discovered that a number of them were loose. The hole opened into a tunnel, large enough for a man to pass through. Was enough a fool to grow excited and imagine I had found a means of escape. I dropped into the tunnel and crept along underground until I came to a wider opening. It was pitch black (I had covered the hole, like a fool) but I knew where I was—smack in the prison's sewage system. The stench was unbearable, and I had wet my feet and my trousers. I groped my way back, having a terror of a time finding the loose stones. I'm sure that every cell has access to the sewers—to let the prisoners think they have found a way of "escaping." I'm sure there is a maze of tunnels running underground, but only with the intention of luring us into the filth and getting us smeared up well. Filth, filth, filth—it is all they can think of. For all their primness, their white and tidy formalities, their minds are obsessed with it!

Further evidence. A few nights ago there was howling of wolves. It woke me in the middle of the night. Have heard wolves many times before, but was unnerved by it. The howling persisted for, I should judge, at least two hours, receded and came closer, and at times one would think the wolves were right outside the door. When the howling stopped, the silence was oppressive. I became aware of how deathly still it is here. There is never a sound of life. Sometimes I think myself the only prisoner. I lay awake waiting for the howling to resume and, finally, hoping it would. By that time I had roused myself and was unable to return to sleep.

Last night there was roaring—as of lions and tigers. And I distinctly heard elephants trumpeting. Perhaps also a chattering of monkeys, but was not sure. I don't believe the whole jungle goes roaming over our grounds at night, so I was not terrified when I heard human screams. But had a vivid picture of the beasts tearing men apart. And yet, perhaps. . . . I would not put it past them. Could not fall asleep again.

They skipped a night, then last night went at it again. I awoke, but did not trouble to identify the sounds. Something even more terrible, I suppose. I was comforted and fell asleep promptly. It made me feel the presence of other prisoners— surely they wouldn't put on the whole show only for me. I have learned to cope with them—at least here—and am proud of it. Will sleep soundly from now on.

And yet to think of the planning that went into it! Power improves the state's imagination—makes it more of a fool, but more of a horror than ever. The trouble they went to, wiring the prison, installing loudspeakers, recording wolves, lions, tigers, human screams! The poor prisoners who know nothing of radio lie in terror, waiting to be thrown to the beasts. Or are already out of their minds.

The state! If I regret anything it is that I was never more of an anarchist.

Last night, awoke in fear. It was not the "jungle." I had
been sleeping peacefully and it is that, I think, which awoke
me. It was quiet in the prison. I walked the floor, unable to
think. But I know what it was, I understood, and if I had
not been a coward I would have admitted it. "What about
it? What about it? What about it?" The question kept running through my head, vulgar and threatening, as if spoken
by a cab driver demanding his fare. I felt a tremendous guilt.
I should have been able to throw myself under the wheels of a
wagon to be crushed, a religious immolation.

But why do I keep deluding myself, and putting it off,
maintaining my spirit, my hope, my blindness? Why do I
refuse to recognize the truth? They have power, and they do
not hesitate to use it. They have begun the oppression and
they will see it through.

It remains to be seen—no, it does not. Why should they
not succeed? What force can stop them? Admit how it is.
The prisons are full; each day the troops go through the cities and the countryside, rounding up the comrades, jailing
them without trial, hanging them or shooting them without
cause. Cause enough! Or else they line up the innocent and
the ignorant and the backward in the city streets and charge
them with bayonets and make our people look on. And then
force us to light the funeral pyres, that we may come to accept
our guilt in the murder of the innocent.

How blind we have all been! Bapu! I would hate him if I
did not hate myself!

He could not say when he actually resolved to fast. In the past
he had frequently gone without food for several days at a time or
restricted himself to a single meal a day when he felt his health
succumbing to prison damp. Having now developed a cough—the
inflammation of an old prison affliction—he had cut off food for
a day, then limited himself strictly until he felt his health improving. Not that he put much faith in fasts, or went nearly so far as
Bapu had gone in regulating his diet. It was quackery at its best,

and he had never hesitated to jeer at Bapu during the latter's nut period, for example, or when the old man had cut out beans, taking a vow as fervent as the one whereby he had bound himself to chastity. But, since prison food was abominable, no one stood to suffer from abstaining, and in a few days Satya felt quite well again. Nevertheless, he did not resume his full diet.

He did not know what was driving him to it—or if he knew, he would not admit it to himself. However, he had soon cut out food entirely, and was no longer fasting, but had gone on a hunger strike.

He expected to gain nothing by it. And for that matter, he was not starving in protest. The protest he should have had to make was so great, no sacrifice would have expressed it fully. Besides, he had lost all interest in the life of the prison, and if there were any concessions to be won, they no longer concerned him.

The first two days his hunger was intense. But even then he did not inquire what drove him to it, or what purpose he could expect it to fulfill. If there were anything he need know, he would learn from hunger itself.

He turned back all his food, leaving the dishes untouched at the door and drinking only a little water. On the third day the authorities, thinking apparently that the food was offending him, offered him delicacies. Several excellent dishes were shoved in through the door: baked eggplant, a rhubarb soup, a bowl of nut meats, a plate of fruit. Satya hesitated. By rejecting these dishes he would indicate that he had gone on a hunger strike. He wondered whether it was advisable to let the jailers know; therefore he let it appear that he had yielded to temptation. He scraped the plates clean, hiding the food in a corner of the cell, and returned the empty dishes. The next morning, when he was let out for exercise, he went to the sewer under the paving stones and threw the food away. He no longer felt hungry, but, experiencing some difficulty in lifting the stones, he realized he was growing weak.

Tempting dishes continued to appear. Satya went through the same procedure for several days, drinking only a little water. Then, growing bolder as he grew weaker (he could hardly raise the stones) he decided to let the authorities know. He stopped going to the courtyard in the morning and let the food remain at the door, to be removed by the guard.

His faculties were still clear; clearer, he thought. He had reasoned it out, trying to find what purpose, deep within himself (since none was obvious) he was serving by starvation. At least, he knew, it had nothing to do with vanity. Bapu's hunger strikes had drawn the attention and the prayers of the whole nation—had been directed against specific wrongs and had always succeeded in wringing a few concessions. Without a doubt there had been vanity in Bapu's hungering. But what of it? He no longer felt a sense of superiority in recognizing the more intimate motives of Bapu's saintliness. It had been politics—all politics—and therefore, certainly, there was vanity in it. But vanity is not inconsistent with saintliness. And not only vanity and not only saintliness: the whole person, with all his imperfections and the whole ideal life, with all its austerities—the two were in harmony, even though one hand did not know what the other was doing. So intertangled were the two that they were necessarily in harmony; and even if one evolved for himself the loftiest metaphysics in order to justify a little physical stealing on the body's side, it did no harm and left no blemish. For the body sometimes stepped naked out of its shrewdness, throttled itself, died willingly, gladly, for the sake of its hunger—even if the hunger, as was so often the case, were a vain thing. All things human were ironic; but the joy of an action is not impaired.

Well, then, if it was not vanity that made him go on a useless hunger strike, what was it? He was beginning to believe in his will alone, and determined to let its working provide the answer. Meanwhile he sat cross-legged on the floor of his cell, motionless for hours at a time. Sometimes he would sleep the whole day away; at other times make entries in his dairy or slump against the wall, exhausted, his features gaunt, the lines about his mouth wavering between pity and pain. At times a strange exaltation would come over him, as though, were he not weak, he might perform some act of defiance, deliver a speech, or call out for the entire world to hear. He would unconsciously assume his old posture, his left shoulder slightly raised, his head in profile, his right arm drawn back.

Awakened again last night. No jungle. News broadcast, piped into my cell. Listened, about the resistance. Statistics, honest apparently—they are not afraid or ashamed. The resistance smashed. Disobedience movement completely abandoned.

Gave me a newspaper yesterday. Printed, evidently, here in the prison. Same news as in the broadcast. Seems they are not lying. Tore it up.

They have techniques for breaking down the person. For making him adopt their values, making him imitate. They have learned everything, not a thing they don't know. But remain fools. Yet what of it? The observation has lost point.

Could it have been otherwise? I do not think so. I do not regret it. We are right, absolutely. Sometimes think we will still win. But there's the rub. Cannot think of being right without winning. Polarity, the whole of life. Woe to them who live fully.

A proud day. Thought of B.M. the moderate, and prided myself. B.M. with his running ear, and little hand pump to drain off the serum . . .

Am haunted by the old man. Bapu, am I aping you?

He gives me no rest. I find sometimes that I curse him. Violently. Sometimes am in a sweat and find I have been thinking of him. My thoughts clearest when I think of him. Do not mind the hunger. Is it tenth day? Lost track.

Pulse seems a little weaker, occasional dizziness; passes after rest. Water is nauseating, but great help. Must remain clear-headed, important to understand. No desire to turn to religion.

A very clear day. Thought it through. Regret nothing. It's not a religious impulse. I still have no faith, never will have. No faith, but fidelity. That, yes! Never recognized the distinction. Not the *existence* but the *insistence* of God. This is all effort of will. But do not mistrust will. It is necessary because man weak. But will strong. Truth is, man by nature selfish and evil, man has no level Ideal never true. But we who know reality need have no fear. We will to make it true. Bapu, I understand you. The whole age in politics today is this: will against fact. Power, the fact. State powerful. We are the will! At the last extreme. After us, the darkness. Our negativism, disobedience, perpetual no! It is necessary! Today, it is the only thing that says yes! I am not too weak for exclamation points!

Yesterday, authorities came. Tried talk me out of hunger strike. Not interested in them. Fools and hypocrites. Told them so. Told them kind to me. Could have been worse. But have some imagination. Left me alone. Knew I would destroy myself. Have not disappointed them. Told me more. Seems true. They have won, time being. People defeated. Docile, outwardly. Cowed, support regime. Refused end hunger strike. Told them, even if useless, necessary. Did not understand me. Say it again. To myself. Necessary, necessary, necessary! I understand.

Not that I can't recognize facts. I know what the truth is. But the other half of fact, unseen! Truth's other name, courage to speak.

Am still alive. Some physical strength. Absurd vomiting. Danger is, may still weaken morally.

The new science of man. Authorities like ascetic scholars of the middle period: they too made a study of pain. How well they understand! Have discovered the affinity of the oppressed for the oppressor. Now comes the new age of the State, the acceptance of suffering. All struggle has rested on belief that men either good or evil. Only necessary to destroy the belief and provide third alternative: the new man, neutral, will love his degradation.

Bapu, these months prison, hated you. At long last, have come to ask your blessing.

The day the above entry was written, guards came and let Satya out of his cell. With their support he walked fairly well, though pausing frequently to rest. The guards opened the door of the outer wall and led him forth into a courtyard. It was a vast yard, one huge wall stretching miles around and embracing many small enclosures, similar to his own. He was made to sit on a stone bench, while some of the other enclosures were opened. A few prisoners were let out. At first Satya did not recognize them, then saw they were party leaders with whom he had been brought up in the van. He rose and went toward them.

They, too, had been detained in solitary, and therefore did not at first recognize one another. But when they saw Satya they knew who he was and who they were, and their faces lightened, and they clasped hands and came toward him eagerly, but slowly, unsteady on their feet. A few had difficulty in standing erect, and these, Satya knew, had been kept chained. All had grown pale with prison damp; a few were now white, a few bald. As they approached Satya they began to weep; but controlling themselves, maintaining discipline, they raised the weak cry, "Long live Satya!" and came forward and embraced him, weeping.

Except for those who had been chained—their wrists and their ankles, fastened together, had worn raw—they had not been molested by the authorities. But a number of them were also starving. When they looked at Satya they understood, and lowered their eyes and knelt before him. He bade them rise.

"Comrades," he said to them, "I am thankful that we are together."

They spoke with one another, sitting on the stones of the court. None had had news of the outside, except what the administration had passed on to them, and none knew what had happened to the other comrades who had come up with them on the prison journey from Allaban. They begged Satya to forgive them for their conduct in the van. A few still had hope, and they spoke words of encouragement to one another, whether or not they believed what they were saying. The movement would not fail, the people would now, at their very worst hour, succeed in wresting their liberty from the oppressor, and they would soon see Satya established as the leader of a free land. But even as the comrades extended their encouragement they refrained from mentioning Satya's fast, and held their eyes averted.

What was it he felt for them? Shame? Shame was what he felt before them; shame and guilt, remembering their accusations and knowing that his failure had made them true. The reunion would have been easier to bear had the comrades still been hostile toward him. He tried to provoke their hostility, blaming himself for what had happened; but they would not hear of it, and they silenced him with the elaborate and flattering courtesy that was the custom of the land. "You mustn't, you mustn't, it's sinful!" cried one of the elderly comrades, always a religious man; he quoted a few passages from Scripture whose relevance Satya failed to see. "You mustn't provoke yourself. If anything, you should feel proud," said another, laying his hand on Satya's arm. "You are a great man! We are with you. We would willingly be arrested a thousand times. We would go through the same ordeal forever!" "You are an illustrious man!" said still another. "A single one of your mistakes is worth more to us than all the success under the sun. We would rather, a hundred thousand times, follow you down the path of error, than follow any other man, even though he had found the right way." "Be calm, be trusting, have patience, have faith, have hope!" they all cried. "We implore you, do not grieve, do not despair, do not tire yourself!"

It was clear to him—as it would have been from the comrades' words, had not etiquette already determined it—that he must in no way refer to his weakness or to his fast. Custom demanded that one never add to the burden of another's sympathy. Thus, while they spoke courteously and soothingly, he was obliged to assume a rough and almost vulgar tone with them, to prove himself unworthy of their solicitude. And yet who were they that they had to observe the formalities with one another? If he was their leader and they were his followers, the truth should have been sufficient for them all. The truth of past failure and of approaching death; the truth underlying the words of flattery—"we would . . . be arrested a thousand times. We would go through the same ordeal . . ."; "a single one of your mistakes is worth more than . . . success . . ."; "we would rather follow you [in] error than . . . any other man *even though* he had found the right way." Above all, there was the truth of inner failure: what love, what charity, what suffering or humility could he summon within himself to take on, before them, the leader's burden? The flattery, the courtesy, the words of encouragement and cliches of hope persisted. No act of life could bear reality.

After they had been speaking for a time, someone proposed that they sing the party's song. Weakly, incapable of sustaining the long notes, they sang the anthem that availed itself of the peculiar syntax of the native language whereby future events could be named in the present tense. But the song prevailed over them and over their poor, hoarse voices; it forgave their weakness, and banished their fear. For music is time and, linked to the native language, it brought the future before them. In the future, as a moral necessity, there lay ripening the inviolable reward and the fruit of all labor. So that, even when the guards came and dismissed the comrades, pushing them back into their enclosures, the anthem, which had been interrupted, went on, slowly and nobly concluding itself in the imagination. The leave-taking was the reunion.

Satya was left sitting on the stones. Several other gates were opened. With difficulty Satya recognized the prisoners: they, too, had come up in the van. They were in good health, not gaunt and slow on their feet like the others; some even had a high color, as if they had been eating meat. But all were wild and unkempt, almost savage in appearance; their faces were bloated and coarsened, as if they had received blows, although no scars or discolorations could be seen. Or, rather, the faces of the comrades seemed, somehow, to have been transformed from within.

When the prisoners recognized Satya they rushed at him and began to kick him and beat him. One of the prison guards intervened and placed a whip in Satya's hands, indicating that he was to defend himself. Satya rejected the whip, rose to his feet, and spoke to the comrades, trying to recall them to their senses. Refusing to listen, they knocked him down again.

The guards drove back the prisoners and formed a ring around them, each grasping the end of the other's whip. The comrades, some seven men in all, were crushed together. This was done, evidently, to inflame their brutality. Meanwhile a barber, carrying a wad of cotton and a sponge, came up to Satya to see if he had sustained any cuts; the barber examined him, wiped a trickle of blood from his mouth, passed the sponge over his forehead, and retreated. For the first time Satya noticed a number of the jail officials sitting under striped umbrellas. They were looking on in great interest, as if following an experiment. Several were taking notes.

The guards allowed the prisoners to break out, and they rushed at Satya again and once more began to beat him. His pain and his pity were identical: "Pity them! Save them!" The unexpressed thought remained in his consciousness as he lay under their blows. But now suffering alone constituted his hold on life.

[1945]

The New Egypt

The Great Event

After centuries, or centuries of centuries, mankind had at last achieved immortality. This great event of our history — but it is ridiculous to speak of it as such, for with this achievement our history, as we understand it, came to an end. How, then, shall we refer to it?

In *The Statistical Tables,* one of the last great books of prophecy, attributed, without much certainty, to Gorelik, an actuary, it is written: *"Men shall huddle together as about a dying fire: even the warmth of it shall be feeble. They shall repent in their hearts all the ages of evil, even while ashes fall from the sky. For the sun shall be burned out. And men, beholding it, shall say, 'Lo, the sun is fallen. Let us repent as we give up the ghost.'"* This prophetic work enjoys the distinction of having been proved entirely wrong. The sun did not burn out and men did not give up the ghost; indeed, they ceased doing so altogether. The date of the last recorded death is known. Therefore one is justified in assuming that the age of immortality began as of that time. But the evidence for human deathlessness was accumulated only gradually and over a period of years; for which reason, one does not speak of the achievement of immortality as an historical event.

The Conditions of Life

A number of important changes in the substance and manner of life preceded the great event that one does not call an event. Existence was so completely rationalized that accidents, of personal, social, or natural history, no longer occurred and the words that designated them acquired a more and more metaphorical meaning and eventually disappeared from common use. Wars, famines, epidemics, even droughts and other natural catastrophes, were now unknown; as a result of which men no longer believed in such a thing as fate or destiny, and insurance companies went out of existence.

True, men still seemed to age, and some, whom death had left standing, appeared all the more shriveled in perpetual infirmity. But the process of aging had lost its rapidity and its finality; and what's more, it had acquired a cyclical, instead of a rectilinear, direction, so that men, like planets, would wander in time, recover for a while their temporal losses, and each year grow several nights backward into youth. True, men still were born, and birth bespeaks its opposite. An endless birth, furthermore, is insupportable even in the most rational society. But for the time being the world, so well organized was it and so powerful had science become, could support itself and defer such measures as would have to be taken to stabilize the population for a comfortable number of years. It should, of course, be mentioned that men still slept, and sleep, once considered the brother, was now regarded as the vestige of death. The truth, however, was that death had died, and the condition of life was life.

The Symbol

It was an age of joy and gladness, of festivals and celebrations albeit these were often tediously prolonged, time no longer being an object. Ceremonies flourished, modes of dress and address were infinitely multiplied, new dances were invented and developed (e.g., *Dance of the Several Willows Renewed after Frost,* a ballet; *Dance of the Eternal Peppermint Stick,* a polka for children); these happy and spontaneous inventions expressed the grandeur of everlasting life. All the same, it was an age of pyramids. The new Egypt was born.

It was perhaps an accident—though the possibility of accidents has just been denied—that the first pyramid was raised. A pyramidal motif appeared in a building that was constructed at the time. Some miscalculation occurred and the builders either ran short or found a surplus of materials on their hands. To prevent loss, the architects decided to build a pyramid in place of the level roof which they had drawn up in their original plans. It was a small pyramid, in fact, hardly noticeable as such; a snub figure, rather flat and inelegant, which, from certain angles, did not even reveal its true geometrical nature. In addition to which, it was quite out of keeping with the prevailing architecture of the times. Nevertheless, the building was a sensation. It was photographed for all the newspapers and magazines, admired by the entire city, and drew visitors, as its fame spread, from outlying cities of ever greater distance.

No one at first attributed the effect of the building, the beauty which it was said to possess, to the pyramid which rose where the roof should have been. Men spoke of the building's grace, of the harmony and proportion of its lines, of the singularly economical way in which the interior volume was contained in the exterior bulk. Many such reasons were invented for calling an ugly thing beautiful; all the standards of taste, natural and arbitrary, that men invoked were used to conceal the truth.

It was, in a sense, only just that men should overlook the presence of the pyramid and fail to take account of it in their theories of aesthetics. The whole quality of recent human culture, so far as the mass of men, and even scholars and specialists could reckon it, had been, if one may say so, antipyramidal. (The actual pyramids of Egypt, as well as Egypt itself, had been forgotten centuries before. In general, few relics remained of the very far past, and virtually no trace of the human dawn.) For as artists, throughout the years, had always yearned for immortality, all art, the very substance of which became one desire, had acquired a quality of hopefulness and longing—a cheerful, confident longing—to which the particular quality of the pyramid was repugnant.

Not until other artifacts of pyramidal shape began to appear—boxes, paperweights, cigarette cases, lamp shades, teakettles, etc.—did men realize that it was the pyramid itself which had captured the imagination. Many hypotheses were advanced to explain the public taste. It was held in some universities that the pyramid, while it had always been a geometrical possibility, was an invention peculiar to the time—the figure which best expressed, in concrete and solid terms, man's final achievement, the conquest of death. The very form was endowed with universal human significance, all that the heart or the cross or the dove had been—one architect, in fact, built a pyramid of stone hearts, crosses, and doves, as well as stars, crescents, olive leaves, dragons, and lambs, which was widely regarded as a work of genius. And as men now expected to enjoy immortality, they razed their houses and rebuilt them in the shape of pyramids, that they might live forever in the symbol of their hope.

Pyramid Criticism

No one knows what heretic it was, what poet or philosopher, who first discovered and dared to reveal the true meaning of the pyramid, or how it was that the knowledge spread throughout the world. Moreover, his name cannot be known, for it was in the nature of things, first noted among the intellectual classes, that men lose their identity when they live forever. One is therefore obliged to speak broadly of the spirit of the age, and to declare that it was inevitable that the new condition of consciousness should turn upon itself—that the condition of life become the examination of life.

Soon it was recognized among the more advanced circles, among the radicals, so to speak, that the pyramid was a figure of death, which conveyed death-feeling. Some actual scraps of evidence of the historical Egypt were unearthed by scholars; they stated their conclusions: Pyramids were known to mortal men. An effort was made to suppress their publications, but before it could succeed, the poets and intellectuals, the better minds of the time, were convinced that mankind, in reaching its ultimate goal, had returned to its original premise and that in the end lay the beginning—the preoccupation with death. Booklets, pamphlets, and brochures, the work of an underground press, were circulated among the population of the cities. In these forbidden publications, all that was known of the true Egypt was set forth plainly, to enable the people to grasp the real character of the age in which they were living. The unknown writers described the dynasties of the unknown Pharaohs, the death rituals, mummification, the arts of healing, and the cults of burial, making it clear that the pyramids were no more than great tombstones under which the Egyptians, fearful and obsessed, sought to defend themselves against death by preserving, against time, the corruptible objects of the known life. Certainly, there was nothing seditious in these writings, nothing that threatened the form of society that had been evolved through the ages, or the ultimate goal of life that this society had attained. But the implication was obvious: as pyramids signified the preoccupation with death at the dawn of man's history, so they cast the shadow of the same anxiety at the full blazing noon.

The Censorship

At about this time, while the knowledge of the history of pyramids was surreptitiously spreading, the government launched a program of pyramid building which was to surpass in immensity all that mankind had heretofore seen. The original plan called for a structure whose walls rose at an angle of forty-five degrees from a base the sides of which were each three miles in length. The completed pyramid was to be enclosed on all sides by rows of smaller pyramids, dimensions as yet unspecified, the whole to be known as The Grove of Eternal Life. But the plans were several times revised; the base dimensions of the central figure were first doubled, then trebled, and the angle of the ascending walls was brought many degrees nearer the perpendicular, to increase the height of the structure.

Now it is however necessary to describe the government that had undertaken the building program, and explain how it functioned, for, in actuality, there was no such thing as a government, as men have commonly understood the term.

The state as an organization in the employment of force, supported by force, had long since vanished from the earth. Human associations were voluntary and sagacious—voluntary, in that men joined freely to achieve their aims, and sagacious, in that these aims were fully and openly discussed by the people. Material accomplishments, in such a society, presupposed an absolute power over nature and an absolutely frictionless economy—both of which had been provided by science. Political accomplishments, or sagacity, the full discussion of aims and the foreseeing of consequences, presupposed an infinity, or at the very least, an absolute bounty, of time—which had been provided by immortality. The government was none other than the exercise of sagacious power in endless time.[1]

---

[1] A similar interpretation may be given the word "country," which meant the entire earth, or any section of the earth so designated. Boundaries had been replaced by "areas of intention"—*i.e.,* particular regions to which given projects, desires or public demands referred.

While there were no officials as such in the government, official functions remained. Some men, by original gift or individual inclination, always arose to interpret the universal conscience and gave way to others as conscience dictated. Two types of planning boards facilitated the work of government: emergency boards, empowered to act without consulting the public in emergencies (which never occurred), and principle boards, whose plans and directives were submitted to public discussions that one might well call endless.

It was the individual members of the highest principle board who first proposed that the gigantic grove of pyramids be built; in the course of endless discussions, their plans were adopted, revised, and put into effect. But when the building finally began, the history of pyramids had already become known to certain sections of the population, and thus it was, after many open conflicts between the radicals and the majority of mankind, that the former were obliged to go underground.

Not that they feared persecution—not, at least, in the beginning. At first they feared only the implications of their own criticism. If pyramids denoted a preoccupation with death, if, in other words, the history of mankind had returned upon itself only to find in the end the birth of a new Egypt, then death had not truly been conquered. Perhaps a new era of struggle with death awaited mankind. These heretical Egyptologists, who called themselves "The Mummies," imposed their own censorship because they feared that their predictions might play an active role in their own behalf—that is, that the foreseeing of a new age might hasten its advent. Intellectual conscience forced them to speak out; but human conscience forced them to mute their voices; and they, who had acquired a true individuality in foreseeing death, were the first to pay the price of anonymity for it. They wore masks in public; when they rose to speak among a crowd of people they raised their voices hardly above a hoarse whisper, simulated a lisp or a stammer, and expressed themselves in parables.

The government was grateful for their self-imposed censorship and did little to make it more rigorous. True, Egyptology was suppressed and, with the consent of the majority of mankind, driven out of the universities. But the most that the government did was to revise its plans for the Great Pyramid in such a way that to build it might well require an indefinite time. Two sides of the base were extended without limit, no provision being made for the points of junction with the other sides that would complete the figure. And from the sides of this base, whose angles now divided almost the entire continent, rose the enormous walls, their angle of ascent, constantly rectified from the base upward, always more closely approaching the perpendicular. It was as if the government had declared: "We who with the common consent of mankind state that man is immortal, demonstrate our faith in eternal life by way of this structure, which we will be forever building."

Saigamon and Perseflores

Two Egyptologists of this period are known to us: Saigamon and Perseflores. Their names are known in spite of the censorship under which they published their findings. Saigamon was a great technician; it was he who collated the discoveries that the many anonymous scholars had made concerning the original Egypt. From such scraps of knowledge, and from his own brilliant speculations, he was able to piece together a reasonable account of the methods the Egyptians had followed in building their pyramids. Many of these methods he adapted to the needs of his own age; he also perfected several processes useful in the large-scale quarrying of stone and devised procedures for the transportation of building materials that were of inestimable value to the government. Saigamon's earlier papers and books were published under his own name; but as his historical researches convinced him that pyramids were indeed death-symbols and that the propositions advanced by the Mummies were substantially true, he began to publish anonymously. His anonymous works were still largely technical in nature, but among his many graphs, diagrams, and equations, interspersed among the mathematical terms and footnotes of his text, he included brief historical summaries of the development and true meaning of pyramid building.

It is with the work of Perseflores, however, that the full implications of pyramid criticism were revealed, although Perseflores himself was more a poet than an historian. Why, asked Perseflores, did mankind select the pyramid as its proper symbol precisely at the moment when it had achieved eternal life? His answer may be given as follows.

A distinction must be made between eternal life and immortality. Eternal life is that life as we know it now, extended into infinity. Whatever quality our consciousness reveals to us at a given moment—this face, here, now, this hand, holding a chisel—embraces its identity in time and assures us that the road to the future lies open, for as whatever essence is known to be now, so shall it always be. The known is the full limit of life *as it is lived*. But immortality, originally defined as the undying, must now be called the unliving. It is that essence, unknown to us, which we longed for when we desired eternal life, still not achieved in the attainment of that life. Death, the barrier to immortality, has been removed. But now our life, eternal life, is the barrier. Hence, the worship of the pyramid, the great, massive, perfect, symmetrical form, symbol of the unendurable weight of our attainment. The pyramid as a death-image expressed the ancient Egyptian's conviction that the life he knew was not the whole. The pyramid as a life-image, which is what we would make of it, expresses our uneasiness that our life, too, is not all. Its great mass would stifle our anxiety, yet it cannot do so. For if this life is all, what is it that we long for? And if this life is not all, then, victors over death, we have lost forever the chance of knowing what that other is, known in the past as life-after-death, and which we must call life-after-life. But while we long for the other, we also cling to this, immuring ourselves in lime and stone and fearing, as men have always feared, extinction and nothingness.

The Entombment

The doctrines of Saigamon and Perseflores spread rapidly through the land. Heretical societies sprang up and pursued their studies in earnest; various Egyptian cults made their appearance. Men gathered in darkness, on the outskirts of cities, in valleys, forests, and caves to read the works of the two great scholars. But for the most part, the public excitement expressed itself in religious rather than intellectual activity, with sacrificial rites and ceremonial dances performed at the shrines of new gods. These gods were death-gods, givers of death, worshiped in the hope of dying.

The government, to eradicate such dangerous mysticism, was at last obliged to institute a program of severe oppression. (By government oppression we understand, of course, the divided conscience of man.) All adults were registered, fingerprinted, and photographed and submitted to extensive examinations designed to test their mystical potential, which was held to be twofold in nature, consisting in death-wish and impulses toward obscurity. The results were discouraging, the very prize of eternal life appeared to be in danger. Accordingly, all men (and women and children who showed signs of contamination) were put to work in mines and quarries; the entire land was organized into laboring gangs that rose with the sun at the ringing of great bells, placed at half-mile intervals over the countryside, and dropped exhausted onto the fields at nightfall when the bells rang again. The building of the enormous pyramid, though an infinite time lay at its disposal, went on in great haste, spurred by the overseers and the building police which the emergency boards, acting for the first time in their history, had organized. All men, the whole country, all of science and industry and human energy, learning and skill, were at work on the pyramid, which consumed acre after acre in its growth and towered miles in the air.

All other building was neglected. Houses deteriorated and fell into ruin (even those that had been rebuilt in the form of pyramids); walls crumbled, roofs caved in, doors leaned from their broken hinges and creaked in the wind. Crops failed, granaries rotted, diseases spread. Soon the great cities were deserted. All mankind, in hunger and pain, diseased but invulnerable, lived in huts, tents, and caves in the fields and on ledges of quarries, chained to their labor.

Perseflores, seeing in the return of slavery a further proof of the prediction of Egypt, was concerned over it and donned a mask and together with his colleague, Saigamon, went forth to speak among the people. They went among the quarries and descended into the mines and everywhere they were known in spite of their disguise, and yet, so great was their reputation, the government was afraid to imprison them. Everywhere they were greeted in divided acclaim with shouts and with stones, the men who applauded being the very same who threw stones.

On one such occasion Perseflores and Saigamon, in broad daylight, descended into a quarry which was so deep and the gorge of which had been cut so narrow that it was pitch black within, and overhead the stars were visible. Electrification had not been able to keep progress with the speed of the work, and therefore, in the very depth of the pit, the stonecutters worked by the light of natural fires. The Egyptologists appeared before them, and when the cheering and the stoning were over, they climbed onto a shelf of stone and summoned the crowd to hear them.

Saigamon held a staff in one hand and in the other a large chart on which was drawn a map of ancient Egypt, showing the course of the Nile and the sites of the pyramids. He stood at the side of Perseflores. Both wore the dress of prophets, sandals and flowing robes.

"Workers, citizens of mankind," said Perseflores, addressing the crowd. He whispered and lisped, as was the custom among the Egyptologists, to show with what regret he felt himself obliged to speak. But soon his voice rang out and the words were clear. "We have come to speak of your freedom. We have seen how you are enslaved and we feel it our duty to warn you that if you once lose your freedom, you shall lose it forever. An eternal man is either eternally free, or eternally a slave. There is no other choice for him."

The fires burned at his feet, the light of their flames shooting up, flickering across his masked face and the masked face of Saigamon, and the course of the Nile on the map in Saigamon's hand. Around the fires stood the workers, holding tools. In the distance, in other sections of the quarry, men were still working, and one could hear the sound of their chisels and hammers, the buzzing of saws, the screaming of pulleys and chains.

"Think, you have an eternal life to live. Is this how you shall live it, forever chisel in hand, at the wheel of the crane, dragging a load up the elevators, across the girders, burrowing ever deeper into the stone earth? Forever to rise with the sun and to sleep the short hours of the night, haunted by the ringing of the dreadful bells, more dead than alive, as the saying goes which still lingers in our language. The work at which you labor shall never be ended. Think, the government shall always demand another stone, another mile; always exact another year of slavery—because they fear you. They fear the spirit that moves you, that makes you inquire into the nature of the pyramid, that leads you to ask, What are pyramids, what do they mean, why do we build them? And you, because you fear them, because you fear their punishment, because above all things you fear the loss of life and you cannot be certain that they will not somehow punish you by depriving you of life—for these reasons you give them your obedience and work on, year after year after year. And so the pyramid shall rise forever and spread over the land, growing with the years, the centuries, the centuries of centuries. And still you will be at work on it—you and you and even you, who now stand before me. You will work without rest and without release. For what release can you expect other than the short annual holiday that the government grants you? Far happier were the slaves in earlier days who had the release of death to look forward to. But you who are without death shall labor forever and bring children into the world to labor forever, and so transmit the burden of eternal life."

The crowd cried out when it heard the word "death." The workers beat their hammers and chisels together and shouted and sang and wrung their hands and leaped into the air. Some hoisted themselves up the wall of the quarry where a wooden platform hung and destroyed the platform, throwing the wood into the fire that burned at Perseflores' feet, so that the heat was overwhelming.

"Peace!" cried the scholar, and Saigamon beat the ground with his staff and waved the map of Egypt to catch the attention of the crowd. "Peace, I say, peace! Eternal men must live in peace and harmony with one another. I pray you, put down your tools, do not heap wood on the fire, cease your outcries, listen to reason! Consider our destiny. (The word 'destiny,' an old one, might well find its place again on our tongues.) Consider, how shall we spend our eternity? What is the price, the cost, the reward of our living? Let me speak the word 'death' with impunity—silence! Silence! Let there be silence! Those who had death to face well knew the preciousness of life. But what do we know? The slavery that lures us is but the outward expression—grim as the very pyramid we build—of the hopelessness we feel who can not look forward to an afterlife. Our life gives the lie to life."

A gang of men climbed up on the shelf where Saigamon and Perseflores stood and seized them and pulled them down to the floor of the gorge. More wood was heaped upon the fire and then the men selected a young girl to sacrifice and bound her and threw her into the fire, while a great outcry went up. The girl lay among the flames, and slowly the entire crowd circled the fire, looking at the burning girl in eagerness, in lust, and in hope. "Be you the witnesses of death," said the men and they branded Saigamon and Perseflores upon the forehead with burning sticks. But when the girl was pulled out of the fire it was seen that she still lived. In great disappointment the crowd fell upon her (Saigamon and Perseflores cried out against them), but though they all beat her and kicked her, she still lived. The girl's flesh was charred, her bones were broken, her eyes were burned out, and only cinders were left in the sockets, but there was still life in her. Then the men placed the girl on the shelf where Perseflores and Saigamon had stood, leaving her in pain, and they turned to the two scholars and commanded them: "Pray for death. Pray that there may be death among us." But Saigamon and Perseflores would not pray, and they remonstrated with the crowd and urged them to be reasonable. "Then pray for disease, that we may die of disease. For we are stricken, but we do not die." But the two men would not pray. Saigamon said: "Live that you may be free." And Perseflores said: "Come forth out of Egypt. Do not build the pyramid, but go forth and be free." But a man arose from the crowd and said, "How shall we ever be free, so long as we do not have the power to die?" And this appeared reasonable to the crowd, for they resumed their dance about the fire, rolled in the embers and the flames, wounded themselves with their tools and wept and pleaded and prayed for death.

So, until the overseers descended in a body and drove the stonecutters back to their work.

When the government learned of the occurrence in the great quarry, they ordered Saigamon and Perseflores arrested and entombed them in a room in the wall of the pyramid which corresponded to the King's Chamber in the pyramids of the ancient Egyptians.

The Watchmen

The work went on, the pyramid grew. Saigamon and Perseflores lingered in captivity. The Egyptian societies continued their avid studies, their rites and excesses, their prayers and vain sacrifices, and the government, which was the divided conscience of man, grew with the pyramid. In time, Saigamon and Perseflores came to be regarded as gods, sent upon earth to keep an eternal vigil— to watch for death and to give hope of an afterlife. Each morning the workers spoke the following prayer, prostrate before the walls of the pyramid:

You are imprisoned in the heart of our hope, locked in stone, yet we cherish you. Pray for us. Watch, we pray you, for a sign, such as eyes that see, see not, and eyes that see not, see. Deliver us from dread of otherness, from the hope beyond life, from the life without hope. For all things living are full of dread and full of hope, and reach for what eludes them. Pray for us and watch over us. And may your call come quickly unto us.

Thus it was that Saigamon and Perseflores became known as The Watchmen.

[1946]

The Misfortunes of the Flapjacks

I WAS THE TRAINER WITH THE FLAPJACKS IN THE ONE EYE League until my own arm went dead and I couldn't massage arms, shoulders, backs, and legs any more. I'm still with the Flapjacks and they still call me Doc, though I'm absolutely no use to them. I spend my time on the bench catching a little sun; every now and then I help the park attendants fix the bases and the foul lines, clear up the infield after batting practice, or pick up papers in the outfield before and after games. Otherwise I can't feel I'm being useful. The boys come to me with broken fingers, concussions, spike wounds, rheumatism, sprains; all I do is apply some iodine and a bandage and tell them to go to a doctor on club expense. This works out well enough when we're at home. The local veterinary likes the team—or else he likes to get away from horseflesh for a change—and he patches us up free of charge. But when we're on the road, we're just out of luck. There is no money, no one had been paid for the longest time. The club owners dropped us in the middle of the season. They put us up for sale, but no one came around to buy so we're on our own. It's a good thing the owners paid in advance a whole season's fare on the railroad and rent at the hotels, or we'd have been stuck.

You won't find another team in the whole country that's had our kind of tough breaks. Ticky Wamburger, our manager, is a madman, really out of his mind—this is not just an expression. Three of our starting pitchers have sore arms and the fourth has an ear infection, on account of which he can't keep his balance on the mound, falls down every second pitch, and gets confused, often throwing his best stuff to first or third instead of the plate. Our best hitter, Eglantine, has gone hitless now for two and a half months and his average is down to .071. We've run out of bats—we left a whole stock of them in Pokegan on our last trip and have been dickering with the Pokegan Eagles to get them back, but no dice. Now there are only five bats left, and all of them are chipped and rough and out of shape and developing cracks.

What else? Spud Pickerel, our shortstop, caught the flu and for a while we tried to play without a shortstop, with only eight men in the game, because none of the boys could be talked into playing short, they were afraid of the errors they'd make; but that was impossible, even for us, as the opposing teams kept poking the ball through short and piling up runs and there was no putting them out; one game had to be called on account of darkness before the third inning was over. I'm ashamed of the scores—in one four-game series the Hornets got a total of 117 runs against us, and our worst licking was at the hands of the Green Lake Trappers, a second division team, who crossed the plate 38 times in a single game. We put in our mascot at short, a fourteen-year-old boy, and that made a big difference right away as the runs against us dropped to around 25. But then the mascot got hit by a pitched ball and was too scared to play, so Pickerel went back into the game before he had recovered, and now he has a bad cough which breaks out every time he stoops for a ball, and that takes care of him. We are the laughing stock of the League.

Our manager has always been a queer bird, so it took us a while to discover that he'd really gone crazy. The kind of talks he'd give us in the dugout before games always had us in stitches. He'd say, "Men, I want you to grickle on the splakker by the top. Cut it on the slant, is that clear?" Double talk. Which did us more good than any plain talk would have done, because with a team as bad off as the Flapjacks, what's the use? But then he began to talk plain to us, and that had us worried. He'd keep us for hours when we should have been out at batting practice, and talk on and on, and it seemed to make sense, but in a queer sort of way it really didn't.

He got himself a little blackboard and some chalk and began to draw diagrams, and he'd say, "Now look here. They've got runners on first and third and nobody out with the score tied. A run can score on a fly, on an infield out, on most anything, and if we try to cut the run off at the plate, unless they've got the hit and run on, the man on third will stay put and that'll load the bases. Best thing in this case is a strikeout. I want you all to play for a strikeout. You, Turkey, play close to third, Pickerel play back, Sammy move over closer to second, and Chuck, never mind first base, get in there close to the box and cover the pitcher. Clyde can watch the outfield from behind the plate and move 'em around. Remember, I want the center fielder in close, and the other boys to hug the foul lines, and everybody to concentrate, look hard at the back of the pitcher's head." Or else he'd begin to work on the problem of how to make a double play with nobody on base. We realized he was crazy, and we felt sorry for him and a little guilty because we thought the tough luck had gone to his head.

As things got worse and we kept dropping games, Ticky seemed to improve. He cut his talks short and there seemed to be less nonsense in them. He went about encouraging us, patting the men on the shoulder and putting in a kind word for everybody. "Nice going," said Ticky, all the while that the going was worse and worse. Well, there's nothing particularly crazy about that— it's the only way for a manager to act when the situation's hopeless, so we thought Ticky was on the mend and we felt much better about him. We'd been afraid that the word would get out that he'd gone off the beam, and then we really would have caught it from the fans, so we breathed much easier now. But then he began to do queer things again. He'd hold his breath, and he got so that he could hold it almost all the while that we were at bat—which I must say was never too long, as we didn't get any hits. He started to knock wood and to carry a rabbit's foot in his hip pocket; he had a horseshoe nailed over each man's locker and he fined some of the boys for whistling before games. (It was impossible to collect fines with no money in the club, so no one beefed.) He got more and more superstitious and jumpy and nervous, and all the time he kept encouraging us, praising us and whacking our shoulders, jumping about and hollering, with his eyes shining and his smile full of pride.

It turned out that he thought we were on a winning streak. We read about it in the paper when we got back from a road trip. Ticky had given an interview to our town newspaper in which he claimed we'd set a record for consecutive games won—"and the end not yet in sight!" he was quoted as saying. The paper treated it as a big joke and was glad to see that they could still get some fun out of us, for they'd given us up and just about stopped covering our games. That stirred up the home town a bit and people came round to see us play for a week or so, we had some money again and the boys got some of the back pay that was coming to them. But all the time, of course, we kept dropping games. The truth was we had set a record for consecutive games lost, with the end not yet in sight—and there was Wamburger hopping about the field with his face red from holding his breath, and everybody laughing at him. It was a great joke while it lasted, but everybody got tired of it, and then no one came to see us play any more. When folks wanted to see a game, they'd drive over to Pokegan, or they'd watch the kids in the sandlot, who I can tell you were a damn sight better than us. The paper ran a big ad on the front page saying they were open to bids from contractors to build a new cellar low enough to hold the 'Jacks. That finished us. The season was nearly over anyway, so the boys began to drop off the team and go home, and we were left with no more than a dozen players to finish the remaining games.

I can't understand what got into Ticky. I don't see how anyone could really lose his mind from managing a bunch of stumblebums, unless he was going to lose it anyway. Get sore, yes, get mean and nasty, yes, and yes, go round with a sneer and an evil look and get into fights, or even say the hell with it and quit. But to go crazy just on account of us, that doesn't seem right. We're not worth it. There wasn't a dry eye when Ticky, in the charge of a doctor, left us, saying he was going off to get tickets printed for the series. The boys were all broken up, and the next two games they put on a show, winning them both, the first game for Ticky and the second for me, who had taken his place as acting manager. They really went out there and played ball, and bad as they were, they made it hum; the pitchers threw their hearts out, the infield was tight as a drum, the outfield made some spectacular catches that would have fallen for triples in the good old days, and everybody got a hit—except Eglantine, our slugger. But they couldn't keep it up, and I was glad in a way, because I couldn't stand to have them playing their heads off for Ticky and me; for Ticky because it was too sad, and for me, because I didn't rate it. I'm no manager. Maybe I do know a few things about the game, I've been around long enough, God knows, but when it came to managing the Flapjacks, I just didn't have it in me, and I told them to go out there and play and do what they thought best, from now on they were on their own.

Well, there are only two and a half weeks left to the season, and as soon as we get back from this trip we'll have ten days at home, and then it's quits. What's going to happen to us, I don't know. I doubt if there's much baseball left in any of us. Most of the boys will go back home, on the farm, in town. Maybe some of them will open filling stations. We won't be seeing each other. I hate to think of what will happen to the ones who still want to play. They'll hang around the clubs, the training camps, and the playing fields in the hope that someone will pick them up, but no one will. Maybe two or three will get on some team and go barn-storming through the South in winter, but when the season starts again, unless they've really burned up the bases and played heart-break ball while everyone else was taking it easy, they'll be cut off and become baseball bums—a special kind of bum who hangs around the parks trying to cadge a ticket or sneak in, and so much the worse for him if someone who knows the game cold recognizes him and says, "Say, you're so-an-so, you played left field on the Flapjacks," and buys him a ticket and a drink after the game out of pity. The Flapjacks are through. Mittsville, where they make pancake flour, has been trying to buy its way into the One Eye League for years, and now, with us out of the way, they'll get up a team for sure, and call it the Mittsville Millers and take our place, you watch and see, and soon no one will even remember the 'Jacks, unless the fans make up a baseball joke and every time there's an error that could have been an easy out, they'll yell "Flapjacks!" Even so, no one will remember us.

The other night when we were staying at the Double Elk Hotel in Salt Creek, where we had just dropped four games to the Salt Creek Ranchers, the manager of the hotel came up to me, and I thought we were going to have some trouble with the bill, but it turned out that the Flapjack owners, before they threw us away, had paid up too far in advance, going into the next season, and now, as everybody knew that there wasn't going to be a next season for us, the hotel owed us money. Did we want a check for the difference? The hotel manager was very proud of his honesty and he made his offer loud enough for all the boys who were sitting in the lobby to hear him. Did we want a check, or maybe we would like a party that the hotel would throw us for the difference, in recognition of our long services to baseball, and the good sports and clean players we had all been. (All the same, I think they were offering to split the difference with us, for the check was only for about two hundred and fifty dollars, and it seems to me that if the owners had paid up far in advance there ought to have been more money.)

Two hundred and fifty dollars, split twelve ways, wouldn't have made much difference to the boys, only about twenty bucks apiece, but twenty bucks' worth of party, that was something else. We rushed into the banquet room, which was small and not much of a banquet room, except for a high ceiling and red velvet curtains. The hotel unloaded a lot of old beer on us that was beginning to turn stale, some raw liquor, and sandwiches that must have been left over from somebody's wedding. They didn't bother with tablecloths or napkins, so the hotel saved on linen, too. We tried to get drunk, but it was no go. Some of the boys tried to get hold of girls from the town, and they turned up with five sad-looking creatures, three old waitresses, a girl from the hat factory, and one from the laundry. We had only a radio to dance to, and no one wanted to dance with the girls, we did it so as not to hurt their feelings. But what really spoiled the party was when the Ranchers somehow got wind of what was up and they all crashed, including their manager, Eddie Forbes.

They came trooping in all at once, a cocky second-place team, all young and tanned and in top condition, looking like athletes even in their town clothes. They brought their girls with them, the prettiest in the town, and the girls laughed at us and said, "Some party, some team." The Ranchers crowded us out at the table and on the dance floor, and pretty soon we were forced into a corner while they were whooping it up and having a hell of a time and bragging how they'd just whipped us four straight without once dropping a game to us all season, and how they had a winning streak on, nine games long, and they would whip the rest of the League and beat the Badgers out of first place. That started a fight and the table was overturned, the beer and liquor were spilled, the sandwiches got thrown around, the velvet curtains were torn, the place was a shambles in no time, two of our players got injuries that would lay them up for several days and not one of theirs got so much as a bad scratch, except that one of their girls got a bloody nose. We took the milk train out of town at two in the morning and the hotel manager and the sheriff were down at the station to see that we all got on, and the sheriff was swearing he'd run us in if we ever showed up in town again.

Wouldn't you know it? We were in such a hurry to get out of there that we didn't think where we were going and we wound up at dawn in Carrington, forty miles out of the way. I tried to get the railroad to take us back, but they wouldn't do it for nothing, as we had just made an unscheduled trip. I argued and pleaded in the office while the boys sat beaten in the waiting room, but it was nothing doing. We didn't have enough money for fare, and the railroad wouldn't advance us anything, or trust us, and they didn't care where our schedule called for us to be that day. "That's your hard luck, Doc. I can't go and ship you free, or I'll be sticking my own neck out," said the stationmaster, and I suppose he was right. We wandered about town with our suitcases and our hats, not knowing where to go or what would happen to us. The truth was we were hungry, but we didn't even have enough money for a decent breakfast for the team.

We were all set to stand on the road and try to get a lift out of town, when I got the idea that maybe we could start up an exhibition game. There was no baseball team in Carrington, but the high school had a team, and as it was late in the season, maybe school had started and we could play the high school team. I went over to the school and talked to the coach. I didn't tell him everything, just that we were in town for the day and would like to put on a show for the kids, if we could find some team to play with. He said sure, the kids would love it, only we must remember they weren't in our class and it wouldn't be much of a game. I said we'd be willing to take our chances on that and maybe we'd spot them a few runs. No, said the coach, the kids wouldn't like that. A straight game or nothing. That's all right with us, I told him, we're straight players, and anyway we're just doing it for the love of the game and because we think it is a good idea to go out to the small towns every now and then and bring some real baseball to the young boys and girls of the nation. Only we'd like to get enough out of it to cover our fare. The coach said there'd be a scandal if they charged admission on the school grounds, he'd been warned about it, but he didn't think anyone would object if we passed the hat, it was all right with him. I could see that he was real eager to play us, and even felt honored in a way. Carrington is far enough east to take an interest in the major leagues, so maybe he had no idea what was doing with the One Eye teams.

I sent a wire to Flood River Valley where we were supposed to play that day, saying that we were delayed and would arrive in time to play a double-header on the next day. Then I told the boys what the arrangement was, and asked them to take it easy and not to show off and let the kids get some runs.

We hadn't had much to eat that day, so we were pretty hungry and weak when we took to the field in the afternoon. Soon we were fighting for our lives. We made two runs in the first, but the kids got onto us and got over being nervous, and in the third inning they scored eight runs and we had our work cut out to catch up with them. We tied the score by the eighth inning, but the kids got a run across in the ninth and beat us, 9 to 8. It was one of the closest games we had played all year, and I think we would have beaten them if we hadn't been so hungry. A good thing we passed the hat before the game started, while the fans still had some respect for us.

Well, only another two and a half weeks. It hardly pays to last it out, we might as well concede the remaining games. It's curtains. But it's hard to get used to the fact that we're through. We're still wearing our uniforms, with the red circle on the chest and the red caps and stockings, and they still look good on us even though they're torn and dirty and our other uniforms got lost in the laundry. We still look like ballplayers, even the men who are close to forty and gray and have potbellies. It's hard to imagine that we'll take off our suits and never put them on again. That's the baseball habit for you. Even some of our younger players, when they want to smoke during a game, sneak cigarettes to one another so I shouldn't see, although they know I don't give a damn, and they can smoke and drink and shoot craps in the dugout for all I care.

I still have the baseball habit myself, and as I watch the game from the dugout, every now and then I have a hunch of some kind—Sam Perkins to pinch hit for Smith, move MacDonald out to center and let Forest play first, put in the left hander, take out Coogan because they're pitching a southpaw, call a squeeze play, a steal, a bunt. I never play these hunches, but I can't help having them, and as I sit on the bench or walk out to the bullpen, or even when I'm asleep at night in the hotel room, I go on getting hunches and ideas, I keep making plans, I still wish I could do something for the boys, help them out in some way.

Right now it's Eglantine's turn to bat. He walks up to the plate swinging all five of our bats, and selects one, a black, chubby stick. I should have benched him long ago, he got only nineteen hits all season and his average is down to nothing. The loudspeaker ought to be saying, ATTENTION PLEASE: FOR THE FLAPJACKS, COOPER BATTING FOR EGLANTINE. But he steps into the box, draws back his shoulders and sticks out his left leg as he used to do in the old days when he was knocking down the fence. He wags his bat, a slow, menacing motion, his elbows are cocked, his teeth are clenched in the tobacco plug, he is stocky and muscular, a powerful man. The pitcher grins and floats the first one over, just hands it to him right across the middle, and Eglantine twists all the way around on a murderous swing, but a mile wide, he can't connect any more. The park yells, "Swi-i-i-i-ing batter!" The next one is right in the same places with nothing on it, you can count the stitches on the ball, and Eglantine knocks the air out of the park as he misses it and goes down twisting like a recoiling spring. Our best hitter, who once led the League at .389—he stands there, working his jaws and wagging the bat, waiting to strike out, and I can feel all the power in his shoulders and forearms and wrists, his muscles straining to connect. I see his eyes squint as the ball sails toward him, and there is that last, pinched strain of energy in his face as he begins his wild swing—and I think, God damn it, all that power and that glory gone to waste.

[1947]

PART II

The Brigadier

The Railroad

The Party

The Fireman, His Story

Three Parables and a Dissertation

THE BRIGADIER

WE HAVE BEEN FIGHTING THE ENEMY A VERY LONG TIME.
So long that I, who entered the war a foot soldier, have had time
to receive more than the usual number of decorations and promo-
tions and to become a brigadier, attached to staff headquarters.
I forget how many times I have been wounded and the names
of the battles and campaigns in which I have participated. The
greater number of them, however, are not to be forgotten: Striplitz,
Bougaumères, Trele, Bzelokhorets, Kovinitsa, Laud Ingaume, El
Khabhar, Woozi Fassam, and so on. I am the oldest man in our
field office, though not in the brigade itself. Lately, the newcomers
have been rising not from the ranks but from the Academy. They
are young men who have not proved themselves in any way; some
have not even fought.

I am settled into my work, which for many years, I am pleased
to say, has been of an absorbing nature. It is difficult to recall the
time when I fretted with impatience to return to what I considered my natural life as a citizen. I am happy that I am no longer
impatient. I have developed, instead, a great eagerness—an eagerness, however, which is thoroughly disciplined and in every way
related to our military enterprise. I do not hesitate to call our
enterprise the most glorious and far-reaching that has ever been
undertaken.

Far-reaching is not quite the word—though it is only in an
unofficial capacity that I admit as much. Let me say that it is not

the word for me to use. As a matter, simply, of objective fact, what we are engaged in is, of course, that—I mean far-reaching—and much else besides. But for myself it is not enough, and the work I do must be otherwise defined. I have been studying the ends of our warfare while pursuing them; I have tried to make them a part of myself. I should not want it to be said that the Objective is one thing, and the brigadier's effort in its behalf is quite another, not related to it as the word one and the number one are related. My work is the war itself.

The office in which I do my work was once a schoolhouse; it stands in what used to be enemy country. A section of blackboard, cracked down the middle, is still affixed to the wall near my desk and on it you can read a lesson in the enemy's language, written by one of his children; when the chalk began to fade, I had it carefully restored and covered with a coat of shellac. I can read the enemy's hand—which is sometimes difficult even for scholars, as the script is spidery and irregular and varies not only with the dialect but with the very temperament of the writer. The broken lines read: ". . . of the cat and the dog? What will she . . ."; here the first line ends, broken off at the jagged edge of the board. "We," runs the second line, "know that the . . . [several words are obliterated] while the bird was singing. . . ." The third and last line: ". . . is what we all love. It makes us very happy." I like to imagine, although I know this is nothing but a child's exercise, that these broken lines, could I only complete them, would tell me more about the enemy than all the work of our specialists combined. As for my subordinates, I have led them to believe that these scraps of writing have something to do with logistics—which is all they care about.

The benches, the charts, the books, and other blackboards of the schoolhouse have long since been removed. The rooms are now occupied by sturdy desks of our own design, developed during the war, and the walls are lined with filing cabinets and hung with maps of the region. The sides of the house have been reinforced against blast with sandbags, and the windows have been covered with intersecting strips of wire and tape, which, when the sun is right, cast patterns of shadow upon our papers. If there were nothing else to do, it would be a pleasure to trace some of these patterns. The glass—these are the enemy's original panes—is very bright and clear. The enemy is known for the quality of his glass work. A strange people.

Our office is a relay station among the various fronts. The position of the fronts has grown so complicated through the years that I never attempt to give our location with reference to the lines of battle. We are well in the center of one circle of fighting, on the periphery of a second, and connected by a long tangent with a third. From time to time our position appears enveloped, and we pack our papers, dismantle our immobile equipment, and prepare to retreat. Subsequent intelligence, however, informs us that the first reports, owing to the complexity of the warfare, were erroneous in many respects and that, far from being encircled, our position may be described as part of an arc thrown round the enemy's flank. The lines of battle, the longer I study them, seem to me more and more like the arms of many embracing bodies.

It is our general purpose, but not my specific task, to supply logistical information to headquarters in the front and in the rear. We are one of a number of stations that coordinate the numerous reports both of the enemy's movements and of our own, and relay these back and forth. These reports never fail to conflict with one another, and no matter how well trained our spies, pilots, observers, and scouts may be, we must keep a large staff working round the clock to prevent mistakes, repetitions, and inconsistencies from appearing in our dispatches. Even so we have blundered many times, and our only consolation, and at the same time the reason that reprimands from headquarters have not been more severe, is the fact that the enemy must work under the same disadvantages. Very often a report so complicated and contradictory that it seems impossible to submit, is nevertheless a true picture of the fighting. You can see what we are up against. And then there are the many spontaneous breakdowns of routine for which no one is to blame, the impatience of my superiors which is always interfering with the work, the orders handed down from above, countermanding orders that have already been carried out, and so many other difficulties that are part of the day's normal detail. To make matters worse a training class for scouts is held in the basement of our schoolhouse and we often hear them laughing or crying out in pain as they tumble about on the mats. I have been trying to get this class removed, thus far without success.

My own work developed as a subsidiary of the main logistical operation. My superiors are not yet convinced of the importance of my task (I have been at it for eleven years!), but some of them are interested, and all my equals and subordinates support me in it, so I am not required to give up my investigations. I work in a semiofficial capacity, filling in and sending out my own reports and as much corroborative material as I can lay my hands on—all this in addition to my regular duties. I am kept very busy indeed, seldom working less than sixteen hours at a stretch. I sometimes think, sitting as I do in an old schoolhouse, that I am both schoolmaster and pupil: a teacher to those who are beneath me in rank and an idiot child to my superiors.

I work on the enemy proper. I am trying to discover what he is, what motivates him, what his nature is. And if you say, as so many of my superiors do, that this is known, I reply that I am attacking his very essence. This is not known. In spite of the many long years that we have been at war with him, and the periods of time, in the past, when we lived at his side in restless peace, we know nothing of him that is really worth knowing and that must be known. I myself am convinced that victory will be impossible until we gain this knowledge—and it is precisely to this knowledge that I am devoting my life.

What do we know? The enemy is darker than we, and shorter in stature. His language, as I have indicated, has nothing in common with our own; his religion is an obscenity to all of us who have not made a specialty of studying it. Well then, as I say, he is shorter and darker, two positive facts. His language, though it would be too much trouble to go into it here, is of such and such a kind—a third fact—and his religion is this, that, and the other thing, which gives us still another fact. So much we know. Still, what is he?

I have gone many times to the camps and hospitals in the rear to interview the prisoners we have taken. It teaches me nothing, but I nevertheless make my regular visits, and just the other week I returned from one of our hospitals. There was the usual sight in the wards; I am hardened to it. (And yet, almost as if to test myself, I try to recall what I have seen. Am I absolutely hardened?) There were the lightly wounded, their personalities not distorted by pain, and the natural qualities of these men could be observed: their churlishness, stupidity, sullenness, or good nature. I spoke with them, I took my usual sampling—so many boys (as with our own troops, eleven-year-olds are not uncommon), so many youths, so many of the middle-aged, so many old men, old campaigners. The usual questions, the usual answers—home, parents, occupation, the government, women, disease, God, the purpose of the war, of life, of history, etc. There is nothing to be learned here that we don't already know. Then the wards of the severely wounded— the amputations, the blinded, the infected. The stench is the same as our own stench (the hospital orderlies deny this, maintaining that the enemy's is worse!). The ones with fever have fever, though their skins and eyes show it differently from ours. The delirious rave, the chilled shiver, the poisoned vomit and groan. There are outcries, the usual hysteria, weeping, coughing, and hemorrhage. One lies in a coma; the stump of his leg is gangrenous, it is too late, he cannot be saved. Another soldier has nearly every bone in his body broken: he has both his thighs in traction, a broken back, a broken arm, his skull wound in bandages. Can he be said to suffer either more or less than one of our own men in similar circumstances, or in any way differently from him? I attend an operation—it is the same thing over and over again. The mental casualties in their guarded ward are no different from ours. Some in strait jackets, strapped to their beds, some screaming, some colorless, lifeless, forever immobile. Here and there a dead body, not yet removed. I lift the sheet; the face is already puffed up. The shock of it is gone, and I can no longer remember what it actually used to be like. I poke a finger into a puffy cheek, leaving a depression which takes a long time to fill up again. It is the same death as our own.

I go to the hospitals, though I learn nothing there, and I go to the prison camps, also in vain. Once I had myself incarcerated, disguised as an enemy soldier. I slept with the men in their barracks, ate with them, was soon infested with the same lice. I was involved in a plan to escape, of which I informed our guards. No one saw through my disguise, and I, in turn, failed to see through the undisguised men and learned nothing. In fact, the few weeks I spent in prison camp were extremely discouraging, for if the gap between the enemy and ourselves is so small that I can pose, undetected, as one of his men, why is it that I can't cross over to him?

I have even suspected my project of a subtle treason. By "cross over to him," I mean of course, "cross the gulf that separates us from knowledge of his true nature." Now I know where I stand in this regard and it no longer troubles me; but at one time I feared that the second expression really meant nothing more than the first and I thought surely that my whole ambition was only to desert to the enemy. Perhaps he fascinated me in the precise sense of attraction, drawing me, through my desire to know, closer and closer to his side. My conscience drove me to my superior, Major General Box. He believes in my project and follows my reports with interest. The General reassured me; it is his opinion that we are all drawn to the enemy, particularly in such a long war, and that the enemy is drawn to us. In certain respects we begin to resemble each other. But this is only natural, and has nothing to do with my project, which, far from being treason, remains the most important of the war.

I was reassured, but was soon taken with a fresh disquietude. A suggestion that the General had made, without meaning to do so, set me on a new course of activity. The General had said that in certain respects we come to resemble the enemy. What are these respects? Perhaps the knowledge that I was seeking really lay in myself? The resemblance to the enemy might have grown so strong in my case that it was my own nature I would have to know in order to know his. I took a leave from the service, the only one I have had in the entire campaign, and spent a month in one of the enemy's mountain villages that had been captured by our troops. I lived away from the men, attended only by goats which forage high up among the rocks in this region. I had a hut to myself, and all the mountains necessary to a great introspection. But I learned nothing, nothing that I did not already know.

It was when I returned to active service that I began the most desperate work that I have as yet undertaken. I selected a group of twenty prisoners, all young, sturdy, healthy men. I lived with them until I grew to know them well; some were like my own sons, and one in particular, a peasant boy named Reri, I will say that I loved. I spent long hours out of doors with my companions, joined them in races and various sports, their own as well as ours. We went on long camping and fishing trips about the country, and I developed so great a trust in them that I even provided them with firearms and let them hunt with me. Evenings, when we were not camping under the open sky, we entertained ourselves in my lodge, drinking, playing cards or chess, listening to music, or holding the most intimate conversations—conversations and confidences that verged on love. We became very intimate; there has never been a group of men whom I have known or loved so well, never a youth as my Reri for whom I have had such a close and tender feeling. It was above all with Reri that I carried on my desperate yet gentle work; I strove to know him as completely as one man can ever hope to know another, and something in his response to me, perhaps an intuitive comprehension of my motive, promised that my effort would be rewarded. He was a handsome boy, taller than the average among the enemy, and fairer in color and complexion. Certainly one such as he could be known, a face as open as his could not long conceal the secrets of the inner nature. Often when I was not with him I would picture his face to myself, trusting that a chance moment of insight might reveal him, and therefore his whole people, to me. And I studied his image, sketching him and taking many photographs while he sat patiently before me. (I have kept these sketches and photographs, and look at them from time to time as I once looked at the living Reri. His image still saddens and perplexes me.) So, with all my companions, I engaged in an unceasing search after friendship and understanding, hoping that love would teach what I was determined to know.

But my ultimate means were not to be gentle, and when I failed again I had to resort, with great reluctance, in shame and disgust, to the final means I had selected to attain my objective. As I had been their friend and lover and father, their teacher in the ways of our people and their pupil in the ways of theirs, so, at last, I became their torturer, hoping now to break them down and force them to yield what they had not given freely. One day I ordered them whipped, the next, beaten; all of them, including Reri. I stood by, directing their tortures and noting their surprise, their hatred of me, their screams, and their pleas for mercy. I could not help feeling that I had betrayed them; but my guilt only excited me the more and made me inflict always greater agony and humiliation upon them. It must have been guilt that was responsible for my extreme excitement, in the grip of which, while supervising the tortures, I would feel an overwhelming hatred of the enemy, and become convinced that my hatred had brought me so much farther than love, to the very brink of knowledge. When my companions died, I trained, in much the same manner, a new group, in which I included some of the enemy's women. The experiment was repeated. This time I did not spare myself, but submitted in their company to some of the same tortures, as if there might still be lurking in me an essential particle of the enemy's nature which was itself either capable of yielding the truth or of preventing me from finding it. The experiment failed again. Again I learned nothing, nothing at all.

I still go to the wards and the camps, and from time to time I still conduct tortures. I have devised many other means of coping with my problem, some of them not yet tested. Over the years, I have grown hardened to failure. I more or less expect it now as an essential element of my work. But although I am hardened and experienced, I find that my work grows more and more difficult. Because of my interest in prisoners, new duties have been assigned to me. Recently negotiations for the exchange of prisoners broke down between the enemy and ourselves, and their number keeps piling up, as ours does in their camps; it is now my duty to arrange for their transportation to the interior. And then there are still the many administrative details of my department, to which I must somehow find time to attend; there are still the hazards and ever greater complications of our old war, which we have not yet won, and which, I have become absolutely certain, we will never win unless I succeed in my task. To know the enemy! It is the whole purpose and nature of our war, its ultimate meaning, its glory and its greatness. Already I have succeeded in my own character, for I have become my task in my whole being. Nothing comes between me and the work I do. I have triumphed in my own character and person, but I must still triumph over the enemy. Sometimes I see his armies standing before me, clearly revealed in their dark, powerful mass, and I rush out of the schoolhouse, out of our office, and I feel that in a moment, but one moment more, I will know the truth. And when I hear our gunfire from the front that winds around us in all directions, I know that if my faith is only great enough, the knowledge will come to me and I will win.

[1947]

THE RAILROAD

THE YEARS I SPENT IN THE CONTROL TOWER WERE THE VERY
best of my life. I look back at them, think of them constantly. It
is as though what I did enclosed up there with the switchboard,
the ticker tape, and the telegraph, the lighted map, the squares
of colored glass flashing on the chart, was not work at all in
the external sense of job or occupation. It was rather a work of
inwardness, as when we say a life's work or a work of love. A
sculptor would know what I mean—imagine that he has a mass
of clay before him and it feels not sticky and cold but warm and
alive to his touch as he works on it, shaping it part by part, giving
it just the form he wants although he does not know what the
final form shall be. . . . My life was never so much my own, never
so completely the work of my own hands.

The tower was a little house of corrugated iron high up in the
girders above the tracks. It could be reached only by a vertical
ladder which was dangerous to climb on wet or icy nights. I loved
that dangerous climb. I would fasten my lunch pail to my shoulder, hooking a strap round my neck, tug at my gloves, look at the
lights blinking overhead, and swing onto the second rung, always
avoiding the first (the superstition of a railroad man). As I went up
I'd see the lines of box cars, then the roof of the station house and
the signal lights retreating in the distance. Halfway up, above the
cinders and the smell of smoke, I would pause for breath. I remember how great my pleasure would be if there were a strong wind,

strong enough to threaten to tear me from the ladder. I would tighten my grip and climb on. At the top I would knock at the trap door and Krasovic, the day man, would let me in. We'd exchange a few words. Krasovic always asked, "What's new down there?" Then, in a hurry to be gone, he'd pull on his oil-stained gloves and his woolen stocking cap and lower himself through the trap door; the white tuft of his cap was the last thing I would see of him. In winter I always turned up the kerosene stove, requiring more heat at night than Krasovic had needed during the day. Even now, the odor of kerosene is to me the odor of solitude and peace.

I looked at the chart, read the ticker, studied the position of the trains. Then I tapped out my signal to the next tower down the line, recorded the reply, watched the light change on the chart, checked the routes—there was enough to do. Even standing at the window and looking down at the track, as much of it as reflected the night lights of the yard—I should have loved to see the entire track converging at the horizon—even this seemed to call for an essential capacity, a skill of mood. I was happy.

The danger of the work delighted me. There was first the danger to myself, though this was minor—the possibility that I might fall off the ladder, that the trap door might give way under me or that on stormy nights, when the rain roared on the iron roof, lightning might strike me. Then there was the danger of train wreck—which concerned me, however, not so much for the sake of the trains, the freight, or human life, as for the perfection of my own work. I do not think that this was heartlessness or indifference to life. It was rather the way of a skill, an art, such as a surgeon's or even a violinist's might be. Not that a skill or an art are greater than life itself; but one's feeling for life and his knowledge of it are wholly contained in the art and are nothing apart from it. The railroad, to me, has always been such a thing. Now a devoted life is never without danger. The danger that lay in my devotion was that I might somehow lose that concrete sense of the task at hand. Oh yes, I might fall asleep or misinterpret, though wide awake, some message or signal or fail to see the warning light go red on the chart—these possibilities were ever present; but linked with them was a subtler danger—the failure to attend to the thing, the actual thing, that the light signified, without which work is meaningless. This danger created the greatest one of all, the danger of danger itself, the fear of falling victim to mistrust and anxiety. In work such as this, a man must have a great capacity for faith, he must believe in himself and in others, in all mankind, from the lowest lantern tender to the engineer in his goggles and striped cap. He must be able to contemplate with perfect serenity an entire army of ticket sellers, freight agents, stevedores, track inspectors, gate-men, signalmen, brakemen, firemen, stationmasters, and say to them, "Peace be with you—we work to the same end."

Peace, faith, serenity—it seems to me that there is no one more virtuous than a railroad worker. That is, virtue in its true sense, which is strength.

The great train wreck ended my days in the control tower. I was not responsible; the investigation cleared me. So many mistakes were made that night all along the line that it was difficult to fix the blame. Certainly, I was not at fault, even though the accident took place only half a mile from my tower. An hour before, I had signaled through passage on Track 5 to the express, exactly in accordance with my instructions, and had made the proper reports to all the stations en route. I had studied the scheduled stops of the fast freight, due to come through on Track 4, and had wired ahead to the crew of the water tower to set them in readiness. A moment before the accident I saw the express, running on time, rush by below me, the fire under the boiler making both sides of the track red. But how could I not feel responsible when I saw the headlights of the freight train and the passenger express join in a single beam, saw the collision and the flames leaping up, heard the crash and the screams, the explosion of the boilers? When I was cleared by the investigation and my job in the tower was offered back to me, I declined it. I asked to be transferred to another department.

If I were to say how many lives were lost, how many millions of dollars' worth of goods and property were destroyed, would that be at all to the point? And if only one bone had been broken, only one crate had suffered damage, would that in any way have lessened the disaster? To this day, I cannot pass the control tower or see signals change, the arms of the semaphores swinging through the air, without being overcome by sadness.

I applied for a transfer to the station house, and for a time worked in a cage as a ticket seller. This was punishment, self-imposed, a term in jail. I could not bear my work, it was monotonous and fatiguing. Gone was the sense of dangerous peace, the keenness and profundity of the tower. The station was noisy, crowded, full of drafts of cold air and smoke which made me shiver and cough. All at once old age seemed to settle on me; I grew nervous, cranky, and thin, I quarreled with the travelers and with the other workers. One day my wife remarked how gray I had turned. I had lost all sense of myself, which is what it means to lose one's youth. But the more I disliked my new position, the more firmly I clung to it.

At last, however, I was convinced that I had been doing a coward's penance. Pity the prisoner who believes in his prison— my work was elsewhere. Tempted by freedom, I applied for a transfer to the telegraph department, moving freight division, which is where I work today.

I am a telegraph operator. In my new capacity I travel about the country in freight trains for months at a time, leaving one caboose only to enter another. I feel unattached to these circumstances, out of place in my new quarters. Only the kerosene lamps that I burn at night arrest my diminishing identity, and bring me back to the past.

It is my job to take messages en route from city to city and relay them to the engineer, the brakeman, and the rest of the crew. The work is of some consequence—but compared to the control tower . . . There in the tower the work I did and the reality it represented were one; here there is a gap between the two which I must somehow contrive to fill.

Yet I know, it seems to me I still know what end I am pursuing . . .

The caboose is a lonely place, though I am not always alone in it. Often the brakeman rides with me and we play checkers and drink coffee and relate our experiences. We talk only of our railroad days, as if there were nothing else in life. But the railroad is an intimate thing to the men it embraces, and we are all content to have it so.

In my case, how much more intimate a thing has the railroad been than even my wife and family! My wife is a good woman. Since the day we were married her world has been our home, and she has made it the kind of home which could well have given some other man the deepest pleasure and happiness. Not that I am disappointed in my family, or that it does not, after all, afford me some satisfaction. But I cannot sit in the rocker on the porch with my feet on the railing, as some men do, a newspaper in my hands, a pipe or cigar in my mouth, and have my eye travel out over the neat little garden and come to rest on the fence post, and not want it to travel farther. I cannot feel the contentment which is supposed to be like a summery hum of well-being in one's ears—contentment in the knowledge that what I see from the porch is mine. Mine, mine, mine, it whispers in the good man's ears, his head nods, his heart is lulled, at peace among its own. I feel inclined to ask, What is mine? Is it the garden sprinkler, rotating madly, is it the yellow watering can the children use, the hedge shears? Is it the house itself with the shingled roof, the checkered curtains in the kitchen window? I do not feel that I own these things or that they own me. There is a happiness that resides in things, and this has its familiar objects which claim it, and which it claims as its own, like the faces of friends in the street. But there is a happiness that is not in things, and this comes to rest nowhere in the world.

What can I say to my wife? Can she be fully aware of the distance between us? We never quarrel, but there is an element of sadness in every one of her emotions, a trace of subjection or defeat. She could have been a happy woman . . . and yet she will never look elsewhere for her happiness. Instead, with a devotion, which, I admit, I find hard to understand and which rather puts me to shame, she looks to the very things that bring her grief.

Thus, our children. My sons, Paul and Tom, have always admired me, and lately, because I have been able to come home only at infrequent intervals, their admiration, intensified by longing, has grown into worship. From very earliest childhood they have loved the railroad, personified in me. The toys I bring them have always had something to do with my work: trains, tracks, station houses, semaphores, water tanks, bridges and trestles, control towers. I have laid miles of track for them about the house and in the garden, thrown up little earthworks, dug tunnels, simulated conditions of disaster, and organized rescues: train wrecks, fires, and floods. Even in their unattended play they have always naturally turned to trains; they line up a row of chairs or boxes and the older one, the engineer, sits in the front and goes, "Chu-chu-chu-chu-chuuu," while the conductor, the younger, stands in the rear and cries, "Ding-ding!"

It must hurt my wife to see them always playing at trains, for she must feel that they have been drawn away from her in their devotion to me and the railroad. Yet she does not interfere with their play, but observes it sadly, a bystander. Indeed, she encourages them at it, feeling perhaps that the children's love for me must be maintained for her own sake. Not long ago, when I returned from an absence of several months, I found the boys at play, dressed in uniforms of the railroad. Paul was wearing striped overalls and cap and a pair of dark goggles; Tom had on a conductor's blue serge with shiny brass buttons. Their mother had gone to great trouble to obtain these uniforms, costumes that children do not commonly wear.

My coming and going saddens us all. Our reunions are strained, for when I return home there always hangs over us the question which even the children hesitate to ask: How long will you stay this time, where are you going next? And when I leave, the boys, with tears in their eyes, beg me to take them along. My wife always makes some remark that indicates how greatly she fears and exaggerates the danger of my work. She stands on the porch and waves a handkerchief in farewell until I am out of sight—much as if I were already on the train.

The life is lonely. I need take but one look at a new caboose as I enter it to see all the men who have been there before me and feel what they have felt. There is the calendar tacked to the wall, the picture of a girl or a sunset on it; there is the almanac and beside it the cup in which dregs of coffee have dried, bread crumbs stuck to the bottom. Scraps of paper with words, names of cities, numbers jotted on them, a crayon, some nails, a pencil stub. The smell of coal dust, ashes, oil . . .

But I have made friends on my travels. One of them is a forester, on fire patrol. He too inhabits a tower. (I say he too; I have never descended from mine.) High up above the trees, scanning the forest with binoculars, on the lookout for fire. And does the forester fear fire? In one sense, yes. But at heart he loves fire and as he looks through his glasses he prays for fire to appear. I know what it means to love danger.

Another of my friends is a fisherman. He fishes in a small calm mountain lake, near which we stop from time to time. A simple, senseless fellow, his face and his forearms covered with freckles. The fisherman has his tackle, nets, and bait—all the necessary, ordinary equipment. But I like to imagine that at his side he keeps a delicate spear which he uses only for one kind of fish and no other. It is a fish of golden color, though not what is commonly called a goldfish. What shall I call it? The fisherman knows how to throw the spear so that it immobilizes the fish, without killing or injuring it. I picture him at his regular business, enjoying a good catch; but suddenly the golden fish appears, for a moment, dimly in the depth of the water. He throws down his tackle, seizes the spear and flings it, eagerly, surely, skillfully, without sound or splash as the point pierces the water. The fish is transfixed. The fisherman dives into the lake, as gracefully as his spear, and comes up, fish in hand. And what does he do with these golden fish? As a rule, he throws them back again; but he had brought a few home to his family and kept them swimming in a large tank on the porch. The fish, I like to imagine, fade in captivity, their golden color turning a muddy blue.

The rather common thing has happened to me again. I have acquired a second family, as railroad men do; this means, in my case, not wife and children, but merely another woman. But for railroad men, precisely because there is no true, permanent relationship, there is no true impermanence either, and a woman is a family. It is not even a second house or home that I share with Martha, but a furnished room in a rooming house, and here the objects are an alarm clock that ticks too loudly, an ivory comb and a wire brush on the dresser, a straight chair and a rocking chair, both of which creak, an iron bed, and a basin to wash in.

Martha is a waitress at the station lunch counter in Salt Lake City. The last few times out that way we have stopped over for several days. On our first stopover we arrived late at night. It was a very hot night. Unable to sleep in the hot caboose, I went to the lunch counter for something to drink. Martha waited on me. From the very beginning, we were like old friends (we regard station waitresses as our own kind) and we engaged at once in that familiar, learned railroad talk which is so dear to us all. But Martha has not long been with the railroad, and her conversation is still fresh. She made several mistakes in terminology which greatly amused me, and aroused my affection by a naïve description of the Western Warrior, which pulls in every evening at sunset. The engine stands on the track, panting, impatient to go on, with an angry expression on its face. The angrier and more impatient the engine, the more lonely Martha feels. It makes her sad to see people meet and separate, to observe the anxiety of the ones who wait and the joy of the reunited; and when the sun sets and the signal lights begin to glow in the distance and she hears the far shriek of the Warrior rushing home again she feels ready to cry . . . An early poetry which every young girl of sensitive nature will create for herself out of the lights, the noises, and the trains when she first comes to work on the railroad. I went home with her.

We are old friends and strangers. The space between these two extremes, normally filled by intimacy, is vacant in our case. I am responsible for the vacancy. I hesitate to give myself up to the relationship with Martha for a number of reasons, the most important of which, as far as I can make out, are the facts that I am so much older than she, that this is not the first or the last of such friendships in my life, and that it is, after all, a relationship not of my own choice or creation, but rather one that was forced on me by the nature of the railroad itself. "Forced on me" is too strong an expression; "given to me" is more accurate. But I hesitate to take it, even knowing that if I do not accept one thing I shall eventually accept another. It is the trick of that vast experience that comes our way as we travel about the country: we learn so much and get to know such a great variety of things, men and women, faces, voices, places, that in the end we become the fools of our own wisdom and give ourselves anew to each experience in the hope that our knowledge will at last bear fruit. After so much knowledge there must come a final wisdom, one last possession that shall contain the wealth of all that we have gathered on earth. But I hesitate to reach for it, for the railroad is infinite and I know what can and what cannot be encompassed in one lifetime. So also with things near at hand, the things that are given; I hesitate to reach even for the nearest thing, for how do I know that through it I do not mean to reach for the farthest? I know too much to trust my knowledge—I am afraid of being the fool with Martha.

But we are in the habit of journeys, and our instinct is also a traveling one and cannot stay long in one place. We are bound to overreach ourselves, to pass ourselves by. We think: the next town, the next station, the next day. And we dissolve as we travel: what was true at one time, in one place, is no longer true in another. There I was at Great Bear's Paw, and I thought one thing; now I am at Red River Canyon, and Great Bear's Paw might never have existed; soon I shall be at Timothy's Pass and I know not what to think. When we are at standstill we are at standstill and when we move we move. But each movement has its center, its still point. Haven't I my center also, my wife and children to think of? But I don't know what to think, and I am yet to encounter a single reality that could survive the distance of a mile. All I know is my regret that the control tower came so early in my life, and that having come, it could not remain with me.

Martha, apparently, takes great delight in me. She would like to keep me up half the night talking of the places I've been to, the cities I've seen, the people I've met on the way. "And then what happened, and then what happened, and then what happened?"— it's an actual rhythm with her, and my ears pick it out, accustomed as they are to the click of the wheels on the track, where the same question also runs on forever. In her excitement Martha enlarges whatever I have to say beyond all proportion. I have tried to make her see that I am more naïve than she is, in evidence of which I point to my presence in her room, her bed. But she fails to understand what I mean. I shall perhaps have to tell her that I have lied to her about my age, subtracting ten years, and that I have a wife and children. But this too, I know, will do no good. She will find me all the more "exciting" (her word), and insist that I account for the ten years I had hidden from her. "What happened, where did you go, what did you do?" She will want to know all about my family and I will have to describe my wife and the house we live in and show her snapshots of my sons in their railroad suits and listen in weariness to her clucking and cooing over them. "Poor girl," I like to say to her, "you have your whole life ahead of you." She smiles like an idiot and still does not understand. Martha will never understand. She will go on offering me her indefatigable affection—until one day, suddenly, she will have grown tired of me and gone on to someone else. And then I too will go.

What do I want with Martha? All I really want is to fling my railroad cap onto her dresser, remove my denim jacket, sit down, in shirt sleeves and suspenders, in her rocker and bend over (rather stiffly) to unlace and pull off my heavy, snub-toe shoes. And when I have done this I am satisfied. Meanwhile, all night long, there are the sounds of the yard nearby, the shunting of trains, whistles blowing, the noise of the jamming together of cars which travels down the line when the engine stops suddenly. It seems to me that I hear the noises of the railroad in my sleep.

I have met her people, who live at the other end of town: her father, a fiddler in a saloon; her brother, a discharged sailor; and her two sisters, one a stenographer, the other a high school girl. One Sunday afternoon we all went to a baseball game, myself standing treat. Her people mistrust me and are forever questioning me about my personal life; they suspect, of course, that I am a married man. It was to win their good will (for Martha's sake) that I suggested the ball game. A strange afternoon. The old fiddler favored both sides and consumed I don't know how many red-hots and bottles of pop at my expense. The others, young enough to be partisan, felt real joy in the victory of the home team. I had identified myself with the visitors, in particular with the center fielder, who was nearest our place in the bleachers, and I took their defeat more or less to heart. It was a close game until the eighth inning when Blake, my fielder, lost a fly ball that let in three runs. I remember the look of dismay that crossed his face when, after running up confidently under the ball and smacking his glove a few times in readiness, he discovered too late that it was no longer in sight and turned round to see it hit the fence yards behind him. The family were very kind to me after the game and made me come home with them to dinner.

The alarm rings at dawn. I jump out of bed to turn it off before it can wake Martha. She stirs in her sleep and sighs. I prefer that she remain asleep. I dress hastily and steal out of the room. The train will be leaving soon. I have only a few minutes to run to the yard. I cross the tracks, feeling for the papers in my pocket and hoping I have left nothing behind. Already the bell of the engine is ringing. As I run it seems to me that it is tolling in negation: Not-this, not-that, not-this, not-that. The headlight of the locomotive is bright in the dawn. It shines on me as I cross the track, and I feel it would like to hold me up long enough to shine directly into my eyes and ask: "Not-this, not-that—what then?" I run for the caboose, the crew in their places calling after me and laughing. Suddenly, I feel very tired and winded, an old man, and I think, "My God, what if I really do not know the answer?"

But I do know. In moments of danger, then I am certain— on the way between one station and the other, between town and town, this moment and the next. Then motion is the only reality.

The country slides by, one mass of green colliding with another. The train sings to me, beware, beware! I hear it in the hoarse wail forward on the approach to a grade crossing, in the squeak of the coupling, the rattle of the cars. The danger is always at hand.

I think of my friends, the forester and the fisherman. Would that my life were as simple as theirs! If I could but watch for fire and send the alarm when fire is sighted, throw all other things aside and cast a spear when the moment came! To seize one's happiness by virtue of a great skill—seize it without injury and let it go again. It is there to be taken with skillful hands, seized, but gently, ever so gently. It is there to be taken—but only for a moment and then it darts away. In what waters? To what depths?

Instead I must wait for the moment of seizure. It no longer attends me as it did in the tower, the moment extended in full, benevolent time. Now I must wait for it, wait ever so long, trembling in fear, and yet not despair of its coming. It will come—it is there.

But disaster? Another wreck? I know that as I stand waiting at the door in the rushing train I am neglecting my duty. A report may come and I shall fail to hear it. This time I alone am responsible.

But the train gathers speed at night and it rushes ahead, the wheels click, the track spins away. I climb onto the roof of the caboose, brace myself, and wait. The race is on! The wind beats against me, soot snows in my face. I cry out, I shout and sing to make myself heard—behavior which, under other circumstances, would surely be madness. But as it is, it is only courage to sing. It is my exaltation in the race and in the knowledge I have, where we are rushing—the risk and reward of it.

[1947]

THE PARTY

1. The Internal Question

The party is said to be in its thirtieth year—but this is only a manner of speaking, a manner of reckoning, rather, which few people take seriously. They would have you believe not only that ours is the true party—which I myself am convinced it is—but that it has existed from the beginning, that our leaders participated in the Founding Congress of the First World Organization and that, as a distinct group, we won the recognition of the president of the Congress—the president himself. (There is said to be a letter from him to Comrade Bain, our national chairman.) But the fact is that the party has existed separately for only seven years; it split off from the parent body, which in turn was born by separation from an earlier party, and so on. It is idleness to trace our lineage back to the Great Days and the Noble Ancestors; for that matter, it is a waste of time (at least, as I see it) even to be concerned with our future. All I know is that we are a small group, a very small group, and, if I may say so—I am speaking in confidence, but I cannot warrant the truth of my words; in everything connected with the party there is always great uncertainty—we have no influence whatsoever.

Behold our trademark: ends never meet. There is always a litter of unfinished business, the rubble of an unexploded doom along the way. Unless we raise two thousand new subscribers by next November our paper, the *Vanguard,* must fold. This is true. Nevertheless, we fail to get subscribers, even lose a few, and still the paper comes out. Perpetual suspension, deferment, a sublet of time. Unshaded lights, tired feet, a package of internal bulletins lost in the subway—this is our atmosphere, our style, and it would even have become a style of architecture, had we buildings to raise. (Our meeting hall was once a dry-goods outlet.) This is hardly the thing to expect of the only true party, the movement to which, when the false directions have been taken and all the mistakes made, the working class will of necessity turn. Necessity should cut a somewhat neater figure, even something in the military line—lockstep, precision, the efficient machine. True, our originals met in cellars, perhaps even in caves, with this one's beard in need of trimming, that one's cuffs wanting to be turned. But that was in another country—no, they made it, the improbable transformation, and so will we. But how, when, by what means?

Call it a disguise. I look at the comrades, at the dandy who hides in one, the mine boss in another; this one recording her disappointments in layer after layer of resentful tissue about the jaw and cheeks and under the eyes; that one harboring failure, preserving its bad taste in the mouth like a boy with soda and straw, his face caved in, his very forehead concave, and he gone all thin with the effort of sucking, to draw out of everything the last bitter drop. One is pompous, another fawning, a third a born informer, but how root him out? And where do I belong, with my own face disfigured in its own unknowing grimace, giving the comrades reason, as they give me, to wonder, "Is it he whom I call brother? Is it to *him* that I am pledged?"

There comes a time, when the leaflets have been run off, when the minutes have been recorded and the last words of the dawdling speech have been pronounced, there comes a time when the very momentum of the movement, that part which moves when all else is still, catches up, no longer to be stalled: seriously now, whom can you trust?

Believe me, I am not quibbling. There is a rule which one can follow in determining such questions. He who is in constant attendance, who has given evidence of his loyalty and devotion, his trustworthiness and capacity for self-sacrifice—for all practical purposes, he is the man. I follow this rule on most occasions, and try to teach myself to follow it all the time. But I have a need, greater than any this rule can satisfy, for actual certainty, the truth, once and for all. There are times when I want to know, when I must know, that our apparent solidarity is a thing as final as a brick wall. A wall, moreover, with nothing beyond it. Without this knowledge, my doubts and fears are insupportable.

It is my misfortune that, unlike the majority of our people, I cannot come to rest in the arms of our leaders. It is ridiculous to doubt, say, Comrade Bain, and I try not to take my skepticism seriously. But I can laugh myself blue in the face, for all the good self-irony does me. It is precisely him that I doubt, our national leader. Is he man enough? I know that he is sincere, he is with us heart and soul, he lives, eats, and drinks the movement, thinks of nothing else, and can speak of nothing else; even the way he pays his fare in the subway has something to do with the party. But I am always uneasy in his presence—even when, properly speaking, I am not in his presence at all, but am one of the crowd, a head with hair, a face with a certain expression, among all the other heads and faces in the hall. I can justify my uneasiness, in a trivial way, by saying that, after all, no less an authority than science has shown us that nothing is absolute. But as I say, such arguments are trivial. All I know is that when I am one among many in the hall filled with people—at all such times, when the audience, oblivious of the stifling air and smoke, are straining to catch every one of Bain's words, are wildly applauding him or nearly falling off their chairs in laughter at his jokes, I alone am unmoved, and only I can entertain doubts of this man. Perhaps it is the fact that he is capable of laughter and of making others laugh that disturbs me so. Whatever the case, it is when he is most a leader that I doubt him most—and it is a doubt that goes far beyond skepticism and is itself a kind of certainty.

But this, if not trivial, is an irrelevant matter. I have only the fact of my own membership to go by—this, so far as I am concerned, is the basis of the party—and it is from this fact that I must always begin, over and over again, my search for the answer: the final assurance, which shall need nothing beyond itself.

Agreed, my belonging to the party is a necessary condition. Whatever my reasons for joining, once I became a member and had actively engaged in party work, I found I had inherited other conditions. No one can escape his inheritance. A man may come into a fortune and turn it down—but he cannot turn down the fact that it has been willed to him. To us has been willed also a fortune; as yet it has no value, except in our own circle, among those who have been similarly enriched. But what a fortune—the whole world! You understand what is meant by the embarrassment of riches. Think—some day the world may actually fall into our hands! Then where would we run? For the time being we have the escape of our work—and who knows?—it may be a perpetual refuge, in which case even the frustration of all our hopes would be a kind of consolation. But it is because we fear our work that we work so hard at it; hence the forcefulness of our singing, our loud voices, even in ordinary conversation, our great—and from a rational point of view, altogether excessive—love of argument, demonstration, protest, our running about, short of breath, always tired, without enough sleep, without rest. At all costs, we must conceal our fear of this thing.

Certainly, we fear punishment; there will come a time when we will be made to pay for our work—but this is nothing to us. We know it, we accept it as a matter of course. We have, in our own way, perhaps without being aware of it, already determined the payment we will make, assigning, this one an arm, that one a leg, an eye, a tooth, a life itself as the reasonable price for our transgression. But what if it is a transgression in spite of this? Would we still have the courage to continue? . . . such thoughts are not in season with the party. I wish I could do as the others do: begin with our premises, go as far as they lead and be thankful for the journey. Perpetual motion is impossible, and no one, not even I, believes in magic, signs, or miracles. Science and history. Reasoning is the thing! Believe me, I do not advocate the desertion of reason—but I cannot reason things out so clearly as the others seem to do, or so effortlessly. Faith? I have faith enough. I have patience, endurance, humility, strength, a governable will, all the proper virtues of the movement. Nevertheless, I have fear, a great fear; do what I may, there is fear. But of what? The truth of the matter is, it is not a fear of punishment. That is only a metaphor. The real fear lies beyond us, as does the real assurance. Which is not to say that courage also lies beyond us. No, courage is real enough, it is the dependable phenomenon. I have seen the comrades face the greatest dangers, the charge of mounted police, rifle volleys, the legal violence of the courts, and beatings in the back rooms of police stations. We have, thank God, we have our courage, a natural thing. But all the same, I wish I were as well assured of our solidarity and could feel it close about me, ever so close but never stifling, the bondage and the freedom in one.

2. The Press

Let us understand one another. I am an intellectual—at least, so considered in the party. I hope you will not, for this reason, mistrust me, as some of the comrades do. (Observation: the ones who are most mistrustful, who always make disparaging comments "on the role of the intellectual in the working-class movement," themselves have all the pretensions but none of the qualifications for this role.) I became an intellectual not as a matter of enlightenment, the discovery of truth after a life of toil; I am an intellectual by nature. Rather, I became a worker as the result of being an intellectual—a worker, that is to say, in reverse. On the first occasion that I spoke up in the party—it was at a meeting, during discussion period, and I rose to obtain, but in my fashion began, instead, to dispense, information on some point—the comrades decided that I should at once be put to work. Because I happened to refer to a certain painter in the course of my remarks, it was determined on the spot that I had "an artistic background," and that I could best serve the party—that sure judge of men—by enrolling my talents in the art department of our weekly newspaper. A few days later, I was informed that I had been appointed assistant art director; and when I protested my incapacity, I was told that I had not only been appointed, but voted into the job. The officers had appointed me, and the comrades elected me, a double certification; and as the leadership and the rank and file always respect each other's will, I might as well accept the position, for if I carried my protest back to the movement, the rank and file would appoint me and the leaders elect me. I accepted in good faith.

This has been my work for the last five years. I am one of the comrades who give "all their time to the movement"; and since this is said of the full-time party workers in a tone of deepest respect, I am something of a hero. But the honor does not overwhelm me, for all our intellectuals are minor heroes; so well regarded are we, that we are kept busy all the time, without a moment to ourselves. Stencils have to be cut and run off on the mimeograph machine, which is always breaking down; the ink pad is dry, the rubber stamps are worn out and have to be replaced; one hundred posters must be ready by the fifteenth, each with a recognizable portrait of the Founder on it—so much for art work. Then, only half our fold-ing chairs are in safe condition to use, there is a bill from the printer which must be stalled another month, unless we can get more advertisements for our Memorial Issue, which will in turn increase the size of the paper and raise printing costs, and has any one given a thought to repairing the banister on the top landing of the staircase?—it would be a waste to call in a carpenter, when some one handy with a hammer and nails could fix it in a jiffy. True, Comrade Ellenbogen is a carpenter by trade, but then, he is a worker, he works all day long and is entitled to his rest. Won't you see to it, Comrade Assistant Art Director? It goes without saying that the more advanced comrades must set an example for the others.

Fortunately, I do not have much time for art work, for the truth is that I am even clumsier with a brush than I am with a hammer. But one learns. I discovered in time that most of the portraits I was called on to produce in adornment of our newspaper and leaflets could be reduced to a few simple elements: high forehead, with or without hair (if hair, then always a shock of it, streaming; if bald, then just a fringe of hair to go around the ears and cover the neck); a nose, a good, powerful nose, on the whole, large, but not too large, and of no very definite shape—a simple line would serve the purpose; and a beard, either full or goatee. After the manner of industry, I worked out a few standardized parts which could be assembled without trouble by an apprentice; and then tradition came to my assistance, for as a rule, three portraits are required, cheek and jowl, which are recognized as much by their position as by their likeness—first the Founder, then the President, and then the Commander. What with tracing the work of my predecessors (a practice which on the whole I despise, as it makes for academicism), frequent erasures, and constant patience, I learned to do well enough. Moreover, I introduced a new principle into our art. It had been customary, when I entered the party, to represent the bosses with huge bellies, pigs' eye-slits and heavy, sagging jowls covered with a brutish stubble. I pointed out to

Comrade Gamper, our editor, that this image had served its historical purpose during the years of the Depression, but now that the Depression was over one could venture, in the interest of realism, to represent the bosses as clean shaven. My suggestion was carried after considerable discussion by the editorial board. A further suggestion—that the workers, always lean, alert, and clean shaven, be drawn instead with stubble, also for the sake of realism—which I was enboldened by my success to make, was, however, turned down with great disapproval by the board. My proposal was called cynical and was said to betray a lack of faith in the proletariat; I was reminded of my petty bourgeois origins as an intellectual, and was told that I had inherited a class prejudice against the workers. It was only Comrade Gamper's intervention on my behalf that saved me from a more severe reprimand.

Comrade Gamper calls himself an old newspaperman. He claims, with a curious pride, to have worked for "the bourgeois press." In what capacity, Comrade? A correspondent, foreign correspondent. In what country, Comrade? A foreign country. Not a further word out of him. No one knows which foreign country, and no one, for that matter, believes him. It is rumored that he was a tailor before he became a newspaperman, and that, far from having worked for the bourgeois press, he had never been in a newspaper office until he entered ours (as proofreader). He has picked up a stock of phrases which he uses without much regard for meaning: "put her to bed and lock her up," "run off," "center-page spread," "offset," "pied lines," etc., and a number of expressions, most likely of his own invention, which have no ascertainable relation to newspaper work. I have heard him shout at the printer, over the telephone, to "cut the top sashing off the primer sheet," and to "stop basting my galleys with a buttonhook"—expressions which confirm our belief that he was once a tailor. Naturally, you can't tell *him* how to edit a paper; but what is not so natural is that there is never the need to tell him a thing. He has an instinct, a workman's sense, for making things fit; one glance, and he knows what must go in and what has to come out, what will not run over and what will fall short, fill out the space or leave a hole. A tailor's sense. But where editing and tailoring part their ways, Gamper, unfortunately, goes on as a tailor. A misfortune because he writes much of the copy himself, and corrects everyone else's syntax and spelling to conform to his own.

There are times when, in spite of all our efforts, the treasury runs dry, the bills mount up and the paper actually does suspend publication. Then there is gloom in the *Vanguard* office. Gamper sits at his desk, his feet no longer stuck into an open drawer, and stares at the wall, the clock, the water cooler. His thumbs are no longer hooked under his red suspenders; he wears his jacket, but not his hat or his green eyeshade. Now he smokes his cigar, no longer chewing it cold. There is no pencil behind his ear, no ink staining his fingers. The paper has suspended publication, and Gamper has suspended his clichés. No more an editor. But he picks up our last issue and turns the pages. He criticizes my art work, curses the linotype operator, damns our contributors. "Look at that head!" he exclaims, and I must remember whether he wrote it himself to know what he expects me to say. He is running about the office again, opening drawers, blowing away the dust, filling the ink wells. His jacket is off, his cigar has gone out, he has put on his eyeshade again and is once more sitting at his desk, feet raised. But there is nothing to do. He plays with the scissors, unscrews the lid of the paste pot and screws it on again. His feet slip to the floor. He lights his cigar, puffs morosely, making the air in the room blue. He imagines there has been talk of replacing him.

The last time we had to suspend publication, we remained idle for six weeks. Toward the end of this period, Gamper discovered that mice had overrun our stockroom and begun to destroy the pile of back numbers. Out he went for a cat, and returned ten minutes later with a scrawny, dirty animal. At once he put in a call to Comrade Lips, the party treasurer, demanding funds for the rehabilitation and upkeep of the cat. Lips refused to hear of such nonsense, but as Gamper kept ringing him and interfered with his work, he sent a delegation of three comrades to the newspaper office to make inquiries and submit a report. By the time the delegation arrived, succeeded in finding the cat (which, unaccustomed to politics, had hidden in fear in the farthest corner of the room where the papers were piled the highest), examined it, took into account the evidence that mice had been at work and returned to make their report, more than half the day had gone by, and the cat had still got nothing to eat. It would have starved to death, had I not persuaded Gamper that the cost of providing it with milk (it could supplement its diet with mice) would be negligible; the order permitting the *Vanguard* to draw a dollar a month on party funds for the maintenance of its cat did not arrive until the whole incident, cat and mice both, had been disposed of. But the cat, whom we had named Spartacus, showed no capacity for supplementing his diet; he grew sleek on milk alone, and our stock of papers, day by day, came nearer to ruin. We were obliged to set traps, at our own expense. (Spartacus had by now proved to be quite a drain on our resources, but as Gamper had grown attached to him, he continued to live in the stockroom.) The traps caught nothing but Spartacus, for as he had been living only on milk, he could not resist the cheese with which the traps were baited. We would come into the office in the morning, to hear him howling in pain. Gamper took to staying on nights in the stockroom to keep his pet from harm, and before long he was sleeping on a bed of papers, among his cat and mice and traps. Soon he was spending most of his time there, and rarely appeared in the office. We would see him from time to time, a pitiful sight, unkempt, unshaved, a wild man living with animals. We tried to keep the party from learning about Gamper, but the news got out, all the more damaging for being so meager, as the comrades supplemented what little they knew with stories of their own invention. He became known as the Catman or the Mouser, it was said that he went on all fours and that he leaped at the throat of anyone foolhardy enough to enter the stockroom, and there was talk of having him brought to an institution. True, Gamper was living more or less in a state of nature, but the comrades exaggerated his condition. I did what I could to demonstrate the falsehood of the stories that were spread about him, persuading Gamper to wash and shave and dress more carefully, to come out for walks, and to mingle with the others. Actually, though he was, in part, affected by the suspension of the newspaper, his behavior was not altogether irrational, and it may even be said that it proceeded from the soundest motives. The basic reason for his living in the stockroom was *economic,* not psychological. His salary had been cut off, and rather than struggle to keep up his own apartment, or to live with his equally hard-pressed comrades, he retreated, as any unselfish man would do, so to speak, to the wilderness, to limit his wants and needs. So much for the comrades who are always repeating, parrotwise, that the fundamental cause of everything is economic, and yet, when the moment comes to put theory into practice, run off in all directions but the one they are committed to. Final proof of the groundlessness of the comrades' stories was obtained when sufficient funds were accumulated for resuming the publication of the newspaper. Gamper came out of the stockroom a new man, rested, invigorated, sound. Restored to his position, his energies redirected in their proper channel, he had no further need of Spartacus, and dismissed him. The traps, left to themselves, caught mice, and the mice, recognizing the objective situation for what it was, deserted the party (let us hope, for the enemy's). The incident was closed, and Gamper was once again shouting unintelligible orders to the printer. But one of the least unkind names that had been applied to him during the period of his aberration unfortunately stuck, though in modified form. The stockroom, because of all the animals in it, had been called the Zoo, and Gamper, the Zookeeper. Now when Comrade Gamper is said to be "one of the Old Guard" (ordinarily a term of respect), it is understood that the word "guard" still means Zookeeper.

3. Picnics and Socials

In summer there are picnics and in winter, socials. Preparations are made long in advance—invitations, collections, various plans for games and entertainment, in winter, a liquor permit to be obtained, and in summer, something like prayer for good weather. Long preparations, and the climax reached in an hour of a single day—come and gone, a natural rhythm. And afterwards the repetition in memory of the day as a whole, and of its parts, relived in serenity, a convalescence.

The party in its pleasures becomes a natural thing; one might almost say it is so designed that its apparatus shall function on certain occasions, freely, of its own motion. Suddenly, the end which the interminable discussions and organizational arguments have served becomes clear and all our work is seen to have existed for this purpose: to be forgotten, transcended, or destroyed. The comrades get drunk, they shout and sing, whirl about the floor, dancing in couples, threes, larger groups; they steal the drum from the band and go beating it, up and down the hall and out onto the fire escape. Where, then, is the objective? What has this to do with the movement?

But it is questionable whether our pleasures really are free. A week after the social the usual notice appears in the *Vanguard*, to the effect that a great proletarian enthusiasm was evinced at the gathering and that all the workers present were impressed by our spirit. As reportage, this notice is completely irresponsible, yet it has some truth, a truth of its own. For in everyone's pleasure two motives are at work, undercutting each other; one is to fling away all restraint and obligation and have a good time at the party's expense, we have it coming to us; the other is to turn even our disregard of the party to some useful end, at least that the outsiders—and all the better if there are any workers among them—shall see how free we are. This conflict cannot be resolved. One may therefore ask, is pleasure possible in the party? Pleasure, mind you, in the real sense, as the world understands it.

Here is a skit, prepared by some of our intellectuals who have a literary background. A comrade comes on and imitates the president of the country, the way he thrusts out his jaw, smokes a cigarette, declares his opposition to war. (The same gestures serve the imitation of other well-known political figures, both at home and abroad.) After every statement that the mimic makes a chorus backstage shouts: *"Ipse dixit!"*—and this is considered amusing by those who understand Latin, and even more so by those who do not. Then the mimic turns his back to the audience, produces a burnt cork, dabs on a small mustache, plasters down his hair, and turns about, his right arm raised in salute. The audience laughs. The mimic again turns his back, enlarges the mustache, ruffles his hair, sticks a pipe in his mouth and faces front, his right hand thrust into his shirt. The audience screams with laughter. I too laugh. But why, may I ask, should such things be considered funny? The faces the mimic makes are the ones we see in our nightmares; the whole party dreams about these men, and not a day passes but that we attach some fresh anxiety to them. How is it that the mimic so relieves our terror? The only answer I can think of is that these faces and these poses confront us with our own divided attitude toward the party, and we escape through the division. We laugh not only to rid ourselves of our fear, but also of the measures we take against the objects of our fear: we laugh at the very notion of fighting these men, and thus, for a moment, get beyond them and the party both.

Or in the course of the skit some one will do an imitation of Bain: his high voice, dimpled fists, his puns and jokes and sophistries. A favorite act of ours. But there is a risk in it—are we including not only the form but the substance of Bain in our mockery? But the representation must have substance. Then what shall it include—Bain's words, sentences, whole speeches? If so, shall we hear a plea for continuing our membership drive into the following year? How is it possible to make fun of the party without betraying our seriousness?

One does not make fun of the party. The very jokes one tells, the political witticisms and pleasantries that draw on the Revolution ("Comes the Revolution, you'll eat strawberries and cream—and like it!"—our basic philosophical joke, a play on freedom and necessity)—these *are* the party. Also the hope of a love affair high in everyone's expectation at a social, the desire for a newcomer, our "contact work"—this too is the party. Our pretty girls and handsome young men, such few as there are, they too work for the party. And Bain and his women—what legends there are! though one legend has it that he is ascetic, for the leader must be all things to all men; who stands in his favor now? And the other leaders, the gift of the gods' love given to this one and that, traveling through the party, an endless communion.

One does not escape the party. Yet sometimes, in summer, out on a picnic, in the woods, or at the beach, it seems that the party has, after all, succumbed to nature. There has been, let us say, good weather, which has sharpened our anticipation but also increased our fears and made our hopes more desperate. But the day breaks fine and clear. We gather in the morning at headquarters, lunches packed, knapsacks strapped to our shoulders, this one holding a camera, that one a bat, an inner tube, a ball. The truck draws up late but not late enough to spoil the day. We swarm onto the loading platform, stand on the benches, climb up the wooden slats, and hang over. The cover is off, the wind blows, flapping our banner, as the truck drives down the street. We wave at the passers-by, whistle at the girls on their way to church, shout and sing, and so on, out into the country.

A picnic, but still the party. The party, but still a picnic. An effort at organization, at holding the comrades together. Games, one-legged races, jumping contests, tree-climbing, apple-picking, stunts and tricks, banjoes, concertinas, soda pop, and beer. Still there are the woods nearby. Comrades Becky and Diego have been seen sneaking away. After them! a hike is organized, we fall into line and go marching through the woods, singing Solidarity Forever. Still there are stragglers. One pair of comrades falls behind, another turns aside, a quick cut off the path and they are gone, not to appear until dark, peacefully hand in hand, their hair matted with leaves.

Or we are at the beach, and again races, handsprings, lunch in the open; swimming contests, instruction for beginners. The day wears on, the comrades, sunburned, seek out the shade, or fall asleep in the sand in strange postures, embracing, their legs intertwined, stricken dead by the sun. A small group holds out, an example of party discipline. They have played cards, drunk lemonade, eaten their sandwiches, saving the frankfurters and the potatoes for the fire at night. Now they are holding a discussion, a quiet discussion. It has been a fine day, they are hopeful. They feel that the time is not far off when the workers, the shopkeepers, the farmers, all the exploited of this country will come to them, recognize the truth, and accept their leadership. They will come soon, they will surely come. Gratefully they will come calling, flocking together, seeking what all men desire: justice, peace, a living wage. The sun is setting, it is cool, the comrades have thrown sweater and jackets over their shoulders. Out on the water, now a speck, now larger, a small boat is making for the shore.

Two men can be seen, rowing. The comrades watch them approach, they are silent, seeing the boat dip down under a wave, reappear on the crest. At last the boat is beached, not far off; it is drawn up on the sand and covered with canvas. One of the men sees our group and he comes running, long-legged, a string of fish dangling from his shoulder. He is burned red by the sun, we can make out his flushed cheeks in the twilight, his sunburned hair, freckles under his eyes. He stands before us, smiles, asks if we know who won the ball game today, and goes back none the wiser, the fish dripping water on the sand.

We light our fire, the comrades gather round it, holding their frankfurters to the coals on branches and sticks. More wood is thrown on, the potatoes are buried in the ashes. All the comrades are together, they eat with great appetite. One can feel the heat of the sun coming out all over his body, and the wind is cool. The stars have appeared, the fire burns lower. Soon it is unattended, it goes out. The comrades have separated into couples, going arm in arm, quickly, down the beach, up into the sand hills, blankets slung over their shoulders. A few comrades are left alone, a few old men, and they stand facing the ocean without speaking to one another.

4. Demonstration

Eleven are in the hospital, seventeen in jail and the lawyer is right now working to get them out. The rest are at headquarters, bandaged, beaten, their faces swollen. Some are still bleeding. Nevertheless, a great excitement. The comrades are boasting how they stood up against the police, disarmed them, grabbed their nightsticks, pulled them off their mounts. It was a success. It was worth it. The city was impressed with our strength. We got our point across to the masses. The workers were impressed. It will reflect itself, just wait and see. The comrades are bandaging their wounds, but they are happy, enlivened, full of an unspent courage. Comrade Helena Biderman is running from one to the other, applying bandages, washing cuts and scratches, cleaning wounds, pouring on iodine, and holding the comrades with her narrow hands while they squirm in pain. Her eyes show her exhilaration, she is nearly faint with happiness. Pleasure is possible in the party, after all.

5. A Devoted Comrade

Helena is one of the "old-timers"—which is to say, she was among those who were expelled from the parent body and who organized our own group. She is sometimes called, derisively, "The Nightingale" or "Holy Mary." She has been given these names because of her sweetness. You may ask why, if she is sweet, should she be held in the least derision? But you must reckon with the nature of the party. What would you have us do, weep when she appears? We are close enough to tears when we see her mount the speaker's platform on her thin, birdlike legs, exactly as if she had claws instead of feet, and ridiculously long for a person so small and delicate as she. A hush falls over us, the silence of respect. The laughter and the heckling which have greeted all the previous speakers come to a sudden end. Immediately, a great sadness comes over us; a sadness which Helena radiates, precisely in the manner in which saints are said to give off an odor of sanctity. The sadness she evokes in us is no ordinary emotion; it is rather a kind of insight, which even the most simple-minded of the comrades acquire in contact with her. Our insight foresees a special suffering for Helena, a doom and annihilation, terrible in themselves, which become even more terrible when they are seen to be her fate. I myself receive distinct impressions of burning from her image: death by fire. Others have said that they think of her crushed or drowned or strangled. We are all moved to prophesy, until we can no longer bear our visions; one of the weaker

comrades breaks down and makes a rude joke, the rest join him
and soon we are all laughing, as if it were one of the lesser comrades who was about to address us. (It is only when Bain mounts
the platform that we do not dare—or even desire—to revile the
speaker.) "The Nightingale" and "Holy Mary" are the most
respectful of the names that have thus been applied to her (I call
her, privately, "The Firebird"), and it speaks something for our
inherent refinement that none of the others has stuck. But she,
remarkable woman, bears us no resentment. She stands on the
platform and waits for the laughter to subside; her body is hidden
by the speakers' stand; only her red hands and her head appear,
as if severed from the trunk, the point of her chin rising just above
the lectern. At last Helena smiles—a child's smile—and apologizes. "I have a bad cold. I hope you will be able to hear me"; or
she apologizes for her speech defect and expresses the hope that
it will not annoy us. Her voice is clear—and of course, she has no
cold, no speech defect, she need not apologize. She should be
proud of her voice, of her sweetness, of the profound respect in
which we hold her and which drives us to such extremes of self-
abasement. We forget our rudeness, we feel at once that it has
been forgiven. Her voice rouses in us sadness and admiration; we
nod our heads while she speaks, maintaining an even, dreamy
rhythm, as if we were listening to music; and her voice has the
quality of music, there are overtones in it that remind the more
sentimental comrades of the sound of violins. Some, in fact, do
weep as they listen to her.

And what is it she speaks of in her wonderfully clear, sweet
voice? Of God and His angels? On the contrary—of the situation
in China, the coal strike, the need for inner-party clarification on
the colonial question. Or altogether on materialism. One must
hear her speak on these subjects to know what poetry means. All
the same, she is a woman of powerful lungs. Her voice, when she
is roused, rings out to the farthest corners of the hall, and then it

is not she alone but a whole choir that is singing. Also, she knows how to make a warlike music. She hops on her bird feet, her head sinks out of sight and pops up again behind the stand, and her white hair is flying. She shouts; not in the ordinary shout of the political speaker, of the hoarse voice and strained throat; hers is still a sweetness shouting, a peacefulness and love bent to the uses of war. It is then that we receive our various images of doom. I sense the burning of her body, first fever, then actual flame. But I must still believe in her sweetness, still believe that her love out-lives her agony and that the fire which has destroyed her has, in its great heat, melted down the iron gates that bar the fulfillment of our desire.

Helena is unique among us; yet what I have observed of her nature reveals the essential being of all the old comrades. A single word expresses it: they are *confirmed*. It is as though Helena had all her life been under special care, designed to bring out and make flourish all those qualities which now so impress us. Compare her to a plant in a greenhouse. Her greenhouse is this hall, and others like it. The smoke in the air, the warmth of compressed bodies, odors of sweat and dust; nights spent in conference, hotel rooms during conventions, street corner meetings, picket lines, strikes, bloodshed, arguments and debates with the leaders of disobedient factions, minutes, reports, leaflets drawn up and distributed, day after day after day—such are the elements that produce the final flourishing of the person. Helena's sweetness is the confirmation. After so much endured, the sweetness is the proof of hope. It is the hope itself. The gestures, the voice, the gentleness and the shouting—all this is the hope, so perfect as to drive others mad with shame. Yet Helena endures. Sometimes when she speaks, carried away by the sadness and the faithful quavering of her voice, I receive no longer impressions of fire but of a still more terrible destruction. I see her cut down by a knife: an arm lopped off, then both arms, both legs; Helena is decapitated, her body halved, quartered, minced. But still her sweetness remains. There is an echo of it, a dying phrase, but the phrase does not die. It goes on. I stop my ears, only to hear, when I listen again, the same voice with its intolerable, indestructible, lovely hope.

6. Factions and Expulsions

It is always the younger comrades who are lacking in hope. This goes against the usual expectation and the common usage of the word; for the young are said to be the most hopeful by nature. But I am using the word precisely in that unromantic sense in which it applies to the older comrades, such as Helena—the sense of confirmation which is to my mind the only important meaning that the concept bears. The young are impatient, too soon disappointed. The world wreaks a sudden vengeance on them. Failing to attain a worldly goal, they turn inward, retreating to their own idealism, and think that they have thereby conquered the world. They do not suspect it is the world which has conquered them. Therefore one may say that is the young who are corrupted, they are spoiled by the comfort they take in their own disillusionment It is the older comrades, superior both to illusion and disillusionment, who have learned to be youthful, and who, in a word, are pure. To be youthful, to be pure—it is to be able to face the world as it is.

The younger comrades take our defeats too much to heart. The death or imprisonment of a leader; the loss of an election or—as we have never won an election, either in our own country or abroad—the loss of a number of votes; the fact that the whole world laughs at us; the failure of a revolutionary situation to materialize in accordance with our expectations or the more disheartening failure of any benefits to come our way even by accident—all such misfortunes, which one must learn to accept as a matter of course, seize the young comrades by the handle, so to speak, and fling them entirely out of the realm of reason. We hear, let us suppose, that our party in France has lost twenty members. Aha, Comrade Abraham Mexico, a lad in his early twenties, takes the floor and demands—reorganization! Reorganization of what, where, why, when? Reorganization! Suppose our group were reorganized, with Comrade Mexico, presumably, at its head—how would that help matters in France? Never mind, the comrade demands reorganization, and he screams and protests, supported by the other youngsters, until he gets what he wants—that is, he gets a promise. The chairman has the secretary make a note of the comrade's proposal for reference to the executive committee. By the time the executive committee gets to hear of the young comrade's request, the situation in France may well have improved of its own accord. But are the comrades satisfied to have been treated with respect, and to have had their proposals submitted to higher authority; are they content to let the party, and nature itself, follow their own course, their own laws? Not in the least. Another cry is raised: "Bureaucracy!" This cuts the elders to the quick: it is the one charge that wounds them, that they really cannot bear to hear. But still they are patient with the younger element. "What about the disaffection of the Spanish workers?" cries La Passionara Dvorkin, so called because of her maniacal devotion to Spain. "The comrades must by now be cognizant of the objective situation! The Spanish workers have put forth their legitimate demands, but their own leadership, their own leaders, mind you, have formed a parasitical bureaucracy that fastened itself to the backs of the Spanish workers and squoze the living blood out of them. Long live the freedom of the Spanish working class!" Very well, Comrade Dvorkin, thank you. The Spanish workers appreciate your efforts on their behalf. But what bearing does your statement have on Comrade Mexico's demand for the reorganization of the party in *this* country? which demand, incidentally, is supposed to be bound up with the question of France, though in a manner that is not immediately clear. Would the comrades care to put their suggestions in the form of a resolution for consideration by the policy committee? Do we hear a motion for a vote? Comrade Ellenbogen, of the carpenters' local, our chairman for the evening, is trembling with anger. A simple, elderly man, he is devoted to the party and cannot stand to hear it criticized. The subtleties of the youngsters are too much for him; he hears the word bureaucracy and he flies into a rage. "Party discipline . . . wreckers . . . young pups . . . expel . . . no good!" These words, spoken in a heavy accent, are the only ones that can be made out until a more articulate comrade takes the floor to answer, patiently, but also angrily, the charges of the young members.

But much as I may admire the steadfastness of the old comrades, I cannot say that their virtues, in all cases, include understanding. I cannot accept their interpretation of the character and personality of the young members, an altogether shortsighted approach which, for example, attributes Comrade Mexico's querulousness to the fact that he suffers from acne. It cannot be denied that his trouble is severe; but to limit his whole being to his pimples is to betray one's own limitation. Or the view which ascribes Comrade Dvorkin's position on Spain and unrelated matters to her virginity. That she is a virgin may in all sad probability be the case. But it is an act of cruelty to limit her being to a condition which is quite obviously not of her own choice; and then to call her La Passionara . . . ! It is furthermore undignified for the human mind to yield so abjectly to the obvious: Spain, land of romance, Latin lovers, hot blood; ergo, La Dvorkin and her Spanish workers. For myself at any rate, it is always something of a struggle to concede the obvious. Moreover in a group so small as our own, where not only the obvious traits but also the innermost secrets of the members are at once found out, a certain discretion must be exercised, even in the use of faculties which it is otherwise our right to use freely. Let me not look too closely; let me shut my ears, not to the truth, but to the bad name which the truth can acquire in a circle so close as ours.

It is with these provisions in mind that I come to the recent expulsion of William Board. Comrade Board, or Billboard, as he was also known in the party, was one of our most trusted workers, noted for his energy and enthusiasm and devotion to the movement. He was also one of our best public speakers and debaters and could make the finest hair-splitting appear as the broadest oratory. If there was work which required a spirited performance and joyous fulfillment it fell, by necessity, to Board. No one else could inspire the youth so well, rouse their courage. Enough. One night, at a meeting, I saw that he was slouching in his seat and yawning, as if he were about to fall asleep. (Ordinarily, he sat erect on the edge of his chair, alert for action.) Several other young comrades were yawning. I assumed that they had all been out late the night before, drinking, or perhaps at a party, and again I had reason to regret my quasi-official status which had cut me off from contact with the comrades of my own age. After the meeting I began a conversation with Board, as much out of jealousy, to ascertain what I had missed, as out of friendly motives. I saw at once that he had overcome his sleepiness and when we went out on the street in the cold air he was entirely revived. Board was vague in his replies; there had been something of a gathering, but not what one could call a party, and far from having liquor to drink they had only coffee, tea, and milk. His evasiveness put me off, so that I was obliged, more or less in self-defense, and somewhat vindictively (I now regret it), to assume my official role and represent the party's interest in our conversation. With typical hypocrisy, I inquired after his health and asked him if he was not perhaps overworking himself. Did he get enough sleep, did he find time for exercise and relaxation? Were the girls (this with a wink) treating him well? Perhaps a short leave of absence could be arranged. His services were invaluable, but after all there is such a thing as fatigue and one does need a rest from time to time, etc. His energetic step—I had difficulty keeping up with him— mocked my anxieties, which in turn mocked my true feelings. Board smiled and assured me that everything was in order. But the next night he was again found yawning. We opened the windows, but it did no good; he continued to yawn, and with him, several of the younger comrades. That same night Board had to make a report on the progress of the work he had been carrying out in connection with the bus drivers' strike. He rose to his feet, stretched and yawned and shuffled his way to the platform, where he slouched against the stand, his chin supported on both fists and his eyes gummy with sleep. The comrades were astonished to see him so enervated; nevertheless, accustomed to his usual manner, and anticipating, appearance to the contrary, another fiery speech, they greeted him with applause. The applause failed to shake Comrade Board out of his lethargy. At the same time several loud cries of "Ho-hum!" were heard from the audience. I could not determine who had called out so strangely.

Board began his speech in a low, dull voice. His arms, which would, ordinarily, have been thrashing the air, now hung listlessly at his sides. He paused frequently, half his words were lost. The people in the back of the room cried "Louder!" Comrade Board replied with a yawn and continued to mumble and drawl something which I, who sat near enough to make out his intelligible words, knew had no relation to the bus drivers' strike. He was saying, as I remember, that respiration is governed by the sympathetic nervous system, and that though a man can will to hold his breath until he loses consciousness, once he faints he will begin to breathe again. This must therefore be ruled out as a method of committing suicide. It was, however, worth noting that the Toti, an Indian tribe, had perfected the method to the point where they could suspend consciousness for an indefinite period—which, for all practical purposes, was as good as suicide, and had besides many other advantages. Here he yawned again. Some of the younger comrades yawned in return. The yawning spread to the other members and I, too, succumbed to it. Long drawn out "ho-hums" were heard, peculiar animal noises. Then, to everyone's astonishment, Board quit the platform in the middle of a sentence—something he had never been known to do. He shuffled to his seat and threw himself down, as one might throw himself onto a couch to sleep.

Comrade Bain sprang up. "It appears that some of the comrades are very sleepy," he began in his high-pitched, ironical voice. "It has never been our intention to keep them up past their bedtime." (The older members applauded this reference to the youth of the offenders; the young comrades continued to yawn.) "These same comrades are notorious for the fact that their main activity in the movement has been sleeping—in one form or another. It is beginning to tell on them." (Loud laughter, continued yawning.) These innuendoes made me think of La Passionara; I found her, mouth wide open, among the yawning faction; and as I had already begun to think of the yawning comrades as a faction, it was only natural to seek out the factious young Mexico. He, too, was yawning. It occurred to me then that we might be witnessing not a spontaneous exhibition of sleepiness but a demonstration of some kind—one that had been planned carefully, far in advance, and that was supposed to serve some political purpose. I expressed my suspicions in a note which I passed up to Comrade Bain; he read it, frowning. It was a frown of extreme displeasure—actually one of hatred; he said aloud, "I was coming to that.

"One of the comrades, as notorious for his alertness as some of the others are for their sleeping, has just called my attention to the obvious fact that this exhibition of yawning—(here he stifled a yawn) of yawning might be in the nature of a political demonstration. I wonder how he can think that I am asleep! Has he ever seen me sleeping? Either publicly or otherwise? With or without my shoes? Aren't my eyes wide open enough for him? Shall I open them wider? Wider? Wider?" He leaned forward, popping out his eyes, until they seemed ready to burst from his head. The audience screamed with laughter, and even some of the yawning faction laughed though they at once resumed their original activity. Thus, hour after hour passed, all serious work at an end, while Bain went about disproving the accusation I had never made in the first place: that he had overlooked the political significance of yawning. He concluded his speech with a ringing denunciation of yawning as a vice of the petty bourgeoisie, of whose historical weakness it gave dramatic evidence. "Remember, comrades, the proletariat does not yawn. It falls exhausted into bed to sleep the sleep, the honest sleep it has earned—and earned rightly, even if it has earned nothing else—neither a living wage nor the essential comforts of life—with its toil!" Nothing was accomplished that night, though the faction was warned and placed under provisional indictment. It was on the following night, when the yawning was seen to continue and to involve more of the younger element, that the yawn-leaders were placed under ambulatory arrest and the trial began.

Board's confession, which was obtained, I can assure you, not under duress, but was given voluntarily—though there are subtle forms of duress whose exercise is purely unconscious; that he was kept under ambulatory arrest, free to come and go, yet, for all that, arrested, may be an instance of such force; how, then, can any authority prove itself absolutely innocent?—his confession is one of the most remarkable documents in the party's history. Board admitted that for several months he had been growing more and more depressed as the recognition of the futility of our work forced itself upon him. Instead of consulting with the older comrades, he retreated into himself as, under such circumstances, it is common for us to do. But to retreat into himself meant, for an activist such as he, a retreat into his work. It was therefore impossible for any of the comrades to detect Board's change of heart; and moreover impossible for Board to realize that his enthusiasm was dwindling. Once begun, his retreat into himself carried him even further away from himself, and from his underlying sense of the futility of the movement. If he had any doubts about himself, consideration of his activity quickly dispelled them. He saw that he was devoting more time than ever to the party; if he felt occasional fatigue, he attributed it, naturally, to the amount of work he was doing, never once reflecting on the purpose it was supposed to serve. He assumed, as do all the faithful comrades, that the purpose of our work is given once and for all; it is fixed, and if it alters at all, it is in the direction of greater urgency.

But there is a human economy with its own laws which do not permit operation at a loss. Eventually, he was forced to give up his attempt to sustain himself through greater activity; and what sapped his strength was not so much the fact that he was bored as the final recognition of his boredom. Here Board went into a long digression on the nature of boredom, justifying it as a motive of human activity and seeking to present it as the underlying condition of all life. I shall give no account of his reasoning, which is sophistical in character, and shall omit his speculations on the meaning of the coincidence between his name and the affliction from which he suffered. Once boredom settled on him and he felt himself forced to abandon all effort to shake it off, he resigned himself to his condition and began, as a matter of course, to yawn at meetings. But even then he remained the good comrade—he stifled and smothered his yawns, as if to maintain a distinction between the inner necessity of boredom and its outward manifestation, over which he still hoped to exercise some control. He took to drinking black coffee before meetings and to swallowing benzedrine and caffeine pills. This cut off the natural outlet of his boredom; but he was essentially a political man, second nature always superseded first, and it was in politics

rather than sleep that he would have to find the true expression
of his fatigue.

Very cautiously he began to confide in some of the younger
comrades, sounding out their opinions and judging their state of
mind. He made it a principle never to reveal his boredom directly,
but to lead up to it by discussing the party's many defeats and the
futility of our work. Even here he remained loyal to the movement
(at least, so he thought), for it was never his intention to demonstrate the inevitability of boredom; rather he tried to reach, always
without success, some other possible conclusion—if only other
possibilities remained. But that there was another way out was
never shown to his satisfaction. And so his loyalty led to betrayal;
where another would have resigned and found a new interest to
absorb him, Board, the devoted comrade, went even deeper into
the party, and his boredom with politics became a new kind of
politics. He had by now assembled a following of some fifteen
young comrades; his faction called itself the Ennui Club. They
met after hours in cafés or in their own rooms to draw up their
program of action, which they called a program of inaction. It
was impossible to change the course of events; all existing parties
were either bent on evil, or were futile, like our own. It was useless to try to call the party's attention to the fact that it was
too small an organization, too limited and old-fashioned in its
methods to have the least conceivable effect upon the world. To
criticize the party in this fashion would only provoke further discussions and debates, to the greater futility of party work. It was
necessary to go underground within the party; if they could spread
their attitude through infection and example they would stand
some chance of achieving their objective.

But their objective—I find it almost too fantastic to mention.
It was "to bore from within"—miserable pun; the party would
change only when it was thoroughly bored with itself. It was to
produce in the members a state of boredom so great that they

would be unable to attend their own meetings, but would instead fill the meetings of rival organizations, spreading the yawn. All politics of the Left was to come to a standstill; then the Right was to be attacked, with a similar result. The same work was to be carried out abroad, until the whole world was too bored to make war, to seek profits, expand its markets, and exploit the working class. And when capitalism had fallen asleep *(sic)* . . . why, then, we would seize power (presumably with the help of black coffee) and establish socialism in our time!

Only to indicate what a pathetic end our youth have come to, I mention the fact, which I would otherwise prefer to omit, that all this was offered seriously by the Ennui Club, as a program for the party to adopt. They were as serious as men can be who advocate nonsense; and yet even their nonsense was earnestly delivered, it being their nature to regard no idea lightly enough for laughter. Serious, faithful, and convinced of their doctrine—good comrades to the end.

Board and his fifteen followers were expelled from the party, along with three suspected sympathizers. Another group of seven youngsters who had originally belonged to Board's faction, but had splintered for reasons too fine to trace, was also excluded from our organization. We lost twenty-six young comrades, all in one blow—a severe blow to our movement, one from which we may not soon recover.

7. The End of All Things

Conceive of the truth as something blinding, into which one cannot look. Then falsehood is darkness, into which one dare not look.

There was always discussion of means and ends, purpose, policy, and doctrine in the party. Full discussion, even (save the mark!) too much discussion. The paper has little else in it; the inner-party bulletins, running to thirty and forty single-spaced

mimeographed pages, still appear regularly, once a month, bulging with clarifications and reclarifications, criticism heaped on
criticism, debates, pro, con, and in between, on what instruction
we should give our comrades in a certain country, should a hypo-
thetical situation arise, though for a fact we have no comrades
there. It is heady stuff, it calls for subtlety. But there's a pathetic
simplicity in it, all the same: what if we are wrong?

Slightly wrong, mostly wrong, wholly wrong?

Some comrades refuse to face the darkness. They look only at
the sun (but do not blink at it!). Others admit that there's darkness, but describe such weird things in it, that there is no making
out what they see. Still others plunge into it, and are lost.

What if we are wrong? Some say, we will win anyway—events
will prove us right. But if we will win anyway, events will prove
nothing, as we may be wrong and still win. This is irresponsible
optimism. If we win anyway, who cares about right and wrong?
God save us from such victories and preserve freedom for men
worthier than we. There must be another way out.

What if we are wrong? There will be time, say others, to discover and correct our mistakes. Science is an endless process of
self-correction, and what is the movement if not scientific? But if
there will be time, there is hope, as much hope as there will be
time. Is there then, indeed, such hope?

If there were, as much hope as one could hope for, who would
need science? But some hope? At least as much as even despair
must have? I do not know. There must be hope of some kind, if
one is to think of the party at all. But whether such hope exists is
another thing. All I can say is that we have a few lessons to learn,
and it is not necessarily the intelligent but the brave who will
learn them.

One such lesson is to be drawn from the expulsion of the
young: we cannot depend on youth any more. Perhaps some day
the young will again fill our ranks, charge us with enthusiasm,

drive us ahead. But today, the young people who have survived the purge are prematurely aged. Their condition is marked not by wrinkles, gray hair, or baldness, but by one thing alone—hope. We say of them, somewhat tenderly, they still have hope. *Still.* The very word implies the past. It is not to the present or even the future that one looks, these days, for hope.

I even feel myself tempted, from time to time, to admit that the position of the Ennui Club was essentially correct. I have said that they took themselves seriously; but I wonder if they can have known how serious they really were. A seriousness in spite of themselves, the superior sense that nonsense can make. Naturally, the party could not pick out the seed of truth from so much offal; in their eyes it was a case, clear through, of madness and irresponsibility, sabotage or, on the most charitable account, bohemianism. Of course, it was all that; and yet, what else could have served the purpose? The purpose, I can now see, though I must suppose it to have been an unconscious one, was to express our impatience with the world—we have a right to it. After all, it is only on the very long view, the historical assumption, that one can say all is well with us. Be patient, the time will come. . . . But where is there time enough for so much history? And how much history is really our own? Only a fragment falls into our hands. Do what we may, we cannot make it fit all our needs—and what about those pitiful needs of ours? And then, is it really history? A fragment?—not even that. No, we have a right to our impatience—we must insist on it. Without it, who should care how slowly time drags? Death itself would be unnoticeable. We must insist on a quick issue, soon enough—the great hope!—to extend our fragment. In our time, our world! Meanwhile, the awakened comrades—even if it be only they who cannot sleep!—suffer the slow drag of time, and legitimately so. How long must the night wear on, when will there be a crack of light, a mere lightening of the atmosphere? Not even a promise—let the dawn greet those who come after us—for us only the faintest of faint hope. Nevertheless, hope. How long must we lie and wait? . . . Do not be so angry, comrades, everywhere in the world there is truth, and in the deepest midnight, perhaps the deepest truth.

Shall I say then, there is no hope—is this the truth? The night does not permit it. All other nights have passed—why not this one? There is no hope, and an end to the matter. But even if there were no hope, there would still be hope. This is not to say, as do some bourgeois philosophers, that it is impossible to live without hope. Far to the contrary—how little they know!—one does live without hope. But how is this possible? Can it be that hopelessness is something that none of us has as yet faced; that it is nothing to fear; that it is—who knows?—a new world with its own wonders? And perhaps we do already live in this world without knowing it; or if we have not yet attained it, perhaps we yearn for it, and it is the one dream we all have, in our deepest sleep, never remembered, our one hope—finally to be rid of hope? A world nothing like our own, but certainly we have pushed to the edge of it. Or have we been pushed? No matter. Freedom and necessity, our standing joke. But who shall laugh at it now? Gladly would we choose necessity and let freedom go, if only we were assured of our necessity. Gladly would we choose freedom, in spite of all necessity, if only the choice were our freedom. But we choose them both, lacking both—jesters that we are! What a ridiculous thing the party is! But a brave thing, the sum of all courage, the greatest venture. Further one cannot go, this is the edge of things. Here ends the human world, and there, in that emptiness, the stars and planets begin.

Well, then, are we right or wrong? And who shall blame either the fear or daring of it?

*   *   *

A great burden has fallen on Comrade Bain; he has been left virtually alone to carry on the struggle not only against the enemy but against the party itself. Helena cannot help him, for in our present condition, we dare not come close to tears; now her sweetness would surely drive us mad. It is not the example of hope that we need, but the compulsion to hope. This compulsion only Bain can exercise. Ellenbogen is inarticulate, Gamper has lost the respect of the organization, Dvorkin and Mexico, who, in spite of their shortcomings, were rising to a position of importance in the movement, have been expelled. This one is a coward, that one a fool; one lacks energy, another, conviction. And as for me, who am I to teach others when I stand so greatly in need of instruction myself? It is for Bain alone.

And who is Bain? But he springs to the task, raises both fists above his head and cries, "Comrades!" Again the audience is divided between the two of us: everyone else, his share, I alone, mine. They hang on his words; there is again the quick response to each gesture and inflection, his jokes (now desperate) bring on laughter, his exhortations, wild applause. It is a congregation in prayer, it is faith. But again, I cannot help seeing him coldly, from a distance, and, as I must believe, clearly. I would shut my eyes to the man I see strutting, even now, in self-importance; but I hear split infinitives, dangling participles, clichés, jokes in bad taste. A high voice, hoarse with recent exertion, rising to a scream again. I would be charitable, forgive the words for their substance; but I hear what I have heard a thousand times before. Why should the substance be dear to me now? And if now I must give assent, then it is the time and not the man who demands it. Still I would lend my good faith to his support; but he brings his pudgy fist down on the stand, and, not content with that, hammers with the other, on and on, a drum roll. His face turns red, the color of the orator's deepest sincerity, but still the pose persists, the strut of defiance, the false optimism, the mechanical argument. Now he is beating his chest, his voice is rising in pitch, spittle flies from his lips, he gnashes his teeth, writhes and kicks, and dashes about the stage, screaming. Is this, then, the man who shall fill us with hope?

His scream goes higher and higher. I am still detached, still cold to him. I am putting my will against his, testing my strength. But I am no longer unmoved; I can feel hatred rising within me, rising with my effort to deny him. Suddenly I feel that the end is come and that he is screaming with the last agony he shall endure on earth. Comrades, the end! . . .

The meeting is over, the applause has died down, the air, cleared a little. We walk down the stairs, our throats stinging with the smoke we have been breathing, with the effort we have put into the song at the close of the meeting. We walk down the street, tired; it is late. We drift apart, some going to a cafeteria, others, home; each his separate way. And each on his way buys the *Times*, which tells him what the news is. The news is very bad.

The news, comrades, is that there will come a time when the party shall be wiped out; it is close at hand, it is here. Though we go underground, they shall find us, though we dig in, they shall dig us out. Even we, whose truth is the only truth. There shall come a time when even our truth shall be no more, and with it, our hope. Not Bain shall save us, not all our sticking together. Nothing. Our solidarity shall not have been great enough.

But only now do I repudiate my hatred, give in to Bain. I no longer hear his screaming, no longer see his agony, its sincere pose. I feel only regret, deep regret, and that makes me give in the more. Our solidarity is not great enough. Again I should like to feel it strong about me, embracing us all with a love that is not in politics.

[1947]

THE FIREMAN, HIS STORY

1. Fire and Water

"Oh, the excitement of it!"

What excitement, when, where? People never stop to think.

You'd imagine they'd be able to come upon the truth by standing matters on end for a moment; you'd think they'd do it even in play, the way children do when for the first time they stick their heads down between their legs and discover the real sky. But no, they're all upright and straight line, and they're lucky if it leads them anywhere before infinity. And yet the first thing that comes to mind, at least where I'm concerned, is the rule of opposites. Mind you, I wouldn't rely on it, but it will do to make a point. Thus: firemen? We have more to do with water than with fire. An exciting life? God preserve the craving for excitement from the long watches in the fire house where we play checkers and cards, fondle and polish our equipment, and choke ourselves with reading adventure stories. And even if the watch between alarms be not an hour long, who can sit and wait for excitement; is it humanly possible?

Consider fire and water. Now, obviously, a man cannot have much to do with fire. There's no training in the element, nor are we baked like clay to endure it. But with water it's a different story. Hendricks, our chief, often orders us out into the yard and lets us have a good hosing. The water is turned on, at first gently, then gradually toward full force. We struggle against it, fighting our way up the stream to see how far we can go without being knocked over. And other exercises: we put our heads in a pail of water to see how long we can hold them there; go swimming on our days off (an exercise, because it's required); bathe not less than once a day (the same reason); and in summer are always running to the shower. The one Hendricks loves best is to make us jump fully dressed, in rubber coat, boots, and helmet, into a tank of water to see how quickly we can take off our clothes; and conversely, to have us jump naked into the tank but with full uniform done up in a parcel, to see how quickly we can get it on. When we have thus gone through water for him, we come out all crinkly and puffed, and you'd think we'd got a soaking to last us for good. But put a man once into a fire and he'll roast.

Call us mariners, we're marinated. If only it worked! Then flame were harmless to the touch, a gentle licking, no rougher than a cat's tongue. And what a delight to play with fire! Hold it in your hands, roll it into a ball and throw it at Klonsky, poor man, so poor a catcher that he's always left off our baseball team. Or arrange it as you would a bouquet with the bright tongues in the center and the blue and yellow branches at the side. Mold little animals of the stuff and give them a saucer of shavings to lap. But even a safety match is wild. Kelly can close his mouth on three lighted kitchen matches, and that's as far as any of us can go.

2. Victims of the Flood

It snowed heavily all last winter and right into spring, when it began to rain. In a week the valley was flooded and everything came apart, house from foundation, door from hinge, cork right out of the bottle. Whatever could float sailed away; what could not, sank. Gone was our lovely new truck with the golden gong; we took to boats to reach the victims of the flood. Up ladders, out hooks, and medicines and bandages; we saved lives left and right, and only two of our own company were drowned, Schneider and Kirkpatrick, peace to their bones. But there's a story within this story to relate, which has to do with our Tom who plays, in off hours, a fine bass fiddle.

Tom got out in one of the first boats and hadn't time to save his instrument. He saw it floating out of reach of the longest hook, the finger board with the carved head pointing up like the prow of a gondola. It went smack into a tree and was crushed. But Tom braved the loss. He was one of our greatest heroes, with next to the largest number of rescues to his credit. All day long we went at it like beavers, in and out of water, swinging our axes, clearing away debris, pulling in kitchen tables and dressers and armchairs, women and children, the quick and the dead, and administering artificial respiration, our work of love. And on into the night, by lantern. On higher ground, we set up, in McLaughlin's barn, an infirmary and soup kitchen, shelter for the homeless. Tom, about three in the morning, crept, dead tired, up into the loft of the barn, burrowed into the damp hay to make himself a place to sleep and was about to blow out his lantern when he saw an elderly woman lying just within arm's reach at his side. She was not asleep. She sat up, embarrassed, shook the seeds out of her gray hair, and smiled at Tom, a shy, grateful smile that showed some false teeth. Fireman Tom instantly felt a desire for this old woman with the false teeth. Tired as he was and old as she was, they dug deeper into the hay without a thought for the others who lay in the loft, asleep, or moaning over their injuries and losses. She was soft as a baby, says Tom. He had never had an old woman before, but now he likes nothing better.

3. The Inner Fireman

Water mocks us, but not as fire does. I refer to the fire in the fire house. The alarm comes to us by wire, ringing a bell on a chart above the chief's desk; the bell rouses us, the chart directs us. But

who, as they say, wakes the bugler? Tom was playing bass and the
boys were playing ball. Two men were playing checkers, a third,
solitaire. I was building a sailboat for my nephew. The chief was
at a meeting of the Board. The boys in the yard were within hearing of the bell and the boys in the house within sight of the chart.
By the time we smelled smoke the fire (in the cellar) was well
under way. Our first impulse was to run out the truck. This done,
we had to turn it about and get it back again. Shouts and running
and confusion, until someone had the lucky thought to pound on
the bell with a hammer. Its familiar noise put everything to rights.
Then we knew what to do and got it done. But the house was half
in ruin and our good name wholly so.

Well, there's a bad joke for you, the fire house burned down.
But whoever is on the bad end of a joke must regard it as a parable. So, is there instruction in this? Not something trivial, but
beyond the wisdom expressed in the saying, play with fire and
get burned? What a truth! A man could put his whole arm in it
and not even get blistered. Such fire burns with the very dullest
flame, it gives neither light nor heat; if anything, it casts a chill.
But what is the instruction of the white heat at the heart of the
flame, the pure-burning part that instantly consumes? If we could
take fire in hand, wouldn't this be the portion for us? As if there
were a human touch subtle enough! But we've never carried subtlety past a smile. There's a subtlety that destroys, more terrible
than all disaster. It is this wisdom that the fire knows, deep in its
inmost residence. Say a god or a devil stays there, to keep the
flame burning within the flame.

But who, knowing this—as what fireman does not—can
devote all his devotion to putting out fires? and who keep him
from setting a fire of his own?

We hope to obtain mastery of the element, pass through it
purified and without harm, either the harm that's done to us or
that we do ourselves. (The fire in the fire house began with some

oily rags and a carelessly thrown cigarette.) Well, despair, we're scorched for the effort. Some day the hope will be attained and then our despair—which is all we know now—will be known for a false alarm. But none the less true, for what else can there be but despair, so long as the hope still burns—and burns us?

4. Wisdom of the Dog

The rule of opposites leads to the obvious. We even have a spotted dog.

Clang, clang, clang! Out rushes the truck. The spotted dog, his name is Spot, barks and runs with us. But only for a block or so. Then he slyly returns to the house. He was to a few fires, early in life, and decided he had no business there; but his returning is also a judgment on our business. It's as if Spot were to say, "Aah, they won't catch it tonight. There'll be other fires—and who knows if they'll catch it then? Skepticism is the only wisdom." And who knows, perhaps it is?

5. Wisdom of the Child

But *clang, clang, clang!* goes the gong. Who can hear this and not believe? Who see and remain in doubt? Drawn grim are the men's faces as they cling to the sides of the rattling truck; one fastening a belt, the other a buckle, all come to grips with their despair. Let there be swift horses in heaven to catch a glory greater than this!

When I was a child, I ran, as did all my playmates, after the truck to the burning house, and never did I doubt the heroism of the men. Amen. Selah!

"Fireman, save my child!" The mother kneels before the fireman, wringing her hands before his stout boots. Such are the uses of melodrama to pervert the very truth. But to apply once more the simple principle, head over heels, of which I speak, should it not be said, "Child, save my fireman"?

God forgive us our undershirts, checkers, and adventure stories, burnt fingers and matches in the mouth. *Clang, clang, clang!* Here we go again to put the fire out—unseat the demon—and who knows?—perhaps occupy his throne!

[1948]

Three Parables and a Dissertation

1. A Horse

There was a soldier had a horse, a good black horse, whose legs were both dainty and strong, whose mane and tail were coarse as horsehair is, and yet glossy and silken, and whose eyes were at once animal and human. The soldier was not so remarkable, for he had less in him of the beast than the horse had of man; he was a kind but simple and ordinary fellow who could ride well enough but not so well as some can. The two of them were friends and confided in each other, though the horse hadn't the power of speech. The soldier talked and the horse listened and understood, which makes a conversation.

The two traveled through the country when there was no war, going from town to town, the soldier looking for work. In this way they met many people, all of whom admired the power and wisdom, the strength and daintiness of the horse. The soldier received many offers for his animal, some of them generous, but he would not think of parting with his friend; and the horse never had reason to feel uneasy. The soldier also met many women in the course of his travels. To some of them he made love.

In a certain part of the country, where they stayed for a while, the soldier met a girl who was pretty in an ambiguous way, so that he could not decide whether he wanted her. Sometimes he thought her lovely, sometimes, not at all; nor could he strike a mean and consider her, say, fair, for there is no single and clear impression to which the idea of a compromise can correspond. He met her many times during the day as he was riding down the road, and again in the evening, and every time he saw her he was puzzled what to do with her. The girl would always stop to pet the horse; but for the soldier she had only an ambiguous smile and an ambiguous greeting, which did not help at all.

The soldier, at a loss, confessed his troubles to the horse, and while he spoke he made up his mind; he decided she was not for him. So he said, "Why don't you take her? Her name is Zelda."

The soldier said this as a joke; for when one must dismiss the possibility of love, it is best to do so humorously. But the horse took his master seriously. It had never occurred to him that he could love a girl. But now that his master had spoken, why, it must be so. And at once the horse found himself in love with Zelda.

If he were free to love the girl, he must be free to see her. Therefore the horse left his master that night and went to call on the girl. He knocked with his hoof on the door of her house. The door was no sooner opened than it was slammed in his face. This the horse could not understand. If one is given freedom, how is it possible that the conditions of freedom should not come along with the gift? He remained for a long time in front of the house, thoughtfully pawing the ground. It is not possible, decided the horse, and he went round the back way and poked his head through Zelda's bedroom window. Zelda screamed. The horse ran away.

Thereafter he never knew a day of peace. He said to himself: "All my life I was admired as a horse; but now that I am in love, I am treated as a monster. Is there something monstrous in being in love? That cannot be. Then is there something monstrous in being a horse? Now that I am in love, it must be so. But how can I help being in love, since I am free to love? Is it my fault I am free? Am I to blame that I'm a horse? But how can I remain content with being a horse? Oh this burden, heavier than any I ever carried on my back!"

The horse thought of dashing himself off a cliff, but it was flat country. He refused to eat and went about in a weakened condition, barely able to drag his legs, and weeping all the time. The soldier did not understand; he thought age had prematurely overtaken the animal, and the horse, thinking that death would be welcome, did not correct his master. He bore him gently and slowly up and down the road in his weakness, though he now despised the soldier for his limited understanding. One day they met the girl on the road. The soldier, whose love for another woman was prospering, did not remember his joke about Zelda until she had passed by without greeting either horse or rider. "Well" said the soldier to his horse, "how did you make out?" The horse broke into a wild gallop, tripped over a root, and fell, breaking his leg. The master was not hurt. "Now," thought the horse, "he will shoot me, and it's just as well."

2. A Clerk

A certain government clerk, who held a minor post in the local branch of the local division of the general office, made an appointment, after much wheedling and intrigue, with another government clerk, who held a more important post in the same branch of the same division of the same office. The minor clerk was seeking to advance himself and was prepared to raise charges against a third clerk, who stood in his way. To make the best possible impression on his superior, he laid out his best suit, his Sunday shoes, and a white shirt which had been boiled and starched in the laundry. Before dressing, he shaved himself. He had had in mind going to the barber, but when he thought of the price of the shave, and of the tip, which in this case would have had to be a little more handsome than usual—barbers have a way of undermining the reputations of those who displease them—the clerk decided to shave himself. He lathered his face, stropped his razor, and set to work, first on one cheek, then on the other. He had cleared his face of stubble, suffering only a few scratches which didn't bleed much. The neck, the most difficult part of his beard to shave, he left for the last. He worked from the chin down, and was finally satisfied that he had shaved his neck well enough, when he noticed quite a number of long hairs growing up from his chest. There was certainly a line beyond which he need not have continued. But whether from carelessness or the habit of carefulness which he had acquired in his work, he went beyond this line, and having brought his razor deep into the thick, close hairs that grew on his chest, he thought he might as well shave all his chest. This he did, not without difficulty. When his chest was free of hair, he noticed that a thin strip of hair ran down the middle of his body, and he went on to shave this, too, as to stop now would have been to leave a gratuitous contrast between the clean and the overgrown parts. The clerk took off the rest of his clothes and began to shave his belly.

It occurred to him, however, that if he proceeded on the principle of shaving himself wherever hair grew, he would have a considerable job on his hands, as he was quite a hairy person; besides, his time was running short and he would have to hurry to keep the appointment. He therefore decided to draw an arbitrary line, beyond which he would not go. This he drew, as he thought proper, just at the groin. But when he came to the groin, he discovered that it was impossible to determine the exact location of the arbitrary line, for his pubic hair did not grow all at once, at one place, but spread over quite an area of vagueness. So he was obliged to shave his groin, which drained his nerve, for he feared giving himself an injury. In this manner, working his razor always faster and faster, he shaved his entire body, suffering more and more cuts as the edge grew dull. He shaved his thighs, calves, shins, ankles, and feet, then his arms and armpits, his forearms and his hands; and when this was done, he felt compelled to shave his eyebrows and the hair that grew on his head. Not until he was completely free of hair did he put away his razor, which was nicked and covered with blood. It was now too late to keep the appointment; and for that matter, until his cuts healed and enough hair grew back to allow him to look presentable, he would not even be able to go to his job, let alone advance himself. He would not even dare go out in the street. He saw that he would surely starve to death before his hair grew back. Therefore he took up the razor and used it, for the last time, to cut his throat.

3. A Cyclist in the Hills

Near the top of a steep hill, which was but one of the lower foothills to a range of mountains, there was a summer camp for poets, short-story writers, and novelists. One day a young man rode up the hill on a bicycle and stopped at the camp to rest. When asked what he did, he said he rode. Wrote what? asked the writers. No, not wrote, *rode*—his bicycle, replied the young man. Was that all he did? Yes, that was all. Then why had he come to the camp? asked all the assembled writers in their pride. He was merely resting there, and meant to go on shortly. Where? Why, on up the hill. How? On his bicycle, of course. What, on the bicycle! Surely he meant he would push it up? No, he meant to ride it. But up a hill! How is that possible? It is, said the young man. The writers were skeptical. They argued with the young man and with one another and concluded one of two things: either he was not telling the truth or, if he was, he was wasting his energy—the proper work for a young man was a work of the imagination.

"But this is the imagination!" exclaimed the cyclist, and he swung his arm about, pointing first down into the valley, then round to the hills, and then on up to the high mountains. And he leaped onto his bicycle and rode up the steep hill, and then up the next hill, pedaling effortlessly, until he was out of sight.

DISSERTATION

No parable without a moral. I would have set down a moral after each parable had I not, in each case, felt some uncertainty as to what the moral might be. The first parable, it struck me, was without moral. I saw it as a matter of deciding whether or not the horse was right; he had, as it were, drawn his own moral, and one might or might not agree with him. But this decision, I thought, involved many things besides morality, some of them even more important. Turning to the second parable, I felt it certainly must have a moral: a man does not simply shave all his hair and cut his throat without teaching us something. Moreover, one does not write of such a man without considering the rule under which his case falls. But it seemed to me that there were so many morals—practically every sentence made a point—that I could not decide which was the right one. As for the last parable, there I did see one moral and only one; but I was so sure of it that I feared I must be overlooking something, and so my certainty was but another form of doubt. Thus I am yet to say what the moral of each parable may be.

I am not a moralist by nature. I do not begin with morality and look for a tale to clothe it—this procedure seems unnatural to me; but I cannot call it the reverse of the natural one, for the other, of beginning with a tale and drawing the moral from it, seems just as unnatural to me. True morality, I should think, is so simple and obvious that even a child must be aware of it, yet it is at no point apparent; it does not obtrude here rather than there, for if the whole world be moral, there is no reason why one part of it should engage the attention instead of another. Fish swim in the water, but no one says, "Look, *that* fish is swimming in the water!"

Then the parables, one, two, and three, should be sufficient to themselves without a moral—which satisfies my own requirement. But what's left over, the problem, if you will—left over, because writing itself has nothing to do with problems—is still of interest to me. If embarrassment with morality be health, I should like to sound it; if it be paralysis of the faculty, then I must know how and why I am affected. I don't know where to begin, and I doubt my own capacity for system, but I shall put down *a, b, c,* and *d,* to spare others what I can of my own confusion.

a. The Horse

The horse has decided that life is not worth living in his condition. He has discovered a freedom greater than it is his nature to exercise; which is to say, greater than the freedom of instinct. This very discovery discloses to him that he is not free. Why, then, here's a moral: "One may have only the freedom of his own nature." But I should say just the opposite is true: for what is freedom if we do not, in winning it, discover both the limit of our own nature and what lies beyond it? We need only indulge ourselves to be free within our own limit—but that's no problem, no freedom, and no morality. The problem is rather, how shall we be free without self-indulgence? Then we must transcend our limit. But how shall we transcend it? for the limit is real. Here cuts the double edge of freedom with its terrible, excellent sharpness: one edge toward ourselves—how sharp the limit is!—and the other, more terrible, away from us—what a deep cut we have taken of the impossible! Sheathe either edge and you are defeated. Without the wound of the limit, you would cut without blood; it is idealism, in the disgraceful sense, to believe in a freedom without limit, it is unreality and cowardice. Sheathe the outer edge and you have a worse cowardice, called determinism, but actually, contentment with things as they are, smugness, the amoral convention. Sheathe both edges and you have dullness on your hands.

What shall our poor horse do? He has decided that life is not worth living if he cannot have the power that belongs to his freedom. This is his choice. Then is he right or wrong? I should say he was wrong. Freedom is a good in itself, even if it imposes on us a burden greater than we can bear. And life is a good in itself, it is always better to be than not to be, etc. But I might just as well say he was right, for to call life worthless in the name of freedom is the greatest dignity, as when a man says, I would rather be dead than a slave. Here we catch a whiff of the real moral atmosphere, having left the lowlands where choices are made by habit and instinct, and entered difficult country, watershed and mountain-top, where all direction is down; this is the very rare air of our freedom. Here no choices are possible, here morality begins. As if to say: "Life *or* death? At this point the two are one."

But isn't there something wrong here? Don't we say that animals have always the better part of love? Our poems admire their ease. Blake in the forest and Walt Whitman in the zoo: we celebrate always the animal part. Animals in their own nature are greater than we, in so far as we share that nature. They are fiercer, wiser, more cunning, more gracious, etc. But it is because he has shared our human nature that the horse is overwhelmed by the burden that he must carry. The worst one can say is that he's not a real animal. But he will do to stagger under the burden; for to bear it is more than any creature can do.

It is worth noting here that the horse sees no ambiguity. If he *can* love then he *must* love; if he *does* love then Zelda *must* be desirable (it never enters his head to think otherwise). Ambiguity is itself ambiguous: some it destroys, some it saves. The soldier, who dismisses it, is saved; the horse, who cannot even recognize it, is destroyed. And we put ambiguity to good use: to be in an unclear position is sometimes the greatest advantage a man can enjoy, as when we give him the benefit of the doubt. But with the animals' simpler nature, no such refinement is possible; their advantage is never in the potentiality, always in the act. Which is why animals are ideally suited to carry our burden in parables.

And which is all the more reason why we cannot dispute the moral that the horse has drawn from his own parable. Was he correct in his conclusion? An idle question, for how could he possibly have been wrong? If this be a moral world, then everything in it is a parable, and one need only know the subject to know the truth. Though our actions be wrong they are always exemplary, and the rule to which they belong is always right. Even if the moral cannot be stated, it is there. But isn't this the greatest burden of all?

b. The Clerk

Morality everywhere. Don't try to advance yourself at another's expense, or even at your own. Don't be meticulous. Never weigh things too fine. The clerk's reflection on the tip, that it would have had to be more handsome than ordinary, was fatal; for a gratuity is gracious or it undoes us. In shaving, as in other acts, let well enough alone, and if hairs remain, let them stand. Or one may say, when a thing has gone well beyond a natural line, there's no use drawing an arbitrary one. And so on and so forth, a moral in every word. This puts it all very explicitly, leaving so little implicit that morality becomes trivial. And in a moral world, where everything is a parable, it is often the case that morality is trivial; the only important moral is like the clerk's last use of the razor, the stroke of death.

But whose parable is this, is it mine? If so, how do I come to write of government clerks when I am not one myself? If not, why does this parable fascinate me and horrify me (and if it does so to others, why to them)? In either case, is the bureaucratic setting incidental or necessary (it seems to me it is necessary: some things simply cannot be imagined without bureaucratic correlatives); is the sexual analogy that one can so easily devise out of the same materials relevant or not? But is it at all important that I be able to answer these questions? Say that this parable is a construction out of known elements: can't it also be an outflowing of the unknown? Is the distinction of any consequence? or one may argue that a man without an unconscious mind—assuming that's possible—is in no way different from an ordinary man: Isn't there a point where our subtlety becomes too fine for itself, and what we write consciously, by calculation, becomes all the greater an unconscious act? I wrote this parable with its moral neither before me nor behind me; I wrote it understanding and not understanding what it means. And if I find it amusing (as, in spite of certain misgivings that I should write such things, I do) is it because I understand or do not understand what I've done?

So when the moral lies everywhere and the choice is impossible not because it is too fine (as in the first case), but too gross (as in this), it is our impulse to look beyond morality (if we can) and find some meaning greater than the one that concerns us. And greater precisely because it does not concern us. Thus, astronomers are the true moralists. But here in hand is still a human thing; the stars do not hang so close to home. What is the meaning beyond the moral? I see only that it is logical; the parable as a whole has reason in it. Not instinct, nor habit, but reason informs it. Draw whatever moral you may, or submit it instead to a psychoanalyst, there's still reason to contend with and shudder at. But what becomes of morality if we shudder at reason, for isn't the moral world pre-eminently a rational one?

c. The Cyclist

Here's a perfect trifle, the poorest of the lot; yet this is the one I understand and can tell you the most about. It is a parable of the imagination, and the moral—the young man is right—is that the world of the imagination is an outer world, as much a real and accomplished one as the world of valleys, hills, and mountains. We travel in it as high as we can, and there are vehicles, whatever our art, that take us there. The genius is he who travels effortlessly so long as he remains in sight; what happens thereafter, no one knows. (Ease and the capacity for taking infinite pains are one and the same thing: of course it is painful to ride uphill—yet look how he goes!) And so on and so forth . . .

But I am so sure of all this, that I fear I must be overlooking something. Can the writers, say, be right after all? That the young man is not telling the truth, or foolishly wasting himself; that a work of the imagination is not an already created thing, but the very contrary of landscape? And then, "Mind has mountains . . ." etc.—it's no such easy ride (even as defined).

And yet it must be so! As if to say, hell with the moral, here's one of our own. My moral is: the world of the imagination is a created, objective world. Having said which, I no longer care if it be right or wrong. (Yet, as I here stand at the threshold of *my own* parable, how can I possibly be wrong?) There is our animal nature, not yet created, in which freedom is the death of us; there is our human nature, in process of creation, where reason, our special part, can be the death of us; and there is the imagination, created, whose reasons and meanings are greater than all the others precisely because they do not concern us. Here, then, is life and—though the word does not even appear—freedom.

But this is so much moralizing—already the word has a contemptible ring! Let me say, once we enter our own parable, and our own life is perforce exemplary, we cease to take instruction from it, and the moral is not the important thing. Then it's as Pascal said, *"True morality makes light of morality. . . . To make light of philosophy is to be a true philosopher."*

d. Summary and Conclusion
This dissertation is my own parable.

[1948]

PART III

Alpha and Omega

An Experiment with Tropical Fish

George

Coney Island Revisited

Wolfie

King Solomon

Alpha and Omega

If my virtue be a dancer's virtue ... verily, that is my Alpha and Omega.

—NIETZSCHE

1. Introduction. The Postman, His Story

They call me Little Giant. In the morning, when my work begins, the bag is heavy. I pull it onto my shoulder with a groan. All day it grows lighter and lighter; my head rises of its own accord, I take longer, quicker steps, my strength, courage, and good humor return to me. Late in the afternoon, when the burden is gone, I am a new man. But it is late in the afternoon, the day's work is done, and tomorrow begins a new day.

This has been going on for years. Mind you, I do not complain. I am glad to hold my position in the service, the more so as I am now an old man and can soon expect a pension. There was a time, not so long ago, when many envied me. Those were the days when nearly everyone on my route was starving; the days when, in addition to letters, I used to load my bag with scraps of bread, meat, cheese, lettuce, the head of a chicken or a fish, lumps of sugar or candy, anything cheap and edible, and not always fresh, that I could lay my hands upon. I distributed food with the mail—first, out of pity, and then out of self-regard, by way of gaining the good will of the people, for the letters I brought them were, more often than not, notices of dispossession and eviction and suspension of relief, news of the death of a relative, nearby or in a distant city. I will not soon forget those days.

But now only one thing concerns me: what effect has this work had on my character? Is it only because of my short stature and broad shoulders, my baggy pants and the rather, on the whole, apelike swing of my arms and stoop of my body that I am called Little Giant? The men in the post office have an instinct for choosing names: they appear to go only by externals, but in reality they work much deeper. Thus, lanky Garrity, our thin man, is called not, as you might expect, Slim, Beanpole, Reach, or Noodle, but Cough Drop, and strangely enough, he really is very much like a cough drop. There must have been something of the same order that made them call me as they do. At least, I like to think so.

My work is somehow similar to that of both angels and hangmen. These creatures, blessed or damned, have surrendered their wills—they are in *service*. But why, since neither has a will of his own, should an angel be held blessed and a hangman damned? So with myself. What am I then, I who do not even read the letters I deliver? True, I know, in a manner of speaking, what they contain. I have developed a sense of content, I can judge by the size, shape, weight, color, and feel of the envelope. But this merely reminds me that I am an outsider in the very thing I am most concerned with. For a time I considered steaming open the letters; I could have arranged to do it without danger of being found out. But I decided against it—rather, I resigned myself not to do so. After all, I am in service, too.

Then how shall I ever know the truth about myself? If there were a mystic society of postmen, such as, granted the proper conditions, might have existed in Roman days, we would have taken the matter up and evolved a rite for ourselves. The mystery would have its initiates. But now the mystery, poor thing, exists by itself and no one is instructed in it.

Concretely, this is how it goes:

One of my houses is a four-story tenement. On the first floor lives a large family. I cannot say how many children—it seems to me that each day I see new faces. The children, ragged and dirty—dressed in burlap and flour sacks, old tennis shoes, galoshes, and so dirty they might just have been plucked out of the ground—rush out to greet me, gather about, cling to my arms and legs, climb onto my back and cry, "Mail, mail, mail, the mailman's here!" There is never any mail for them, and there hasn't been any for years—not since I brought the family its last relief check. Times have changed and things are looking up.

On the floor above lives the prostitute. There is never any mail for her either. Once there was a court order for eviction, but somehow she got around it. She comes to the window and looks out, sees the children swarming at my feet. Occasionally she clears her throat and spits; the gob of spit spatters on the sidewalk. More often, she gives me a forlorn look. I have no comment to make, neither of judgment nor condemnation, and with the direct, unblinking glance that I give her in return, I try to tell her so.

There are two other tenants. A dancer on the third floor, and on the fourth floor, a man with watery eyes who, from the way he drags himself to the window, appears to be a paralytic. There is always mail for the dancer—spicy, fragrant envelopes in many colors, addressed in backhanded, quaint, irregular, square, delicate, or spidery script. Letters often from foreign countries, from France and Italy, Finland, Canada, and Spain, and from remote corners of our own country such as Curtain Falls, Onion Terrace, and Mahogany Creek. Fluffy letters written on tissue, bulky letters, clippings—all of them, I am sure, in praise of the dancer.

The man on the fourth floor also gets mail. Large envelopes, magazines, pamphlets, books, all very scholarly and serious, to be sure, but never a personal letter. It is strange that the people to whom I bring the most mail are the ones I know least. The large family of children and the prostitute I see every day, and though it is always the same, yet something new always passes between us. The dancer I also see daily—sometimes, barefooted and wearing her thin dancing costume, she takes the mail directly from my hand—but she is always preoccupied and remote and never looks at me, so that I do not really know her at all. I very rarely see the paralytic. He must have a hard time dragging himself up and down the stairs.

Such equations, I have noticed, are by no means uncommon: large families—no mail; steady customers (so to speak)—unknown to the postman; occasional customers—his best friends. The supreme touch, I should add, is that I myself seldom get mail. Precisely what this means I have not been able to find out. But I imagine it has some meaning, and is of interest, not only to postmen, but to the world at large.

2. The Pleasures of Family Life. Antontonio Jeveves

Martafolia hung the last stocking on the line. "Zing-zing! Ding-a-ling! Chuka-chuka-chuka-chuka!" Lugubugu came tearing round the bend, steam up, throttle open, and collided with the post. The line snapped. All the freshly washed clothes fell to the ground.

"You watch where you go," said Martafolia, mother of how many? and picked up the clothes and carried them into the house to do her washing all over again.

The child screamed several hours. There was a lump as hard as a stone on his forehead. He kicked out his legs, stiffened, collapsed, lay like a dead chicken on the ground, groaned and contorted himself and struck one pose after another, screaming. His brothers and sisters did not know what to do with him to make him keep still. They carried him down into the basement and laid him on the carpenter's bench, his head on the grindstone.

"I know what. Let's play hospital. Lugubugu must be sick. You must be the nurse. You must be sick too. Lie down in the washtub. You must be another nurse. I must be the doctor."

"What can I be?"

"You two must take turns being dead and being the undertaker."

Lugubugu screams, and Ellabella, the eldest, never at a loss, builds a play about his screaming. Stuck away in her pocket book is a packet of picture cards—movie actors and actresses with their favorite smiles: Lola Cowley, Mark Thorp, Bucky Anderson, Charmaine Charmante. These must wait for another occasion to call them forth, when the child's desire distributes its other roles: I must be beautiful (Who do I look like?), brave (Stand back! Stickemup!), tender (I know, yes, I know, darling, but we still have each other), wanton (I'd let you kiss me good night, but I'm wearing pants). And the accessories of desire lie in a heap in the treasure chest, a cheese box, behind a loose plank in the wall: a used-up lipstick, discarded high-heel shoes, cap pistols, a doll's head, severed from the trunk.

Lugubugu falls asleep and they perform an operation on him with a rusty shears, snipping the air at his throat, the fuzz of his ears, and, very delicately, his eyelashes.

Antontonio Jeveves is a janitor with many houses to take care of and a family of his own in each. He has, all in all, in one place or another, some sixty children, not counting dead or jailed. He has three wives, two of them legal: Martafolia (see above) and La Paloma Pigeon; his common-law wife is Clarissa Melissa, now big with child, who still has hopes of marrying him. His other women are Stella, who lives on Orchard Place in Cleveland, Sarah, who lives in Boston, street address unknown, Mary, Helen, Jewel, Rachel, Pearl, Gertrude, Pima, Pia, Ria, Mia, Nina, Parthenia, Virginia, Becky, Bessie, Anna, Suzy, Aida, Paula, Polly, Cookie, and Gertrude (known as "the other Gertrude"), most of whom give their names as Smith. Antontonio Jeveves has had children by nearly all of them.

Social workers, who have at one time or another been on his trail and have learned a little about him (though not, for instance, that he has more than one wife), have invariably given him up as an incorrigible idiot and stricken his name off their lists. Antontonio holds them in contempt. He made advances to one of them, a fairly young and, in a bloodless way, pretty woman, and nearly had himself turned in to the police. He attributed his failure, the first in many years, to the fact that he had been neglecting his nails, and for several days, waiting for the social worker to return, he kept after his nails, digging the dirt out with the blade of a screwdriver. He would very much like to meet this woman again.

Antontonio knows that there are all kinds of women in this world (what doesn't he know?), and that some of them might, conceivably, have some reason to refuse him. But to tell the truth, he is eager to encounter one of these women, and for many years has been in search of her. (The social worker does not count, because, thinks Antontonio, he met her only in her professional capacity, and besides, she was not his type, her hips were too narrow. Here he performs a little trick, for whenever he does meet a woman who refuses him, he immediately concludes that she was not his type and therefore doesn't count; just as another man, whose concern, the very opposite, is to find a woman who will love him, will also say that his failures do not count. But in spite of his little tricks, Antontonio's reckoning is substantially accurate in these matters.) He curses the luck which keeps him a poor man and cuts him off from access to the upper classes where, he feels sure, he would have no difficulty in finding a woman to refuse him. But on the other hand, he reasons, if he had money and could open doors that are now closed to him, he would again meet his old failure-in-the-form-of-success, and there he would be, right back at his starting point. Even so, poor as he is, and dirty, ugly (except for his beautiful, long, straight nose with the delicate nostrils), scarred, and tattered—even so, he has met and enjoyed more than what one would grant him as his natural share of these women. There is no accounting for the upper classes, thinks Antontonio. What do they see in him? It all comes from being a janitor, from having worked round their homes. "Oh please sir, won't you please fix my faucet?" And Antontonio, a complaisant man, fixes her faucet and her daughter's, too. But what's the use of kidding yourself? Antontonio knows all about such romances, and he resents being included in the same category of afternoon- or odd-moment lover with the milkman, the iceman, the vacuum cleaner- and brush-salesman. He feels that if he had a somewhat wider space for his explorations, if he could only move about a bit more freely in these circles, he would soon find what he is looking for.

Well, true now, there have been women who've said no. But Antontonio knows these nos, and is thoroughly weary of them. In each there is a sprout of possibility, just under the surface, thrusting its way up into the light. It is not a no, dead at the roots, an outright, absolute blank of a no, the no of a stone, past, present and future the same. It is the no of an onion (Antontonio eats onions raw); peel off the outer layers of negation, the middle layers of possibility and probability, and you come to the green core of willingness. Enough of such nos. Antontonio wants the absolute thing.

Why does he want it? He is as eager for it as another man would be for the very opposite, for yes—and for the same reason. He wants the truth. He feels that if he could find a woman who was thoroughly dead to him, then perhaps he would begin to understand. He would study her as he studies a bit of machinery that needs fixing, examine the matter from all sides, probe into it, this way and that, and cast as much light as he could on the subject. He would study such a woman until he found, so to speak, the part that was missing; he would know in what respect she differs from the other women, and then, precisely because he knew why she does not want him, he would know why the others do. Then perhaps he would learn why he runs to them, adding woman to woman and piling up heaps of children, each with a straight, long nose like his own. Is it because he wants them or they want him? Or neither; or both? If both, in what proportion, and if neither, what then? He would very much like to be able to answer these questions. Now, while his sixty-first child (so far as he knows) is waiting to be born. He feels it is time.

One night he hit the pregnant Clarissa Melissa over the head with a beer bottle. (He was feeling rather depressed at the time, and some half dozen or so of his children were crying in concert. Antontonio thought it was because they were hungry, and Clarissa, because they were wet. In either case, they had neither food nor clean diapers to give them, so let them cry.) He hit her, but not hard enough to break the bottle (on the return of which a five-cent deposit could be collected) or to break Clarissa's head. She did not fall unconscious, so, to occupy his time, he felt he should hold a conversation with her. He asked her immediately, without beating about the bush—such directness is one of Antontonio's greatest charms—he asked her why. Why did she think he came to her in the first place, why did they go about it the way they did, and why did they have so many children? Clarissa Melissa thought it was because they were poor. That, thought Antontonio, was a good answer, and it increased his respect for the intelligence of his common-law wife. But on second thought he saw that it was no answer at all. For if he was what he was because he was poor, what good did it do him to be told that he was poor? If he had money, he would no doubt have been able to answer many questions—but then what need would there be to ask any?

Likewise, now, as a poor man, he asked many questions—but how can a poor man answer them? Clarissa Melissa hadn't much use for such subtleties and told him so, adding that in her opinion it was high time they were married. Antontonio hit her over the head again, not very hard—he was sensible of her condition—and taking the bottle with him to collect the deposit, he went off to see another of his women.

Unlike other men, he takes greatest pleasure in his children not when he comes home to them, but when he leaves. No sight is as rewarding to him as the sight of his many children, playing in the alley or the yard—at a distance of a block or more, when the dreadful noise they make grows dim and pleasant to the ear. He walks away with his head turned back and his heart filling with love. Just before turning the corner, he takes a last look, and there they are, blocks away in the empty lot, the whole family of them rolled together into one mass, impossible to tell one from the other. He blows them a kiss and goes proudly on his way.

Perhaps he does it all for the sake of the children. He loves children, of course—and who knows, maybe even more than other men do? Ever so much more, to such an extent that it is something morbid? He can't be sure, for he has so many children, that even his thick emotions must be spread thin to cover them all. If he had only one child, or two at the most, then he would know for sure. But then, again, the question wouldn't even come up. There was a time, after all, when he was a father of only one by his own first, proper, legal wife, Martafolia, and then he never even thought to ask.

But perhaps that's it, who knows? Perhaps it is all for the sake of filling the world with his stock, neighborhood after neighborhood and city after city, and he still a comparatively young man with, God willing, many long fertile years before him. Who knows? Meanwhile, he goes about his work, a regular and decent man with no bad habits—rises early, starts the fire, carries out the ashes, carries down the garbage, leaves some food outside the door of the man on the fourth floor, mops the hall and the stairs and goes on to the next house and the next house, pausing, mid-day, for beer and a sandwich if he has money, and scratching his head and his neck if he has not. And when evening comes, depending on where he is, he goes in to one of his women, and if there happens to be supper, has a bite to eat with her; then takes her to bed and snorts like a bull and a little while later snores like a saw-mill. And while he sleeps—who can tell?—perhaps a seed has begun to sprout into a child with a long, straight, delicate nose.

3. The Prostitute, Her Story

Allow me my dignity. When I was a child, my mother, also a whore, said to me, "Never listen to what others say." I have followed her advice.

Most things bore me. I no longer derive pleasure from the so-called pleasant things of life. My plum must be all lined and wrinkled like a miser's purse, though—if I may be cute for a moment—I have never been miserly with it.

A word on language. By "plum" I mean vulva. Early in life I formed a strong dislike for the terms of my trade: *sexual intercourse, penis, vagina, prostitution,* the various diseases, etc., etc. There is something terribly vulgar, pedantic, self-conscious, and condescending in these words, and I stammer and feel I am going to blush when I use them, as from time to time, say in conversation with a doctor, I find it necessary to do. The synonyms, which are called four-letter words, though many of the most essential contain five letters—and I can think of one of eleven—the synonyms would serve the purpose very well, but their use by a person of sensibility is full of danger. Above all one must be natural—especially in performing what self-conscious or inhibited folk call the natural functions. The difficulty in the thing is reflected in the word. A brutish person, a simpleton, or a foreigner who is just learning the language can use "dirty words" (as they are called) with a clear conscience. But the rest of mankind is compromised. And who is not compromised? How well I could explode the myth of "the healthy truck driver!" But some other time.

To avoid compromising myself (and as it is, I sometimes think I am the most compromised of all) I have coined my own language. Plum is vulva or vagina (also flap and gobbet); penis is whacker, thrucker, dishik, or McCarthy; sexual intercourse I call jim-jam, etc. I do not object to being called a whore (especially with the Middlewestern pronunciation, *hoor*), but "prootitute" I dislike and prefer badger. As for the word "prostitution," which I abhor, or the trade itself (as my mother used to say, "*das Geschäft selbst*"), I say woodpile.

I've been on the woodpile all my life, ever since I began to assist my mother. (Her gentlemen called me "Mother's little helper." Thus it was that I came to regard my work as a kind of help, given in free will to mankind. It was also from this innocent phrase that I learned to appreciate the beauty of *double entendre*, and not only double, but threefold, fourfold, and so on, until the whole world blossoms into a garden of hidden meanings.) I regret nothing. I've certainly had my time, and what with one thing or another, fizz, flapdoodle, stug, and caracoca from here to Borneo and back, I can truly call myself a woman who left no lesson of life unlearned. God bless it, even now, an old woman in a creaky bed, bitten by bugs, I can feel it descend on me with a bang and a wallop, the life I've led! What a clear, clean conscience—and what I value most, a sense of peace.

Soak me in salt water and you won't purify me. Preach at me, pray, rave, threaten me, pour lye on my flesh—but me you cannot touch, nor can you undo one single thing that I have done. My life that has put me within reach of all, has also placed me out of reach, out of reach of the hatred which burns in the gut of the whole envious pack of you that would raise me from my fallen estate, as you call it. It gives you no rest; but me it gives great rest and a deep sleep—it is a pillow under my back. I have plucked many a soft feather, my hearties, to comfort my deserving backside. What wouldn't you give for one of my secrets? But the truth is, I have no secrets. I have had nothing that I have not shared. Ponder that.

All the same, it is wise to have the good will of the public. So my mother taught me, and so I have learned from my own experience. There was my colleague Rosalie, who was stoned, just as it happened in the Bible. But one moment, please. My impressions and memories rush at me, and I am entangled in them, but they shall have to wait. Why do I call Rosalie *colleague?* Am I being cute again? The worst thing about whores is their cuteness. The hats some of us wear, the cunning little smiles and dresses, the little-girlishness! The angel of death in a bridal gown—we are incurable romantics. One hag I know, a real bag of a badger, went to the trouble of painting on her nose lifelike and life-size— freckles! Would you believe it? Another wore a braided pigtail with a ribbon in it all her life. And when her hair fell out as the result of one of the many occupational hazards and diseases to which we are subject (see, more of my cuteness), she got herself a wig which also had a braided pigtail. Pouts, sniffles, giggles, even pimples—the little girl pursues us. We think to regain what we have lost. . . . Thank God, I've had none of that nonsense. But my own affliction, perhaps even worse, is the cuteness of acuteness—my abnormal sensitivity to words. I've just said that I have a clear conscience, which is true. I don't consider myself a sinner— but I have all the symptoms of one, chief of which, in my own case, is a troubled speech.

But the public, its good will . . . Rosalie was stoned one morning on the way home from the grocery. One stone bruised her ankle, another cut her cheek, a third hit the bottle of milk she was carrying and her coat and dress and shoes and stockings were drenched in milk. She was also cut up by the broken glass, but she didn't mind that half so much as the shame of having to walk down the street in broad daylight, all covered with milk. Everyone who met her on the way laughed out loud—and even perfect strangers who couldn't have known who she was, it seemed to her that they, too, knew and were laughing. It was the grocer's son who did it, a lad of seventeen named Timmie, may the crut give him no rest. Several days before, he had accused Rosalie, falsely, to his mother, of having offered to cancel her debt at the store in trade. Because of this accusation, the grocer's wife drove the weeping Rosalie out of the store with a broom. But the grocer, a wise father who knew his own son, saw no reason to believe the charge without also believing the kid had accepted the generous offer. And so he beat him with the same broom—in the course of which beating, the son confessed his lie, and Rosalie's custom, but not her good name, was restored. . . . I can't help remarking on the utter ignorance of our psychology that this episode reveals. The grocer's brat, having no experience of the world, was in a perfect position to indicate the depths of the misunderstanding that so-called good and industrious folk have of us. It is never a whore's malice, her venom, contempt, or desire to degrade her alleged betters that would lead her to make such an offer. The offer itself is rare—and if it is made at all, it is a sign of the whore's own degradation, the misery and poverty and last extreme to which she has come. But these good people imagine that we have nothing more to do than go about plotting and planning to ensnare them—sure, run up a debt and then wipe it out with one job, an easy life. As if they would ever extend us credit beyond thirty cents—and when they do it's a sure sign that they want to ensnare *us*. Which, in fact, this whole incident proves. They think they have it coming to them, they want it, the stinking hypocrites, they want it their own way, which is a whoredom dirtier than our own, and whose false motive is the cause of the

bad name we must bear. We bear it for the sake of their unclean-
ness. May the crab sadden their days and nights.

Another unpleasant run-in with the people—this time, my
friend Phyllis taking the rap. She was living decently and quietly
in a semiretired way in a good neighborhood and paying an
exorbitant rent for her flat. (Landlords, like bugs, can smell your
blood.) One morning she awoke to find her door decorated with
two huge symbols, male and female, joined—a competent drawing of considerable detail, in red paint. The poor girl worked at it
desperately, for the house was up, but it would not wash away. By
the time she had run to the hardware store and come back with
turpentine, the landlord and the neighbors had gathered at her
door. The ladies, who had been enjoying themselves tremendously,
retreated when Phyllis appeared, slamming their doors in her face;
then opened them a crack and looked on. The men giggled and
passed obscene remarks. The landlord made her scrub off the
offensive drawing with the whole house looking on, then kicked
her down the stairs and would not let her come back for her
belongings. No one said a word in her behalf.

What redress do these poor girls have? None whatsoever.

Some of the girls say, jim-jam the public! This is not my attitude. Ours is a public calling, and it is useless to pretend that we
can go our own way, taking no heed of the world. True, the pro-
fession amounts to a guild, of sorts, but it does not protect us or
represent us in any way. I know, in some countries they register us
and inspect us like so many cattle, and a certain percentage of our
earnings goes to the state. I don't see much hope in that. Even if
you were to put us on civil service with competitive examinations,
sick-leave, paid vacations, and old age retirement funds—so long
as the lie remained that we are outcastes, occupying a special,
degraded position, it would not help one bit. The falsehood would
remain, the people would suffer from it, and we would suffer in
turn. It is our lot to suffer from the evil in others' hearts.

What falseness and evil I have seen! It is evident in men from the very first moment of their approach. The way they look at you or talk to you—the way even that some avoid talking to you, keeping their mouths shut and pointing or grunting to make themselves understood—but expecting you, of course, to sing them hymns! There are some, however, whose silence is a blessing. They say nothing because they feel, as I do, that words are unclean—but in their actions, in their look, in the touch of their hands and in their very bones there is a sweetness and a purity. It is these rare men who are our only hope, and the hope of the world. But the rest! I've seen strong and weak, crippled and sound, the long and the short, the black, the white, and the in-between and in all of them a fury, a possession as by devils, of hatred, lust, uncharity, niggardliness, arrogance, stupidity, false pride, and lies, lies, lies. A man's whole nature is expressed in the simplest act. There is a way of unbuttoning a button which is like cutting off a head. And to lie down in bed is to leave yourself open, wide open to judgment. It's a wonder how little they realize that we know them and can see deep into them, clear to the back. And not only we, but the whole sex, because a man lays himself bare in such an obvious, clumsy way, poor thing, and doesn't even know that he is known. But we especially have a power over them that is absolutely implacable. Perhaps that is why they hate us, or pretend, or feel that they have to hate us. It is only a strong man who has nothing to fear that can grant us, with his blessing, our right to live.

I am reminded of money. Make no mistake, I love money. Gelt, mazuma, mahoola, kale—I can't get enough of the stuff. The things I have done for mere money I would have done for nothing else in the world—not for long life, good health, good looks. If the choice had ever been put to me: either do this, or remain as ill-favored as you are, I would certainly have refused. But the trouble is that such choices are never put to us, which is another reason the world misunderstands us. The choice always is: either do this, or you will not have this money. I for one always jumped at the money, promptly went down on my hands and knees, my knees and elbows, or stood on my head to get it. When it comes to money, there just is no choice.

And yet, believe me, though I say I love money, I also hate it, I really do, with all my heart. It embarrasses me, it disgusts me, it reminds me of the world's disesteem. But more important than that, it reminds me of the disesteem in which I hold myself. Money brings out the real whore in me. I am self-conscious in speech and obsessed with the avoidance of certain words; and uneasy before money. Quarters, pennies, dimes, dollars—they burn a hole in my hand. Words and money, money and words—you will find them at the bottom of the woodpile, in all its secret, dismal places. But all the same, when it comes to money I will instantly overcome my fastidiousness (and later hate myself for it) and there isn't a thing I still wouldn't gladly do for money, though the strength that some of these things require is now no longer mine.

Mr. Hubert Jackson is the ugliest man I know. He has been coming to me for years, and from the very first I wished I could drive him away. But he has the pertinacity of an old client and, apparently, a satisfied one. Hub follows me from place to place whenever I move or am forced to move; he has his distinct step on the stairs, his knock on the door, which I wouldn't mistake in a thousand. I hear it and immediately, as one would respond to a lover, something inside me says: It's he! My heart goes faster, though my hands turn cold and I shrink away in disgust.

Now, praise the Lord, he is too old for the woodpile. But this is not an unmixed blessing, and grateful though I am for it, I must say that it makes matters worse. For one, it prolongs his visits—and sometimes, when the caprice seizes him, I am at my wits' end to chase him away. Then, when he sees me squirming in his presence, he loves to sit down and talk. "You know, we've both grown old together," he says, more often than not blowing his nose with a dirty handkerchief, as if to strike the note of confidence, or, without so much as a by-your-leave, taking a hairpin from my dresser and digging the wax out of his ear. He looks into his handkerchief after he has blown his nose, or if it's wax he's been after, he holds it up to the light on the hook of the pin and studies the quarry for a while. He knows how much these things disgust me. And then, because he knows how much I hate to recall his share of the past, he repeats, several times, "Grown old together . . . old together." There is engendered that false and clammy old-couple sentimentality which I would dislike with any man, and find absolutely intolerable with him.

But he does not keep on very long at this level. Before long he has switched onto a more familiar, and what is for me a more disgusting, plane, and he piles on the intimacy, as thick as slush. He begins by kidding me. Perhaps the religious pictures that I have hanging on the walls will catch his eye—say the picture of Him, enlarged, with the open streaming eyes, like a close-up in the movies, which hangs over the head of my bed. Hubert Jackson stops at nothing.

"What's He doing here?" asks Jackson. And when I don't answer him, he goes on, "Oh yes, I forgot, you told me. He dropped in one night and just stayed on." Or else he will say, "Very nice and cozy up here, just the two of you. But tell me, sometimes you must look at each other. Who blushes more, you or Him?"

I have stopped saying, aghast, "Hubert Jackson, don't you fear God?" It only encouraged his blasphemy. Now I keep still and hope he'll soon play himself out. But he goes on in this manner, offensive to man and God. Is there no way of getting rid of such a man?

I tell him he must leave—I am expecting someone. He offers to stay on—perhaps he can be of some assistance to me—I am, after all, not as limber as I used to be. Or I tell him I am unwell, will he please go. He smiles very knowingly, congratulating me on my prolonged youth. The vileness! What does he want with me?

A rhetorical question. I know perfectly well what he wants. He wants to make me play the whore for him, although he is too decrepit to do it in the regular and proper way. The last time he tried it proper, it was such a hideous scene that even Jackson has not had the courage to try it again. Although he has an abominable pride before God, like all such people, he hasn't even a spark of dignity in himself—but the scene I am alluding to was too ugly even for him to bear. He knows, however, that I have too much decency to remind him of it, which is why he has the courage to face me. Now he is casting about for an opening, some new trick to catch me on. I know what is coming and shrink back. Jackson knows me too well.

He begins to speak in the vulgar language that he knows I detest. The words the old lecher uses! I clap my hands over my ears, but he goes on. I can see the movements of his lips, forming the obscene words. I shut my eyes, but I know Jackson is still at it, confident that sooner or later I will look at him again. I do what he expects me to do, look at him, take away my hands and ask, "What do you want?"

"I want you to say '——.'"

"I won't!"

He takes out his wallet and places it on the table. "C'mon, girlie, say '——.'"

"I absolutely refuse!"

He takes out a dollar bill and lays it before me. "Say '——.'"

"No!"

'——.'

"No!"

"——. Come on, little girlie, say '——'!"

At last I give in. "——. Now get out of here!"

"Not so fast." He places his hand over the dollar bill. "Say it again. And say '——' and '——.'"

"——. ——."

"Again! . . . faster . . . say it again! Say it, girlie. Roll it on your tongue!"

He excites himself inordinately. I'm afraid that one day he'll pass out on me, die of a stroke. His face grows red, his hands tremble, his eyes pop out of his head. When he finally leaves, I feel dragged and spent and put to shame. My only defense is to take the money, when he has at last had his fill of dirty words, and to take it with as great a contempt as I can call forth in myself, exerting every ounce of the whore in me. I make him feel my disgust, I make him see what he's like, how dirty, mean, and vile, and give him a shot of my insight that penetrates his shriveled old-man's loins and sticks like a barb in his spine. I don't even hide my self-disgust, the better to spew it out in his face. But he stares back at me in the same contempt, grinning in malice and triumph, feeling he has won his object, and we stare at each other in silence and hatred for several minutes before he leaves.

And he's right, too, the wretch! When he leaves, I feel so humiliated that I can think of only One to turn to. But I am too unclean, and I blush at the thought of His seeing me. I lie face down on the bed, not looking up, but it seems to me that He is looking down, and He, too, is blushing. . . .

*   *   *

So it goes, from one thing to another. Words, money, the public— all these simple things become complicated and unendurably ugly. Are they ugly in themselves or do I make them so? I began by suspecting the things, but now I suspect myself. Where does my clear conscience come in, the fact that I regret nothing, am glad of it all? But what shall I pin it to? I am reminded of the game children play and which we played at my birthday party when I was seven years old—and what trouble my dear mother went to, to get children to come to the party! Pin the tail to the donkey, it is called. There is the donkey on the wall, and here I stand, blindfolded, tail and pin in hand, dizzy, having been spun round and round. Go, grope, look for it, and see, while everyone laughs, how far you can come from the mark. Fantastic mistakes: the sofa, the clock, the umbrella stand. But now I know what the trick is. It is to pin the tail to yourself. One sharp jab and it's over—you're fixed up for life.

Hubert Jackson makes fun of me for keeping all these religious pictures. He thinks, Ah, so this is where you've stuck your tail! In a way, I don't blame him for laughing. It's so old hat among us to turn to religion in later life. It's just another one of the many clichés that rob our life of its freshness. The whore with a heart of gold, the whore with a daughter in a convent, with a sick mother, a mad father, a starving brother who is studying law, an ailing uncle, discharged from the police force on account of bursitis. The whore who goes to church ten times a day, and, in a single hour, crosses herself enough times to weave a rug. That's all stupid and trite, and so is the reformed whore, grown fat and rich, who supports all the local charities, is a pillar of the parent-teachers' association, keeps a clean house, and is a mother to her girls. The poor things lack sophistication; they hang the tail in the most obvious place and go away feeling proud and justified, because they think they've hit the mark. Not one such whore has ever doubted that she'll go to heaven—and, I suppose, rightfully so. We all have, you see, a clear conscience—we just don't know what to do with it.

In my own case—well, I could just as easily have made the same mistakes, and at one time I did: the Last Supper, the Agony in the Garden, the Stations of the Cross, Christ Crucified among Robbers, and the Descent from the Cross, all of which scenes hang from thumbtacks on my walls, are a testimonial to my errors, as are also the pictures of Mary and Joseph in Egypt, Pontius Pilate Washing His Hands (this over the sink; I said to myself when I hung it there, "Think well what you wash your hands of"), and Lazarus Raised from the Dead. I have always had a religious streak a mile and a half wide, and lately you can tap gallons of tears from me just by saying the word "suffer." Of course, I control myself, I try to remember the difference between what's true and what's exaggerated. But after all, can you blame me, or any of us, if we take to it as ducks to the duck pond on a rainy day?

After all, think, it is natural for us. There's Mary Magdalen, and the woman who was taken in adultery, and Christ said, "He that is without sin among you, let him first cast a stone at her." Rosalie, who was stoned, wept bitter tears every time she read this passage, and covered it with kisses; the page on which this is written—she willed me her Bible before she died—is smeared with lipstick. And then when I think of my own life, the things I've done, the places I've been to, the men I've known, the lowest of the low, I think of Jesus, poor among the poor, and Christ in Hell. I don't mean to compare myself to Him, understand me, although some will even go as far as that. It's rather that when I begin to look around for something to cover myself with, any old rag to cover my shame, I hit upon *that*—and it's not a rag at all, but a piece of the finest silk, and on it is embroidered a message in red thread, and the message is meant particularly for me—and then I don't feel shame at all.

Didn't He say, take? Take insults, calumnies, misunderstandings, stones, bruises, wounds. Turn the other cheek. I have taken, and so have we all. I have turned both cheeks at once. And He said, give, give out. I have given. Give unto Caesar. I have given unto him. And to Peter and Paul and Tom, Dick, and Harry, and Hubert Jackson. Take in, give out—it is the message, the rhythm of the woodpile and the rhythm of life.

And then as the preacher said who used to come among us, an old hand at converting the girls, "He was the greatest whoremaster of all. Didn't the Disciples procure for Him, Paul establish the syndicate, and Peter open the first house?" (He meant well, Christ forgive him these words, and me for remembering them.) "Bow down, you sinners, kneel, and then look up with shining faces to greet the Great Man who is come to lay it on you!" We kneel, we fling ourselves down, we sigh and cry out and gasp and clutch with our hands and dig with our nails, sink our teeth, and call on His name. "Open the gates of righteousness, that I may enter and praise the Lord!" And then, with shining faces, cry "Sweet Jesus, I am coming! Hold me tight in Thy embrace!" But spent, let down, ashamed, we think, unworthy, of His Passion, and like wet, uncomfortable babies, having wet ourselves with tears, cranky and disconsolate, we whimper "Jesus, Jesus, Jesus," His sweet name. In the asylum, in the hospital, in jail—nurse Christ, nurse us, doctor Christ, heal us, lawyer Christ, plead for us. Love us, sweetheart Christ, and father Christ, hear us, and do Thou weep for us. We have ourselves been dragged up the hill of skulls. Thy will be done, Jesus Christ, the same today, and tomorrow and forever. Forgive us, Christ, this humble flesh. The Father, the Son, and the Holy Ghost. Amen.

But this overdoes it. I don't like blasphemy, I don't mean to be blasphemous (or blasphemious, as our preacher used to say) and I don't think I have been. But there's a limit, after all. To begin with, we are sinners, and though Christ said go and sin no more, we go and do sin more. Our sin is a mortal one, and we will burn for it, for sure. What's more, it is gall in His wounds, and lacerates His poor hurt flesh. And yet I think He forgives us for it, for it is a humble sin, the very humblest sin there is, and done, the way we do it, not at all in pride. We are not like the rich man who has as much chance to enter heaven as a camel has to pass through the eye of a needle. We are not proud, not rich, nor do we take His name in vain, even when we call upon it in our beds. Nevertheless, we are sinners, and that leaves us out. His house is for whores who whore not, and we, for a fact, do whore. Now, if because I *am* a sinner I must be left out, all the more must I stand outside the gate because I do not even *consider* myself a sinner. I don't, and that's all. It's a matter of conscience, and my conscience, when all is said and done, will not support the claim. It is too clear—and though I am troubled with words and with money and with the complication of simple things, I seek not to be troubled, and see no reason to be so.

What then, is this not pride, to say I do not consider myself a sinner? A remarkable thing, take my word for it, it is not. That's the way it is, just so, simply so. I say it in simplicity and humility, humbler flesh has never been, and though I feel a tickling in my bones, I know it is not the smart of sin I feel, but a trickle of pleasure in the marrow, now almost dry, and I wish this trickle could flow and flood again, and it is not in pride that I wish it to be so, but in simple pleasure in the time I have had, and in regret that it shall not come again.

I think of my days and do not regret them. Rather, I am glad, and it does my heart good. I regard it as a plain and a pure thing, plain as rain and pure as snow. I know why the old Greeks, or was it the Egyptians or the Hindus? would keep the girls in their temples, for a pure thing it is. Mary, Mary, white as snow— but it seems to me that She is proud, not I, and I am pure, not She. (Forgive me, Mary.) Why is She now so still? I think of the girls in the temples and I think it would do Her good to have another Son.

A pure thing it is, pure in itself, unpurified. Just that, and nothing more. The act without consequence, the word without meaning. That alone. How often, therefore, is the bed without a sheet, the pillow without a case, the lamp without a shade. Even here in my room the bulb hangs, unshaded, from a chain over the bed, and you either turn it on or off, behold it or behold it not, and it can burn or just as well not burn. But when it burns, and seems to sway, and the bed moves, and seems to travel far into space, it is that alone, and we are all strangers.

It is neither a good thing nor evil, but pure, alone, by itself. And whether with the young man, his first time, and his pimples bright and round as cherries, or with the old man, dry and winded, or with that man, best of all, between age and youth, who knows how it is and how it should be—and then, sometimes, it is no longer sham, but true—even so, with one and all, we are all strangers. The impurity is in Jackson, who would make it a familiar thing, to laugh at, not in myself, who would keep it strange and stern. It is the thing itself one has to have mind, heart, and courage for, the jim-jam, nothing more. To that of the insects in the crack of wood, the mice in the pantry, the animals in the field, the beasts in the jungle, and the birds in the air, we add our own, grounded, unable to fly, but our own, our human and inhuman thing, to crown them all, the greatest and the best.

Then the thing burns and is cold as ice, words fail and there is a stream of words in strange languages, one lives and dies and goes through the stages of life, crying baby, oh boy, daddy! We are all strangers, mother to son, you and I, and peace to us all. But suddenly we are strangers no more. Then bang, and the lights go out and the lights go on, it is all one, the darkness and the flashing lights, and in the act of devotion, the devotion itself, the Son of Man has come and redeems us one and all.

But Christ, I am mocked. My face mocks me, wrinkled and sagged like an overblown bladder emptied of air. My hair mocks me, tangled in the comb. My body mocks me, a tired, sticky, flabby thing, the widow of itself. My eyes mock me, dim, and not, after all they have seen, clear, the dimness burned out of them, but dimmer than the landlord's baleful look. And I must hustle for rent, drag myself up and down these stairs, beg, threaten, cheat, dissimulate, blow liar's dust, and sneeze mercy on the saints; crouch, crawl, whimper, simper, fall, pick myself up, hobble, limp, skip, run, walk, creep, scratch, bleed, cry murder in broad daylight and Christ at night. Nothing touches me, grown old, grown cold. Nothing pleases me. I complain, grouch, grumble, and scold—at the children below, the dancer above—they darken my days. Nothing pleases me, nothing touches me, nothing gives me a bang and a wallop, a thrill, a tickle, an itch any more. Last night I threw the clock at the door, and broke it, glass and all—I thought I saw an ugly thing there, painted in red paint. The day before a woman pulled my hair Sew up the flap, I'm off the town. Off Crisco and cabbage and fantail for good. Lights out, roll up the flag. Empty the ashtrays. Carry out the pails. Mop the floor one last time and lock up. Take off the sign. Closed for alterations, forced to close out, changed hands, under new management, under six feet, face to the wall.

But Christ, if the fat could still fry!

4. The Dancer

Talia springs naked out of bed and puts on her leotard. This happens every morning. The time is eight-thirty, neither one minute more nor less. She has time to brush her teeth—which she does standing on tip-toe, thereby enabling herself to see the full reflection of her face in the bathroom mirror, and to engage in the day's first exercise, the strengthening of her leg muscles—and to drink half a glass of tomato juice, which she has poured out and set in the ice box the night before, before the arrival of the morning mail. At the postman's ring, she leaps out the door, another exercise, and goes bounding barefooted down the stairs, taking them either two at a time, or jumping down three or four at each landing, as a schoolboy does. Sometimes she gathers the mail directly from the postman's hand, and, if she thinks of it, collects the bulky packages and parcels of the paralytic who lives on the floor above her. There are always many letters for Talia, and, inwardly, she is delighted to receive them, although she does not express her joy, for it is not in accord with her regime to release emotional energy so early in the morning, before the day's work has begun. Talia runs up the stairs, gracefully, lightly, two at a time, and arrives not winded at her door. Then she sits cross-legged on the floor and opens her mail, pouting at the day's first disappointment. Her big toes also pout, standing out from the others, which are turned in toward the soles. There is an expression something like disappointment on her big, bluish toe nails. The letter she is waiting for has not yet come. She flings them all away, frowns and sighs, and would certainly sulk—but by now it is nine o'clock and time to begin the day's routine.

The first record she puts on the phonograph is the time-study in metronome, which she had recorded, at considerable expense and trouble, under her own supervision. The beat seems irregular—there are many different cadences, rests, irregular rhythms; but the beats of the metronomes have a carefully measured relation, one to the other, and after one has heard the record several times he perceives the over-all relationship which unites the single time-patterns into a whole. Talia is convinced that this is her own personal pulse and beat, the rhythm of her heart and lungs, the cyclical rhythms, expansions and contractions, the movement of her thoughts.

She begins to dance to it. Her motions, like the sounds that accompany them, at first seem unjoined, sporadic, irregular. But there is also a pattern in her dance, which soon becomes apparent. In the beginning, the movement is concentrated in the lower part of her body and her legs, which are sturdy, with square muscles. The toes grip the floor and release it, her feet working like hands.

Now it is her thighs and lower trunk that carry out the main movement of her body. Her feet move in smaller circles, their rhythm ebbing and coming to rest. Her arms and hands are not yet involved in motion. It is her thighs that carry the upward movement, suggesting the rising of water in the tree trunk.

The tree is now rooted, it can only sway, as in wind, which is brought to mind by the heaving of her belly. But this heaves like a sail in the wind, as one says, bellying. Then the tree is a tree no longer, but becomes a mast in full sail. But the mast is again a tree trunk, not yet cleared of its branches, which are her arms. The arms protest the transformation of the dance and refuse to bear sails. The fingers express ten alternatives, the wrists two, the arms and forearms supporting them. But even the protest and the alternatives are caught up in the transformation, and enter it, no longer distinct.

Now the movement changes and the image can no longer be tree or mast or sail. There is the movement only, withdrawn to itself at its fullest point, full of possibility which it does not discharge. Meanwhile, the rhythm of the record, nearing the end, goes:

tick-tock   tick-tick-tick   tock
tick-tick-tick-   tick   tick-tick   tick
tock   tick-tock-tock   tick   tock-tick-tick-   tick

Now the dancer's head rocks from side to side, its motion at first jerky, then tapering off. Now the body is still and composed, and the head says in its wisdom, slowly nodding, that it is best to dance in one place. Then, as the record ends, it too comes to rest; as in the last moment of a spinning top, shudders and stands still, and what remains of motion, its departing soul, passes out of the top of her head in a moment of comprehension and silence.

Talia has her other exercises, other dances, other records. Some she performs, like the time-study, with her attention turned in to the essence of the dance; then she keeps the curtain drawn over the full-length mirror that covers one wall of her room. Other dances require her outward attention; then she draws the curtain aside and watches herself in the mirror, criticising her gestures and smiling at whatever is right, subtle, or exact in them.

She pauses for lunch. Today, to suit the purpose of her dancing, and, as she thinks, the better to regulate her bodily economy, she is on a liquid diet. Talia drinks a glass and a half of pineapple juice and three quarters of a glass of milk. Then she rests on the couch in a position that she has herself discovered, after some research, to be the most restful and invigorating. Her limbs are neither relaxed nor tense, and her weight is so distributed that she both bears and yields it, sharing it with the couch. While she rests, she hears the stumbling, dragging noise the paralytic makes on the floor above, pulling himself about his apartment, and the noises of the many children in the courtyard. Their voices are shrill, frequently they quarrel and the younger ones wail and scream. There is a pattern in everything, the world is without chaos, and even chaos has an order—the order that it has. This Talia knows in her instinct for order. She has tried, with some success, to integrate the elements of a simple life—the things she sees daily, the daily events, sounds, rhythms, smells, feelings—into an over-all pattern of the most general proportions, which pattern she guards like a treasure and in guarding, seeks to perfect it. But the noises of the children do not fit the pattern—and this has for her a kind of horror, the kind that disorder calls forth in an orderly mind. Now she listens to the noises in the courtyard. There is a sound such as a tin tub would make, dragged over stones. A sound as of marbles rolling on the sidewalk, forever. The girls are jumping rope, and there is the noise of the rope striking the pavement, and the song the girls sing:

> *Buster Brown*
> *turn around*
> *Buster Brown*
> *touch the ground*

Talia listens in pain; a pain, as of the fear of death, which tells her she will never finish or perfect her work. . . .

It is time to return to the dance; time for three more dances until the arrival of the afternoon mail. She springs up, flexes her muscles, and tenses and relaxes her toes, which are now all pink, devoid of expression, and covered with the dust of the floor.

Again, records and phonograph, again dances, the mirror covered and uncovered.

The mailman's coming is made known to her by the shouts of the children in the yard. A glance out the window—she sees them climbing up his legs and back, hanging from his arms, from the bag, embracing his neck; and he plods on to the mailboxes, bearing their weight, neither laughing nor annoyed.

As before, she runs barefooted down the stairs, takes her mail, runs up with it, and sits cross legged on the floor, hastily going through the letters. And as before, discards them in disappointment and gets up to dance again.

It grows dark, but she is still dancing. Certainly, by now, she is perspired and exhausted, and what sadness there must be for her in dancing alone, unseen and not leaving the house, must have made itself felt; but she has taught herself to incorporate even her exhaustion and sadness into the dance. So, too, the noises of this time—the whore who lives on the floor below has several times knocked on the ceiling with a broomstick in protest against the music and the thud of her feet, and the paralytic has dragged himself down the stairs to pick up the day's mail, which Talia has neglected to bring him.

Dinner, two glasses of milk and the remains of the tomato and pineapple juice, and again the dance. Her movements now are heavy, and severe with self-criticism. But there is no time to go back, to rehearse, repeat, refine. Each dance is new, and its execution and perfection must be spontaneous. There is no time to go back, for now is approaching the climax of the day's effort, which is the performance of an unrelated act, ungoverned in movement and uncontrolled.

Talia sees a hook in the woodwork, high up on the wall; climbs onto a chair to test it and finds it is strong. She puts a last record on the turntable, takes a rope out of the closet, makes a noose at one end and ties the other end to the hook; then places the noose over her head, and holding the slipknot firmly that it may not constrict her throat, she kicks the chair away and dangles from the rope, kicking and squirming, gasping for breath, and slowly choking. She hangs for the duration of the record, which like the first consists of metronome beats. When the record ends and whirrs and scratches under the needle, she scrambles out of the noose, kicks herself free, and falls, with a swollen face, heavily, not gracefully, to the floor, rolling over several times.

The panic movements of the hanging act have provided the topic, the theme for tomorrow's dance. Now it is bedtime. She undresses, turns off the light, and gets into bed, selecting a position which she thinks is best for her, considering the day, the time, the theme, and the pattern. Talia holds this position all night, neither tense nor relaxed, in her sleep.

5. The Paralytic

It was not always so. He had, at one time, the full use of his legs. As a child, he loved to ride his tricycle; as a boy in his teens, he went on many long hiking trips, and even as a young man, when he had already begun to limp, he loved to walk about the city, along the river, in the park and in the country. And he had full command of his other faculties as well; his health was always good and he was cheerful and optimistic. Even in those early days, he had a turn for books and speculation, and loved to seclude himself—but these attacks, which is what his family took them to be, were only sporadic, and even when he was seized with his scholarly fits, he remained the gay scholar, good-natured and bright, who lightened his serious work with walks and social affairs.

Winniker has suffered a general decline. He is lean, has a large, square head which no longer fits his neck or shoulders, a wrinkled, yellow face with watery eyes, and on his forehead and hands liverish spots have begun to appear, although he is just fifty. His legs are now almost of no use to him, though he can still walk with the aid of a stick. The stairs are an ordeal, but he is forced to live on the top floor, for he cannot get about well enough to find another place, and knows no one who would be kind enough to find better accommodations for him. Exchanging apartments with the tenants on one of the lower floors, supposing they would hear of it—the dancer, the prostitute or the janitor—is out of the question. He can't approach them normally, as another in his position might be able to do, and whenever he meets one of them on the stairs he is overcome with a shyness that forbids conversation. He stands stock-still, turns red, averts his eyes, and waits until the stairs are clear, so that no one should see him struggling with his infirmity. There is, besides, some satisfaction for him in the fact that he lives above the dancer. It makes, as it were, for a well-established point.

Winniker has lived what he considers a full life, and therefore does not very much regret that he must now live withdrawn and alone. His youth was not misspent, by which he means that the pleasures available to his earlier days did not entirely pass him by. Now the pleasures are gone. Sickness and age have cut them off, but Winniker lives by the afterglow of his golden age, summoning it up, when he is gloomiest and most dismal, to reassure himself that he has lived well. But he manages to live pleasantly enough in remembered pleasure, and has even achieved a kind of serenity—though he has enjoyed this serenity only infrequently. He feels that the serenity which must be achieved, with a life devoted to it, as to an object, is not of the true kind which comes of itself. But even if his knowledge of the true serenity is for the most part theoretical, it has on several occasions come to him as the truth should come: prepared, but not contrived, uninvited, but not unexpected—a long-awaited surprise, a shock of peace. This true serenity is related to his major work and devotion, and whenever it has come it has been an expression of his joy in his work.

Winniker studies the dance. He has studied it in every phase and aspect, in its evolution and retrogression from place to place and period to period—studied its forms, motive, purpose, inspiration, its effect on the individual participant and spectator and on society at large. It is to him a concrete thing and a vast symbol, indefinitely abstract; he sees it everywhere in nature and in imagination, a thing prior to life and more primitive, life itself, and greater than life. And because it is so vast and great, the dance is to him the most representative activity, everything joining it in an ever-widening gyre.

Winniker's interest in the dance developed concurrently with his paralysis. At first he was unaware that the two existed side by side—there was his anxiety over his paralysis, but the dance was his refuge from anxiety. It was the dance itself that made him realize that there was a connection between the two states of terror and peace that alternated in his mind. . . . One night he attended the ballet (so long as he was able to walk without too great difficulty, he continued to go out, in fact, "ran about" wildly, from place to place). During the performance he felt so moved, and was transported so far out of his anxiety, that he unconsciously began to express his own joy, and the joy of the ballet, with the motion of his body. But his feet—at the very least, he had wanted to carry out the gliding rhythm—refused to respond—as if for the first time, so great was his surprise; and then he realized the intimate and terrible relationship between his joy in the dance and his incapacity for it. He left the theater at intermission; the shock had so unnerved him that he had temporarily lost even the degree of control he had hitherto been able to maintain over his legs, and had to be helped into a cab.

Then began the study that has occupied him ever since. The first question he asked himself was: Do I love the dance because I am paralyzed, or am I paralyzed because of my love for the dance? Winniker posed the question with wonderful subtlety, turning it this way and that, inverting it and restoring its original formulation, and arranging the probable and tentative answers in groups, series, pairs, and classes of pairs. He recognized at once two poles, between which his thought was torn   the obvious and the recondite. Thus he saw that the hypothesis, the love of the dance is born of paralysis, was too obvious, and that the other hypothesis, that paralysis was born of the love, was too recondite. Was there not, he wondered, a third alternative, neither one nor the other, but nearer than both to the truth? An impossible necessity, an excluded ground between extremes? In which direction Winniker moved for a while, seeking the ultimate in the initial venture, the absolute answer at once. But he soon saw that his way was not prepared and that he must first study.

He began to study himself. No longer as the young student, grasping everything that came to hand, but now as the mature scholar, confident that his isolated interest is universal in scope. Thus the problem, What am I? became a world problem, as did also, and above all, the question, What is the dance? But this last question had first to be answered from within the questioner, so it became, What is the dance, that I am what I am?

Slowly, gradually, his work began. He published articles, essays, books, and reviews and became known as an authority; books, periodicals, monographs, doctors' theses, magazines, reprints, lectures, addresses, and miscellaneous papers were sent to him in the mails, as were also photographs and films, charts, diagrams, costumes, and musical instruments. He amassed a valuable library and a veritable museum, all from the publications and artifacts which other authorities, admiring his work, begged him to accept with their compliments. He soon had the means to work uninterruptedly, the facilities for study, and the double incentive of the desire for knowledge and greatness, which was renewed and given even greater force by his work.

But still Winniker was unsatisfied. He did not deprecate his great accumulation of knowledge, nor was he unaware of its orderly arrangement in his card files and his mind. It was a treasure which he would be proud to leave to the world. But as yet it represented only knowledge, which he considered to be but the first stage of work. After knowledge comes being, and this, he felt, he had not yet attained.

To be, as well as to know, what one knows! To be the war dance, the love dance, the rain dance, the bridal dance, the dance of fertility, of the benevolence and anger of the gods—and to have these dances issue from him, from his instinct, as they had issued from the instinct of the race. To be in himself that which makes one say, of one dance, that it is the assurance of immortality, and of another, that it teaches devastation, the subjection of the world to death. Then, only then, is the great representation achieved—Winniker, fully human, the man of all men.

But how does one achieve being? He remembered in his early adolescence he had come across a learned "Manual of Marriage"; reading it, though he had tried to preserve in himself the attitude of scientific detachment which the author had urged on the reader, he had nevertheless become aroused—and felt ashamed of himself for desecrating the proper spirit of the work. But now he felt, of course one should be aroused! A man responds with his whole being: the boy, in a furious study, to sex, and the astronomer to the stars, sucked up through his telescope to the sky, to become a constellation. And may the dance find the dancer, with eager feet.

But how? His own being gives no clue, his feet are still. And the world about him is not congenial—the noise, the cramped quarters, the long stairs to climb, and the filth. Even his books and artifacts, once so highly treasured, have become a clutter of useless things.

Right now in the courtyard, interrupting his study, the janitor's children are playing a game, the rules of which demand that they beat the waterspout with a stick. Bang-bang-bang! Bang-bang-bang! Between blows of the stick he can hear the words of a conversation conducted by Mandalay and Panteley Jeveves. They are discussing the question, "Are pregnant women lucky?" Mandalay says, Yes, they are, if you turn around three times when you see them coming. But Panteley maintains, No, you've got to touch it first.

Between Winniker and Talia there has for several years been an unacknowledged relationship. He met her on the stairs soon after she moved into the building, and at first had nothing but contempt for her: he mistook the sound of her metronome records for tap-dancing. Not that he held anything related to the dance alien to himself; but associating the young, rather muscular woman with a pinched face, whom he continued to meet, to his embarrassment, on the stairs, with the sound of tap-dancing, he concluded that her interest in the dance was not serious; and it was to protect himself from what he imagined would surely be her scorn of his work that he scorned hers. Such defensiveness, unbecoming and inappropriate to any authority of Winniker's reputation, was, however, the direct result of that reputation. He wanted to avoid the disappointment of meeting her and finding that she did not know who he was. He was, moreover, by that time, very bitter—though unconscious of his bitterness—toward all healthy and, in particular, athletic people, and extremely suspicious of them.

But as time passed and he continued to hear without letup the metronome beat in the morning and at night, the other records that accompanied Talia's dancing, and the thud and shuffle of her bare feet, he acknowledged his mistake to himself. Evidently, she was no tap dancer; and since she worked indefatigably, with only the briefest pauses, and, far from dancing in night clubs and theaters, never seemed to leave the house, he felt obliged to admit that she was a serious student. But this, in turn, led him to the conclusion that she was a mediocrity, and he devoted a considerable sympathy to her under a general benevolence to honest, sturdy workers, all thighs and no talent. And then, her records disturbed him. All day long he cursed her music—though he had devoted a large part of his work to a study of the function of music in the dance. Music and bare feet, bare feet and music— and he, Winniker, must work with their noise always in his head. But in truth, it was the proximity of the dancer dancing that disturbed him most, the image of the unseen, active body. He found himself devoting more and more of his labors to human anatomy— a related topic, certainly, but altogether remote from the theme he was at that time working on. The longer he studied anatomy—in particular the bony structure and musculature of the legs and feet—the more closely he was drawn back to the preoccupation with his paralysis, which he had only lately managed to put down. Now it worked contrary to his instinct to consider the dance with reference to his incapacity; whether his objectivity, gained at such great cost, were truly objective, a desire to possess the object and nothing more, or whether he had thereby adopted merely a method in the most desperate subterfuge, hitting upon it precisely in the hope of a cure, he knew that self-concern, at the present stage of his work, was retrogressive and a danger. Nevertheless, the image of Talia gave him no rest, and whatever way he determined to regard her—as a serious student, a mediocrity, even as a fairly gifted dancer whose friendship might prove valuable to him—no sooner had he struck an attitude toward her than he found himself recoiling from the threat which she somehow exerted against him into a preoccupation with himself and his disease.

At last he resolved to put an end to his uneasiness by confronting the thing itself that unnerved him—he would have to see her dance. Then he would be on his guard, no longer vulnerable—and if she proved vulnerable, he would take advantage of her weakness to put her forever out of his mind; if she proved strong—and, it was to be hoped, truthful and representative in her dancing—then, perhaps, their association, placed on a level footing in the open, would be of advantage to them both. But he was incapable of directly presenting himself at her door and asking permission to watch her dance. It would most likely offend her. Furthermore, the necessity of descending the stairs and entering her room on his uncertain legs before her unsympathetic eyes—and all the worse if she chose to be sympathetic!—would certainly offend him. There was no one to employ as an intermediary, except the Jeveves children or Jeveves himself, one of whom brought him food and a newspaper once a day; but the Jeveveses were not of reliable intelligence. And he could obtain no one else to act as intermediary without putting himself out beyond the limit of his patience, his endurance, and his pride. He considered dangling a note from a string outside her window until it should come to her attention; but most likely the children in the courtyard would notice it first—and besides, the whole situation was ridiculous, as was also a variation of it, that he slip the note under her door. There was evidently no way of approaching Talia. And to rely on a chance meeting on the stairs was absolutely out of the question, as this method involved the embarrassment of all the others, to the highest degree.

Then it occurred to him that it would best suit his purpose to observe her, unseen. In this way he could take her true measure, and not have to reckon with her awareness of his judgment. He thought of peeking through her keyhole, of placing mirrors and reflectors outside her windows, of lowering himself on a scaffold to the edge of her window and peering in; none of these procedures was feasible. Fortunately he soon hit upon a simple expedient, the simplest and most direct. He asked Jeveves to bring him a drill, and set to work at once, boring holes in the floor; the holes, when completed, would look down through her ceiling. The work gave him the immediate satisfaction of knowing that he had the solution of a problem in hand; at first it was not exhausting, and he could turn to it as a rest from his other activities, or a means of combating the distraction of the records and the thudding feet from the apartment below.

But he soon found that it was more exhausting work than he had expected. He had to bore very carefully and quietly, not to call attention to himself. It went slowly, with little progress to show at the end of a week's labor. His arms and back tired easily, and sometimes, when he had kept at it for an hour or more, he would find that from great exhaustion he had temporarily lost the use of his legs altogether. It was difficult enough to bore through the floor undetected; sinking the holes through the ceiling presented an even greater difficulty, for unless he proceeded with extreme care, the plaster would crack and chip, fall onto the dancer's floor, and give him away. There were now well over two dozen holes in the floor, at various parts of the room, to afford a view of the dancer from all angles; before extending these holes further he let water down through each hole, a drop at a time, to bind the plaster. Then, working very cautiously, he enlarged the holes in the floor, and before lowering the drill bit to the ceiling he set his lips to the hole, prepared to suck up the wood shavings or loose plaster. Winniker was months at this part of the work, before he completed a few holes. Through them he could catch a glimpse, now and then, of an arm or a leg in motion, the gesture of a hand or the top of Talia's head, but never the whole figure or the whole dance, nor would his effort be rewarded until he had opened all the holes. Meanwhile, his own floor was covered with plaster and wood shavings, and the holes that had been opened admitted even more of the disturbing music and thudding of the girl below.

Talia, all this time, had not been unaware of Winniker. Her encounters with him on the stairs had greatly excited her curiosity, the more so as he would stand stock-still and refuse to move until she had gone into her apartment. Nor was he deceived by the mere closing of the door; guarding himself against a crack left open, he waited until he heard the lock catch before venturing to move on. By his extreme embarrassment on the stairs, and the thumping, dragging noise he made above her, she guessed at his paralysis, and began to feel for him an impersonal pity, for the most part curiosity. As Talia thought, out of pity, but in reality, to obtain a better view of him than the brief glimpse in the hall gave her, she began to bring him his mail. But the stratagem failed. On several occasions he pretended not to be at home; and when she had at last made unmistakably clear to him the nature and purpose of her knock at the door, Winniker, in an unexpectedly gruff voice— it was the first time she had heard his voice, and for some reason had imagined that paralytics speak sweetly— ordered her to leave the mail outside his door. Thereafter she brought his mail much less frequently, only when impelled by a very strong curiosity, as when the noise he made, dragging himself about, claimed more of her attention than she had assigned to it in her patterning of the surrounding world. But even so her curiosity was limited; she did not know or care to find out who he was or what he did. His whole existence was contained for her in the fact that he made a certain kind of noise, which she found it necessary to relate to other noises.

As soon as Talia began to come to his door, Winniker realized that his project was in danger. Though he kept the door locked, he feared that she might some day gain access to his apartment and discover the means he had devised for observing her. He therefore instructed Antontonio Jeveves to buy him a rug, and when the good janitor brought it to him, Winniker spent the day, in great difficulty, laying it over the holes. He made so much noise, struggling with the heavy brown paper in which the rug came rolled, that late that afternoon, when he had finally succeeded in unrolling it and had placed books and dishes along the edge to keep it flat, Talia again brought his mail. She knocked at the door.

"Leave it in the hall," said Winniker, in a gruff but weak voice. He was lying exhausted on the rug, where he had been trying to think of a simple way of rolling up the rug whenever he wanted to work on his peepholes or look through the ones that were already finished.

But Talia's curiosity, though essentially as superficial as ever, was very strong that day. She knocked again. Winniker realized that he had neglected to lock the door after the rug had been delivered. He pulled himself up and began to shuffle to the lock, when the door opened. He stood stock-still.

Talia, her face pinched and her arms laden with parcels, barefooted and wearing her leotard, said, "I've brought you your mail, Mr. Winniker." Accustomed to the solitary life, each acquired character and social sense, as if from nowhere, when confronted with the other. The dancer turned sly, the dance authority, contemptuous. They stared at each other.

"Leave it, leave it! I said leave it!"

"May I come in for a moment?"

"You may not. Please go!"

"Where shall I leave these packages?"

"Anywhere. On the floor."

"I can't. My arms are full. You'll have to help me, or I'll drop everything."

"Then drop it, the devil take it! Drop it and get out of here."

"It'll break. This package, here, under my arms, sounds as if it has glass in it."

Winniker stamped on the floor with his stick. "Will you please go?"

"In a moment. Here—" She came into the room, moving toward him as if she were about to drop the packages; staggered, grasped the parcels, lost them, and caught them again. "Help me!"

"The devil! Will you get out of here?" Winniker, forgetting his embarrassment and rule never to be seen walking by a stranger, stumbled toward her, holding up his stick.

Suddenly Talia stood still, as if she were the paralyzed one. The spasmodic movements of her hands and shoulders stopped. She watched Winniker in great enthusiasm for the quality of his movements, observing his faltering legs, his head thrust forward and trembling on his thin neck, the crimp in his back, the twitching of his shoulders, the excited, spiderlike motion of his fingers, the stumbling, uncontrolled course of his feet. Her face lighted up in inspiration and she gave him a brief, satisfied smile; then flung the packages down on the bed, skipped out of the room, and went bounding down the stairs.

Later that afternoon—exhausted though he was, he had completed several more peepholes, working with extreme effort— he watched her do an imitation of his walk, executing a dance about it. She had gained her object, at once satisfying her curiosity, and extending the pattern, deriving a theme from his disease. And while he, too, had gained his object—that afternoon was the first time he had been able to catch more than a few disconnected glimpses of her dancing—it was in great disgust that he found that the object he had so long been pursuing, proved, on capture, to be nothing more than himself. Winniker was furious.

Whether from fury at the futile, senseless interruption of his work, the months lost in pursuit of a false object, or whether from the mere passing of time, with no cause other than an inner and inevitable one, Winniker's paralysis has grown worse. He has thrown himself back into his work, hoping to regain lost time, but he must now work slowly. His arms and hands have at last been affected, and he now has difficulty in turning pages and taking notes. He still has voluntary motion in his hands, but his coordination is poor and his nerve impulses are sluggish; an extinct monster. He now sits at the table all day, and no longer drags himself about the room; he limits his movement to the absolute minimum and has stopped going downstairs for his mail. Now it is brought to him by the Jeveveses or Talia, when the parcels and packages have cluttered up the vestibule. Talia no longer attempts to come in to him, but from time to time she leaves foolish notes with his mail, such as:

> These came for you.
> —Talia

or

> I brought these up.
> —T.

The notes are written in various inks on colored note paper—gray, lavender, deep blue, and in white ink on black; the paper is always scented. It is as if Talia had begun a flirtation with him, or (he peeped down at her once again and found her dancing the same paralyzed dance, now elaborated with all sorts of extreme, disconnected gestures), or it may be that she feels grateful to him and, too proud and selfish to thank him openly—too selfish, perhaps, even to realize that it is gratitude she feels—she has selected this means of thanking him.

After a week without notes, she left a particularly offensive one at the door:

> Are you ill? Haven't heard you thumping about in some
> time.
> —T.

A few days later, another note:

Worried.

—T.

Then another note, which Winniker did not read. She came up the next day and found that he had not taken in the mail and note from the day before, or the food and newspaper that Jeveves had left for him. Talia knocked on the door and got no answer; tried to open it and it was locked. She ran down the stairs, alarmed, but nevertheless leaping gracefully at each landing, with her spine straight, her chest thrown out, and her arms outspread. The janitor, seeing her burst into his apartment, cleared the bed for her, knocking off several children who had been sleeping on it and shoving them into the kitchen. Martafolia was out shopping.

"Hot stuff, all right," said Jeveves, sitting down on the bed and reaching to pull off his shoes.

"The hot water has been fine all week," said Talia. "It's Winniker. He doesn't answer. We must get to him."

"Old man. No walk," mumbled Antontonio, hopefully wondering if he had the right to consider her words a refusal. He decided he had not. "No good. Old man."

"Quick, give me the key to his place. Key, key—a passkey. Do you have it?"

"Have got." He removed a huge ring from his pocket, the keys sticking out like the spines of a radial sea animal. "Lots keys. More." He produced another key ring from under the pillow, reached for one under the bed, overturned a milk bottle and a stream of keys poured out. Antontonio swept them all into his pocket. "We open door."

He tried each key in Winniker's lock. None of them fit. "We break door," said the janitor, and did so.

Winniker was lying in bed, a sheet pulled up to his chin, staring dead ahead of him. "Mr. Winniker!" Talia did a split at the side of the bed. "Are you all right? What's the matter with you?" He did not answer. "Can you hear me? Do you know who I am?" Winniker lay still, alive but motionless. Only his watery eyes moved, glancing at the janitor and at Talia and quickly looking away. "Can you move?" She pulled his arm out from under the sheet, raised it and let go. It fell lifeless to the bed, rolling a little, as if it were going to fall off.

"Knockout," said Antontonio.

Two days before, as he was working at his desk, he had felt himself growing heavy and cold, and had just managed to crawl into bed and pull the sheet over him, when he lost all power of motion. He had lain there ever since, hearing the children's noises, the mailman's ring, the janitor bringing food, Talia coming up with the mail and coming again the next day, her knocking and calling his name, the door broken in—but he had also lost the power of speech, and could make no sound in response. He could move only his eyes and his lips, soundlessly.

"Sick man," said Antontonio. "You stay with him?"

"I can't," said Talia, springing up. "It's late. I must get back to work."

"Me too. Go fix boiler. We get it old woman, who-ha, she live second floor, she stay." They went down the stairs together, Talia running ahead and leaping in very gracefully at her own door.

Jeveves knocked at the prostitute's door. He told her what had happened to Winniker and asked if she would sit with him, which she agreed to do. Watching her climb the stairs, he realized he had again forgotten to ask the question that he asked of all women but which, for obvious reasons, he had never asked of her.

The prostitute took one look at Winniker, screamed, blessed herself, and ran down the stairs. She came back presently, her arms laden with religious pictures, and holding a bottle of hair oil that she had grabbed in her haste. She tacked all the pictures onto the wall above Winniker's bed, and then sat at his side, wondering what else she could do for him. She talked to him, but he did not answer, touched him, and he felt dead—warm, but dead—and did not respond; she shook her fingers before his eyes, and they blinked. "Poor man, poor man," she muttered, and began to say a prayer over him; but she felt false, and she suspected, from the look in his eyes, that he did not want her to pray for him. When I die, she thought, there will be no one to pray for me. But prayer was not necessary, the fact of dying was enough. What you wanted was something different from prayer, without words. But what was it; what could you do for another, not knowing what it was, what could you do, not having learned in your own life what it is? How will I die, who will do it for me? she thought. Still, she wanted to do something for him, and after a while she got up and began to straighten up the house. What a mess it was! All the books and daggers, knives, shields on the wall, the strange masks—it would have been a good idea to wear a mask on the woodpile—the dancing costumes, shoes, skirts, scarves. He had these things on his wall, and she had her pictures—it was all a matter of where you hung your tail. She arranged the books and papers in neat piles on his desk, aligned the books in the bookcase, dusted all the objects and swept the rug, laying on the strokes of the broom with considerable vigor and making the layers of puffy, dimpled fat dance at her elbows.

At the onset of the stroke, Winniker realized that he was going to die. Though he left his desk in haste, he left it reluctantly, and for an hour or so, as he lay awaiting death, he regretted that his work was unfinished, and that he had not stayed with it, to die at his desk. But when death was delayed in coming, and he saw that he should still have some time to live suspended over death, he gave his mind to his work again, thinking he might use up his remaining time in the best way that he knew, by following to its conclusion the particular problem he had been engaged on. But try as he would, he was unable to remember what he had been working on when the stroke came, and alarmed at the loss of his last power, he tried to get up and go to his desk, though he knew that he was unable to move, and tried to call out for help, though he knew that he had lost his voice. Winniker struggled with the paralysis, fighting it with greater will than he had ever done and all night long he lay afraid and struggling with it. But when morning came, he was more at peace with himself.

All that day, even when the door was broken in, he had been at peace. Now he considered it no loss that the work he had been doing remained unfinished. What was it, after all, but knowledge, further knowledge, a gap stopped here, a hole plugged there? The sieve would remain open, for all his effort. What mattered was that the stage beyond knowledge had not been attained—the being of the dance. There was this to regret, this to regret deeply, and nothing else. But as the day passed, he came to realize that he had reached the ultimate stage, had all along been on the edge of it, and had at last entered it wholly. The realization seized him in joy: it was his disease, growing in him since early in life and at last overtaking him, it was his paralysis, to which he had yielded step by step and day by day until it had achieved its final power—it was the paralysis that represented the ultimate being of the dance. By yielding all motion to paralysis, he had yielded to the dance and become part of its being, which was absolute motionlessness, forever at rest. So, in yielding completely to life, a man dies—and knowing this now, Winniker lay serene, at peace, and no longer afraid to die.

But one thing Winniker regretted. Now he felt the need again to have followers and disciples to whom he could impart what he had learned and have it live in them. To be vouchsafed being—but only for a moment, and not to grow great in it! Not to expand and explore its plentitude! To take up the dance again and go on—

who knows?—perhaps even to a further stage, still higher. To have but one man to whom he could pass on the truth—with his eyes, since words now failed him; perhaps even to a number of men, perhaps to a generation, perhaps, if it were not too great a hope, perhaps, eventually, to all mankind, that they might all know the sublimity of the dance!

The prostitute had by now dusted and swept and cleaned everywhere, and was taking up the rug to mop the floor, when she discovered Winniker's peepholes. She dropped down on her hands and knees and peered into the apartment below, where Talia was dancing to the music of the phonograph. "Well, I'll be!" she exclaimed, but the dance seemed false to her and did not please her. Winniker's holes, however, gave her great delight, and she felt a sudden love for him, as if they shared the secrets of a common self. She remembered, in tenderness, the days when she had worked in a peepshow, and it gave her a sense of triumph and achievement to find herself, at last, on the outside, looking in.

[1948]

An Experiment with
Tropical Fish

⌒

THE FOLLOWING EXPERIMENT WAS CONDUCTED WITH A group of tropical fish consisting of one mated pair each of guppies *(Lebistes reticulatus)*, swordtails *(Xiphorus helleri)*, zebras *(Danio rerio)*, and angelfish *(Pterophyllum scalare);* and one unmated catfish *(Corydoras paleatus)* of undetermined sex. One pond snail and one red snail were also present in the tank, which contains $2^{1}/_{2}$ gallons of ordinary tap water. The aquarium is lighted from above by a small lamp fixed to the top, and a number of plants *(Cabomba, Ludwigia, Myriophyllum)* are rooted in the layer of gravel along the bottom.

The experiment was suggested by the behavior of the male guppy, who, on several occasions, was observed to be swimming backward. As this behavior was first noted while the male was in the presence of the female guppy, it was erroneously attributed by the observer to the sexual impulse and considered to be of a character connected with the mating activities. Further observation disclosed that the male continued this activity (a) when the female was in another part of the aquarium, (b) when her back was turned, (c) when he was hidden from her view by one of the plants or, (d) when she was otherwise unable to see his movements. As this refuted the sexual interpretation, the question was raised: Why does the male guppy swim backward?

Continued observations during the next four days disclosed that the guppy not only swam backward but exhibited a number of other unorthodox swimming movements: he would immobilize, in turn, the pectoral, dorsal, anal, and caudal fins, singly and then in various combinations, obtaining from these combinations a variety of rolling, stalling, and looping movements not ordinarily encountered. That these movements were deliberate and not the result of an impairment of the swimming mechanism was borne out by the fact that during all this time the guppy was able to swim perfectly well, and that he executed a number of other maneuvers of an apparently experimental nature in which he floated, glided, sank, and rose. The hypothesis suggested itself that *the male guppy was testing the nature of the water.*[1] During this period, the temperature of the aquarium was kept within the constant limit of 72° to 78° F., the fish were regularly fed, once a day, with a well-balanced fish food and enjoyed several hours of direct sunlight and several hours of artificial light from the aquarium lamp.

After the first week in which these observations were made, the guppy, who until then had been solitary, engrossed in his experiments, was seen to seek out the company of the other fish. He solicited the companionship of the female guppy in particular. The observer, having been warned by the initial error, was careful to interpret this behavior correctly. That it was not in the nature of a sexual overture was clear from the fact that (a) the male exhibited none of the stunts and tricks which tropicals have within their repertoire for catching the attention of females, and (b) the response of the female differed from the usual response to a sex-

---

[1] The first application of the theory of knowledge to the scientific study of fish was made by Professor Sidney Passin, in whose Ichthyological Papers (Greenwich, 1938), I have found many valuable suggestions. I must also express my indebtedness to Kitty Brucato and Rover Block for their help in keeping the aquarium under constant observation.

ual situation in that it was neither coy nor firm, but showed a marked and evidently sincere lack of interest, and an actual boredom once some kind of communication had definitely been established by the male. The nature of this communication was not known to the observer, but that it had been established was indicated by the repeated attempts the male guppy made to hold her attention while he demonstrated, in summary form, the various experimental movements he had engaged in earlier. Winning no encouragement from his mate, he turned to the other fish, approaching them during their feeding and grazing activities and hovering over them insistently. Eventually he succeeded in attracting an audience. The fish and the snails gathered in a clearing of the tank and hung round him in a semicircle while the guppy went through the familiar gyrations. He moved in one direction, then at right angles, first with one, then with another combination of fins, pausing, after each figure had been completed, to turn to his audience and direct a pattern of air bubbles at them. It was clear from this and from the preceding episodes that *the guppy, having performed a number of experiments to test the nature of the water, was now publishing his findings in the form of an illustrated lecture.* A study of the air bubble patterns[2] further bore out this conclusion, as did the subsequent behavior of the audience. The fish, at first skeptical, attached greater credibility to the lecture as the demonstration proceeded. At the conclusion of the talk, they broke up into several small groups and appeared to be discussing the guppy's findings. The male swordtail and the catfish were the first to repeat the guppy's experiments, and their example was soon imitated by the others, who, with the exception of the angelfish, executed these gyrations with the greatest enthusiasm. The angelfish, possibly because of the peculiar angu-

---

[2]This study, "Speech Patterns of Tropical Fish," will be published by the observer in a forthcoming paper.

larity of their bodies—something like that of the flounder—experienced some difficulty in performing the maneuvers and remained unconvinced of the guppy's thesis. During the next few days, the aquarium was the scene of constant experimentation and discussion of such great excitement that a number of the plants were dislodged from the gravel and had to be reset. Careful study of the air bubbles enables the observer to state the guppy's thesis as follows: *That we live in an element* [water—I.R.], *that this element is all-embracing, that it has certain properties of flow, resistance, and pressure which enable us to float, swim, maneuver, and maintain our buoyancy, and that we are depen dent on this element for our life and nurture.* With the exception, noted before, of the angelfish, all the members of the aquarium accepted the thesis and acclaimed the guppy for formulating it. Now the female guppy admiringly sought his attention.

During all this time the aquarium was kept at constant temperature, the fish were fed regularly and the condition of the water was excellently clear (see above).

2

In the next phase of the experiment, the condition of the aquarium was altered. First the temperature was lowered to 68° F., and maintained at this level for three days, creating a partial chill. The fish were unaffected by the drop in temperature and continued all their normal healthy activities, but discussion and investigation of the guppy's theory rapidly declined and on the third day ceased altogether. On the fourth day the temperature was lowered to 67° F. No overt acknowledgment of this change was made by the fish, and the guppy himself offered no comment, though a certain perplexity of movement and expression was clearly observed, and the affectionate relationship between him and his mate was replaced by an attitude of mutual distrust. All the fish seemed to feel the chill, but none was affected in health. On the afternoon of the fourth day, the first reference to the guppy's theory since the change in temperature was made by the angelfish, who, as indicated by his air bubble patterns, passed several remarks disparaging the study of the element. The rest made no comment, and on the fifth day the angelfish apparently felt himself emboldened to declare—out of hearing of the guppies—that all such activity was not only nonsense, but dangerous and harmful to the aquarium. On the sixth day the temperature was again raised to the proper level; this was immediately followed by a resumption of scientific activity and of the optimistic mood that had been previously observed. On the seventh day the temperature was again lowered to 67° F., and for the first time the oxygen economy of the tank was disturbed, by the removal of the greater part of the water plants. Also for the first time, the aquarium was given an excess of light, to encourage the growth of algae, and an excess of food was fed to the fish. The bottom of the tank, which had been periodically cleaned with a dip tube, was now allowed to accumulate decayed matter and droppings. The aquarium was kept under constant observation. The fish responded to the lowered oxygen content of the water by frequently approaching the surface and thrusting out their mouths; they tended to stay at the top, and no longer swam in the deep water. Within two days the tank was clouded over with algae, decayed food products and droppings.

These physical changes in the environment were accompanied by an immediate cultural change. Even before the health of the fish was noticeably impaired, a mood of pessimism, anxiety, and despair began to prevail; and this took deeper hold of the aquarium with the subsequent disturbance of health. No further scientific activity of any kind was observed while the environment was kept in a state detrimental to a healthy economy; instead, the prevailing opinion, in the forming of which the male angelfish took the lead, soon became one of expressed hostility to such activity. The air bubble patterns of the male angelfish showed a consistent formation: the guppy's pattern was always included in his own, bracketed at either side by air bubbles, in the nature of quotation marks, of an unmistakably derisive character. The other fish were quickly persuaded to a scorn of their previous commitments, and on several occasions the zebras, the least stable of the fish, were influenced by their new persuasion to nip at the guppies who, though grown mutually distrustful, huddled together for protection in a corner of the tank.

After thus discrediting the guppy's researches, the angelfish announced a theory of his own, to replace the theory of water The angel declared that fish, true enough, live in an element, but this is neither the true life nor the true element. There exists an element outside water in which fish have their true being. For water is not only not all embracing, it is actually the most limiting and limited of all the conditions under which fish live, and it is ultimately detrimental to the true life and the true nurture. Life under water is a species of slavery, from which humiliation a fish can escape only by aspiring to the true life in the Realm Beyond Water. There only does a fish exist not as an object among other objects—food, plants, and the like—but as a subject, a fish *qua* fish, and consequently a free being. Belief in the Realm Beyond Water is not only the true belief; it is necessary for the health of the aquarium. For look what happened to us as the result of the false theory.

The angelfish instituted a set of rules, which the other fish, in their weakened condition, accepted without murmur. These rules, demanding unconditional submission, were introduced, according to the angelfish, to save the aquarium and prevent recurrence of the catastrophe caused by the guppy's researches. The substance of these rules was that no experiments on water or inquiries into the nature of water were to be made. All questions and inquiries into the nature of the Realm Beyond Water were first to be submitted to the angelfish for approval; and all other proposals affecting the public good, such as recommendations concerning the feeding order and proposals for spawning or mating, were likewise to be submitted for approval to the angelfish. (In the opinion of the observer, the stipulation concerning the mating activities was quite unnecessary, for all trace of such interests had long since vanished.) The angelfish were to be first in the feeding order and in every other order, and the guppies last. All association or communication with guppies was forbidden and punishable by death.

The first death that occurred in the aquarium under the new regime was that of the female zebra, who was found floating on her side at the top of the tank and removed by the observer on the eighteenth day of the experiment. Autopsy disclosed that she was suffering from parasites and corrosion of the gill plates and intestine. Some time after she had been flushed away by the observer, the angelfish acknowledged her disappearance from the aquarium, stating that it marked her translation to the Realm Beyond Water. No other deaths have as yet occurred, though all the fish show increasing infirmities.

Study of the guppy's air bubble patterns, during this time, discloses that with the exception of a single attempt at refuting the angelfish—he ventured near him, in the presence of the others, and asked to be told how one could possibly live out of water—he has not communicated with the other fish, and there is even no communication between him and his mate. He no longer conducts experiments, and his theoretical interests are confined to the recapitulation, in private language, of his earlier conclusions, and the formulation of a few new principles which, as far as the difficulty of translating his private language will allow, run as follows:

The element not only sustains the only possible life, it contains within itself properties which, were it only possible to conduct experiments, would surely be shown to be auspicious for a fuller and even more pleasurable life than was once known in the aquarium. The element is all, there is no other. If there were another, it would be but another form of the same element. Only when the inner economy of the element is disturbed and the health of the fish impaired, is the existence of a different and allegedly superior element imagined. As the strength of the belief in this other other element varies inversely with the health of the fish, this belief therefore provides a reliable measure of the health of the aquarium. Other things being equal, nothing besides the element is necessary for a flourishing aquarium, and scorn of the element endangers the aquarium. There is in the element an ultimate principle which is—

Here the difficulties of translation are insuperable. The word can only be given as *booble,* after the sound with which it is uttered. The meaning of this word, and of several others that follow it—*bool-bool-bool* [with a liquid *l*]—can only be guessed at. As the life of the guppies was menaced by the opposition, the observer has since removed them to another aquarium where healthful conditions prevail, in the hope that the male will be encouraged to resume his researches. But as his increasing recourse to private language suggests, he may have suffered too deep a disappointment.

The first aquarium is still under study, but a limiting condition has made itself apparent in the stench which has begun to rise from the water. This may soon render close observation impracticable.

[1950]

GEORGE

"'BODIES BORE ME. A WOMAN'S BODY EXCITES IN ME nothing more than a vague pity. There is something pathetic in a body, the way it looks at you—there's an expression about the navel and the nipples, any part of a woman's body which resembles eyes (to say nothing of their eyes). Do you see what I mean?' He pointed to her. 'What could be more absurd? No, at times like this, I tell you, I ache, I ache all over to be a pure intelligence.'

"I remember these words, they made a deep impression on me. I felt something extraordinary was going to happen—even after everything that had already happened. And as soon as my friend George had finished saying this, he looked about the room with that manner he has of saying farewell—a thousand farewells to things of no consequence, tables, chairs, the drinks half drunk, but not once at the naked woman. . . . He cast his farewell glance about the room, and before we could realize that he was actually taking leave of things, he walked out of the window.

"I ran to the window at once—in time to see him land. Fortunately, the apartment was on the first floor, he didn't hurt himself. But there was never a chance of his hurting himself, and had he gone out of a penthouse window, the result would have been the same. He didn't fall, he *settled* to the ground. I was in time to see a little of the wafting movement, as a feather, a leaf—incredibly light!—with which he descended. Right side up, steady on his feet. He adjusted his hat—I should say that he picked it off the table as he was leaving the room—turned up his coat collar and walked off with his characteristic air, preoccupied, eyes to the ground, just as though nothing had happened."

"How do you account for it?" I asked, suspecting a hoax. This is often Stanley's way of getting back at me for some advantage, imagined or real, I may have over him. "How come he landed so lightly?"

"Nothing to it," he replied, and I could feel this was a prepared statement. "Men are often sustained by their doubts."

"Please. I'd like to hear—"

"It's a long story. If you put on some more records and turn the volume down, I'll tell you. There's nothing like talking against a background of music. Especially these days."

"Why these days?—Mozart?"

"Anything, who listens? . . ."

"What have 'these days' got to do with it?"

"Nothing. I'm only trying for epigrams. Ever since George walked out of the window I've been talking nonsense, I'm so envious of him. Now give me a drink. . . .

"It was at a party, everybody was there. George came late, I think he was the last to arrive, and he stayed only an hour; not over an hour and a half at most. That's important, that he was the last to arrive—the party was already in full swing. There was nothing unusual in his behavior. He came in, greeted his friends, poured himself a drink—our hosts had already begun to neglect the company—talked to a few of the girls—

"But I'm telling this wrong. I shouldn't say there was nothing unusual about him—you'll expect miracles."

He paused and took a long time with his drink. His bulging brown eyes—like eyes which had once popped out in wonder and never settled back, though it was undoubtedly a thyroid case, a condition uncommon in men—went over the rim of the glass and furtively about the walls, over the paintings, the books I have, coveting my possessions. A look of disappointed wonder, as of someone who had been waiting in vain for the marvelous to recur, but I could feel all the envy in it. . . .

"You know how parties are. Most of them have no character at all—drinks, dancing, wisecracks, everybody's together, but nothing—no communication—and the party only drives people farther apart. They avoid each other for weeks after one of those parties. Then some do have a sort of character but it's all wrong, and that only makes it worse. A really good party—perhaps there hasn't been one since we were six and played blindman's buff and were too young to know our blessings. This was one of the bad parties. I sensed it from the beginning, and I came early. By the time George arrived there was something positively evil going on. Superficially it was all right, a lot of talk and noise and music in the room, couples dancing, everybody drunk and laughing. But an undercurrent . . . George sensed it immediately. As I say, the party was well along when he came in and it hit him full blast. It's a disease . . ." He blinked his eyes self-consciously, as though to see whether I considered him immune. "People get together, have a few drinks, and before you know it they've caught the infection from one another.

"Everyone was having a 'good time'—that's what made it so repulsive. The married were playing musical chairs with their wives, everybody take the wife on the left; the unmarried might as well have been married, there was no telling them apart. A nasty flirtatiousness that's out of place in the Village. Sex, sex, sex, everything sex, and as vile as it can possibly be. Village parties can be models of decorum; I've been to a great number. This was one of the worst. Decorum, because true Villagers, at their best, are fundamentally serious people. Sensible, relaxed, and above all, responsible. A man sees a woman that he likes—an old friend he's lost sight of, a new girl who's come into the circle. He goes over and talks to her. But a man's not alone in the world, neither is the girl. They both have commitments. That can't be helped. They talk. While they talk, there's a playfulness about the eyes. . . . Each, if he were to be open with the other, would admit that this chance meeting has given him a new purpose in life: contact, the promise of fresh pleasure, human solidarity, call it what you will. It's understood. Also understood is the fact that they each have their own worlds, even if they're the same. That's what's involved when a man and woman come together. It calls for feeling, tact. If the playfulness about the eyes continues, they make a discreet arrangement. A telephone number, an appointment. No one need know. In this act of discretion, even if nothing else happens, they have already known the greatest intimacy. It's one of the highest moments of human experience. The natural feeling of creatures for each other, who know the world for what it is. It's even, if you please, a kind of chastity. . . .

"That's the true Villager at his best. He doesn't drag the bed out in the middle of the floor and go thumping away, in front of God and everybody. He knows what's involved in going to bed with a woman, and she knows it, too—actually, the knowledge flows from her. After all, it's her decision. It's one of the most awe-inspiring things to see, to watch the decision being reached in the first few moments, while the eyes find the range.—All right, I'm incurably romantic!" He had caught me looking at him, surprised that he was capable of such sentiments. I was painfully aware of his bulging eyes.

"At any rate, that's your best example. The rest of them, oh what pigs! There they were, leering and wiggling, reciting dirty limericks and copping a feel. High school at its worst. No, college—in a small town—the inbred, incestuous finger-diddling of the faculty and their wives. Screaming their frustrations, a rage of impotence. No tact, no discretion, no hope, nothing in the eyes, which are bleary and wasted-looking, streaked with blood. Right out in the open, damn you, that each may bloat himself on the

244 ~⌐ ISAAC ROSENFELD

other's chagrin and meanwhile keep an eye on his partner, the other's license justifying his own. And nothing will come of it. A hangover, nothing more. The concupiscence is preserved intact. Until next time, the next party, when it will again come screaming out, only to be shelved once more, with a headache, among the thousand hypocrisies of a conventional life. Really, I'm ashamed for my friends.

"Now picture all this as it was when George arrived. Our hosts' two children, wakened by the noise, were locked in one of the bedrooms and crying most of the time. Someone had already been sick and had passed out. There were already a few broken records, cigarette butts and ashes were mixed with the gin. The house already had that overheated, disorderly look, all the freshness had gone out of it, that look of weary horror houses take on in accordance with events. And there was an explosion coming.

"Phil and Martha, you may have heard of them. Martha left her husband about a year ago to have an affair with Phil, and of course Sam, Martha's husband, was there. Husbands are always invited to these parties—or maybe somebody brought him. Sam was watching every move they made, and everybody else who was not too drunk to keep his eyes in focus was watching the three of them. Phil and Martha were dancing in a violent way—I can't describe it, it's a form of quarreling. They've been on the verge of breaking up. At one point they must have insulted each other, they always do. She loves it. It gives her an illicit little thrill to see how far she can drive the man. Suddenly, he struck her, slapped her, smack on the cheek. You could hear it. She fought back with her nails. Some people jumped in to separate them. Sam remained in his chair, staring at them as he had been doing all along, with the same smirk on his face.

"I can't tell you what led to the next outburst. Gloria. Maybe it was a simple fretting at inattention—she had lost the initiative earlier in the evening and had been sulking *hors de combat,* giving off an occasional shriek at someone's obscenities. Maybe she once had or still has that feeling for Phil that I was talking about, only he never came to her or she to him in silence and discretion as people should when their eyes meet. I don't know what combination it was of humiliation, rage, or shame, envy of Martha or of Phil, love and hatred of them both. Or maybe it was even directed at Sam—who knows what these motives can be? But the two of them were no sooner separated, with people standing about them on either side of the room, shushing them, holding them back, and covering up—it was an accident, a mistake, a joke—a third detachment hovering over Sam to keep him in one piece—and all of them hopping with excitement as though they had just seen the ultimate excess of transgression—than Gloria got up on the expiring end of a shriek, stepped into the light of the clearing that had been made by the rush of people to opposite sides of the room—and began to remove her clothes.

"She went at it methodically, righteously, with a firmness of duty (I saw it all from the beginning), as though she were undressing to go early to bed, in need of a good night's sleep. She unbuttoned the neck of her dress without any particular show of violence and not the least evidence of lewd intent. She even removed a few pins from her hair, and I saw her swallow her lips, as women will do, not to smear her dress with lipstick before she pulled it over her head. But she threw the dress out on the floor. This had a little defiance in it—and it caught the public attention. From that moment they never took their eyes off her. They saw her standing in her slip—and a few people, detaching themselves from the previous shock, rushed up to restrain her. 'What are you doing?' I heard them say. 'Gloria! For God's sake!'

"She held them off with her determination, stepped out of her slip and bent to unfasten her stockings from her girdle. She went fast. There was no haste in it, but no delay. She kicked off her shoes, rolled off her stockings, and letting her underpants fall around her bare feet, stepped out of them, moving over the heap of clothes to the center of the room. She was now in her girdle and brassière. She also had a string of pearls round her neck; I hadn't noticed them before.

"Our host and hostess came running. They had long since abandoned their function, forgotten the drinks, the crackers and cheese. This revived them. Mary, a big woman, stood over Gloria, as though to hide her nakedness, and Aaron stood by, divided in his own lechery between a sense of responsibility and a desire to peep. This was true of all the men. I make no exception of myself (although I have the advantage over the rest while I'm telling the story). Gloria brushed Mary aside and stepped in front of her. This was the one difficulty her determination had to face; she made it, and her sense of power, of sheer will having its way, which I am sure had never been so great in all her life, only gained from the encounter. Off came her brassière, this, too, flung on the floor. At the last she was having a little trouble wriggling out of her girdle, and all the while she was peering about the room, probably to locate Phil. She's quite nearsighted. Then she stood naked.

"I don't know if you've ever seen a woman naked under such circumstances. You get a curious impression—first of all, surprise. If you've never before seen the woman's body it surprises you— the actual moment of nakedness is startling, that's true in every case. Now there was a gasp—and silence. In this silence, the record which had been playing while Phil and Martha danced still ran on, and you could hear the kids crying in their room. But the moment passed, it became a fact. She stood with full and hanging breasts, the necklace dividing them, on stout thighs, dimpled at the buttocks and wider across the hips than you would have expected from her clothes. Her pubic hair was oddly at an angle and several shades darker than the hair on her head. But it wasn't only her nakedness that was startling—it was the fact that she had it all to herself. An absolute difference—the rest of us were dressed. It was such an odd thing—like dragging mortality into the open. No, hardly that. I can't describe it, I never have got it straight in my mind. I've seen models in life class, but that's altogether different. Here it was as though Gloria's uncovered body were saying something—but God knows what. About Martha and Phil, no doubt, but she had entirely superseded them. About her own frustrations, the misery of sex—the same sort of shrieking statement that everybody had been making that night at the party—but with this difference, that what Gloria was saying was absolutely true. Too true, no one wanted to be reminded of it, whatever it was

"No one got the meaning, not even George, though he must have felt it in his bones. And not Gloria for sure. Everyone was too embarrassed, caught between looking and peeking. I don't care how sophisticated they're supposed to be—every single soul at that party was terribly embarrassed. Here they were looking, and mind you, at the same time *peeping*—the men, at any rate. Looking at what was unmistakably the fact of a woman's naked body—which by now was something huge and dominating, and had grown to the proportions of a colossus. But right out from under that bland, knowing, winking, appraising, blasé, and wrinkled little mask of indifference that they made themselves wear—oh yes, we know all about it, put on your clothes, you'll catch cold my dear—every last one of them was stealing a glance, anxious for his own virility. The married and the unmarried, the lenten and uxorious alike. You could hear it crackle in them, these brave cocksmen. Man, this is it! Oh baby, mama, WOWEE—Look! Then why was it that their blood ran no warmer, that they felt no stir, not a trickle even, and were it not for the flagellation each of them undertook to beat his maleness to attention, this exposure to the absolute would have left no mark at all? Because they don't know. They don't know what sex is, neither man's nor woman's. Nor do I. While I tell you this I'm master of the scene, and judge of all, but I'm lying. I, too, don't know. Or I forgot at that moment what it was, that without the playfulness of love about the eyes, there is no sex, no male or female and no joining them, and nakedness is nothing but a surrender to violence, as Gloria's was, exposure to a rain of blows!

"Oh, it was intolerable. I'm taking a long time telling you this, but it was over in a minute or two. No one could have borne it any longer. Already there were giggles and wisecracks (but mind you, no obscenities! No one had the courage of his lechery) and the ones who took it the worst—to be sure, Phil and Martha among them, in a rage—had settled on the proper discount: Really, this is so dated! Just like the thirties, don't you know . . .

"It was then that George said and did what he did.—But you've got to know about George. You've never met him?"

"Once, long ago."

"When he was in his prime. Then you have an impression of the man. Mind you, I make no case for him. He's neurotic, sick. Look at it one way, and walking out of a window was just another in a string of eccentricities, like the time he walked across the subway tracks at Times Square, and not even on a dare. Or the years he spent in a basement on Perry Street, smoking the tea, or his crazy marriage. You've probably heard all that. But one thing about George, he knows. He knows what it is to go up to a woman, and his eyes always come alive. He's a model of decorum, of reserve, he has feelings, he knows what the world's like. Not that he hasn't done many mean, stupid, even cruel things in his time, but he has the morality of a bandit chieftain—where you'd least expect it—a sense of justice, of life. Watch him sometime at a party, watch how he handles people. You'll see what I mean.

"I could tell. The moment he came into this party he knew it wasn't for him. It offended him—he's been fighting against it all his life, this frantic, dirty spirit, this misery they were all so full of that night. It wasn't that these were the wrong people, that he didn't belong. He knew all of them, they were all his friends. And it's not even that he's older. Some of the men, and it wouldn't surprise me if even a few of the women, are older than he. It's just that he's been through this and has put it behind him. Detached himself, clean.

"When he saw what was going on, it must have disappointed him deeply—he always looks forward to parties. I could see he wanted to leave. Still, he was among friends, some of whom he hadn't seen in months. He went up to them, he tried to make contact, he met some of his old girls, found a few new ones. It was no good. They were all putting him off.

"And he saw what was coming. He saw the violence between Phil and Martha—as he had seen it all along. He predicted the affair, and explained her motives, and Phil's and Sam's, and it all worked out as he said. Not that he's such a genius, and don't think he doesn't make mistakes. He simply has contact. That night he even took Phil and Sam aside and tried to talk to them—one at a time, of course—and he even said a few words to Martha, whom he's never been able to stand. It didn't help.

"When Phil hit Martha in the face, he was the only one who didn't run up to take sides, shushing and clucking like a hen. He looked to see what Gloria would do. It was because I saw him do this that I set my eyes on Gloria and saw her strip act from the beginning. A pained expression came over his face—this he hadn't expected. He looked at her while she stood naked with the real man's look in his eyes, as he had done before, as he does with all his girls, but it was no use. Gloria was too far gone, and besides, she's nearsighted. She may not even have known he was there.

"The people hadn't recovered from the first shock, and now they were having another. He stood by. He would have tried to do something, but they were all against him, they had rejected him. When the giggles and wisecracks began to come, he turned away quietly and got his hat and coat. He came back into the room in his coat. His old girl Gloria was naked, and he had his overcoat on. He laid the hat down on the table and turned to her once more.

"But his spirit gave out. It was all too ugly, too insane. He couldn't stand the men ogling her impotently, the women picking her figure to pieces. It was then that he spoke—in a loud voice, it carried over the phonograph record, the giggling and the comments, the children crying in their room. It wasn't a premeditated statement, not even a good one. He was too provoked. When he said, 'Bodies bore me,' that wasn't what he meant to say—it was even cruel—or when he said, 'I ache to be a pure intelligence,' that wasn't right either—far from it. It was even ridiculous—it had too much pique in it, too much hurt pride at being overlooked, bypassed, his influence spurned. But does it matter? What he meant came through in spite of it all. It's even a credit to his integrity that he said something foolish. He said it, that was enough.

"Then he walked to the window, on the way picking up his hat and setting it straight on his head. The window was partly open—it was one of those high windows, more like a glass door. He flung it up and walked through.

"Does it matter that this may have been a stunt, after all? That having witnessed the first climax of the evening in the fight between Martha and Phil, only to see it surpassed by Gloria, he had determined to cap them all with a climax they'd talk about for years? (After taking his bearings and reassuring himself he was on the first floor.) Does it matter that he didn't come lightly wafting down, as I said, but landed with a crash and lost his hat—another few feet and he would have killed himself for sure? As it was, he was laid up with a sprained ankle, but it's a credit to him—this I did see; we all ran to the window, even the naked Gloria—that he picked himself up and walked off, without a limp. And without looking back. . . ."

He had talked himself out. We sat and listened to the records; Mozart. Stanley drained off the rest of his drink and once more his eyes went over the rim of the glass, stealing over my belongings. But this time the envy did not immediately appear: he was too full of admiration for George, still too close to him. He regarded me sadly with his bulging, watery eyes, eyes that could never look at a woman with playfulness in them. But for the moment, sharing George's power, he was exempt, and still oblivious to the pain of his discipleship.

[1952]

CONEY ISLAND REVISITED

IT WAS NOT UNTIL THE OTHER DAY, WHEN I RETURNED ON a visit to Coney Island, that I recalled an important episode of my youth which had been buried all these years. The recollection shocked me; I had forgotten that I was once capable of doing such things. It made me think, not that I had come a long way, but that I had started very far back, farther perhaps than most.

I was standing outside the phony spook show when I realized something I had known all along, that eighteen years ago I had worked there. Curiosity had brought me on an idle afternoon; I had been away from the city for several years, and had set myself the program, not quite deliberately, of revisiting old scenes as a way of getting back in touch. Coney was nearly last on the list. I never thought much of the job I had had there—it was summer work between my first and second years in college. Oh, I expected to see Sam, who ran the show, and maybe George the barker, and Vittorio from the aquarium next door and Bill Levi from the Whip around the corner. Not once did I think of Gladys. Sam, I learned, was dead; the aquarium had closed and been replaced by a shooting gallery, and the Whip, like the spook show, was still operating, but under new management, and no one remembered Bill Levi. It was only after I had spotted the kid in the beanie who took tickets, relieved the barker, and poked around in the machinery that I remembered Gladys, and I remembered her by way of myself, for the kid in the beanie was just what I had been. The last thing I expected to meet on Coney Island was anything related to myself; as I say, I never took the place seriously. But when I had made my inquiries and learned what I might have known to begin with, that everyone was gone, and found myself betrayed into foolishness ("Step aside, Mac, can't ya see the people wanna geddin?") I realized I might possibly have been asking after something of a deeper order; and then I saw the kid, who confirmed this suspicion.

He was sneering, just as I used to do in the old days, and no doubt for the same reason: because the summer was hot, and the work hard, sweaty, and irritating, stretching over long hours for poor pay. It was absolutely indispensable, now as it was then, to separate oneself from the job—one had to have a little ledge to stand on all to himself; otherwise perish. I used to pitch this ledge very high. The higher I stood, the greater my contempt, and the more precious the moments of freedom I won for myself by this trick of balancing above the crowd. I remembered how I used to mix T. S. Eliot with my spiel (in those days there was hardly anyone in freshman English who did not know a good deal of *The Waste Land* by heart): "Step right up ladies and gentlemen mingling memory with desire for the greatest thrill show on earth only a dime the tenth part of a dollar will bring you to Carthage then I came burning burning burning O Lord thou pluckest me out ten cents!" Or when I was fooling with the machinery I would pretend there was a part stuck which had to be lubricated by spittle, and I would wait until some jerk stood before me, just as I now stood before the kid, to spew a mouthful of saliva into the smoking straps of the machine. When he sneered at me it all began to come back.

I became more fully conscious of the mechanical dummy twitching its chest in laughter, at once seeing and remembering how also in those days we had a contraption outside the entrance dressed, not as this was to resemble a clown, but much more effectively in a split dress with ropes going round it, to represent a young woman captive in a torture chamber in token of the spooky torment within.

He, hee, hee, ho, ho, ho, ohh, oww, ha, ha, ha, he, an endless hysteria, endlessly revolving; and I remember the quotation from Schopenhauer with which I used to struggle for detachment from the job: "A man's capacity to endure noise stands in inverse proportion to his intelligence." These may not be the exact words, but in the old days, you may be sure, I had them right. In this moment of doubled consciousness, joining myself to the kid in our sneering, sweaty detachment, an old fantasy of mine came back. I used to wonder, in the hours spent listening to the dummy with its overtones of torture and sexual perversion (death by tickling; bare feet, armpits, private parts; finger, feather, velvet whip), what, I used to wonder, would be the case if one always had to live here in this noise for a whole twenty-four hours a day, seven days to the week, month after month—not the mere ten hours or so that I took in a day? I imagined a man tied to his seat in a roller coaster: would this man live? I saw him chained to the Cyclone or Thunderbolt, taking the huge dips and nauseous, clattering turns over and over again, without a moment's break, the wind knocked out of him, the world turning round and round in a swirl of broken images, spokes, wheels, girders and beams, a revolving Meccano set, with the rat-tat-tat and pop and bam of the shooting galleries, and the insane, insufferable HO, HO, HO, of our demonic female masochist forever ripping in his ears. He can't get off his roller coaster, there's no stopping it, and no *coup de grâce* on which he can count to put an end to his suffering after a week, a month, a year of agony. Strangely enough, I always saw him surviving. Somehow he would manage to hold his spirit together, recover himself, and draw a free breath, perhaps in the moment when the coaster paused at the top of the first high climb. With his head knocking on his collarbone, he would even manage to sleep of a night, dreaming of the ocean, of gliding through space. This man would live. . . . And now at last when I re-entered the old fantasy with which I used to flatter my heroism, I remembered Gladys for the first time in years.

Where the shooting gallery stands there used to be an aquarium, built like an underground garage with a sloping ramp down which the suckers walked to a RARE AND THRILLING SPECTACLE OF MAN-EATING SHARKS ELECTRIC EELS GENERATING A CHARGE OF 3000 VOLTS ENOUGH TO KILL A MAN AND RARE BEAUTIFUL TROPICAL FISH GATHERED FROM THE AMAZON AND OTHER REMOTE CORNERS OF THE UNIVERSE AND SHOWN FOR THE FIRST TIME IN CONEY ISLAND OR ANYWHERE IN THE UNITED STATES STEP RIGHT UP . . . this was Gladys's spiel. She stood with a microphone in a little glass booth next to the ticket cage. Her unpleasant voice, because she held the mike too close, came over the P.A. speaker with the whine of a drill; and whatever was not unrecognizably distorted came through in a blaring Brooklyn, full of transposed *oi*'s and *er*'s, every vowel a diphthong. I found her when I came on the job, heard her hour after hour, except for occasional breaks, and felt I would go mad if I had to go on hearing that voice. Our own noise I somehow grew accustomed to; perhaps it was the habit I soon fell into of inventing images to accompany the sounds of torment and delight. But Gladys' voice was intolerable, and her appearance—I had a clear view of her, usually in three-quarter profile and from the waist up—her appearance was precisely as I should have imagined it in my snobbery and rage. From that voice alone I might have deduced the staring, blankly impudent green eyes, loaded with mascara and arched over with a stripe of black pencil; the expressionless, heavily powdered face, dead white down to the neck, and the rest of her visible skin, her shoulders and thin arms, very brown, though I don't know how the sun reached her in the booth; the young, pointed bosom, which infuriated me (she was, I should say, sixteen, no more than seventeen), moving me to nothing like tenderness but to violent thoughts. At once I gathered my hatred of Coney Island and all its vulgarity into the image of this stupid young girl: she became for me the body and voice of everything meretricious.

I must have endured no more than two days of her shrilling. Certainly it was not much later than the third day when I found myself screaming over our own barker and the maniacal laughter, trying to shout her down. SHUT UP FOR GOD'S SAKE SHUT UP! I caught her attention at once. Her voice stopped in the middle of the endlessly revolving sentence, she held the microphone away from her chin, and into this girl's impudent blank eyes there came the hint of an expression of wisdom and amusement. She answered me, moving her lips without a sound, and indicating the captive woman who howled at my side. I don't know what her lips spelled out but the sense of it must have been, we're in the same boat, mister. There was no other possible answer. To my great unease, I felt at that moment that Gladys was vastly my superior.

There were still many days before I would feel desire for her; I still had so much snobbery to live down, and had not yet discovered that in desiring Gladys there lay a snobbery which I might live up to. But at once I entered into the relationship which she had fixed, and began to communicate with her in dumb show. I communicated only my disgust in syllables of imprecation; but I had my lips and teeth and the tip of my tongue working in her direction, and she answered these communications, as though they were made in a language she was master of, sometimes with a smile or a grimace, sometimes with a silently mouthed sentence, but always with the knowledge of a sexual tradition against which I had no defense.

Then it happened that we took a walk once after hours, going along the boardwalk and down to the sand. I was unprepared for this, and in my capitulation was brought to desire that very same vulgarity, the image of which I had so despised in her. From then on my communications changed: I entreated her, in the same silent lip-language, begging for dates, walks in the sand, and she would often go right on shrilling at her microphone about man-eating sharks until I had made the same request three, four times over; when she would address her answer, so that I might be at some trouble to catch it, to the viciously tormented dummy which jerked in my sight all day.

This relationship was what every college man desires, a liaison with a girl of inferior rank and intelligence—it is only from girls of this sort that they will not consider it beneath their dignity to humble themselves enough to learn. This does not justify me; what does (if it does) is the fact that, for a time, she burned the snobbishness out of me (only to burn it in deeper) so that I was hot with my whole sexual nature for every trace and gesture that her body registered of what I had taken for mere vulgarity. The broadly smeared lipstick, extending in a false Cupid's bow over part of her upper lip, through which, on hot days, oozed drops of her sweat, the mascaraed eyes, the powdery face, the pointed breasts, forced into a tight, unnatural brassière, the ill-matched barrettes and bobby pins with which she kept the curls and waves in her scanty, limp hair, the clichés, the mispronunciations, the intrusion of *he-sez, she-sez, I-sez* which made an incantation of her speech—all these traits revealed a double meaning, linked no longer with noises and spinning lights alone, but also with moments of silence in the damp sand at night, when I heard only the surf, roaring like lions, and the little cries which I had not known it was in a girl's nature to make. Then I might almost have yielded up my proud and foolish battle of Coney Island in which the conquest of Gladys was a victory for me. I might almost have fallen away, as she did when making love, from awareness of everything that divided us. Many times when we went naked for a night swim, I had the feeling that the waves meant to wash me clean of this. But during the day the sight of Gladys provoked me to a rage of lust, as though it were really vengeance I was after. There lay a vicious satisfaction in the thought, which came to me often in the midst of our turmoil, that after working hours I would have this girl in the sand, under the boardwalk in a spot (she must have gone there with other lovers; many couples kept their trysts in the same place) which a little connivance with the police who patrolled the beach secured to the use of the Coney Island staff. And her voice continued to infuriate me as it rose above all the other noises that made me ask whether life under such conditions was possible.

As I grew bolder I made strange demands, wanting to exploit my conquest to the full. I insisted that she insert lines and tag ends from the poems I knew into her pitch; this she refused to do, she objected to the mockery. But when I rewrote her spiel, filling it with polysyllabic words, she gladly accepted the revision for its elegance. I went to the trouble, not only because it amused me to hear her stumble over the words, but because, when this girl used expressions of any degree of abstractness, it excited me inordinately. I made a parody of our position, and when I brought her things to read, in place of books to improve her mind I presented her with pulp and movie magazines, a stack of which she had already gone through on her own. So also with the gifts I made her of the cheapest trinkets and perfumes. Much of this escaped her, and I took care not to be too subtle; but when she caught the cruelty, she thought she must have failed to satisfy me, and thrust herself into a deeper and deeper ardor on the sand.

And then I hit on my most daring scheme of all, which was to have us retire to the spook-house for our love-making. Gladys agreed even to this. She thought the proposal horrible, but it must have seemed to her that I was testing her courage or her loyalty, and she met it with an eagerness greater than my own.

This required care. It would be necessary to do it during hours, while the cars, in which the customers sat, came crashing along the dimly lit walls; there was no point to it with lights out. We arranged to accumulate breaks so that we would have half an hour coming at the end of the day, and all day long we questioned each other, moving our lips through the noise, "Would you have the nerve?" "Would you?"

"What if they see us?" asked Gladys, when I stopped for a moment outside her booth.

"They'll think it's part of the show."

An ordinary excursion to the beach lacked relish now. I was proud of my daring, I hadn't thought I would be able to go so far. But all of that day, as our eyes met, I saw in the looks Gladys gave me a meaning I hadn't intended at all.

At last I heard her conclude her recitation about fish and saw her hand the mike to an assistant and make her way round the corner to the hot dog stand, where I followed her, as though we were going for refreshment. She took my hand.

"Would you like something to drink?" I asked her. She shook her head.

I led her down an alley to the back end of our concession, where we came to a trap door the men used when they made repairs on the moving track that shunted the cars along.

"Should we . . . ?" asked Gladys, before we went down.

"Should we what?"

"Go the limit," she whispered, and squeezed my hand.

"You're not quitting?"

"No, but I thought maybe—" She interrupted herself and leaned down over the trap door to kiss me.

It was dark inside and smelling of oil. We groped in the underground passage for the ladder and climbed up to the ghostly blue light, waited for a car, loaded with men and women shrieking like idiots, to pass, and ran along the ledge behind one of the many walls in which ghosts and skeletons swayed in niches. I had given thought to it and selected the place well—a rather wide platform at one of the turns in the track, dark except when a car passed, when lights would flash on, with a ringing of bells and rattling of chains and the swooping down of a mechanical bat, to show a decomposing body rising from a coffin, red bulbs blinking in the eye sockets and bony hands reaching to tear at the spectators' hair. We waited in the darkness, Gladys whimpering in fright, but whispering, "Go ahead, honey, I don't care if they see us." My hands were cold and wet. The track rattled on; at the last turn there was the hoot of an owl and then a shot as the last car crashed out through the swinging doors. Down the track lights blinked, blue and green as in the subway, and a huge mechanical spider made its way back and forth along the wall. The laughter of the dummy echoed back into the room.

I had lost heart for it and was thinking only to get out, but Gladys, loosening her clothes and fumbling at mine, kept urging me in a whisper. Another car came crashing in, and the lights and screams and contrivances of murder and strangulation began to operate. We lay tight in each other's arms and my eyes were shut. The carload of people came shrieking by, shrieking, for all I knew, at us. Soon another car bore down. We held on, pressed against the wall, and Gladys was slowly beating her fist in my chest. After a while, suddenly the ceiling lights went on and Sam, the owner, trailing cobwebs and a length of gauze, came running along the ledge to catch us half naked, Gladys still urging me, "Go ahead, you coward, give it to me," with a venom I had never thought she might feel toward me. . . .

I had walked away from the concessions. Now I found myself on the boardwalk, looking out over the beach, the bathers of a thousand arms and legs, the surf, the sea wall. . . . the reliving of this experience came to an end when I realized that I no longer heard the dummy's frenzied, tickled HO-HO in my ears. I came to, shocked to think I should ever have been capable of doing such things; but in the intervening years, how much had I altered? Had I really made my way to freedom? I continued to look out, my eyes reaching for the silence of the ocean.

[1953]

WOLFIE

⌒

1. *Das ewig Weibliche zieht uns hinan*

It was long a wonder how Wolfie managed to live. He was one of the most miserable creatures in the Village, without a friend, everywhere ridiculed, scorned, and despised; and utterly poor, the clothes on his back were his entire wealth. These were a blue suit, which looked greenish in the light, a blue workman's shirt of the kind worn more often by sympathizers than by actual workers, and a dusty brown overcoat covered with lint and chicken feathers, such as one picks up from a leaky pillow. With the overcoat he frequently wore a knitted scarf or muffler (maroon, as I recall); his mother must have knitted it for him. By the way he wore it and by its soft woolly look, one could tell that Wolfie was very fond of the muffler and that he derived a certain psychological warmth from it the way a child will who insists on going to bed with a particular blanket or animal made of cloth. It was a great big fringed, fluffy thing—you may have seen Continental students wear them with one turn and the ends hanging loose, front and back. Wolfie wore it all wrapped round his neck in many turns, and it gave him a very sickly appearance.

Perhaps his family, who lived in Nebraska, sent him money. But it can't have been much, and I don't know how he picked up enough for his needs. He had no regular job. Though he had a master's degree in sociology (from Omaha), no school would hire him, not even the Rand School for evening lectures. Apart from his review of a book on trade unions in the *Old Guard,* he never appeared in print. From time to time he may have got a few meager ghosting commissions, and during the various fund-raising campaigns may have persuaded the editors to take him on as a letter writer. To be sure, no one actually thought of Wolfie as a writer, but he managed to maintain a vaguely literary air, mostly by gossiping about writers.

But he was a big *macher,* with his air of fantastic enterprise and the squinty leer with which he kept the Village informed of activities in the intellectual world. It was always as though he had it fresh, his elbows still warm from the rubbing. Politics, literature, swindles of all sorts, the very hottest and the latest; wherever there was conniving, cheating, grifting, horning, or plain adultery, Wolfie had it, steaming bucketsful right from the horse's behind. Reliable information, he had clippings to prove it; the knotted orange-paper accordion-pleated envelope under his arm was stuffed with the goods. Making allowances for misrepresentation in transit, a tip from Wolfie was sound, you could stake shoes and collar on it and your daughter's education. The very people who made fun of him to his face—and who didn't?—stood in fear of him, knowing perfectly well that if they had anything to hide he would find it, if he had not already done so. But they never treated him with respect, no one did.

Because it was impossible. The kinky filaments that grew sparse and woebegone on his head (thick only over the ears), the battered, tufted, boxer's eyebrows, the cunning, pale, fearful eyes, the broad nose, the cornetist's pursed red lips with spittle in the corners, and the pitted face invited mockery, and that was his portion. So I imagine he must have had a correspondingly swollen notion of his own true worth; surely he paid people out from an enormous fund of self-regard. The flying spittle and the exhalations that accompanied his stories were aimed in retribution for the neglect he suffered, and his greatest contempt, naturally, was reserved for those who dared to be friendly and benevolent, who would stand him a bottle of beer in payment for his gossip. He must have thought of himself as a highly trained mind, and a poet.

Wolfie did actually generate a poetic atmosphere as he stood on street corners or at bars, surrounded by several, telling his stories. The girls of whom he spoke underwent transfiguration. He would dribble and leer like a rutting satyr, and from his thick lips would pour legends of good women: Helen, Cressida, Queen Guinevere—dancers, models, art students, receptionists, hostesses, housewives, and the ones who posed for photographs, all taken with a tropical blossoming of nubility, so that you could even catch their scent in the air. He had their phone numbers and addresses in a little book, and loved to riffle the pages while he talked. All their intimate and cunning secrets he had wiretapped, and you could hear them whisper and moan within his grating voice. All their downy parts stood forth from his recitation and everything, that was rose-tinted, soft, and volcanic. He lost himself in a rapturous ogling and waved his little book in their air, not able, and eventually not caring, to conceal the smart and smirking hurt of his disappointments, while antlers popped and branched on his head. And while he talked of the feminine and the grin split wider over his face, his audience, sooner or later, to a man, would be oppressed, as by too heavy an air, too thick a perfume—they were all vulnerable. An image of the feminine would tease their eyes, and even the oldest veterans of the chase would come to feel something of Wolfie's own smart at beauty and the quest of love.

He waved his book under our noses, he sneered at us and observed our temptation, but at last he was unable to resist giving out the numbers and addresses. This would consume hours, whole evenings, but in the end—not that anyone wore him down, he would come to it of his own accord—he would part with the information and send the more successful men as envoys of his lechery. Days later, when he met them in the street, he would suck out the details.

He had no girl of his own, not really. Late at night, when the crowds were leaving the bars and cafés, Wolfie, done with his rounds, would sometimes call on a widow, the mother of an eleven-year-old boy, a rather heavy woman, who lived in a basement on 22nd Street. He would timidly knock on her door, never sure of his reception; she was always cross when he woke her. Sometimes, when she was alone, she would let him in, after calling, "Just a minute, honey, let me put something on," and appear, in a wrapper and curlers, heavier than he remembered her, her feet broad and flat in carpet slippers. Scowling if he had brought no present ("At least a bottle of beer, my mouth feels dry at night"), she would lead him through the small apartment, hung with mottoes and pictures of the martyrs, to her bedroom, which was separated by no more than a curtain from the alcove in which her son slept. The boy would often whimper in his sleep, and his mother would go to him, to return cursing. "God damn it, he's wet the bed again. Get up, Wolfie, change him!" And Wolfie would get up.

2. The Other

But the real misery of Wolfie's life was not poverty, women, or ill favor, it was Falkenberg. This was a gentleman, a few years older than he, who lived by misfortune in the same rooming house as Wolfie, where he occupied a three-room apartment. (Wolfie had but a single room, with a hot plate and washstand in the closet.) Although Falkenberg looked like a death's-head with his huge forehead, concave cheeks, and prominent teeth, he was conscientiously devoted to the life of pleasure, made a great success of it, and was known for his exploits. He taught social theory at a number of establishments and occasionally appeared in the professional journals, and rather looked the part with his conservative dark suits and English shirts, and the handkerchief in his breast pocket that went with tie and socks. From the habit of lecturing, he had acquired the expectation of profound silence, attention, and respect when he talked, whether he said good evening on the staircase or appeared at Wolfie's door, which was opposite his own, to borrow a cup of sugar or a match. Each word of his fell in place, like a row of even teeth, and the whole utterance was grave and precise, according to the method of science. He spoke slowly, as though to allow people time to take notes, and with an ironic twist, having plainly been intended for better things.

Wolfie started it, he picked up Falkenberg's spoor when the professor moved into the house and went among his friends with an excellent imitation, sucking in his cheeks, patting himself on the breast, and saying, "Hmmm-hmm-mmm-cough cough." This was quite harmless, but within a week, Wolfie, who had learned something of Falkenberg's habits and was therefore on the watch, managed to meet him three nights running on the staircase and twice in the hall, each time with a different girl. Falkenberg gravely said good evening with a pause after the words before he moved on. Wolfie replied in the same gravity and added a bow; then flew down the stairs to bring news to the world. He was delighted in his neighbor.

But these meetings continued, and Falkenberg, who knew nothing of Wolfie and cared to know less, soon discovered that something was afoot. Wolfie's face would pop out at him, squinting and sneering and breathing at the girls, and its expression frightened him; it seemed, by his own decorous standards, so insane. He made his own inquiries and when he learned who Wolfie was he decided to deal firmly with the man. The next time they met—it was on the staircase and Falkenberg was accompanied by a young lady, probably from one of his classes; Wolfie had seen them together once before—the professor was very curt with him. He did not return Wolfie's greeting or step aside to make room for him on the stairs, but planted himself in the way and thrusting a terribly disdainful pale face into his, exclaimed, "You will please confine yourself henceforth to a polite form of address, and make no further insinuations!" Wolfie was stunned. He stumbled, blushed, found no reply, and slunk obediently down the stairs. At the landing he looked up prepared, at least, to do an imitation, but the professor presented him with a gray homburg and a frigid back, and the girl, with a pair of pleasant legs, visible, on the staircase, well up to her thighs.

The following morning, while Wolfie was still in bed, there came a knock on the door. Wolfie had no real existence in the morning, it took him hours to shake off sleep; besides, he had trouble with his eyes, which were swollen and gummy when he woke up, so that he could hardly open them. He knew this was Falkenberg (early though it was, he pictured him in the gray homburg and even imagined that he was knocking with a cane) so he pretended to be asleep and shut his eyes once more. The knock was repeated, several times; Falkenberg even cried, "Open up!" and tried the handle of the door. Wolfie groaned, pushed himself out of bed, reached for his dusty overcoat, which was lying on a chair, slipped it over his shoulders, and in his bare feet and underwear, picked his way over the mass of papers, cups, and soiled linen which was strewn over the floor.

Falkenberg was not wearing his homburg. He was in a tasseled dressing gown and patent leather slippers; his hair was plastered wet over his skull and an odor of toothpaste and shaving cream came from his face. He took one step into the room and checked himself. Wolfie, as though plugged into his nerves, felt Falkenberg undergo shock at finding himself in so dark, small, and disorderly a room, so dirty and close-smelling; he felt Falkenberg's horror, as though he had roused a hibernating bear in a clothes closet, or wandered into the den of a predatory beast, cluttered with ribs. "What do you want?" said Wolfie, barring the way, but his voice was smothered in hoarseness and he could smell his own foul breath. His eyes smarted and ran.

"I would like to clarify our relationship," said Falkenberg, setting one arm akimbo, as he probably did in the lecture room. "Last night I found it necessary to speak sharply to you. (Pause.) I hope this will not again be necessary. There is no reason why we should not be on friendly, that is on gentlemanly terms. Now I would like to borrow a couple of eggs."

"Eggs," said Wolfie, stupidly.

"Yes. Two." A sudden little complacent smile twitched between his mandibles and caused nauseous envy to run through Wolfie. He caught himself looking for marks, signs on Falkenberg's freshly shaved and lotioned face, in his self-satisfied eyes. "If you please," added Falkenberg, quite politely, but with a touch of impatience.

Wolfie went to the window sill for the eggs (he had no refrigerator) and handed them over without a word. Falkenberg shot a look at them before accepting the eggs from Wolfie's hand, and with a straightening of his neck and the trace of a nod said, "I thank you. I will repay you," and shut the door.

3. Myra

Falkenberg began to make many appearances at the door, mornings, evenings, at odd hours, coming and going, until it seemed to Wolfie that their positions had been reversed. He came always on a pretext, to borrow something or (occasionally) return what he had borrowed; to inquire what time it was and whether it had turned warmer or colder overnight; and even to send Wolfie on errands, to the drugstore for nosedrops when he had a cold, and to the grocery for grapefruit juice. Hardly a day passed without several such visits. Wolfie began to fear the man, much as Falkenberg had once feared him; he saw his skeletal face everywhere, in crowds, on subways, in advertisements, grinning with teeth, the eyesockets dark with innuendo. Wolfie wondered what he was after—but with half a mind he knew, and his knowledge increased his fear of the man and gave him no rest from sick envy. He now had his own horror—that Falkenberg had caught on to the motive which had driven Wolfie to him in the first place, and was now working it in reverse. He saw it coming in all the calculated insults and academic sarcasms, the lectures on the necessity of retaining the gentlemanly character of their relationship. And when Falkenberg resorted to a patronizing tone, referring to the two of them as men of the world, and flattered Wolfie on the scope and variety of his interests, Wolfie knew he was trapped for good; worse still, by his own devices. Of course, he knew what he wanted—phone numbers! But this was obvious, and for that matter he was welcome to them—let him have Marge and Liz and Betty and even Dorothy Taylor with the red MG, good riddance to them all. Let him drag them, kicking and squealing, to his apartment, singly or in pairs, in sets of three and four, whole clusters and chains of them. Straight to the apartment across the hall, why not—why not all of them at once, for all the good they had ever done Wolfie? He would run to the drugstore, the liquor store and delicatessen, and between errands raid the apartments of all the girls he knew and deliver them up on stretchers. Oh, yes, he knew what he was good for!

He delayed as long as possible, to force Falkenberg into the open. What would he say, the pompous lecher with the Phi-Bete key dangling from his fly? Wolfie played deaf and dumb, really not the faintest idea, oh, you don't say, quite remarkable, pip pip, toodle-oo. And Falkenberg with his grave pauses and precise formulation, pursued him, circling in closer with his tongue out, chewing his homburg in a frenzy. Down on your knees, fatso, mynheer, wheedle, grovel, lick my boots—both of them! Men of the world, eh?

At last Wolfie gave out a phone number, a dud, long defunct, now belonging to a Polish janitor. Falkenberg came running back, he demanded justice, and puffed and spouted with hardly time for pauses: taste, refinement, comradely obligations, the pleasures of civilized life. Wolfie gave him the number of an elderly baby-sitter which had somehow got onto his list, and ducking out before Falkenberg had time to cry fraud, he spent the evening in bars, telling the story for beer. Eventually Wolfie was forced to give out active and desirable phone numbers, and the thing he feared drew nearer.

Now when Falkenberg was coming home with a haul, he would notify Wolfie beforehand and order him to stay off the staircase and well out of sight; and if Wolfie disobeyed the warning, he was haughty and cool, a stranger. But as the girls all knew Wolfie they would stop, on their way to perdition, to say hello and linger for a chat, and frequently wind up introducing the professor to their old friend. Wolfie would acknowledge the introduction graciously, and while Falkenberg sweated with impatience—even in the dark hall Wolfie could see sweat form on his thin upper lip; oh, how it helped him to see this!—he would detain the girls with questions and narrations and, as often as not, warn them of the fate that awaited them in Falkenberg's apartment, and invite them to seek shelter with him. These familiarities outraged Wolfie's neighbor. The girls felt sold, procured. And yet, thought Wolfie, twisting the knife in his own bowels, Falkenberg had his pleasure of them, while he, who had courted them clean, had nothing but a friendly smile. Every morning he had reason to regret his involvement with Falkenberg, when the latter, on his way to class, came to complain and stayed to recount the evening's luck. He would give each girl a rating. Wolfie endured it, gummy-eyed.

"If he were paying me," thought Wolfie in self-disgust, "at least if he were paying me— What am I doing it for?" Enough. He would drive Falkenberg away, expose him to the world, kick him out of the house. He did nothing of the kind. When Falkenberg appeared on a gentlemanly mission, Wolfie bit his tongue and dipped into the book for more numbers. He was willing to undergo this humiliation and help swell the stinking carious heap on Falkenberg's bed, if only by enduring this shame he could acquire the strength to withstand the greatest shame of all, toward which he saw himself heading. But the temptation, which had burned in him from the beginning, only grew stronger, the more he delayed; and he knew that sooner or later he would surrender the phone number, out of the whole long list, of the one girl he had loved.

This was Myra, whom he had met two years ago at a party. He had sat next to her on a crowded couch and at once come into contact with the warmth of her body. Even before he had heard her name and caught more than a hazy impression of her face, he found himself edging away from the touch of her thigh—it was too much for him. Without being aware of it, he had grown used to expect the stiffening of withdrawal. But her eyes participated in the smile she gave him, her cheeks were round and spotted with moles, her nose delicately bifurcated at the cartilage, and brown were her eyes and her hair, mild brown. She listened with interest to his stories, made intelligent answers, and encouraged him with laughter and facial expressions. She did not reject him. (Myra was new in the Village, having just arrived from Pittsburgh.) When he came to the point and asked for her phone number, she gave it easily, naturally, without coyness, a delightful thing. He was left with a mouthful of unused venom and a sneer, drawn in antici-pation of refusal. It was too good to be true, there was a hitch somewhere, but (experienced in these matters) he saw none. She accepted him. She even said something, which he did not precisely catch, about friendship, and her eyes burned welcome. Wolfie recorded the number with a flourish.

All the same he was armored for trouble when he called on her. He would play it cool, with provision, no chance of a fluff-up. But he was overwhelmed: by the burning fireplace, the warm orange glow of the room, the soft tones, the Mexican rug on the couch, ready to be turned back, it seemed to him, surely, at his pleasure; most of all by the spontaneous reproach, better, to his ears, than a thousand endearments, "You're late." He walked in, trembling, to something he had never known.

She exuded friendliness and good intentions, went straight for the heart and spoke so gently to him, with such a homing care for his troubles, that when the time came for the first lunge, Wolfie let it tick away and could not bring himself to scramble after it. Many times he was on the verge of making his pass, as their heads leaned together over photographs, while their finger-nails, on the coffee table or the same square inch of the Mexican rug, beat out the tempo of phonograph records; but each time he hesitated, shoring up another moment, and the load on his chest pressed upon him till his eyes bulged. He had grown still, ox-tongued and thick, but she calmed him with her melo-dious talk, and he had only to listen. Her words were wisdom and enchantment, the substance of hope. For example, employ-ment. When she spoke of her job, copy-editing for a trade journal, and complained of the dullness, he knew how she must be lan-guishing, and he drooled. He licked his lips and his eyes misted over, already he was flourishing on these fruits.

Suddenly he bolted up, almost knocking over the coffee table, and, his face aching with pleasure, clumsily excused himself for a moment's absence and ran to the drugstore—not for contracep-tives. He came in whirling and limp to the perfume counter, the powder puffs, and settled, within his own price range, on a box of chocolate-covered cherries for fifty-nine cents. He returned with the offering wrapped in green paper and tied with white string, but he was pack-laden with Oriental spice. And when

Myra exclaimed, in all sincerity, "Oh, Wolfie, you shouldn't have done it!" and laid a cool hand on his fever, Wolfie was smitten and his donkey ears burned with happiness. This was the girl he was going to marry.

This went on for a while and he let his heart swell. Myra did not tease him or exploit him, she was gentle, kind, and always sincere, and told him truly that she valued his friendship. They went to movies and rode the Staten Island Ferry, ate in Italian and Chinese restaurants, splitting the bill when Wolfie had money, Myra footing it when he had none. They went on late night walks, fingers locked and arms around waists, read poetry aloud, listened to music, told each other about their childhood, and Wolfie, from time to time, gave her instruction in political science, and everything that lay stale in his mind was revived as he talked. Only when he said good night to her did he touch her, briefly. In the fullness of time, he had come to the point of kissing her; he once or twice laid a hand upon her breasts and had even on occasion lifted her dress. But he waited, there was time enough. How much calmer and more patient he had grown, more careful in appearance and so much lighter in his step, and a trace of handsomeness, features and thin hair to the contrary, even began to appear in his face. His happiness made him see things: this was it. He was on the point of looking for a regular job.

And then, one night, Myra asked him not to call again. She was sincere as ever, though she stammered a little. She gave no reason, and begged him, please don't ask me. He gathered up his books and carried them away.

Long Wolfie lay in pain, howling. He beat his knuckles on his bare head, suffered and raged and tortured himself, as he lay awake, with images of Myra's naked body in all the sexual postures and excesses. Their walks, evenings together, whole poems he had memorized, the warmth of her participating eyes—all this rankled in his heart as he saw her in lust with the Mexican rug at last turned back on her couch. Sand through spread fingers. That he, of all people, should have forgotten the law of the chase! That this should have happened to him! He lay in his room at night and feared to go out, where every street reminded him, where the lights of the houses shone with a warm orange glow. Here they had walked, here eaten, there stood at a shop window. . . . The whole world became the visible legend of his loss.

When this diminished, when the crystal, as Stendhal calls it, began to dissolve, the old Wolfie, his eyes swollen and his sneer limbered up, resumed his old habits and returned to his old haunts, where no one, apparently, had missed him. He got back on the beat and once more began to make simultaneous appearances all over town, with his envelope under his arm and the glitter of information in his eyes. He dreaded and longed for the sight of Myra, thinking he must inevitably run into her (Whom would she be with?), but this never happened. Here and there he heard she was with this one, then with that one, it was rumored with still a third, but Wolfie shut his ears and would handle no gossip related to her. So be it, be reconciled, he said to himself. With the season's first cold, he got out his muffler and wound it round his neck.

4 Gettysburg

Two years had passed, but on the day that Wolfie yielded to the evil temptation and gave Falkenberg the phone number, all his anguish was renewed and he saw Myra's face with original clarity. The moment he had given the number, he wanted to recall it, Falkenberg would have been none the wiser. But if he had been capable of doing this, he would not have yielded in the first place. Ah, well, perhaps nothing would come of it. For all he knew, Myra might long since have moved away, she might even have left the city. And even if Falkenberg got in touch with her, that did not necessarily mean she would consent to go out with him; and even if she did consent, that was no proof anything more would come of it. After all, she had once gone out with him, too. . . . No, really, there was no reason to attach such importance to the matter, it had as much likelihood of falling through as any other date. But in his heart Wolfie knew that it was bound to happen; would he have acted as he did if the outcome had not been certain?

He did not wait for Falkenberg to come to him, but went of his own accord and knocked on the professor's door. He had never been in the apartment, and had never been conscious of any desire to enter it, but now that he was in he had to see the whole thing, intimately; he would have loved to poke in all the corners and turn everything upside down. Falkenberg, with an ironical expression, as if to say, "To what do I owe this honor?" admitted him into the living room, where Wolfie remained standing, *lumpen*. Falkenberg's expression changed to annoyance, he frowned as though trying to read small print, and Wolfie took this to mean that the professor was assuming, as the reason for the visit, that he, Wolfie, had come to collect. What was it now, how many eggs? Wolfie kept his own counsel and grinned, rather idiotically. He enjoyed Falkenberg's discomfort at having admitted the predatory beast, the feral man, into headquarters, and he did what he could to prolong it; but at the same time he suffered an embarrassment of his own and felt it leaking out through his pores—he wanted to see the bedroom!

The living room, at any rate, was much as he might have imagined it: drapes, rug, couch, and chair; the books stacked in cases on either side of the fireplace and a row of overflow arranged on the mantelpiece; a desk with papers in neat piles; a small table for magazines (like a dentist's office! thought Wolfie) and a larger one, round and oak, with the varnish removed, for meals. To one side, in an alcove, was the kitchen (he caught a glimpse of white walls and sink, nothing disorderly, no garbage, no odors); opposite, the bathroom, darkened, clean, and proper as a church. (Wolfie, who had none, was obliged to use bath and toilet in the hall.) The door to the bedroom was open, but from where he stood Wolfie was unable to look in. Everything in the apartment was in order, the place had been swept, dusted, aired through the ministrations, quite obviously, of female hands. Why couldn't he, Wolfie, live like this?

"Won't you sit down?" said Falkenberg at last.

Wolfie was considering—should he march through the place and as one, say, who was simply curious, pop his nose into the bedroom too? But it had to have more point than that. He was groping for something infinitely subtle and malicious to poison the barb and spread paralysis through the bloodstream. Obviously it would not do to say, in so many words, "Here is the phone number of the woman I love. Now let me look at the bedroom where you will sleep with her." But his heart was pounding, and as he considered the point of his visit, he himself began to feel paralyzed. He sat.

"Y-yes . . ." said Falkenberg, slowly backing into a chair. "Is there   is there anything I can do for you?" He let the words out one at a time, careful not to get hooked, in case, sensed Wolfie, who was extraordinarily sharp while the paralysis crept in his blood, just in case he, Wolfie, had not after all come to collect. No point in one man of the world's repaying another unless he had to, eh what?

"Oh . . ." he replied, in a manner as near absolute vagueness as he could strike. "Yes . . . yes and no." Then while he grinned, flashing and sheathing the knife, he hit on the best method of slicing up Falkenberg. It was late afternoon; Wolfie would hang on. Falkenberg might have a girl coming up—to cook his dinner, of course! From the look of the apartment, this was quite probable. Wolfie would put off inspecting the bedroom and handing over the phone number until the girl arrived. What a moment! "Good evening, Miss. Charmed, I'm sure. Why Falkenberg, what a soft bed you have! Here's another phone number!"

He lived through the scene in vivid hallucination and was crowing over it. His lips must have moved, perhaps a whoop did escape him. Falkenberg was startled and rose from his chair. He took a few steps in the direction of the refrigerator (to get out the eggs, thought Wolfie, who now had prophetic vision) but stopped and turned midway in the room. "Was there—there wasn't anything you wanted?"

"Oh, I say old man!" exclaimed Wolfie in a piping voice. "Shall we have tea?"

"Tea? Oh. No, I don't have any tea."

"Pity. But I say, I must have some at my place. If you don't mind tea bags. It goes so much farther, you know. Shall I run and look?"

"No, no, no, don't bother. (Pause.) What time is it getting to be?"

"Five thirty-five, by your own clock." Wolfie pointed to the desk. "Well then, let's have coffee. . . ."

Falkenberg hesitated. Wolfie, who was hopping up and down on the couch, read his thoughts and saw that he had him now. Apparently, it was not the eggs Wolfie wanted, but what did he want? It was getting late, this was no time to be sociable. (Aha! thought Wolfie, so a girl is coming up!) Better get rid of him. But he must have come for a reason, maybe he had something, maybe . . . Better be nice to him . . . The professor shrugged his shoulders and went for the coffee pot.

"What a nice place you have!" cried Wolfie. "Imagine—I never saw it before. Is this your own furniture?"

"What did you say?" asked Falkenberg from the kitchen, over the sound of running water.

"The furniture, is it your own?"

"Some of it is."

"Really. I didn't know you had furniture. Which is yours?"

"Oh, the table and the desk. The soft chair. The pictures, of course."

"Is the bed your own?" asked Wolfie, and clapped a hand over his mouth to keep from exploding.

Falkenberg came out of the kitchen, wiping his hands on a towel. "I've put up the water. We'll have coffee in a moment. (Pause.) How," he resumed, with the special intonation he reserved for such questions, "has life been treating you?"

Wolfie brushed the question aside. "I see you have a bedroom." He was like a possessed man, speaking with tongues. "Please don't think I'm prying. I don't care to see your place at all, and I didn't come for that reason. I'm not even going to ask to see the bedroom. Absolutely not. Why should I? Though I might be interested to see it, the way people come to see Gettysburg and other famous battlefields. But you have a right to your privacy—and it must be hard enough for you as it is, with so many people in your life. I'm not one of those who imagine that a full life is an altogether enviable thing. I know what a burden women can be, and I sympathize with your burden—I assure you I do—and I'm even aware of your secret desire to be an ascetic. You don't know how much I respect you for it! Then what am I doing here? You know, that's one thing I like about you, old man. I've been here ten minutes and you haven't once asked me that question. You believe in putting a chap at ease, just as I do. We have a lot in common. Do you know something? If I weren't already a friend of yours I would look at you and think, 'Now there's someone I could really be friends with!' That's a fact. But that's why I've been saying to myself, 'I must drop in on him sometime. Why should I always make him come to me? It's not fair. Why should he be beholden to me?' Or does that make me beholden to you? In these delicate matters it's sometimes difficult to know.

"Anyway, here I am. Besides," he added, screwing up his eyes so that they completely disappeared, "besides, you enjoy our little chats, don't you, professor? So what if I have been a little curious to see how you live? Well, yes, I have been curious. I want to see what goes on here. That is, I know what goes on—I just wanted to see the setting, so to speak. I was sure you wouldn't mind. . . ."

He had broken into a sweat. How should he give him the phone number? Hand it to him on a slip of paper without saying a word? Mail it, anonymously?

"Tell me the truth," he blurted out. "Are you waiting for someone?"

"I beg your pardon," said Falkenberg, not so much startled as cornered, and glancing at the clock. But he recovered himself and answered in tones of full discretion, "Just a friend. We are planning an article for the *Journal* and I've asked my friend over to discuss it."

"Let me compliment you!" cried Wolfie. "You couldn't have put it better. 'My friend' sets it on just the right plane, so that I would be showing a dirty mind to think of your friend as *she,* and playing into your hands if I thought it was a man. Above such considerations entirely! The life of the mind, that's the ticket!"

By now Falkenberg was quite alarmed, as in the old days, and his death's-head gleamed in fear. Even his speech broke down; he mumbled something about the coffee's being ready.

"I'm so sorry. I've come at the wrong time!" Wolfie rose and ran to the door. He was literally trembling. So there was a girl coming up! Somehow he had fastened onto the conviction that this was Myra, coming of her own accord; that Falkenberg had independently become acquainted with her, and they had been seeing each other for months. In a moment she would appear in the apartment and find *him* there! He had to clear out at once.

But to Falkenberg he said, "Why should I leave? Just because you're expecting *her?* Let her find me here and see what's become of me. I'm no better than a pimp! And let her see—"

"What are you talking about?" exclaimed Falkenberg. His face had grown terribly white. "I want a full explanation—at once!—or—" But he was much thinner than Wolfie, and besides, excitement affected his bladder. "Or I'll ask you to leave!" He backed toward the desk and put his hand on the telephone.

The police! thought Wolfie, it would be a wonderful idea if the police came. He would accuse Falkenberg—of what, he was not sure, but something would offer itself. Molesting women.

"What are you doing here? What do you want from me?" Falkenberg was jiggling a knee, and it shook his voice.

Wolfie, at last, saw a frightened man, and his delusion began to lift. "Do you mean to say," he asked incredulously, "that you don't know whom I mean?"

"I have no idea. And if you don't speak clearly—politely—I'll—"

"Myra," said Wolfie, the one word, as though it were a curse.

"Myra? Myra who?" Falkenberg let go the telephone. He was still puzzled, but greatly relieved to find the conversation back on familiar ground. The color returned to his cheeks.

"Then you really don't know her . . ." Wolfie was also relieved.

"No—I'm not sure. You'd have to tell me her last name." He shrugged his shoulders and said with a smile, "You know how it is."

"Never mind then," said Wolfie. "I was going to give you her phone number. But if you don't know her, there's no point."

"That doesn't make sense," observed Falkenberg.

"I guess not," admitted Wolfie. But he regretted the admission, it weakened his case. Now what? "All I meant to say," he temporized, "was that I was going to give you her number, and I may still do it. But if I don't want to, I won't. It's up to me."

"Well, of course." Falkenberg paused, but evidently he considered himself not nearly so indifferent as he wanted to appear, and he added, in his most offhand tone, "What's so special about her?"

"I say!" exclaimed Wolfie. "I lost something—a collar button—do you mind if I look?" He rushed past Falkenberg.

"Hey, where are you going?"

"I'll only be a moment. It's probably under the bed." At last he was in the bedroom.

The light was turned off, but by the light from the adjoining room he could see, well enough, that it was a perfectly ordinary bedroom like all other bedrooms. Curtains on the window, a chest of drawers along one wall, on top of it a mirror and a comb and brush set edged in gold, such as a woman might use but by no means out of the question for a man. But it was to the bed that he turned, as though he expected to see the augury of everything to come: here her head would lie with her hair spread, so, and here, the bulk of her body under the covers. . . . He turned to the bed as though he would actually find her there, awaiting the fulfillment of events. But the bed was simply a bed, with pillows, a head- and footboard, and covered with a striped green spread to go with the curtains. He saw nothing.

"What are you doing here?" cried Falkenberg.

"Oh—I'm sorry—I made a mistake. I must have lost it somewhere else."

"Are you crazy? What are you looking for? Get out of here!"

"Now I remember! It was at the washstand. I dropped a cuff-link at the washstand. Isn't it funny how one gets mixed up?" He moved out of the room like a ship through fog.

Falkenberg went after him, hesitated at the toilet, went on. Wolfie was already in the hall, breathing. It gave him some satisfaction to see (he had not suffered altogether in vain) how Falkenberg was shifting from fear to lechery, back and forth. Wolfie stood at his own door, his hand on the knob, waiting for the professor to speak.

This he did, before long, in a voice both pompous and kittenish and with a suggestion of sucking through a straw. "Wasn't there something you were going to give me?"

"Oh yes, but I'm not sure it's worth it. She's a perfectly ordinary girl."

"I see."

"Though if you like—" He played with the door knob.

"It's up to you."

"Never mind then. I've given you the wrong impression."

"Ah, yes. (Pause.) I see, I see."

"You understand, it means nothing to me—whether I tell you or not—if you see her or you don't see her."

"I'm aware of that. All the same—no, it's a matter of indifference to both of us."

"That's right—to both of us!" But suddenly Wolfie saw the possibility that he might, just as he stood there, turn the door knob and walk into his own room without a word. For some reason this terrified him.

"She's so beautiful!" he cried. "I was in love with her. I still love her! I've never loved anyone so much in my whole life!" He was burning. He wrote the number on a slip of paper, crumpled it up, and flung it into Falkenberg's face. He would have wanted to fling himself on Falkenberg's neck.

But he ran into his room and slammed the door.

5. *Pervigilium Veneris*

Now began the most difficult time of all for Wolfie, while he waited to see what would happen. He kept constant watch on Falkenberg, followed him downstairs, after a safe interval, when the professor left the house, and trailed him, from the other side of the street, at a distance of half a block, to see where he would go. (This he had never done before, to anyone.) He inquired at the various establishments where Falkenberg taught and drew up a schedule of his hours, so that at any moment of the day he knew where to find him and had at least a vague idea what he was doing. From the time Falkenberg left the house in the morning to the time in the evening when he returned, Wolfie had him covered. And when he returned in the evening, Wolfie would be standing in the dark, in his own room, peering through a crack in the door. If Falkenberg came home alone, Wolfie would wait to see what arrangement he had made for the evening; whether he was staying in, expecting company, or planning to go out again. If anyone called on him, Wolfie was at his post to see who it was. If Falkenberg went out again, Wolfie trailed after him, and if he came back with a girl (which Wolfie on the whole preferred, as it left his own evenings free) Wolfie would stay close enough to make sure it was not Myra, then light out on his rounds, at a winded trot, to make up lost time. Somehow, Wolfie also managed to keep up with the world on his own behalf and to make enough appearances, as though by chance, on the staircase or in the hall, to seem perfectly natural to Falkenberg and allay his suspicions.

Nevertheless, the morning visits ceased. Falkenberg was civil enough when they met and not much more chilly than usual, but he no longer stopped by to give account of the evening's adventures, and this rather worried Wolfie. He maintained his vigilance, and suffered in doing so—it was low, mean, and contemptible of him to snoop on his neighbor; but he also enjoyed it, and he kept up his sneer. Myra's name was never again mentioned between them, and Falkenberg did not even indicate whether he had called her. A week went by; ten days. Then one night—it was quite late—Wolfie, in the dark, at the crack of his door, heard footsteps on the stairs and low voices; and for a moment, Myra appeared. He saw her face in profile as she turned to go into Falkenberg's apartment.

Wolfie removes his shoes the better to preserve silence. Picture him in his stocking feet, with several toes protruding from a hole; alone in his room, in the dark, among the litter and detritus of months, stercoricolous, hyenoid, a joy-popper. His whole body is tense with listening, but he hears only the noises of existence, radios in the rooming house, voices, the creak of floor boards and of stairs; and from the outside, the louder, duller noises of traffic on the river and the streets. Myra is absorbed in these noises, dissolved and lost, somewhere in the night. But he tells himself, she is right next door.

He feels a pain in the midsection, in the pit of the ribs, a contraction like hunger, but if it is hunger, it is more than his own. A sharp pain, nauseating and severe—he would like to vomit, shout and cry all at once. He is breathing with difficulty, his nose is blocked, and he holds his mouth open, panting like an animal. Sweat is all over his body.

Time goes by, he doesn't know how long he has been standing in the dark at the crack of the door. It seems to him he is standing in several different places: at his own door, at Falkenberg's door, and somewhere far away—a grassy place—is it a field, or is there sand under his feet? He would love to lose himself altogether in contemplation of the far distant place, and he feels himself swayed and swept, but he is held to the rough, cracked panel of painted wood against which he is pressing his nose, and to the dim light in the hall and Falkenberg's door which he sees through the crack. He has been trying, for the longest time, to determine something,—what was her expression when he saw her for a moment, passing so near his hiding place, he had practically breathed upon her, so near, he could have whispered to her and she would have heard? Was it perhaps a reluctant look, was there the least chance of that? Or was it the look, never given to him? He thinks, what a dreadful thing it is to see this look in a woman's eyes: absolute, nothing else is such exposure. But the Wolfie who is standing far in the distance calls to him and makes a gesture of compassion: "Come away, be reconciled."

He opens the door and moves into the carpeted hall on tiptoe. What does he hear at Falkenberg's door? Music, a recording of a string quartet. They, too, once listened to quartets. He stands, held by the music, even nodding in tempo. So be it. The violins are issuing a statement concerning loss and reconciliation, all sorrows, give, hold nothing back, and be purged. So be it. No promises, no hint of eventual fulfillment, that arms must once again hold what is dear, that lovers must meet in the ripeness of time and have harvest of each other—of this, not a word. Accept what is, say the several voices. Many are the portions dealt to man, and what falls to each is his own.

But Wolfie stiffens and rejects. Records! he sneers. Strange that he had never before troubled to note Falkenberg's methods of seduction. And no doubt drinks, the girl's spiked, while the music plays, and the right lighting, count on that, then a touch of the hair and a breathing, softly, into the ear, the rehearsed look in the eyes and the death's-head glittering with teeth. Well, he's still at the records, thinks Wolfie. Man on first. He goes back to his own room.

There he paces the floor, still in his stocking feet, scattering the scattered papers, the shirts with empty sleeves entangled. Later, he does not know how much later, he creeps back to Falkenberg's door. The music has stopped. He hears conversation, thank God for that, but can't make out the words; Falkenberg's voice, as he can tell by the rhythm, is still formal, observing the pauses. . . . He makes several trips and stands at last before silence. No music, no voices. There is no light showing under the door. He can't remember whether a light showed earlier. He presses his ear to the door, but is uncertain whether he hears a sound at all and whether it comes from the apartment. The pain under his heart is vivid and unbearable.

At first he knocks softly, so softly, hardly a touch, that no one but he can have heard it. But the sound provokes him, and with the first transgression past, he knocks louder—it seems terribly loud to him, as though he were banging directly on his own eardrums. He takes panic at the sound, and flees, heading down the stairs until he remembers his shoes; stops dead still on the staircase in a frenzy of sweat and shame, trembling and holding his breath. Falkenberg's door remains shut and from all the other doors proceed the regular noises of existence. Softly, stealthily he tiptoes up the stairs, slips on his shoes without lacing them, and takes his coat—but he does not go out that night. He falls full length upon his bed.

At first he lay in a stupor, overcome with disgust. Clearly, painfully, he saw his own wretchedness, through his own eyes and through the eyes of the world. What had become of him? It was a sin to live this way, and an especially grave sin for him, who had life and capacity and was no pompous lecher like Falkenberg. He, Wolfie, knew what love was and if he had not won love in return, it was because he had not been deserving. Myra, forgive me my sins. But who was she? Another Village tramp, for the likes of Falkenberg. He had thrown his life away on them. . . . No more. He would rise out of his sloth and his filth, he was still young, it was not too late. He would move out of the house in the morning, out of the Village altogether, and live uptown near the river or in Queens; find a job and work hard, and work hard on himself and learn to control and direct his life toward a decent and worth-while objective. He would live alone, waiting patiently, learning the right way and saving his money to buy good clothes and a regular hat such as all men wore, a car, a nice apartment; and while he worked and waited, developing his inner power and strengthening himself, buying the morning paper on the way to work and the evening paper on the way home, and no longer sneering at the others who did so, from somewhere, surely, a good woman would come to him. A woman who, perhaps like himself, had also known degradation and had fought against it, and who would recognize him for what he truly was and they would join forces to conduct their fight together: for the truth. He would marry her and love her all his life, and they would raise a family. A whole world lay before him. He would never again sneer at the bourgeoisie and not even call them by that name, but be everlastingly grateful to live like them, secure and with dignity. Wasn't it Flaubert himself who had said, *"Ils sont dans le vrai"*? Let them lie together, Myra and Falkenberg, in that stinking dirty bed, dirtier by far than his own; let them rub and strain and press their sweating bodies together in a jungle fever, and let the whole world join in. He, Wolfie, alone would persevere and fight and cry No!

But the image tortured him and he could not put it down. Next door, only next door she lay. Did she know that he lived here, was she aware that he lay here, across the hall? Surely, Falkenberg had mentioned it. . . . Why hadn't he run out when he saw her pass his door and confronted her, or when he was knocking on the door, why hadn't he persisted or broken the door down? He could still have prevented it. There, only across the hall . . . He tried to turn his mind away (he would fight!) but the thought of her joined to Falkenberg, the vivid bestial images, leaped before his eyes, and he felt the overpowering desire to play with himself. He did this, sneering at himself and the resolutions he had made, but he gave himself over to it and imagined he was lying with her and mimicked her outcries of passion.

There was no relief, the pain was worse. Oh, sure, he would reform and fly right, a fine one! Profound, immeasurable disgust . . . How would he endure this night? If only it would pass quickly! Be reconciled, he told himself again, have courage. But for what? So that he might again supply Falkenberg with phone numbers when the affair with Myra had run its course in ten days or two weeks from now? For what? What had happened to him? What would become of him? He saw himself sinking deeper and deeper into filth and sloth and winding up in a madhouse or a suicide. The news would spread through the Village and as quickly be forgotten. Why, why had this happened to him? Where was there help? Where in all this world could he turn?

He lay spent, shivering and feverish. If only he could sleep! He sank to the level of semiconsciousness but could go no further. Again he saw himself standing far in the distance making a gesture of reconciliation, there were lights in the sky, a soft wind blew. So be it, said the voices, speaking the truth, without false hope or false promises: give. But he recognized the music he had heard at Falkenberg's door, the string quartet coming from inside, and with all his heart breaking, crying deliriously, he called for Myra. He sobbed and wept, calling her name, and at last, it seemed to him, she came and stood beside his bed, not the Myra from across the hall, but, as it were, one who had been long dead, come to intercede for him: one of the mothers, in a white gown. She laid a cool hand on his fever and employed various powers to comfort him. Now lights of many colors, in the distance, began to blink and draw nearer at her command: orange and green and a flooding and dissolving blue. And now suddenly a troop of performing dogs on their hind legs, and a huge rubber ball slowly spinning in the air. Myra took him by the hand and led him forth; she pointed upward and drew him after her, up, up, and he felt himself carried along, weightless. But when he looked again it was not she in white but a clown with a white face and a huge, smeared mouth. The clown said something and laughed and Wolfie still wondered what he was laughing at and whether he was laughing at him, when the orange and green lights blinked out, one by one, and there was darkness and he slept.

[WRITTEN 1956; PUBLISHED 1957]

KING SOLOMON

1. With His Women

Every year, a certain number of girls. They come to him, lie down beside him, place their hands on his breast, and offer to become his slaves.

This goes on all the time. It is a simple transaction, a lovely thing: "I will be your slave," say the girls, and no more need be said. But Solomon's men, his counselors, can't bear it—what is this power of his? Some maintain it is no power at all, he is merely the King. Oh yes, admit the rest, his being the King has something to do with it—but there have been other kings, so it can't be that. Nor is it anything else. Consider how unprepossessing he is, what a poor impression he makes—why, most of the counselors are taller, handsomer, and leaner than he. To be sure, he has an excellent voice, but his voice comes through best on the telephone, and he has an unlisted number which no one would give out. Certainly not, say the men. Still, the girls keep coming, and they lie down beside him with their hands on his breast.

It is not enough to say the counselors are jealous. After all, there is something strange here, the like of it has not been seen. But who shall explain the King?

Solomon himself makes no comment, he does not speak of his personal affairs. He may drop a hint or two, but these hints are contradictory and vague, and he drops them only for his own amusement; perhaps he, too, doesn't know. Every few years he publishes a collection of his sayings, most of which he has never said, but the sayings have little to do with the case, and their melancholy tone is held to be an affectation. The wisest counselors pay no attention to his words. If anything is to be learned, the wise men say, it had better be sought among his girls.

But the girls also say nothing. The rejected go away in tears, in anger or regret—in which case one cannot expect them to speak coherently or with regard for truth; or they are determined yet to win his love—and again they will tell lies. As for the women he accepts, they are useless. Almost at once they become so much like Solomon, adopting his mannerisms of gesture and speech and sharing his views of things, that they say only what he would say—and Solomon does not speak his heart. Besides, the counselors think they are stupid. Oh, they are gifted, no doubt of that, and none lacks charm. One dances, another sings, a third makes cheese; some bake, some spin, some are skilled at floral decorations. Still others wear their hair, or cultivate the expression of their eyes, in some mysterious way, impossible to fathom. Or altogether their talent lies in their bare feet, a way of arching the instep or turning up the toes. Yet so far as outsiders can judge, these girls are unqualified to minister to the King, and the counselors waste no time asking questions.

So it has become the custom in the court to study Solomon's women in their work: perhaps the manner in which they serve him will make it clear. The counselors watch over the harem, each chooses a woman to follow about the palace, over the grounds, and through the town. One woman . . . there she goes! . . . sets out early in the morning with a basket, trailed by a counselor. She makes her way to the largest and most crowded kosher market, where she will stand in line for hours, haggling and hefting, crying highway robbery! And what delicacies does she buy? Surely pickles and spices, the rarest and the best . . . Not necessarily, it may even be turnips. So who is the wiser? And as for the obvious conclusion—that Solomon sets store by economy—this has long since been drawn. He even lunches on leftovers.

Another goes to the laundry with his shirts. Solomon wants them done just so, and she gives out instructions on the washing, starching, and ironing, then waits in the steamy atmosphere for hours, till the shirts are done; and carries them back on her head, walking swiftly, deftly, with infinite pride. Why such pride? This is precisely the mystery.

Others clean his shoes, open and sort the mail, tend the garden and the vineyards, keep his musical instruments polished and in tune. A few go to the well for water—a curious assignment, as the palace has had hot and cold running water for years. Perhaps he sends them to the well on purpose, to confuse the counselors. But if this occupation serves only to deceive, why not all the rest? This may well be the case. King Solomon has a staff of regular servants, quite capable of looking after his needs.

Therefore nothing has been learned. The counselors are always confronted by the same questions at nightfall, when their need to know the King is greatest. Much of the time, he sits quietly with a girl or two, pasting stamps in an album, while they massage his scalp. On festive nights, the counselors note the revelry and participate, when invited, in the dancing and carousing. Over and over again they have resolved to stay sober and observant, but always they give way; the moment they enter the King's apartments they are overcome by the radiance which waits—or which they imagine waits—for them there. All is gold, ivory, inlay of silver, velvet, damask, and brocade; incense and odor of spice and musk, with sound of timbrels, flutes, and drums; carvings, hangings, carpets ankle-deep. Not that all of this enchants them; many counselors complain that the King has no taste in entertainments, that he relies, for instance, too heavily on tambourines, which he has his dancing girls flutter in their hands till the jingling gives one a headache; that much the same or better amusements can be had in the cabarets about the town which—so much for Solomon's originality—have been the source of many a spectacle of the King's court—and they even have newspaper clippings to prove the point. Nevertheless, they succumb to the King's merrymaking, join it or are swayed by it, and even if it makes them puke with disdain, still they lose the essential detachment. And then at the hour when the King retires to his chamber with his chosen love, all is lost, the counselors are defeated and go disgruntled to their own quarters, to lie awake or dream enviously through the night.

All the same, a pertinacious lot. What stratagems, disguising themselves as eunuchs or hiding in vases or behind the furniture to learn what goes on at night! Here, too, they have been disappointed. Though Solomon burns soft lights beside his couch, no one has witnessed anything—or at least has ever reported what he saw. At the last moment the hidden counselors have shut their eyes or turned away; no one has dared look at the King's nakedness, dared to watch his love. A few, it is said, have so dared, but these have either disappeared (the consensus is, they left of their own accord) or, remaining, have worn a dazed and guilty look ever after, so that people say they went blind. Still, sounds have been heard floating in deep summer air over the garden and the lily pond, mingling with the voices of frogs: sighs, outcries, moans, and exclamations—but the intrusion has been its own punishment, maddening those who have overheard the King and driving them wild with lust or despair. Sooner or later, the counselors have been compelled to stopper their ears. Now when these sounds issue from the King's apartments, the counselors take up instruments and play, softly but in concert, to hide his sounds within their own.

None has seen the King's nakedness; yet all have seen him in shirt sleeves or suspenders, paunchy, loose-jowled, in need of a trim. Often in the heat of the day he appears bareheaded, and all have looked upon his baldness; sometimes he comes forth in his bare feet, and the men have observed bunions and corns. When he appears in this fashion with, say, a cigar in his mouth and circles under his eyes; his armpits showing yellowish and hairy over the arm holes of his undershirt; his wrinkles deep and his skin slack; a wallet protruding from one hip pocket and a kerchief from the other—at such moments, whether he be concerned with issues of government or merely the condition of the plumbing, he does show himself in human nakedness after all, he is much like any man, he even resembles a policeman on his day off or a small-time gambler. And sometimes, unexpectedly, he summons the cabinet to a game of pinochle—then all are aware he has again transcended them.

Some of the counselors have formed liaisons with his rejected mistresses, women he has grown tired of and no longer summons to his couch. Often it seemed to them that they were on the verge of discovery, but persistence undid them. These liaisons have invariably degenerated into marriages, the counselor become a husband, the mistress, a nag. Then the counselor has forgotten his purpose, and the mistress, her knowledge; what the curiosity of the one and the bitterness of the other were to have produced in union, has been dissipated in recriminations: hang up your clothes, don't spend so much money, brush your teeth before coming to bed. Men and women have grown old in this dissembling, but nothing has been learned. From these fruitless experiments has come the statement, erroneously attributed to the King: vanity of vanities, all is vanity.

Of late, King Solomon has turned his attention to the young. He has organized bicycle races for children, entertained them with magicians, taken them on picnics and excursions to the zoo. He loves to sit on a shady bench with a youngster on either knee, a boy and a girl, about four or five in age. They pull at his beard, tug at his ears and finger his spectacles till he can no longer see through the smudges. Sometimes, the children are his own, more often not. It makes no difference, the King has many sons and daughters. He tells stories, not nearly so amusing as they should be, old stories which the children grew tired of in the nursery, or poor inventions, rather pointless on the whole. And he seldom finishes a story but begins to nod in the telling, his words thicken and stumble; eventually he falls asleep. Solomon is a disappointment to the young, seldom will children come twice to his garden. Yet for them he is truly a king: robed and gowned, golden-sandaled, wearing a crown, his hair trimmed, his beard washed lustrous, combed, and waved, and the hairs plucked out of his nostrils. And in this splendor, in which he seldom appears, not even for the reception of ambassadors, he loves to bounce a rubber ball and play catch with the children. He is unskilled at these games, they call him fucky-knuckles. A man turning sixty, an aging king.

But how clear is the expression of his eyes as he plays with the children—if only one knew what it meant! Perhaps he longs to reveal himself but does not know how; or does not know that the people await this revelation, or is unable to see beyond the children, who are bored with him. Perhaps he has nothing to reveal, and all his wisdom lies scattered from his hand: he is merely this, that, and the other, a few buildings raised, roads leveled, a number of words spoken, unthinking, on an idle afternoon. Occasionally, when he recognizes the expectation of the people, he tries to remember an appropriate saying from one of the collections he has published. Most of the time, he is unaware of all this.

The children are fretful in the garden, they wait to be delivered. They have been brought by mothers, nurses, older sisters, who stand outside the gate, looking in through the palings. The mothers and nurses whisper together, their feet and eyes and hands are restless, they look at his shining beard. Later in the afternoon, when the children have been led home, perhaps one of the older girls, one of the sisters, will enter the same garden, approach the spot where the King lies resting, lie down beside him, fold her hands upon his breast, and offer to become his slave.

2. The Queen of Sheba

From all over they have come, and they keep coming, though the King is now an old man. It may be owing to his age that he has grown lenient, admitting women to concubinage whom, the counselors swear, he would have sent packing in the old days. He has reached the years when anything young looks good to him. This may not be true, there may be other reasons; but the counselors have a point in saying that the standards have fallen, and they prove it by telling the story of the Queen of Sheba.

A letter came, it was the first application to be received by mail. From a foreign country, the woman signed herself The Queen. She flattered Solomon's wisdom, word of which had reached her from afar; her own ears longed to hear his discourse, her own eyes, to behold his person. An unorthodox application, written in a powerful, forward-rushing, though feminine, hand on strangely scented paper: the King said it reminded him of jungles. He inspected the postmark, clipped off the stamp, and pasted it on a page by itself in his album. His expression was hidden in his beard.

The woman meant it. Boxes began to arrive, plastered with travel stickers. They came on sand-choked, sneezing camels, in long trains, attended by drivers, natives of the Land of Sheba. The next day, more boxes, and again on the third. Gifts of all description, of money and goods, spangles and bangles for the entire court. It made an excellent impression, but Solomon, who distributed the gifts, did not seem pleased. On the last day but one came another shipment, as large as all the others combined. . . . Here the counselors pretend to know the King's mind. First of all, they say, he was annoyed at having to put up so many camels, whole droves of them—his stables were crowded, and there was a shortage of feed for his own animals. Then the camel drivers, rough and barbarous men, were inflamed by the sight of Solomon's women, and the King had to double the guard and pay overtime; this killed him. But their greatest presumption lies in saying that Solomon, when he opened the last and largest load of boxes, which contained the Queen's personal effects, thought, "Adonai Elohenu! Is she coming to stay?" No one knows what the King thought.

He may well have been glad that the Queen was coming. No queen had ever before asked to be his slave—and she was a queen for sure, and of a rich country, think of the gifts she had sent. Solomon put his economists to work and they submitted a report: the financial structure was sound, and the country led in the production of myrrh, pepper, and oil. Now to be sure, the Queen's letter made no direct application; apart from the flattery, it merely said, *coming for a visit,* as an equal might say. But the interpretation was clear. An equal would not come uninvited, only one who meant to offer herself would do so—unless the Queen was rude; but the gifts she had sent took care of that. Yet as a queen, writing from her own palace, she could not have expressed the intention, it would have been treason to her own people. Nevertheless, she had every intention: otherwise, why would she have gone to the trouble? The fact is, there was rejoicing in the palace, Solomon himself led the dancing, and he declared a holiday when the Queen of Sheba arrived.

She came in a howdah, on a camel, preceded by troops of archers and trumpeters. Solomon helped her down and washed and anointed her feet in the courtyard. This didn't come off so well. Sheba used coloring matter on her toenails and the soles of her feet, and the coloring ran; Solomon was out of practice, he tickled her feet a few times and made her laugh. The ceremony was supposed to be a solemn one, the people took it very seri-

ously, and they were offended by her toenails—feet were supposed
to be presented dusty; as for the giggling, it was unpardonable,
and the priests took offense. A poor set of omens. Besides, Sheba
was not quite so young as the autographed picture, which she
had sent in advance to Solomon, would have led one to expect.
Her skin was nearly black, relieved here and there along her arms
and shoulders with spots of a lighter color, a leopard design.
Her black hair, which she had apparently made some effort to
straighten, had gone frizzled and kinky again in the heat of the
desert crossing. Her lips were thick and purplish brown, her palms
and the soles of her feet were a light, bright saffron yellow. She
wore anklets of delicate chain, gold bracelets all over her arms,
and jewels in both obvious and unexpected places, so that the
eye was never done seeing them; their light was kept in constant
agitation by the massive rhythm of her breathing, which involved
her entire body. A sense of tremendous power and authenticity
emanated from her breasts. Some thought she was beautiful, others, not. No one knows what the King thought; but he may well
have felt what everyone else did who came to witness her arrival—drawn, and at the same time, stunned.

But the King is glad in his heart as he leads Sheba to the
table, where he has put on a great spread for her. He is attended
by his court and surrounded by his women—and how lordly are
his movements as he eats meat and rinses his mouth with wine!
At the same time he is uneasy in the Queen's presence, his usual
resources may not be enough—after all, this is no maiden lurking
in the garden to trip up to him and fold her hands upon his breast.
The meal goes well enough: Sheba asks for seconds, and seems
impressed with the napkins and silverware. But suddenly, right in
the middle of dessert, she turns to him and demands, in front of
everyone and that all may hear, that he show her his famous wisdom. This comes as something of a shock. The implication is twofold: that so far he has spoken commonplaces; and secondly, that

he is to suffer no illusions, it was really for the sake of his wisdom that she made the difficult trip. The people turn their eyes on the King, who handles the awkward moment with skill; he clears his throat on schedule, and raises his hand in the usual gesture, admonishing silence. But nothing comes.

In the official account of the visit, which Solomon had written to order, he was supposed to have

> *. . . told her all questions: There was not anything . . . which he told her not. And when the Queen of Sheba had seen all Solomon's wisdom, and the house that he had built, and the meat of his table and the sitting of his servants . . .*

etc.,

> *There was no more spirit in her. And she said to the King, It was a true report that I heard in mine own land, of thy acts and thy wisdom. Howbeit, I believed not the words, until I came and mine eyes had seen it; and behold, the half was not told me: Thy wisdom and prosperity exceedeth the fame which I heard. Happy are thy men . . . which stand continually before thee and that hear thy wisdom*

After which there was supposed to have been a further exchange of compliments and gifts.

Now this is not only a bit thick, it gets round the question of Solomon's wisdom. What *did* the King say, when put to it by the Queen? That there were so many feet in a mile? That all circles were round? That the number of stars visible on a clear night from a point well out of town was neither more nor less than a certain number? Did he advise her what to take for colds, give her a recipe for salad dressing, or speak of building temples and ships? Just what does a man say under the circumstances?

Certainly, he hadn't the nerve, the gall, to repeat the abominable invention to her face of the two women who disputed motherhood of a child. She would have seen through it right away. And surely he knew this was not the time to quote his sayings; besides, he always had trouble remembering them. Then what did he say?

His economists had worked up a report on the Land of Sheba. He may have sent for a copy; more likely, he knew the essential facts cold, and spoke what came to mind: industry, agriculture, natural resources. Of the financial structure, the public debt, the condition of business. Of the production of pepper, myrrh, and oil, especially oil. Grant him his wisdom.

Certainly, the Queen was impressed, but one need not suppose that the spirit was knocked out of her or that she said, "It was a true report that I heard in mine own land . . ." etc. Chances are, she paid no attention to his words (except to note the drift) but watched him as he spoke, taking in the cut of his beard, the fit of his clothes, and wondering, betimes, what sort of man he was. She saw his initial uncertainty give way and his confidence grow as he reached the meaty part of his delivery. And all along, she observed how he drew on the admiring glances of his girls, soaked up their adoration, as they lay open-mouthed on couches and rugs at his feet, all criticism suspended, incapacitated by love. Love ringed him round, love sustained him, he was the splendid heart of their hearts. She must have forgotten the heat and sand images of the desert crossing, she, too, lapped from all sides and borne gently afloat . . .

So much one may imagine. But the Queen spent a number of days or weeks, perhaps even a month or two in the King's company, and of what happened during the time of her stay, let alone the subsequent events of the first night, the official chronicles say nothing. A merciful omission, according to the counselors, who report that it went badly from the start. When the King had finished his discourse, they say the Queen felt called upon to answer.

But words failed her, or she felt no need of words: she was the Queen. What she did was to lean forward and, in utter disregard of the company, take his head into her hands, gaze at him for a long time with a smile on her thick lips, and at last bestow on him a kiss, which landed somewhere in his beard. Then she jumped onto the table, commanded music, and danced among the cups and bowls, the dishes and the crumpled napkins. The counselors were shocked, the girls smirked painfully, the servants held their breath. Nor was Sheba so slender as the autographed picture may have led one to believe. When she set her feet down, the table shook, and the carafes of wine and sweetened water swayed and threatened to topple. Solomon himself hastily cleared a way for her, pushing the dishes to one side; his hands were trembling. But she proceeded with the dance, the chain anklets tinkled, her fingers snapped, the many jewels she wore flashed wealthily. Her toes left marks on the tablecloth, as though animals had run there. And run she did, back and forth over the length of the table, bending over the counselors to tweak this one's nose and that one's ears. But always she glanced back to see if she had the King's eye.

She had it, darker than usual. To her, this meant that he was admiring her, gravely, as befits King and Queen, and her feet quickened. How stern he was! Already she felt the King's love, harder than any courtier's and so much more severe. She increased the tempo, the musicians scrambling to keep up with her, and whirled. Round and round she sped, drawing nearer the end of the table where the King sat. It was a dance in the style of her country, unknown in these parts, and she did it with the abandon of a tribesgirl, though one must assume she was conscious, in her abandonment, that it was she, the Queen, none other than Sheba, who abandoned herself to King Solomon. That was the whole point of it, the mastery of the thing. Pride did not leave her face, it entered her ecstasy and raised it in degree. Already cries, guttural, impersonal, were barking in her throat; then with a final whoop she spun round and threw herself, arms outstretched and intertwined, like one bound captive, to fall before him on the table where his meal had been.

It was a terrible mistake. The women and the counselors knew the King so much better than she, and their hearts went out in pity. The Queen had offered herself in the only way she knew, majesty, power, and reign implied, throwing herself prone with a condescending crash for the King to rise and assault her. What presumption! He did not move. He sat infinitely removed, almost sorrowing over this great embarrassment. The music had stopped, there was an unbearable silence in the banquet hall. The King rumbled something deep in his beard; perhaps he was merely clearing his throat, preparatory to saying a few words (if only his wisdom did not fail him!). Some of the servants took it to mean more wine, others, more meat, still others, fingerbowls. They ran in all directions. Sheba lowered herself into her seat at the King's side. Her dark face burned. . . . Somehow the time went by, and the evening was over. Solomon led Sheba off to his chamber, as courtesy demanded. Even as she went with him, it was apparent that she still went in hope; even at the last moment. The older women wept.

Day by day, the strain mounted. Sheba was sometimes with the King, they played chess or listened to the radio, they bent their heads over maps, discussed politics, and played croquet. But there were no festivities and she did not dance again. She bore herself with dignity, but she had grown pale, and her smile, when she forgot herself, was cringing and meek. Sometimes, when she was alone, she was seen to run her finger over the table tops and the woodwork, looking for dust. She could not bear the sight of her waiting women, lest the revival of her hope, as they did her toilet, become apparent to them, and would chase them out of the room; only to call them back, and help her prepare for an audience with the King. Finally, she quarreled with some of the girls of the harem. And when this happened, Sheba knew that the day had come and she began to pack.

A pinochle game was in progress when the Queen of Sheba, unannounced and without knocking, came into the room to say she wanted a word with the King. He dismissed his counselors, but one of them swears he managed to hide behind the draperies, where he witnessed the scene.

The King was in his undershirt, smoking a cigar. He apologized for his dishevelment and offered to repair it. The affairs of state, he explained, were so trying lately, he found he worked better in deshabille. Had he been working? asked the Queen with a smile. She thought this was some sort of game, and she fingered the cards with pictures of kings and queens. Solomon, knowing that women do not pay pinochle, told her the cabinet had been in extraordinary session, trying fortunes with the picture cards. The times were good, but one must look to the future, and he offered to show her how it was done. No, I don't want to keep you, said the Queen of Sheba, I beg only a few words. Speak, said Solomon.

"Solomon, Solomon," said the Queen, "I am going away. No, don't answer me. You will say something polite and regretful, but my decision can only be a relief to you." She paused, taking on courage. "You must not allow this to be a disappointment to you, you must let me take the whole expense of our emotion upon myself. I did a foolish thing. I am a proud woman, being a Queen, and my pride carried me too far. I thought I would take pride in transcending pride, in offering myself to the King. But still that was pride, since I wanted the King for myself. You did wisely to refuse me. Yes, you are wise, Solomon, let no one question your wisdom. Yours is the wisdom of love, which is the highest. But your love is love only of yourself; yet you share it with others by letting them love you—and this is next to the highest. Either way you look at it, Solomon is wise enough. Understand me—" She took a step forward, a dance step, as though she were again on the table top, but her eyes spoke a different meaning. "I am not pleading with you that you love me or allow me to love you. For you are the King, your taking is your giving. But allow me to say, your power rests on despair. Yours is the power of drawing love, the like of which has not been seen. But you despair of loving with your own heart. I have come to tell the King he must not despair. Surely, Solomon, who has built temples and made the desert flourish, is a powerful king, and he has the power to do what the simplest slave girl or washerwoman of his harem can do—to love with his own heart. And if he does not have this power, it will come to him, he need only accept the love which it is his nature to call forth in everyone, especially in us poor women. This is his glory. Rejoice in it, O King, for you are the King!"

The counselor who hid behind the drapes said he regretted his action, to see how his King stood burdened before the Queen. His own heart filled with loving shame. Solomon looked lost, deprived of his power, as though the years in the palace and the garden had never been. He made an effort to stand dignified in his undershirt, he bore his head as though he were wearing the crown, but it was pitiful to see him.

"The Queen is wise," said he. Then he broke down, and the counselor did not hear his next words. He did hear him say that the Queen was magnificent, that she had the courage of lions and tigers . . . but by now his head was lowered. Suddenly, he clasped the Queen to his breast in an embrace of farewell, and the Queen smiled and stroked his curly beard. They did not immediately take leave of each other, but went on to speak of other matters. Before the Queen of Sheba left the country, King Solomon had leased her oil lands for ninety-nine years.

But on the day of her departure, he stood bare headed in the crowded courtyard to watch her set out, with her trumpeters and archers mounted on supercilious camels, all of them bold and reflecting midday sun. He extended his hand to help her up, and she, with her free hand, chucked him under the chin. Then she leaned out of the howdah to cry, "Long live the King!" King Solomon stood with bowed head to receive the ovation, and it was terrible for the people to see his humility, humble in acknowledgment of his power. Now more than ever they yearned for him.

When Sheba moved off, at the head of the procession, Solomon led the people onto the roof, to watch the camels file across the sand. He stood till evening fell, and the rump of the last plodding animal had twitched out of sight beyond the sand hills. Then he averted his face and wept silently, for it is a terrible thing for the people to see their King's tears.

3. With His Fathers

So the counselors have a point when they say the standards have fallen. Once the Queen of Sheba herself was unable to make it; and now, look. But no wonder, her like will not come again, and besides, Solomon is old. He has been running the country forty years and has begun to speak of retiring; but the people know he will never retire, and so they whisper, it is time for the King to die.

How does this strike him? To look at him—his beard is white, his spotted hands shake, he walks bent, his eyes are rheumy and dim—to look at him one would suppose he dwells on the thought of death. But he is no better known now than he was in his prime. The only certainty is that the King is old.

But what follows from this, how does it reveal him? Or this?—that he had an attack of pleurisy not long ago, and since then his side has been taped. And what does it mean to say that he now has more women than ever cluttering up the palace, one thousand in all, including seven hundred wives? (Is it merely that the standards have fallen?) It was necessary to tear down the harem (while the women, to everyone's displeasure, were quartered in the town) and raise a new building, so large, it has taken up ground formerly allotted to the garden. They are a great source of trouble to him, these women, and the counselors complain—that's where all the money is going, to support the harem. Harem? Why, it's a whole population, the country will be ruined! And the priests complain, every week they send fresh ultimatums, objecting to the fact that so many of Solomon's girls are heathen; they have even accused him of idolatry and threatened him with loss of the Kingdom and the wrath of God. And the people grumble, it's a shame, when they find his women loitering in beauty shops or quarreling right out in the open, as they have begun to do, in the very streets. But Solomon ignores the discontent and goes on collecting women as he once collected stamps.

Why? Or what does this mean?—that he seldom takes the trouble to interview applicants, but establishes a policy for several months, during which time the rule is, no vacancies. Then he will change the rule and take on newcomers by the dozen, most of whom he does not even see, the work being done by the counselors. And how complicated the work has become, compared with the old days, when all that was necessary was for a girl to lie down beside the King with her hands upon his breast. Now there are forms to fill out and letters of recommendation to obtain, several interviews and a medical examination to go through, and even then the girls must wait until their references have been checked. The filing cabinets have mounted to the ceiling. What sense does it make?

And above all in view of the following? The counselors vouch for it, they swear they have seen the proof. That King Solomon now takes to bed, not with a virgin, as his father, David, did in his old age, or even with a dancing girl, but with a hot water bottle to warm him. Think of him lying in bed with a hot water bottle. If this report is true, then doesn't something follow? For this is the extreme, between life and death, where all thoughts meet; an extreme, not a mean; and a wrong guess is impossible, everything is true, as at the topmost point, where all direction is down. It follows that he warms his hands on the water bottle, presses it to his cheek, passes it down along his belly. Now when he thinks of his prime, he of all men must wonder: what was the glory of the King? Who bestowed the power, and what did it consist in? When he had it, he did not consider, and now it is gone. Passing the rubber bottle down to his feet and digging with his toes for warmth, he sees he did everything possible in his life, and left no possibility untouched, of manhood, statesmanship, love. What else can a man do? There is no answer. Except to say, he was in God's grace then? And now no longer? Or is he still in a state of grace, witness the water bottle at his feet? And perhaps he is only being tried, and may look forward to even greater rewards? Such are the advantages of being a believer. If he were one, he would know—at least believe that he knew. But a man who knows only that once love was with him, which now is no more—what does he know, what shall he believe, old, exhausted, shivering alone in bed at night with a hot water bottle, when all's quiet in the palace? And if all's not quiet, that's no longer his concern.

No, if there were any rewards, he'd settle for a good night's sleep. But sleep does not come. He hears strange noises in the apartment, scratching . . . Mice? He must remember to speak to the caretakers. . . . at last he drowses off, to sleep awhile. And if he does not sleep? Or later, when he wakes, and it is still the same night? . . . Does he think of the Queen of Sheba and wonder, whom is she visiting now? Does he remember how she danced upon the table? Or the song he wrote soon after her departure, with her words still fresh in his mind, resolved to pour out his love for her, but from the very first line pouring out, instead, her love for him? Let him kiss me with the kisses of his mouth, for thy love is better than wine. It has been years since he heard from her. . . .

Meanwhile, the bottle has grown cold. Shall he ring for another? He shifts the bottle, kneads it between his knees. *And be thou like a young hart upon the mountains of spices.* Look forward, look back, to darkness, at the light, both ways blind. He raises the bottle to his breast; it does not warm him. He gropes for the cord, and while his hand reaches, he thinks, as he has thought so many times, there is a time and a season for everything, a time to be born and a time to die. Is it time now? They will lay him out, washed, anointed, shrouded. They will fold his arms across his chest, with the palms turned in, completing the figure. Now his own hands will lie pressed to his breast, and he will sleep with his fathers.

[1956]